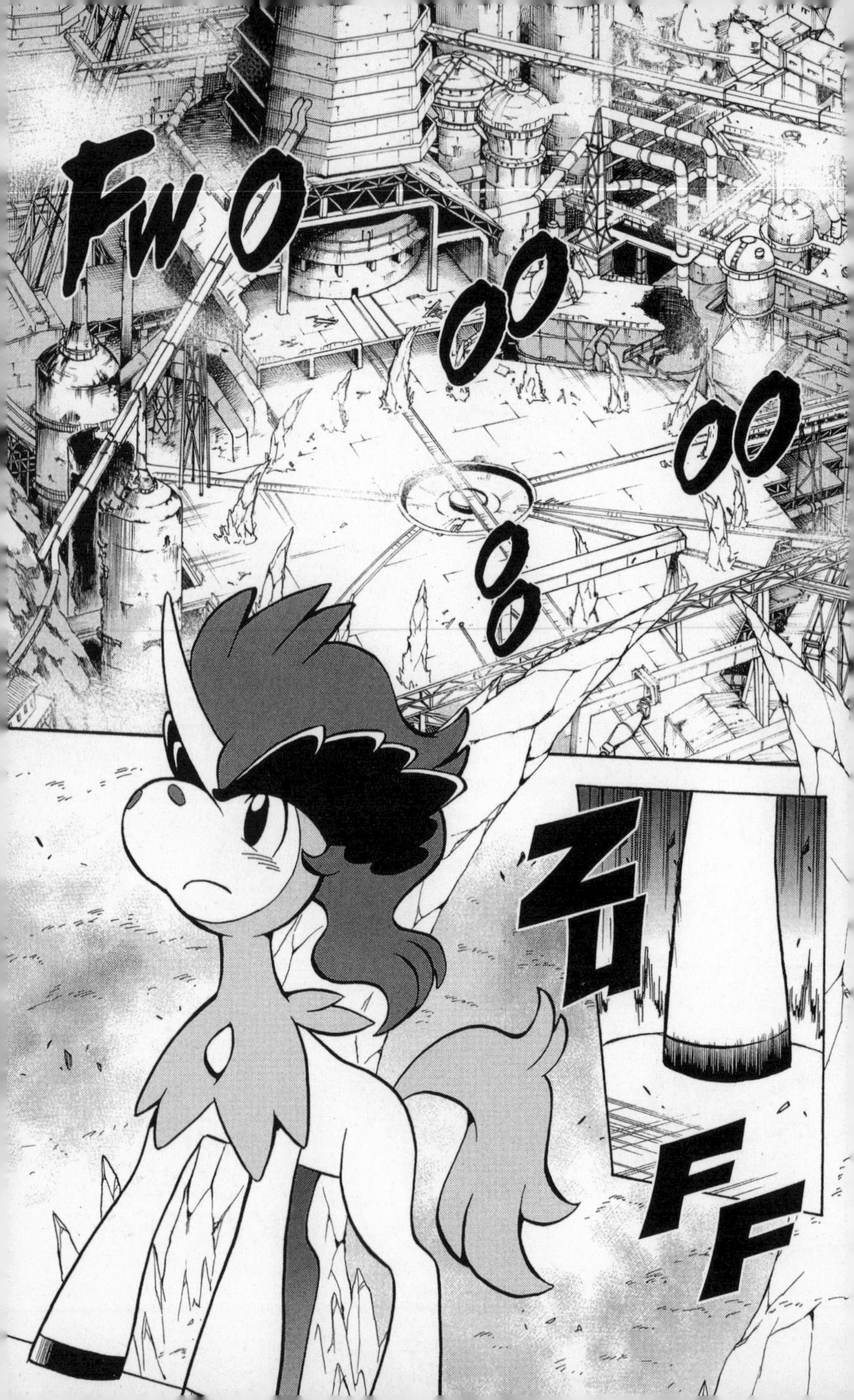
FWOOOOOOO
ZUFF

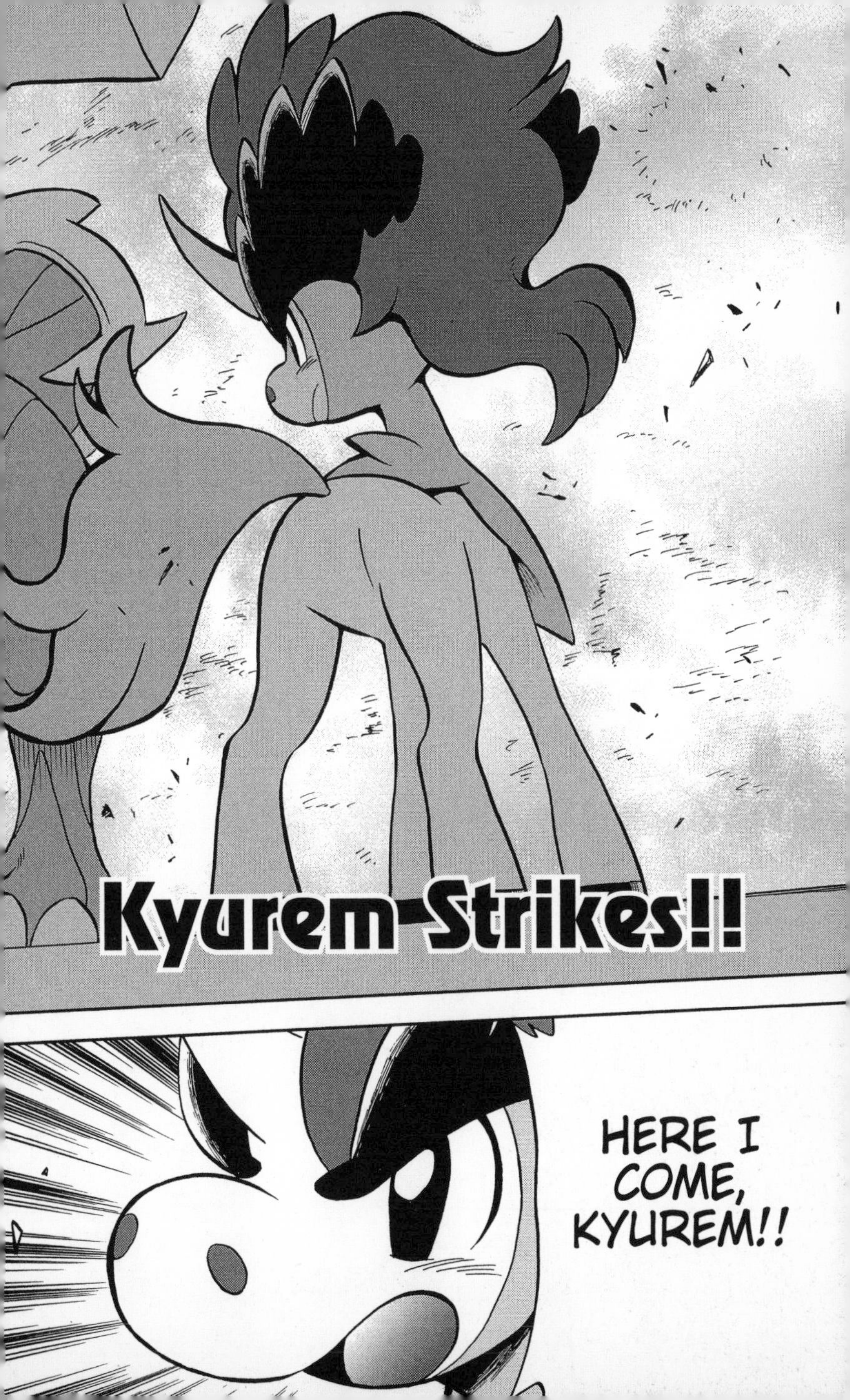
Kyurem Strikes!!
HERE I COME, KYUREM!!

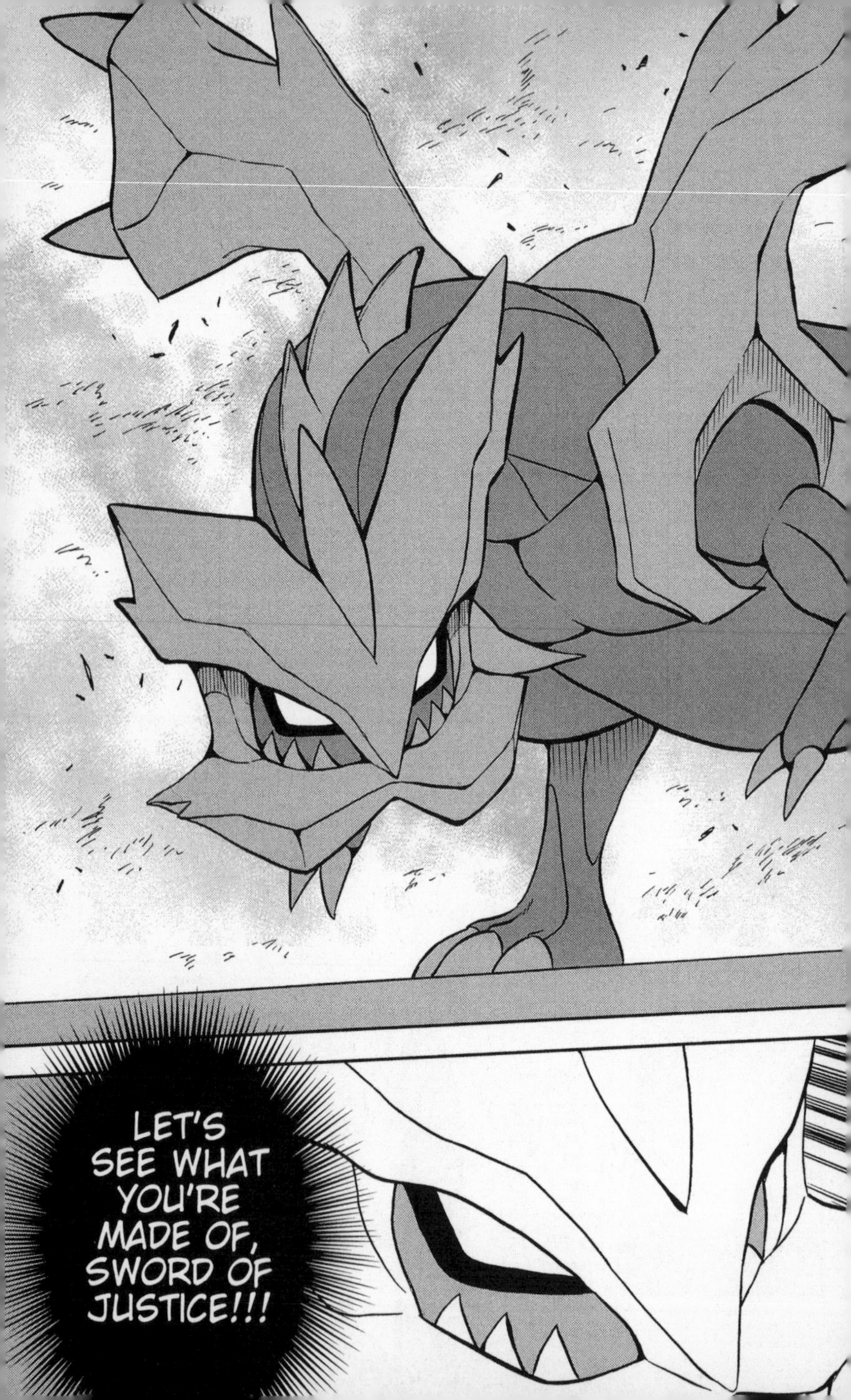
LET'S SEE WHAT YOU'RE MADE OF, SWORD OF JUSTICE!!!

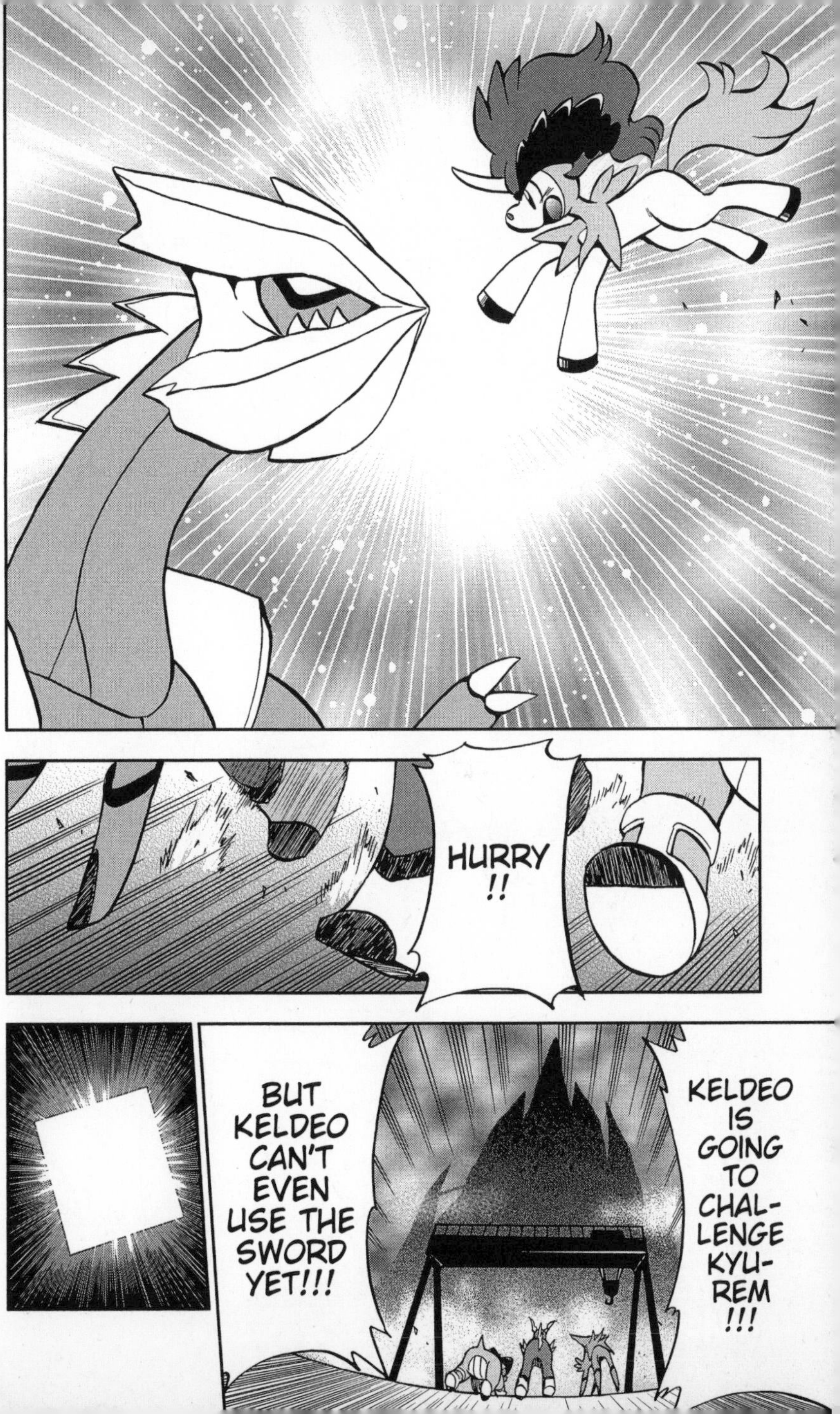
HURRY!!
KELDEO IS GOING TO CHAL-LENGE KYU-REM!!!
BUT KELDEO CAN'T EVEN USE THE SWORD YET!!!

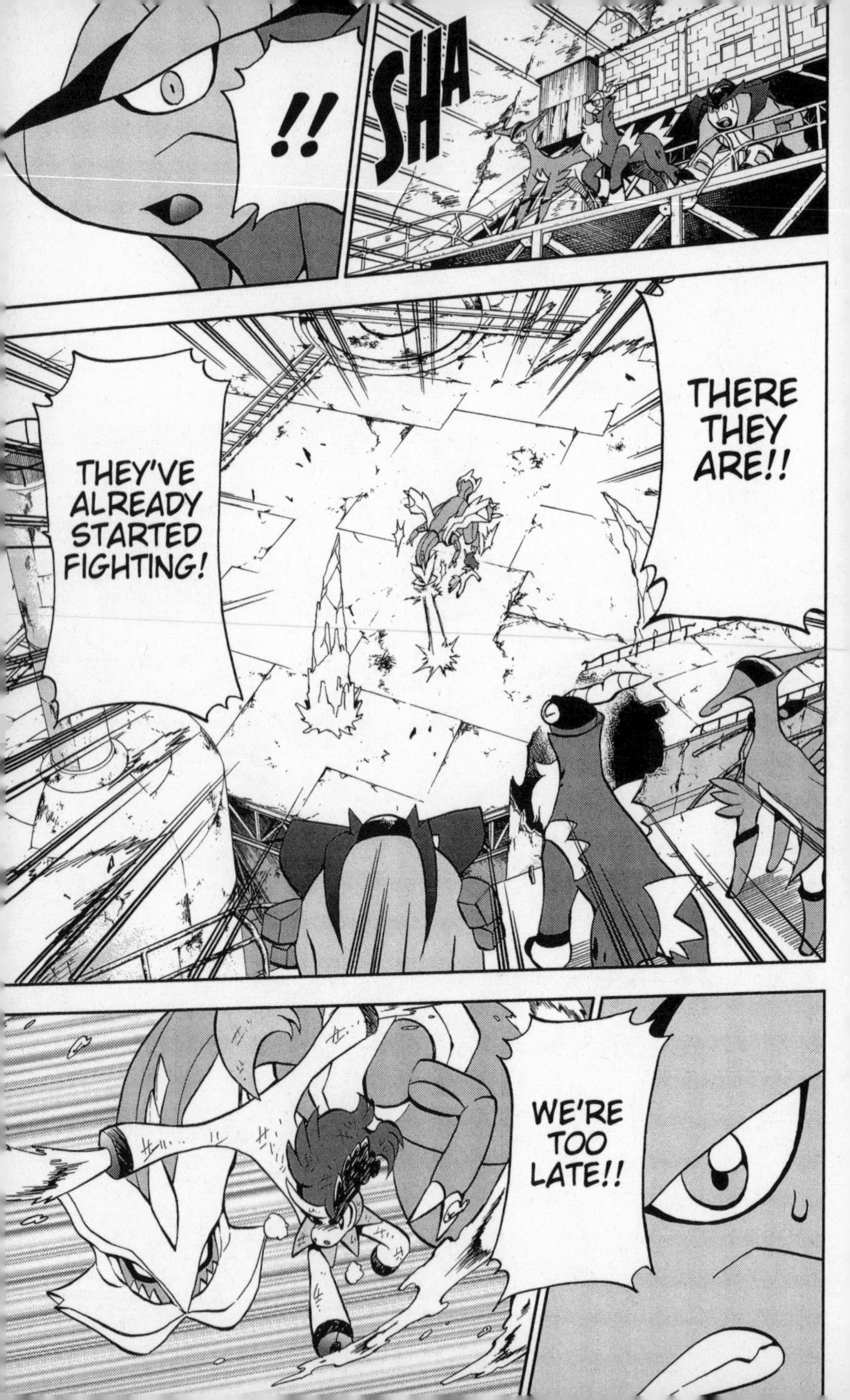
SHA
!!
THERE THEY ARE!!
THEY'VE ALREADY STARTED FIGHTING!
WE'RE TOO LATE!!

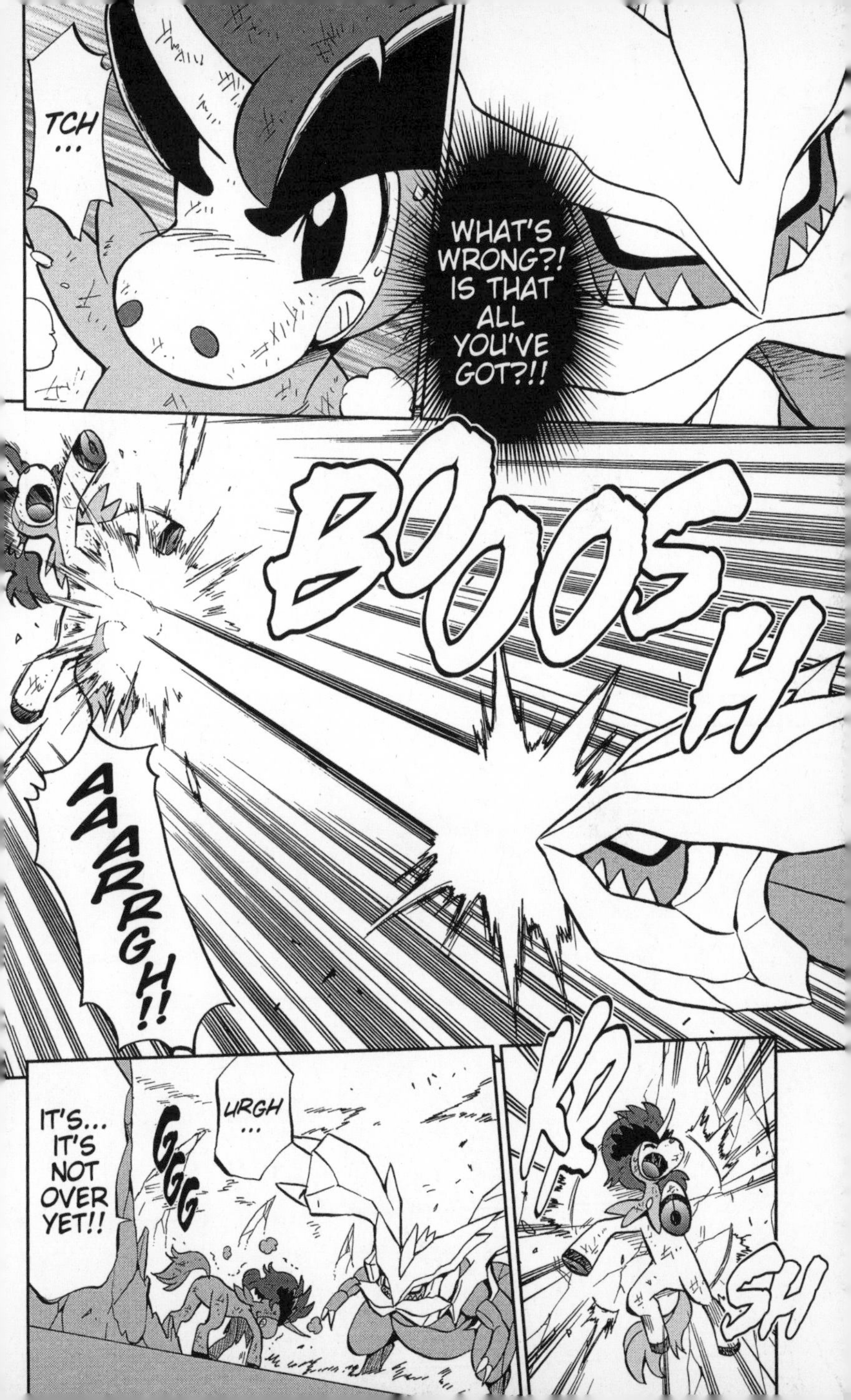
WHAT'S WRONG?! IS THAT ALL YOU'VE GOT?!!
TCH...
BOOOOSH
AAARRGH!!
KR
SH
URGH...
GGG
IT'S... IT'S NOT OVER YET!!

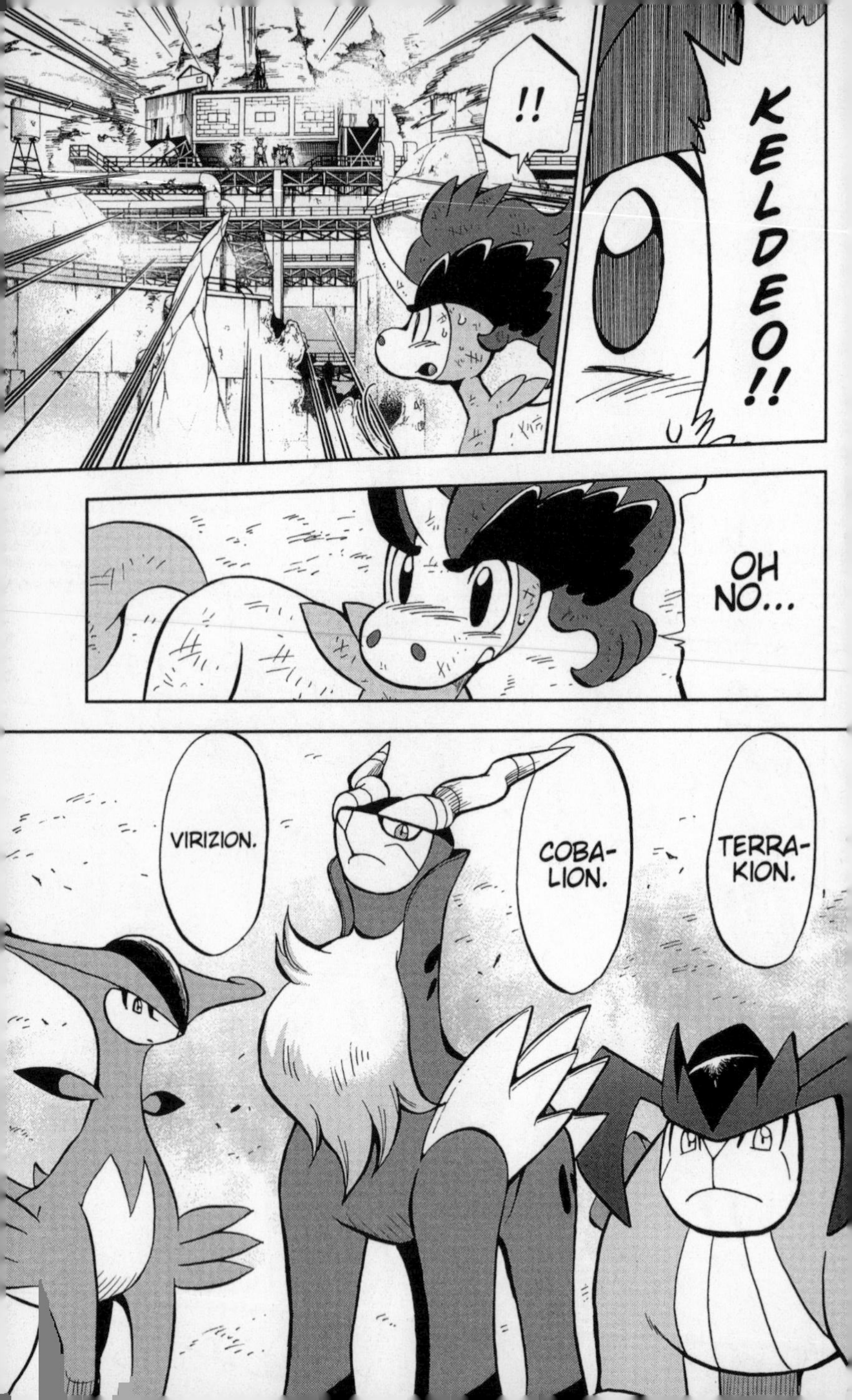
KELDEO!!
!!
OH NO...
TERRA-KION.
COBA-LION.
VIRIZION.

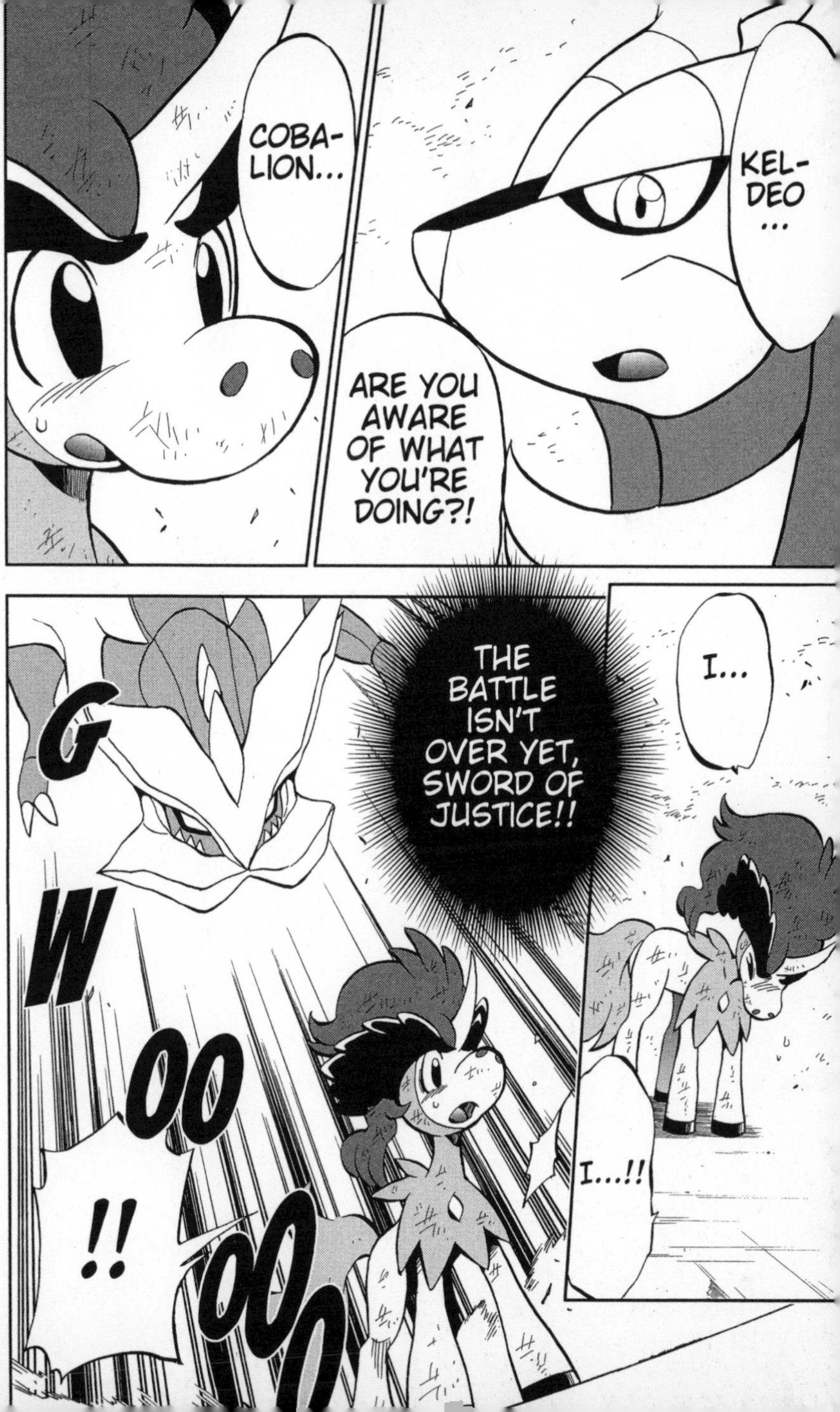
KEL-DEO...
ARE YOU AWARE OF WHAT YOU'RE DOING?!
COBA-LION...
I...
I...!!
THE BATTLE ISN'T OVER YET, SWORD OF JUSTICE!!
GWOOOO!!

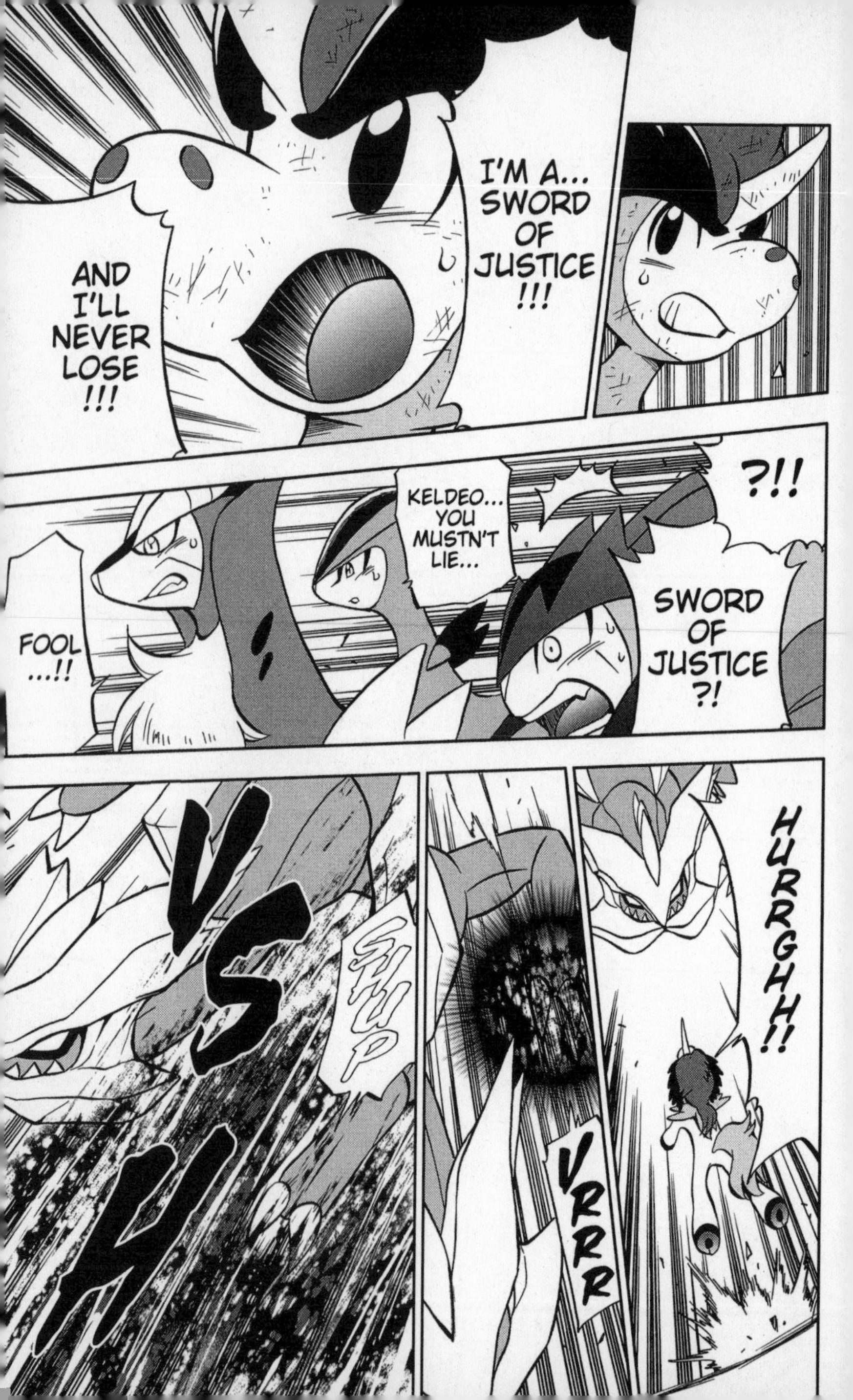
I'M A... SWORD OF JUSTICE!!!
AND I'LL NEVER LOSE!!!
?!!
SWORD OF JUSTICE?!
KELDEO... YOU MUSTN'T LIE...
FOOL...!!
HURRGHH!!
VRRR
SHUP

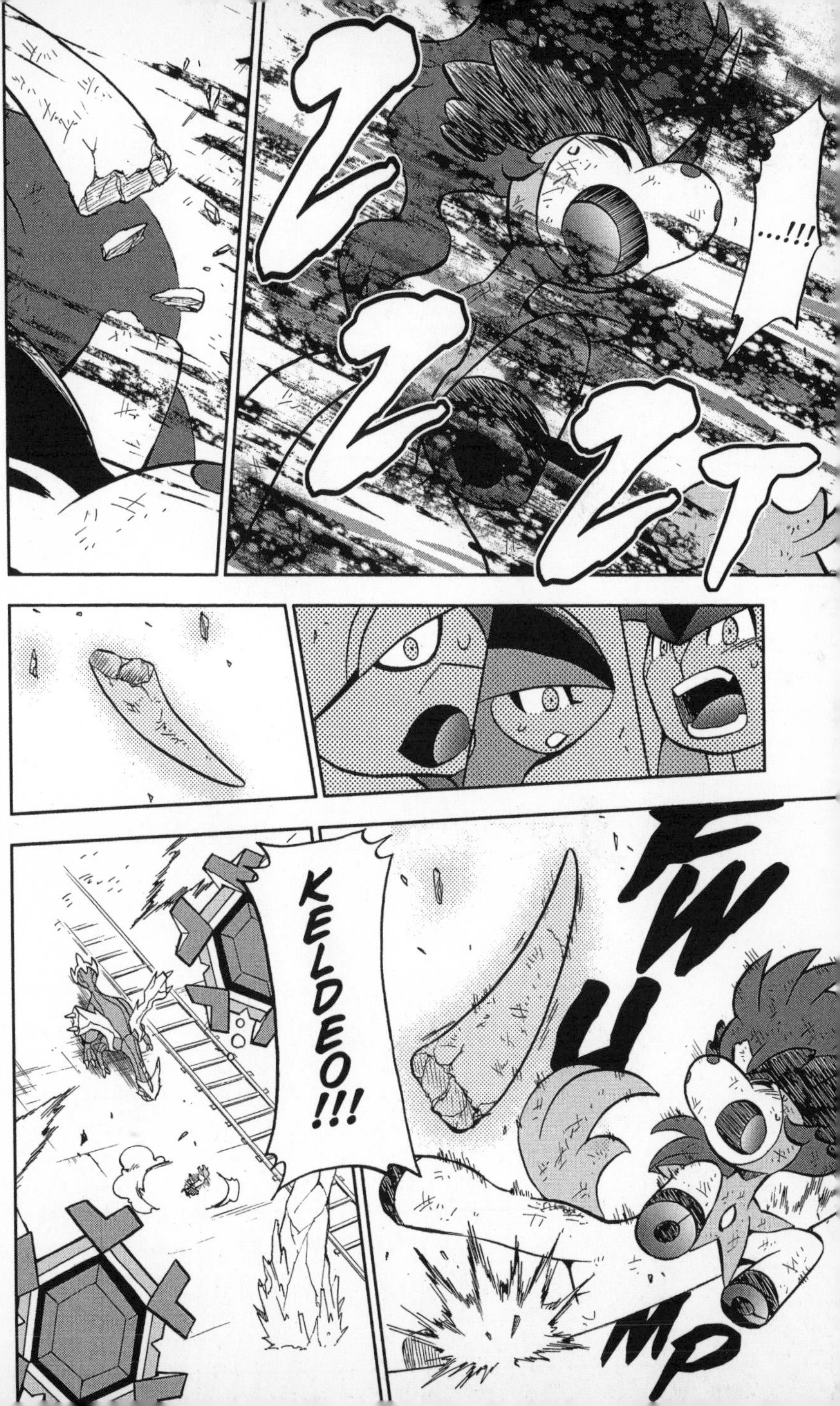
...!!!
ZZZT
FWUMP
KELDEO!!!

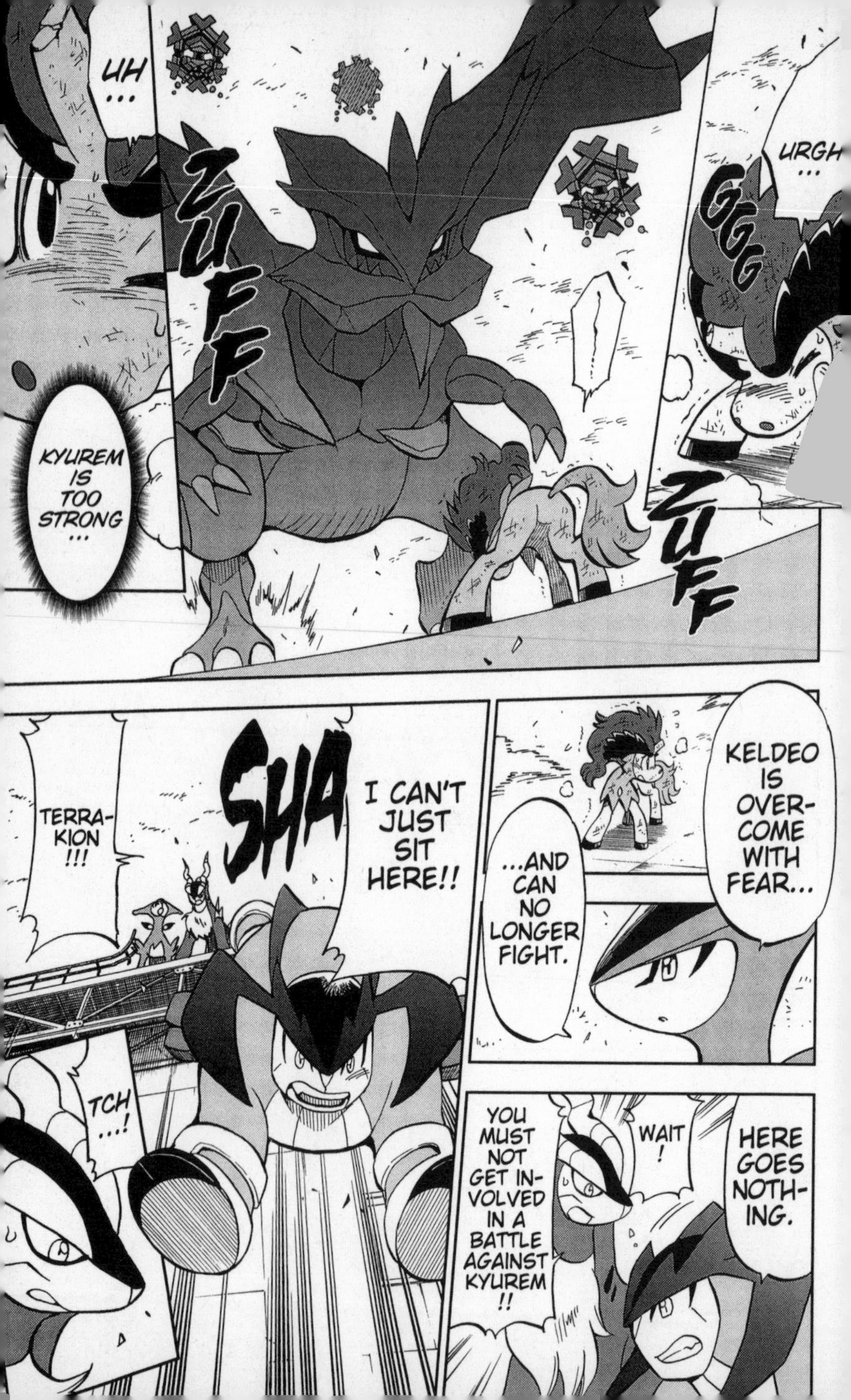
URGH ...
GGG
ZUFF
!
ZUFF
UH ...
KYUREM IS TOO STRONG ...
KELDEO IS OVER-COME WITH FEAR...
...AND CAN NO LONGER FIGHT.
HERE GOES NOTH-ING.
WAIT!
YOU MUST NOT GET IN-VOLVED IN A BATTLE AGAINST KYUREM!!
I CAN'T JUST SIT HERE!!
SHA
TERRA-KION !!!
TCH ...!

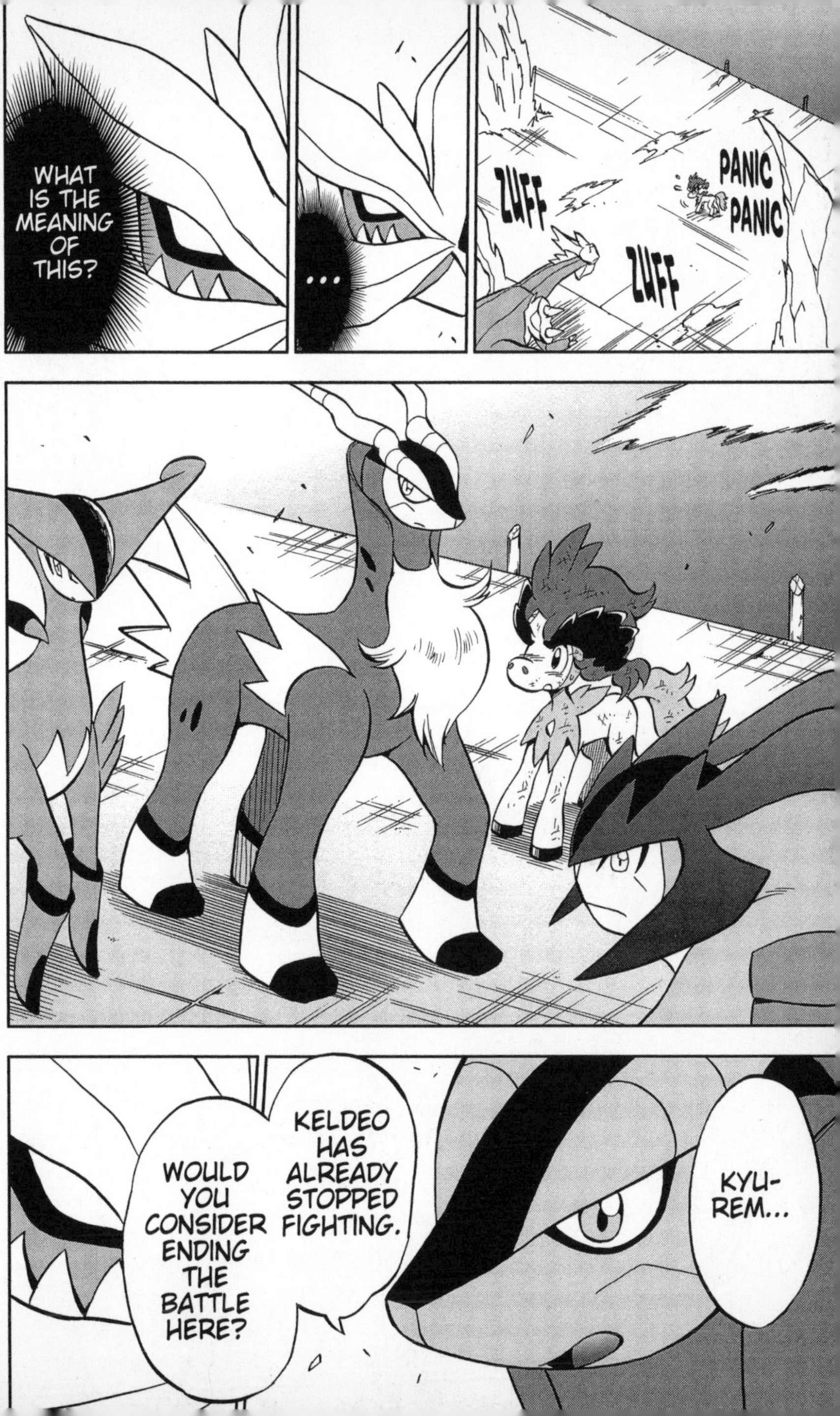
PANIC
PANIC
ZUFF
ZUFF
...
WHAT IS THE MEANING OF THIS?
KYU-REM...
KELDEO HAS ALREADY STOPPED FIGHTING.
WOULD YOU CONSIDER ENDING THE BATTLE HERE?

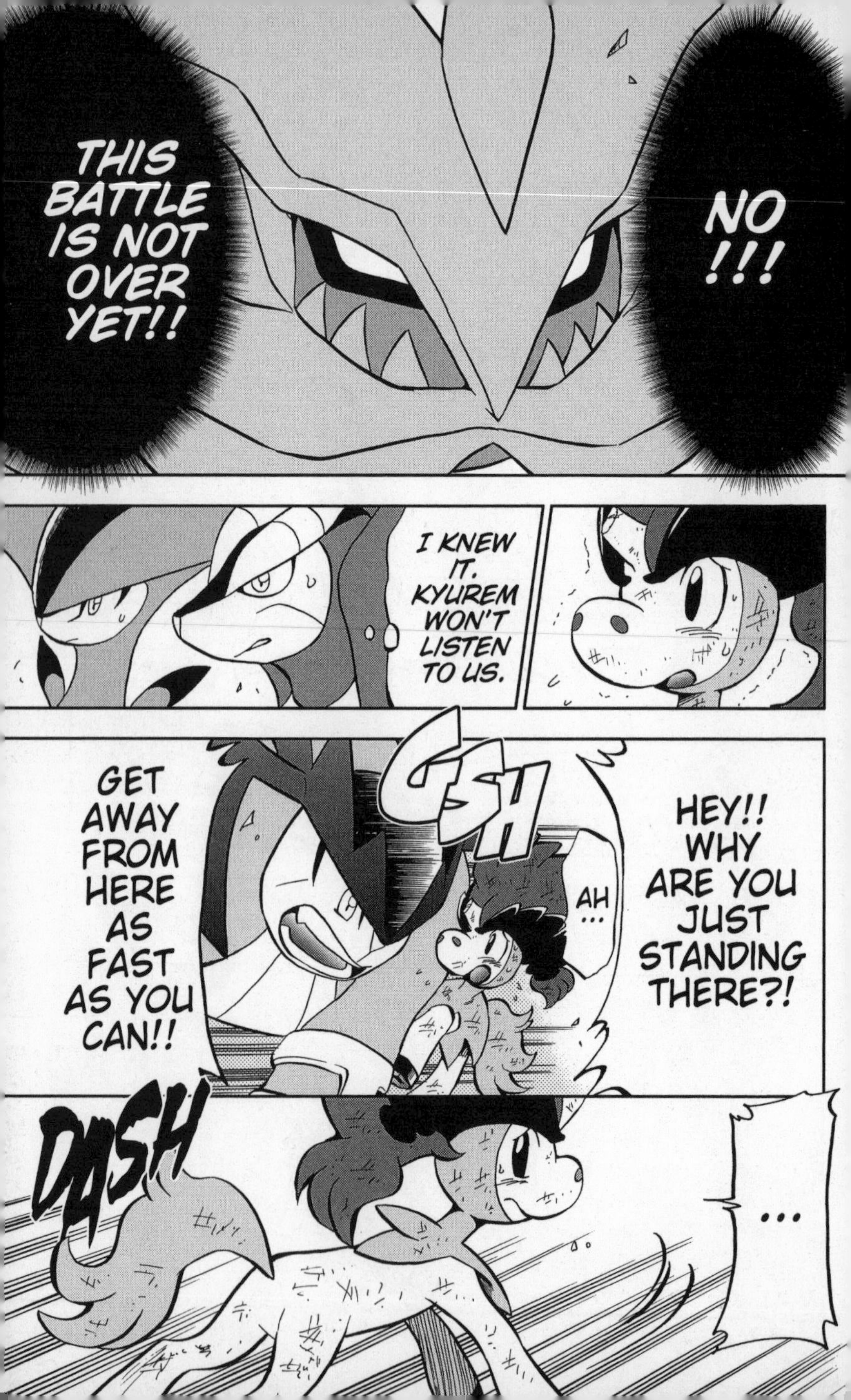
NO!!!
THIS BATTLE IS NOT OVER YET!!
I KNEW IT. KYUREM WON'T LISTEN TO US.
HEY!! WHY ARE YOU JUST STANDING THERE?!
AH...
GET AWAY FROM HERE AS FAST AS YOU CAN!!
...
DASH

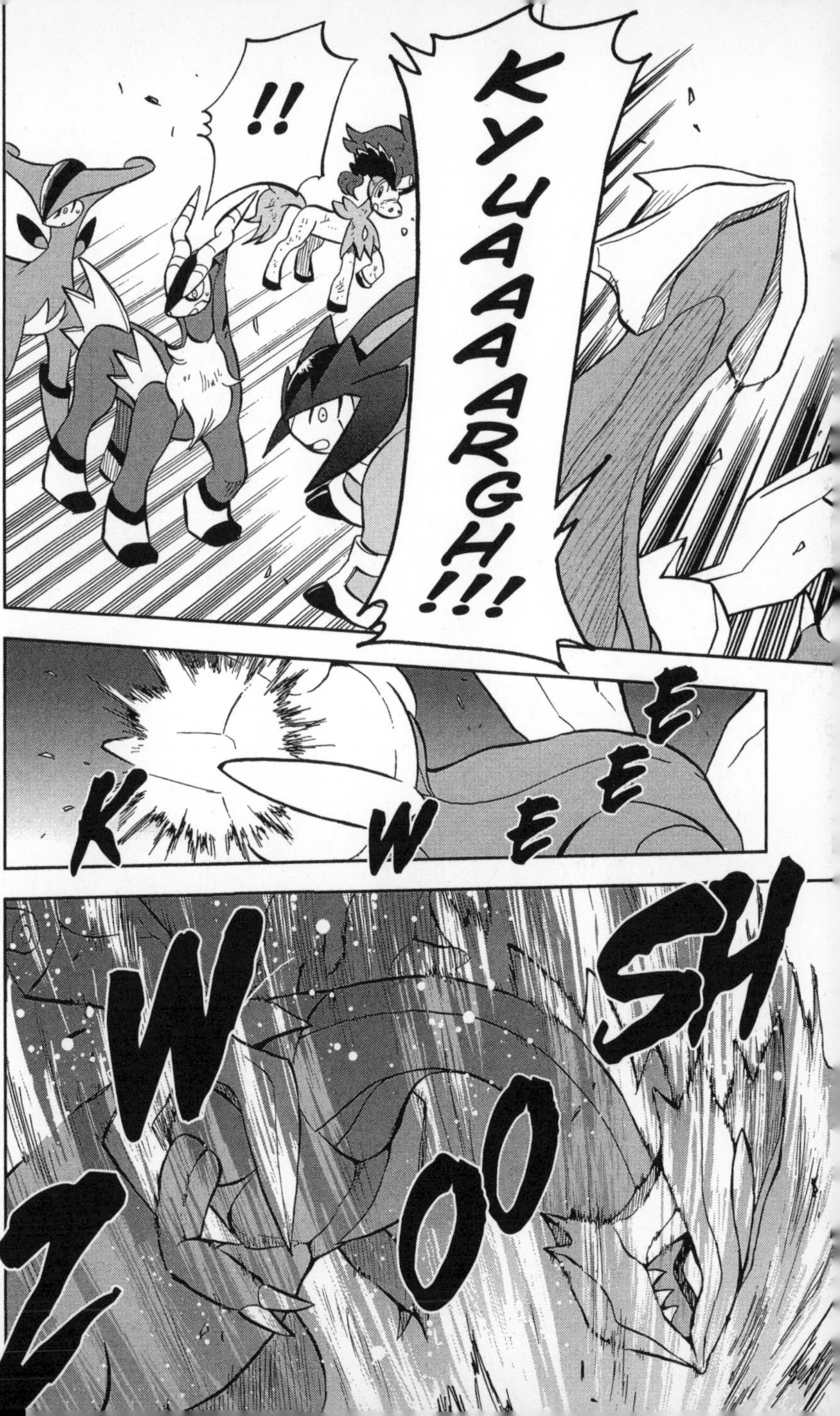
KYUAAAARGH!!!
!!
KWEEE
ZWOOSH

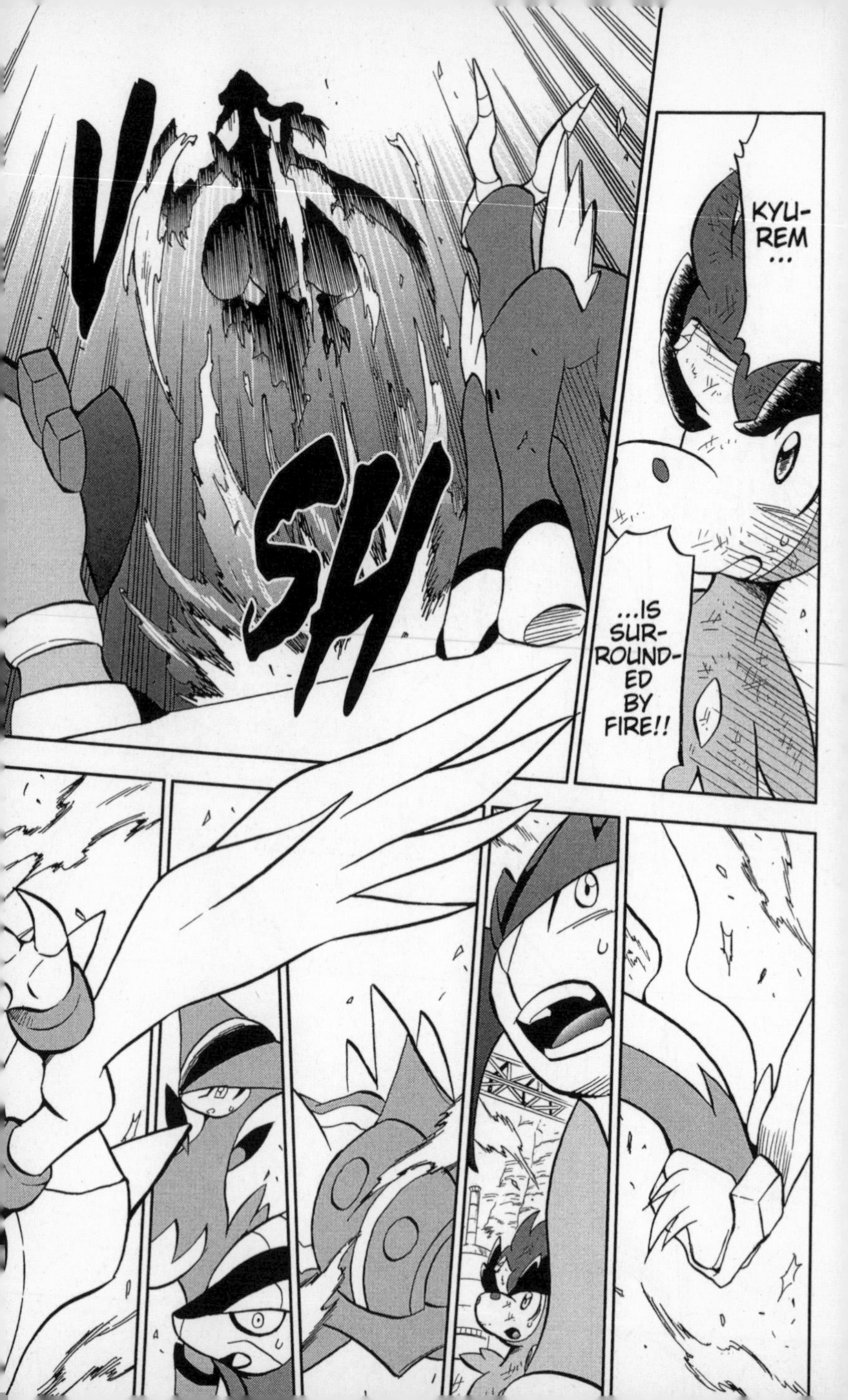
KYU-REM...
...IS SUR-ROUND-ED BY FIRE!!
VA
SH

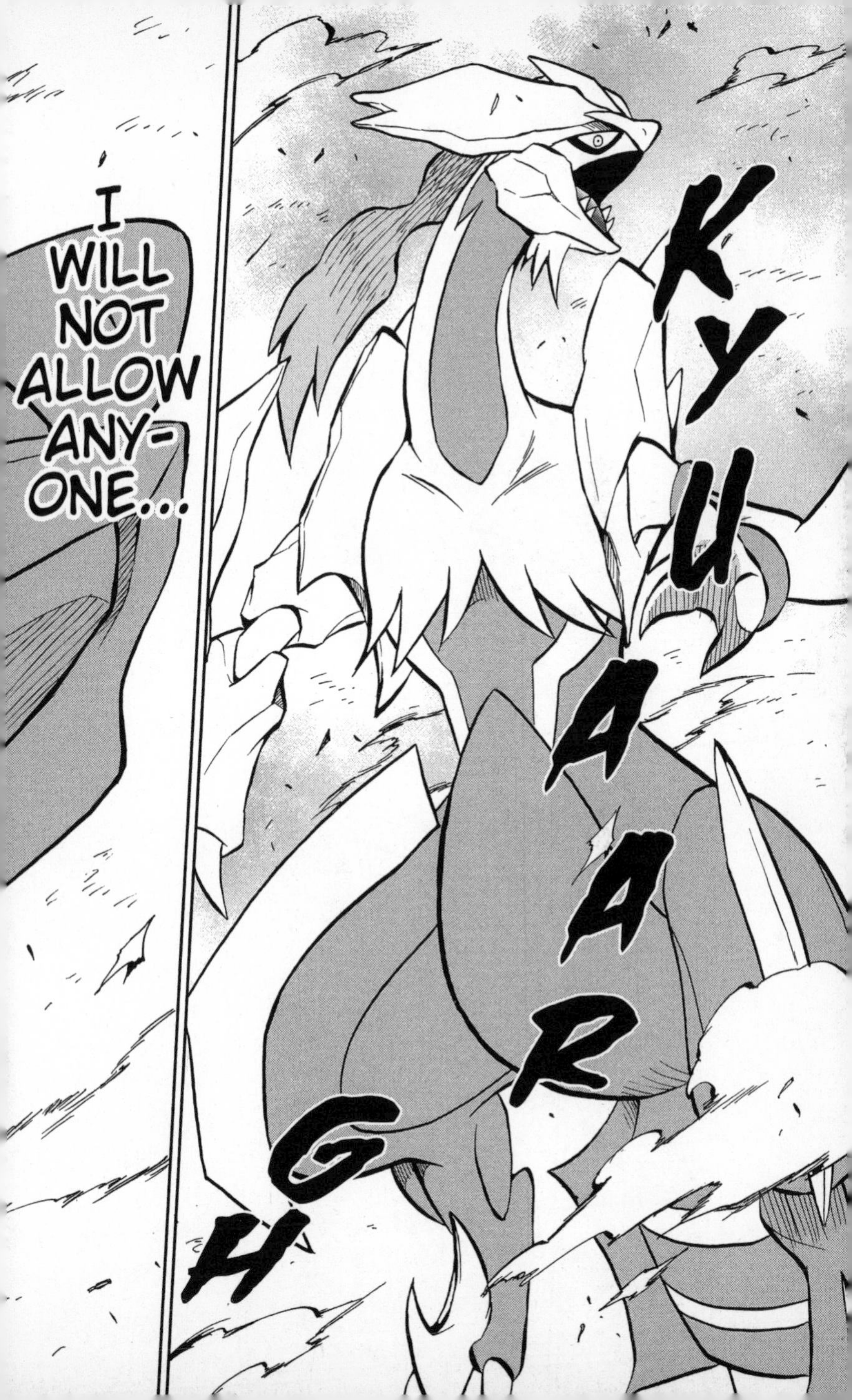
KYUAARGH
I WILL NOT ALLOW ANYONE...

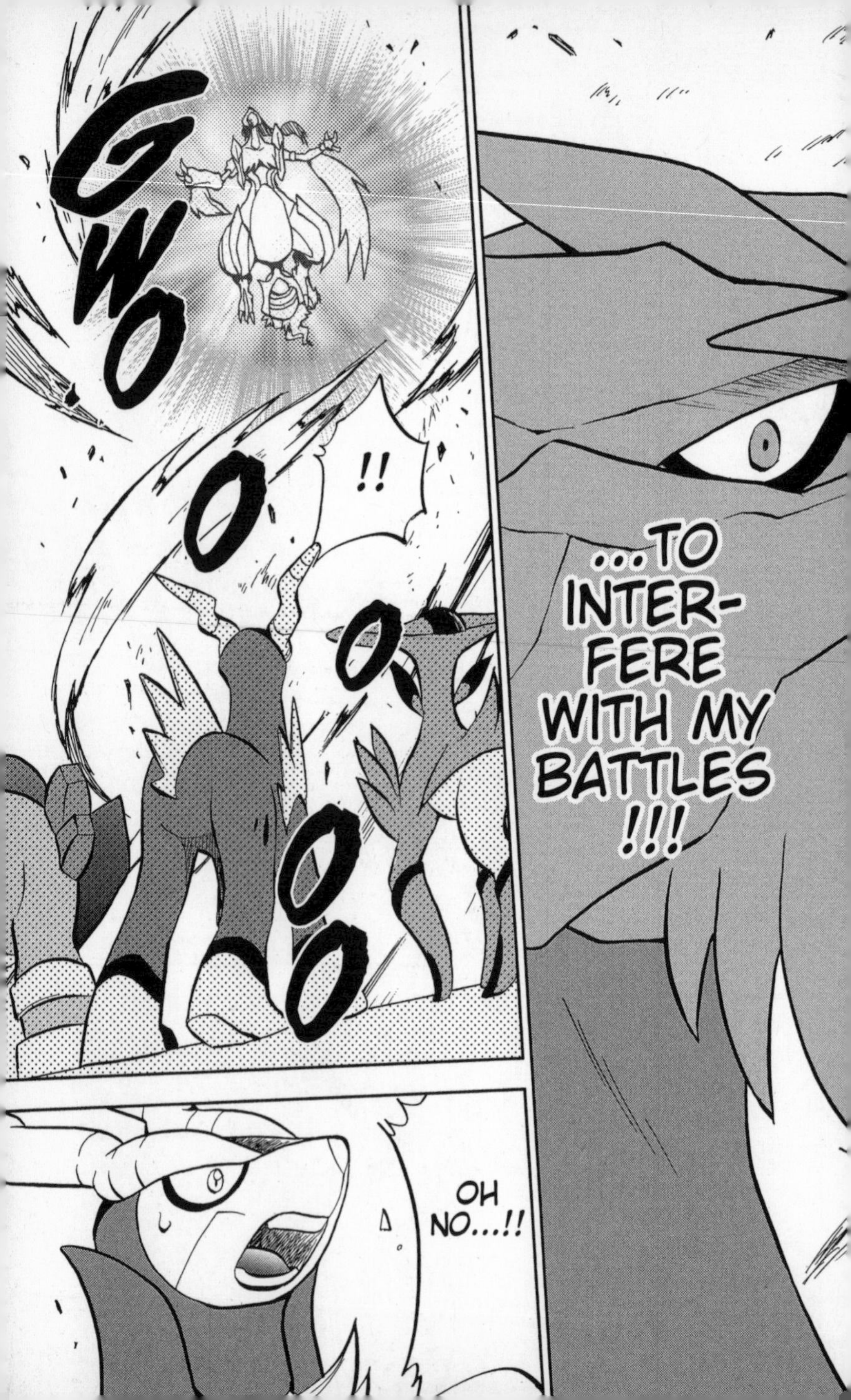
...TO INTER-FERE WITH MY BATTLES !!!
GWOOOOOO
!!
OH NO...!!

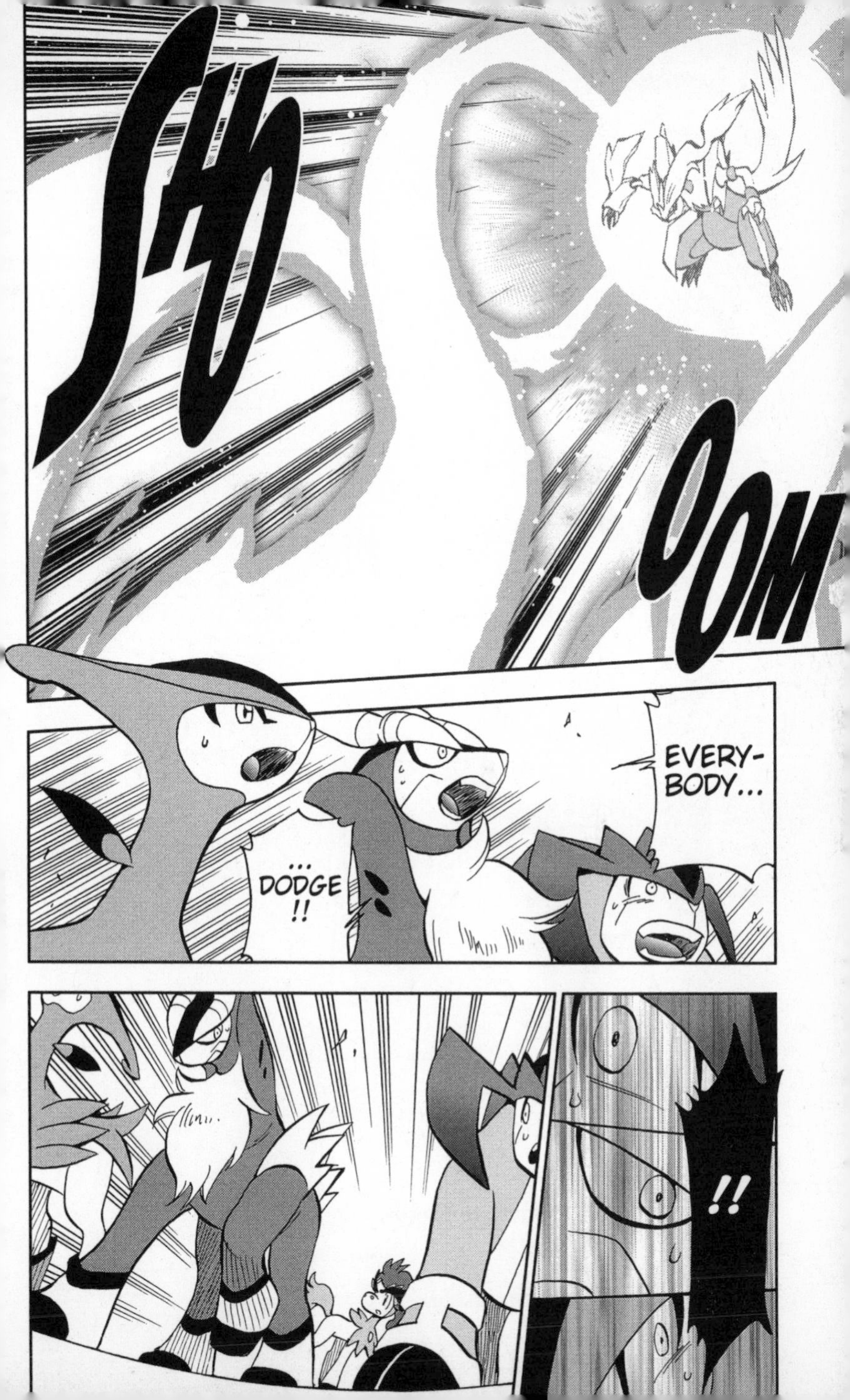
SHOOOM
EVERY-BODY...
... DODGE !!
!!

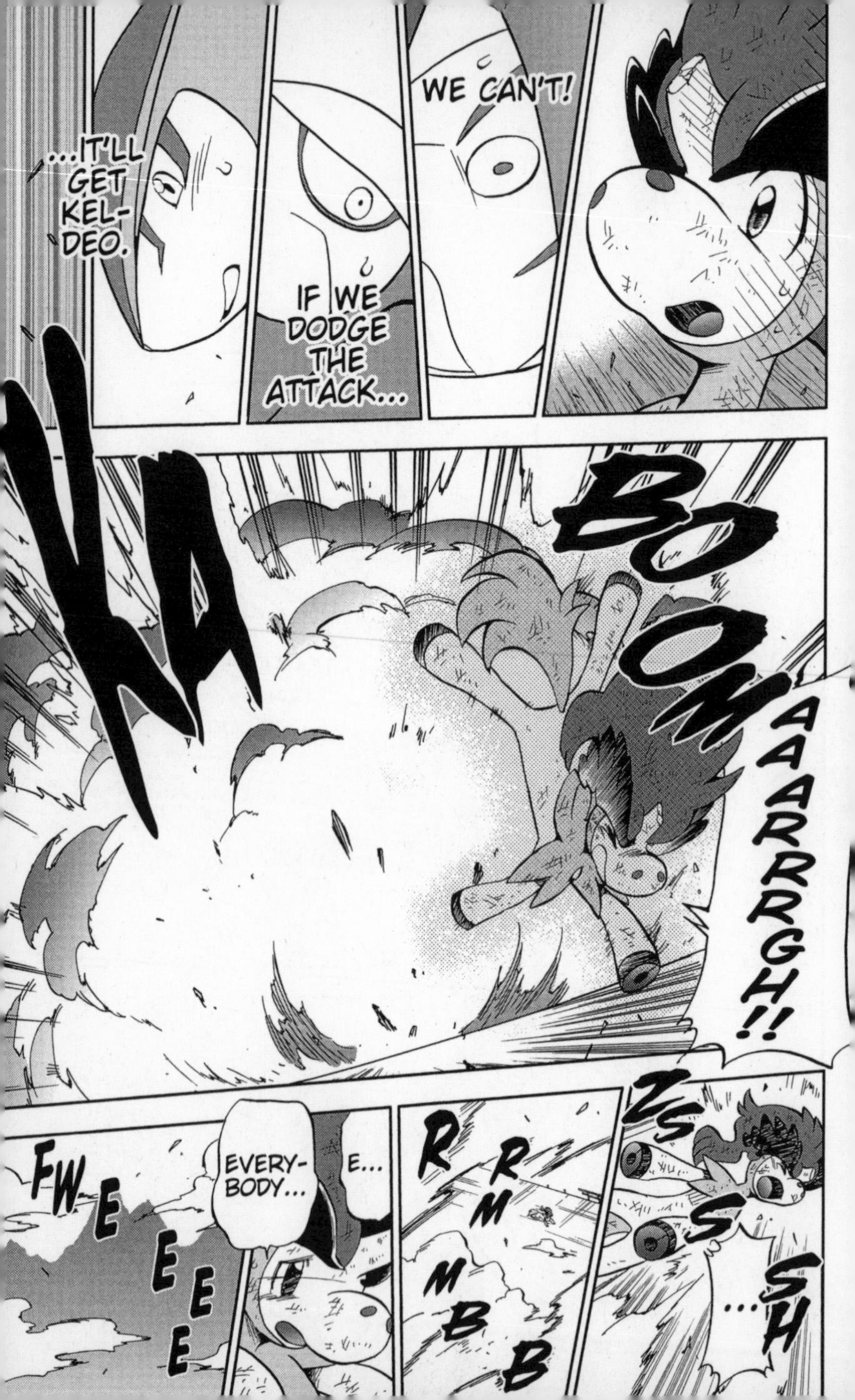

WE CAN'T!
IF WE DODGE THE ATTACK...
...IT'LL GET KEL-DEO.
KA
BOOM
AAAARRRRGH!!
ZSS
...SH
RRMMBB
E...
EVERY-BODY...
FWEEEEE

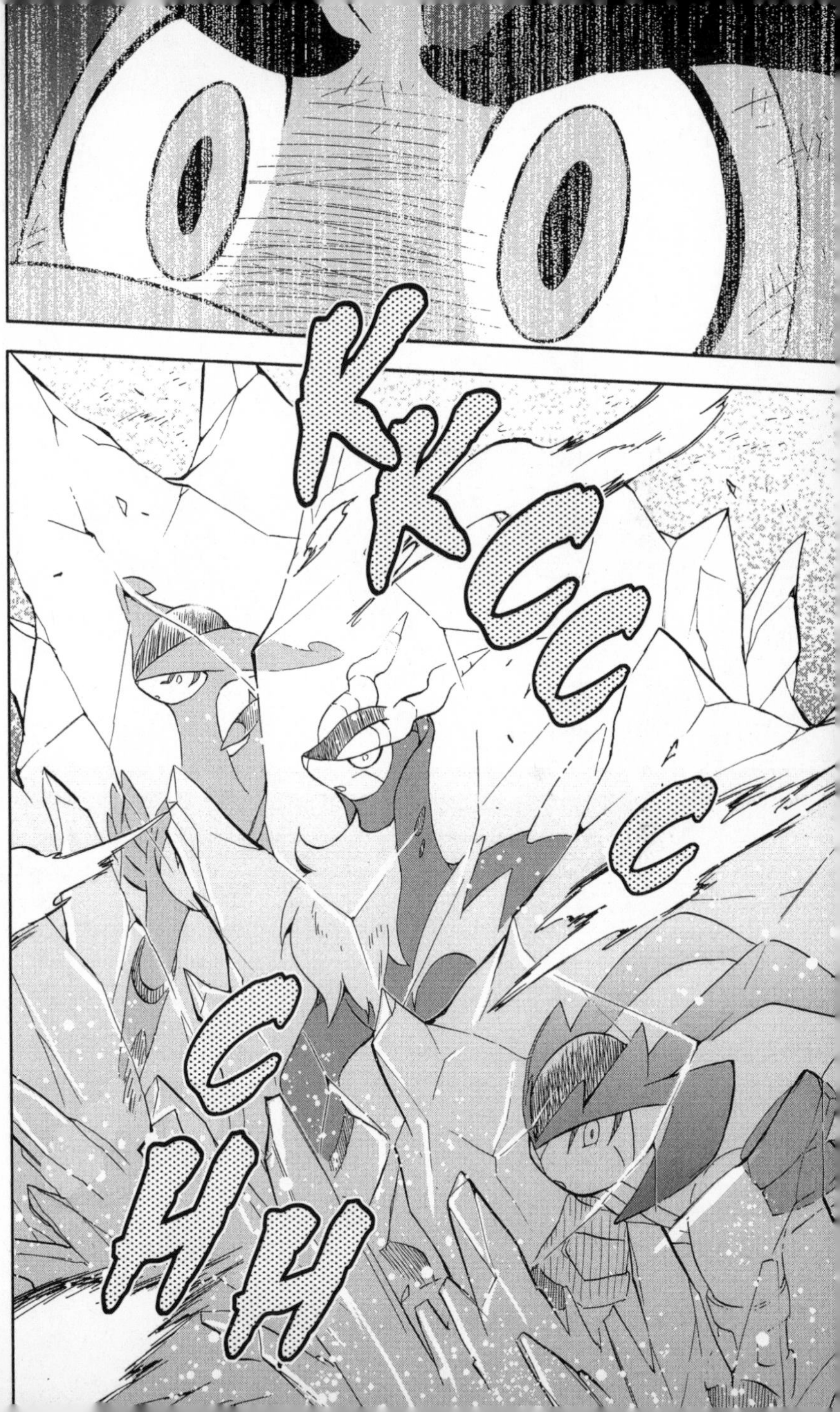
KKCCCC
CHH

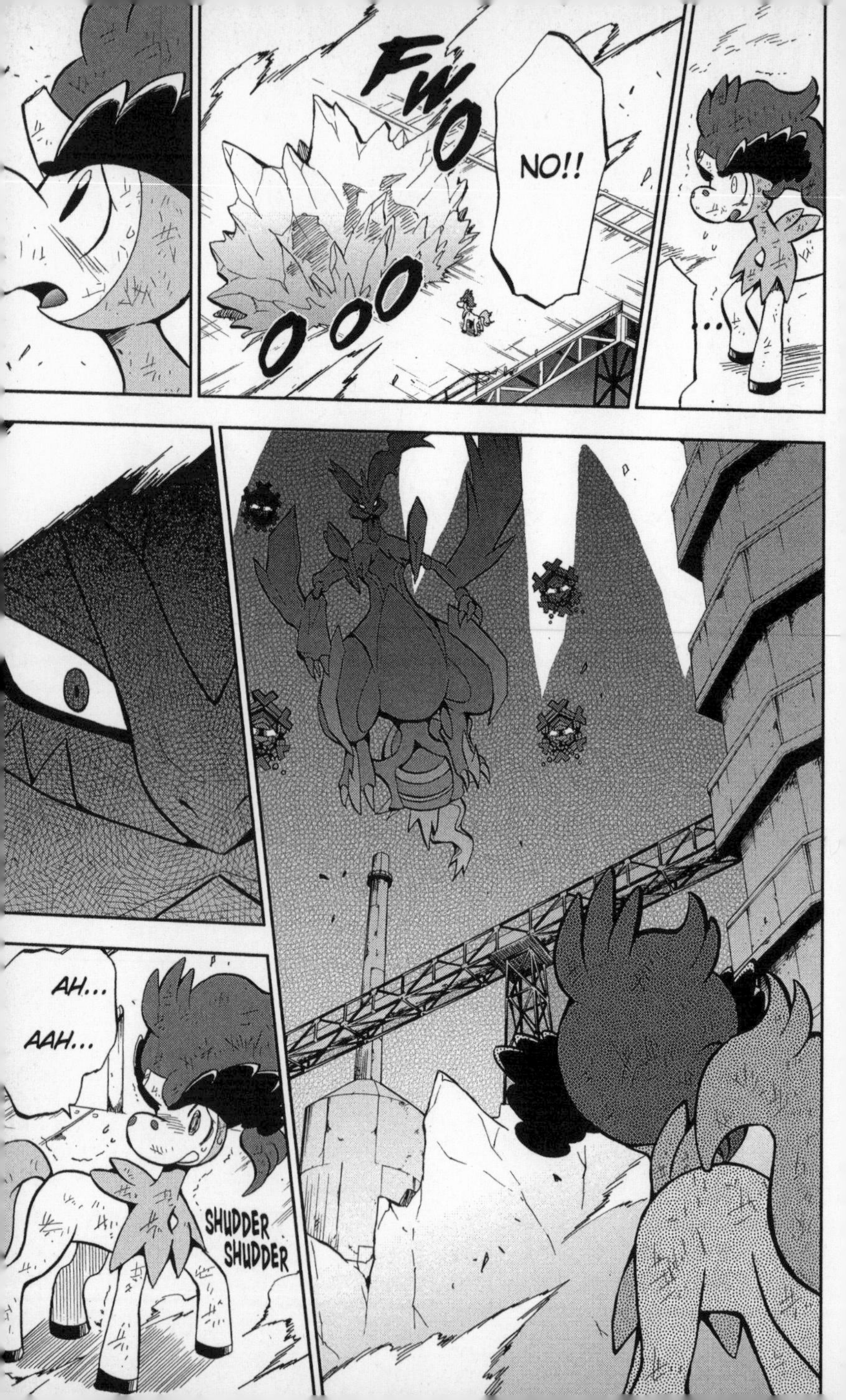
...
FWOOOO
NO!!
AH...
AAH...
SHUDDER
SHUDDER

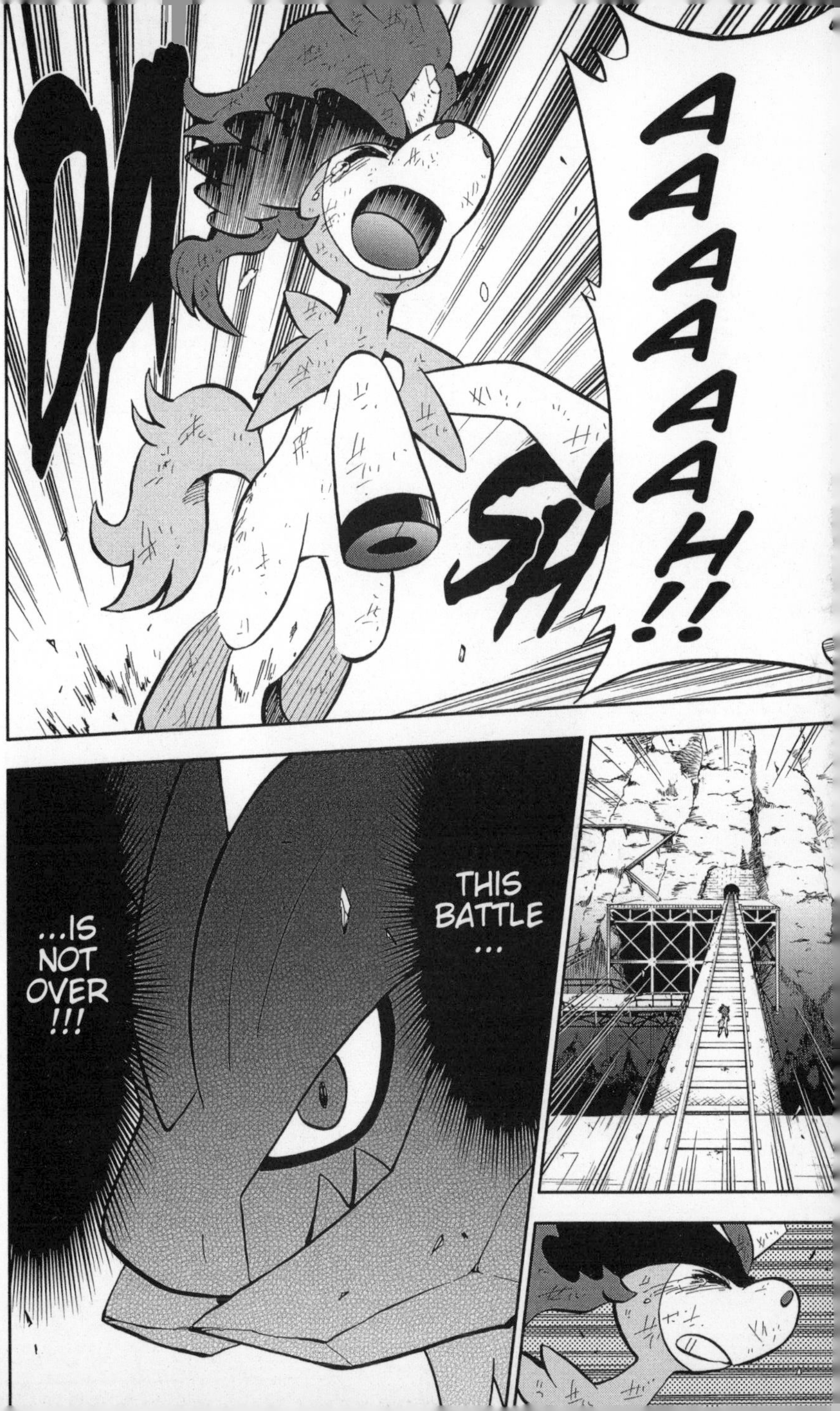
AAAAAAH!!
SH
DA
THIS BATTLE ...
...IS NOT OVER!!!

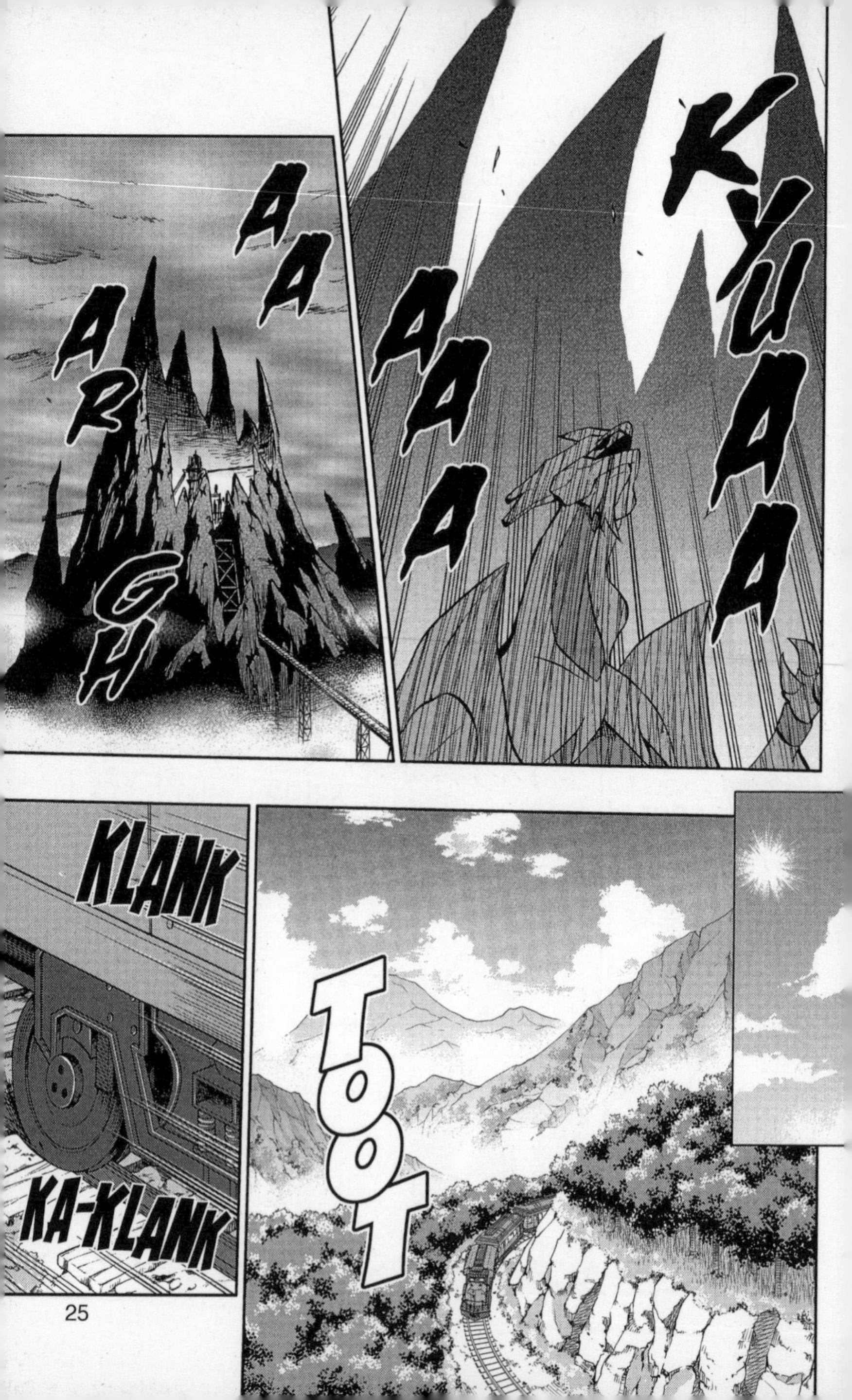
KYUAAAA
AAAA
AA
ARGH
TOOT
KLANK
KA-KLANK

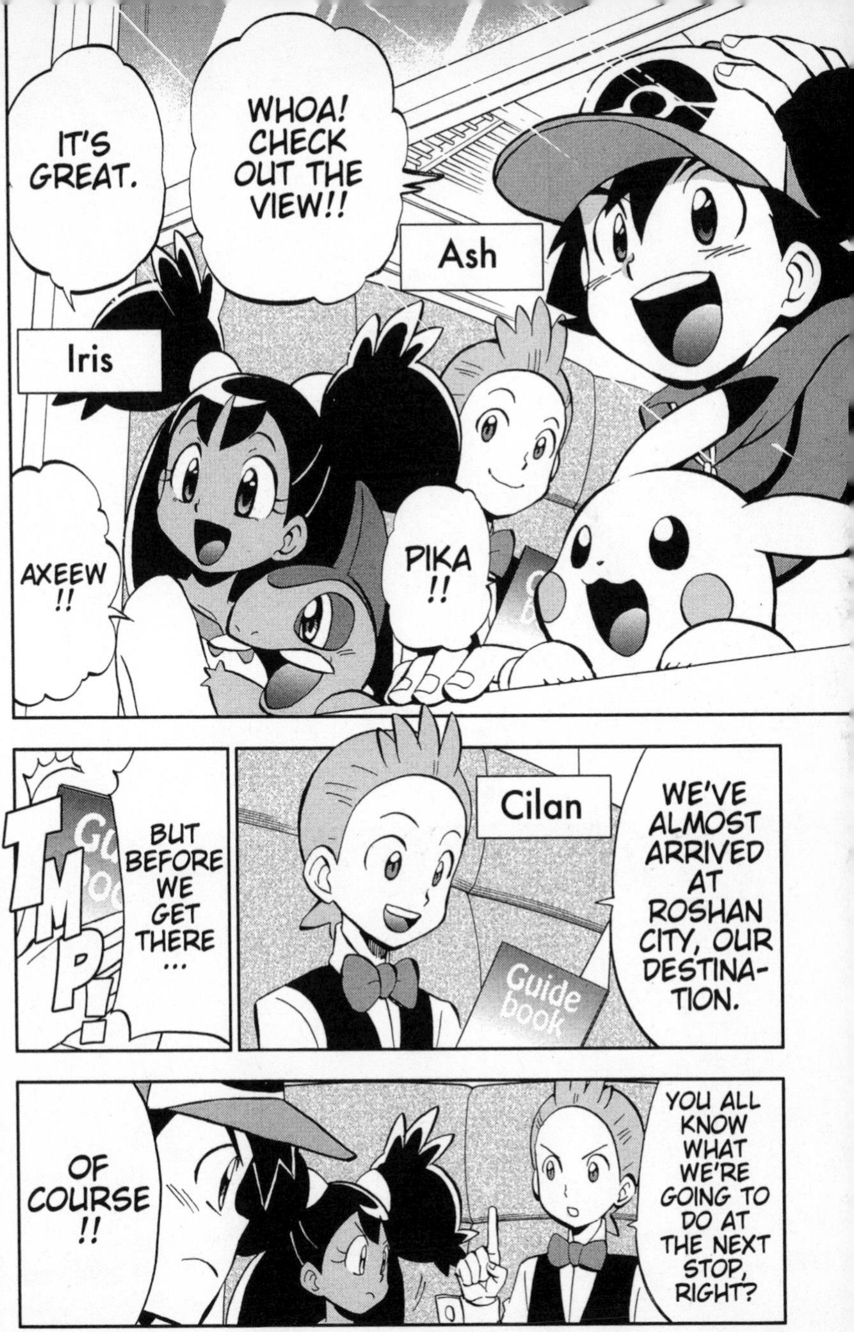

WHOA! CHECK OUT THE VIEW!!
Ash
IT'S GREAT.
Iris
PIKA!!
AXEEW!!
Cilan
WE'VE ALMOST ARRIVED AT ROSHAN CITY, OUR DESTINA-TION.
Guide book
BUT BEFORE WE GET THERE...
TMP!
YOU ALL KNOW WHAT WE'RE GOING TO DO AT THE NEXT STOP, RIGHT?
OF COURSE!!

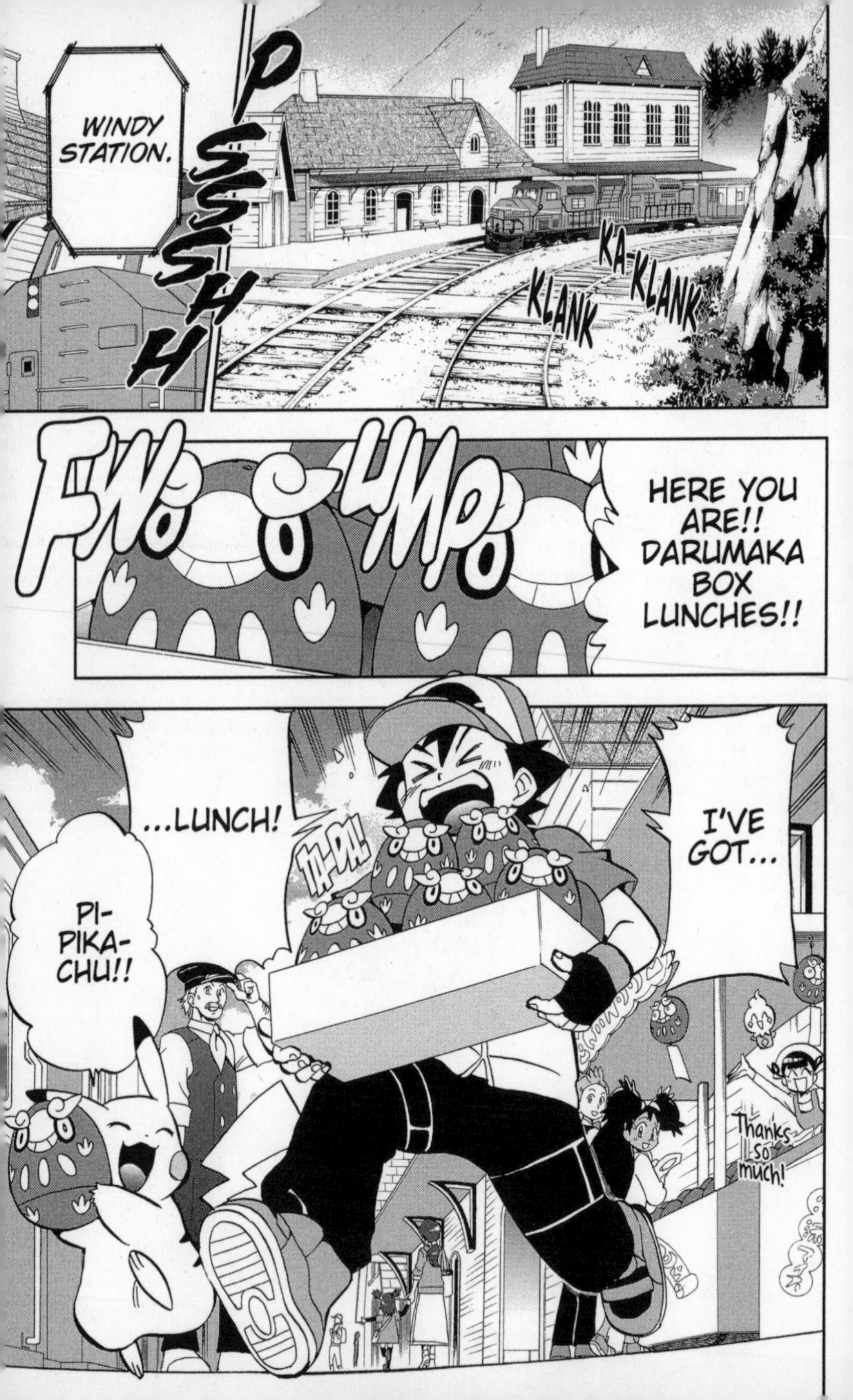
KA-KLANK
KLANK
PSSSHH
WINDY STATION.
HERE YOU ARE!! DARUMAKA BOX LUNCHES!!
I'VE GOT...
...LUNCH!
TA-DA!
Thanks so much!
PI-PIKA-CHU!!

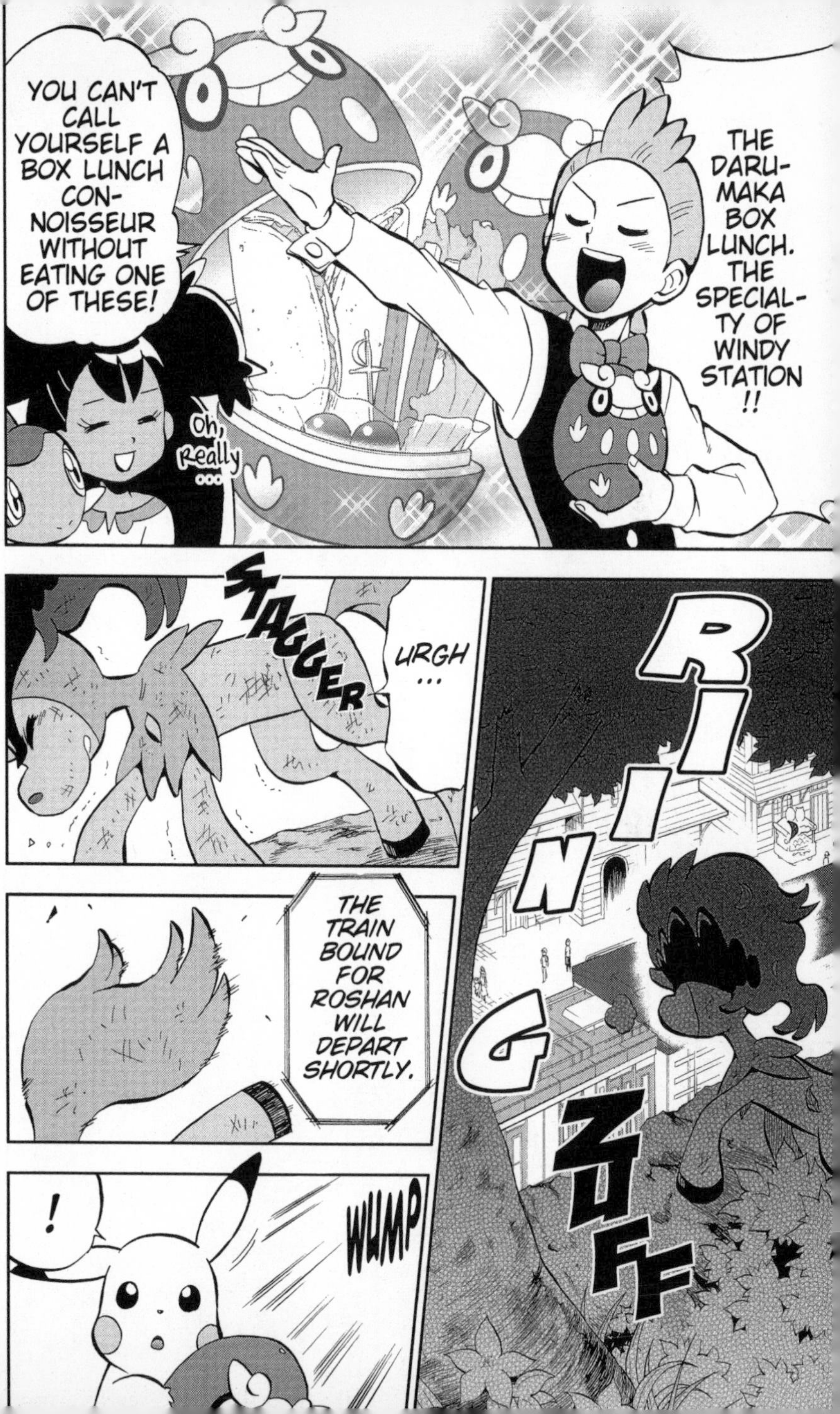
THE DARU-MAKA BOX LUNCH. THE SPECIAL-TY OF WINDY STATION!!
YOU CAN'T CALL YOURSELF A BOX LUNCH CON-NOISSEUR WITHOUT EATING ONE OF THESE!
Oh, Really...
RIING
ZUFF
STAGGER
URGH...
THE TRAIN BOUND FOR ROSHAN WILL DEPART SHORTLY.
!
WUMP
!

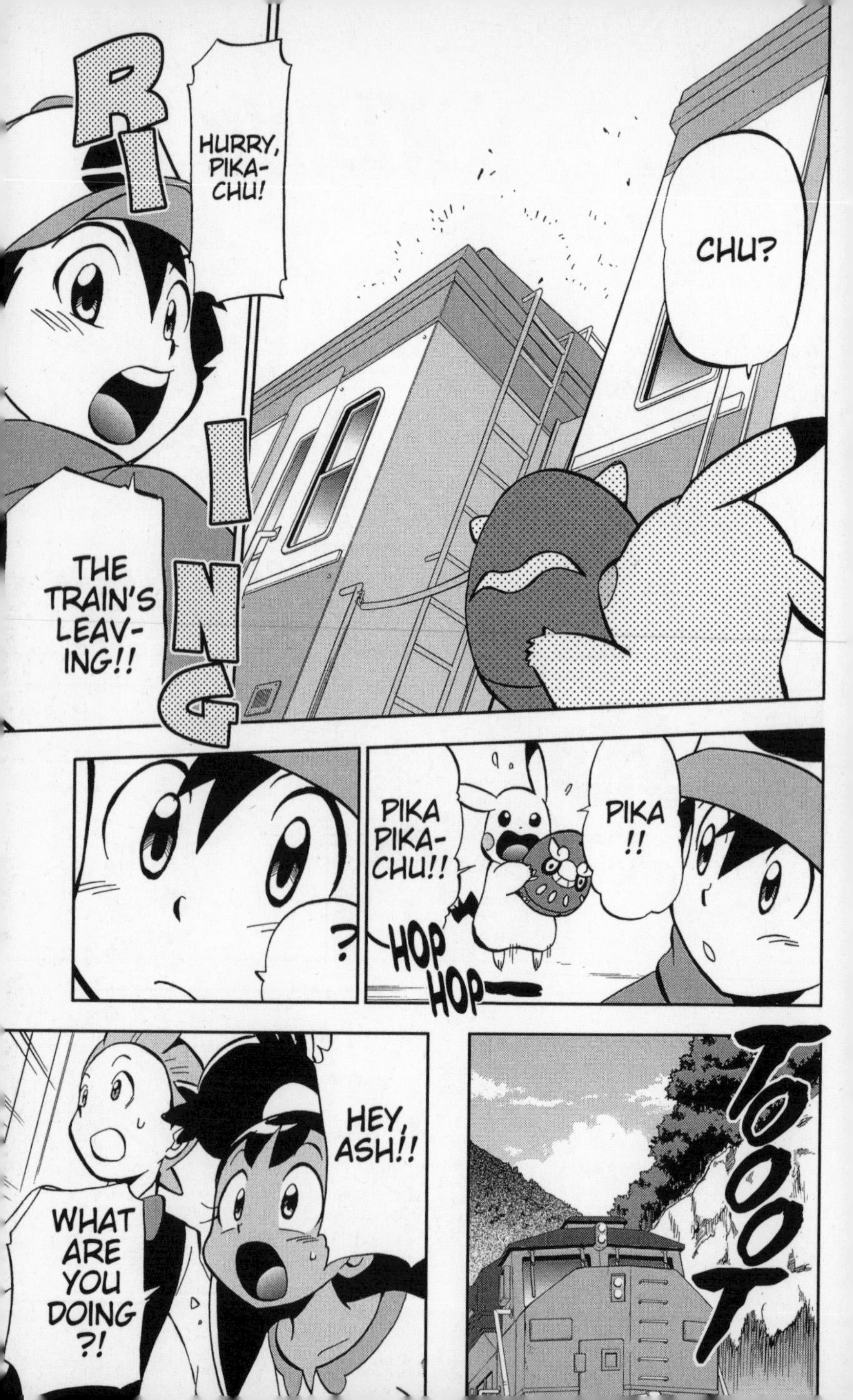
HURRY, PIKA-CHU!
RING
THE TRAIN'S LEAV-ING!!
CHU?
PIKA!!
PIKA PIKA-CHU!!
HOP HOP
?
TOOOT
HEY, ASH!!
WHAT ARE YOU DOING?!

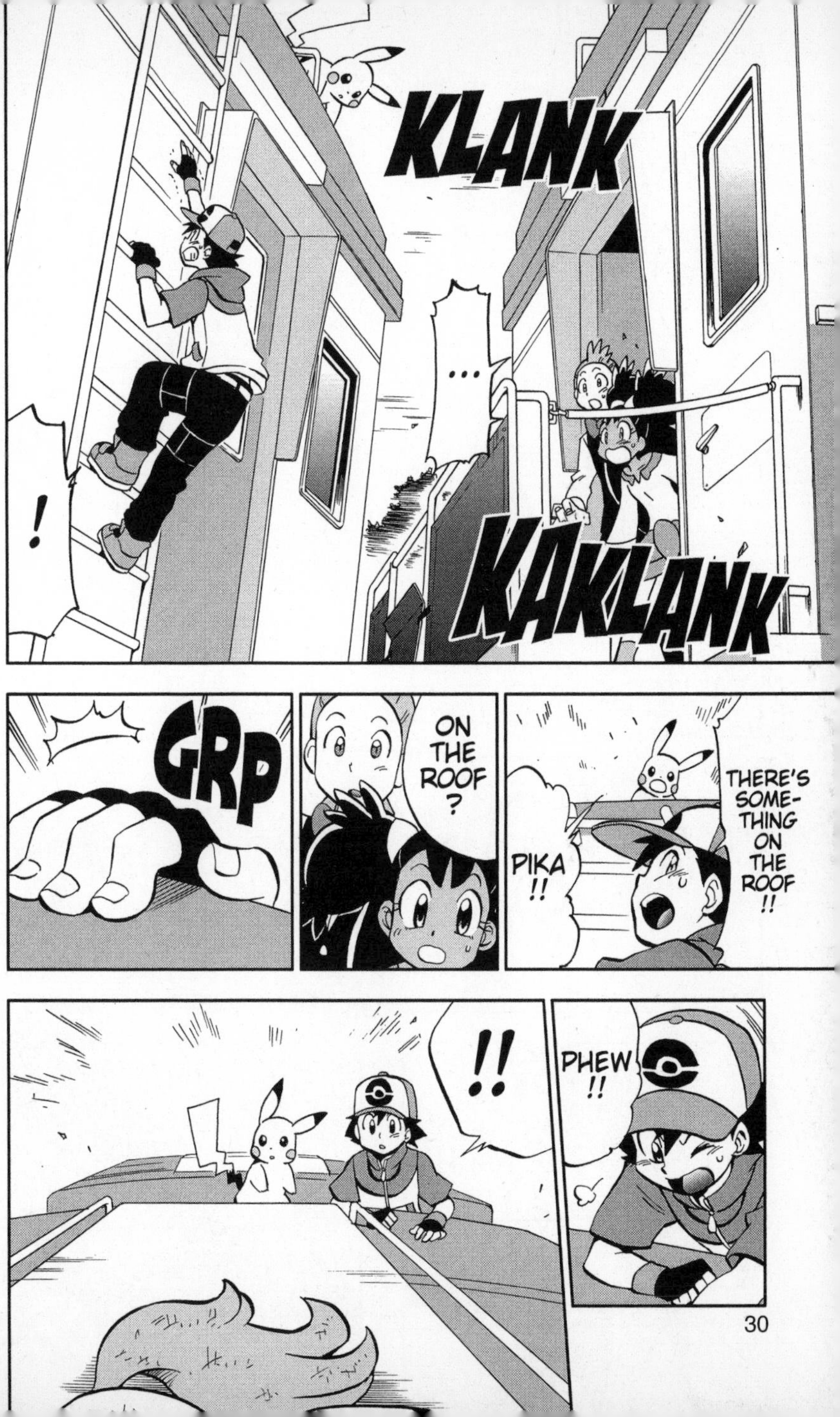

KLANK
...
KAKLANK
!
THERE'S SOME-THING ON THE ROOF!!
PIKA!!
ON THE ROOF?
GRP
PHEW!!
!!

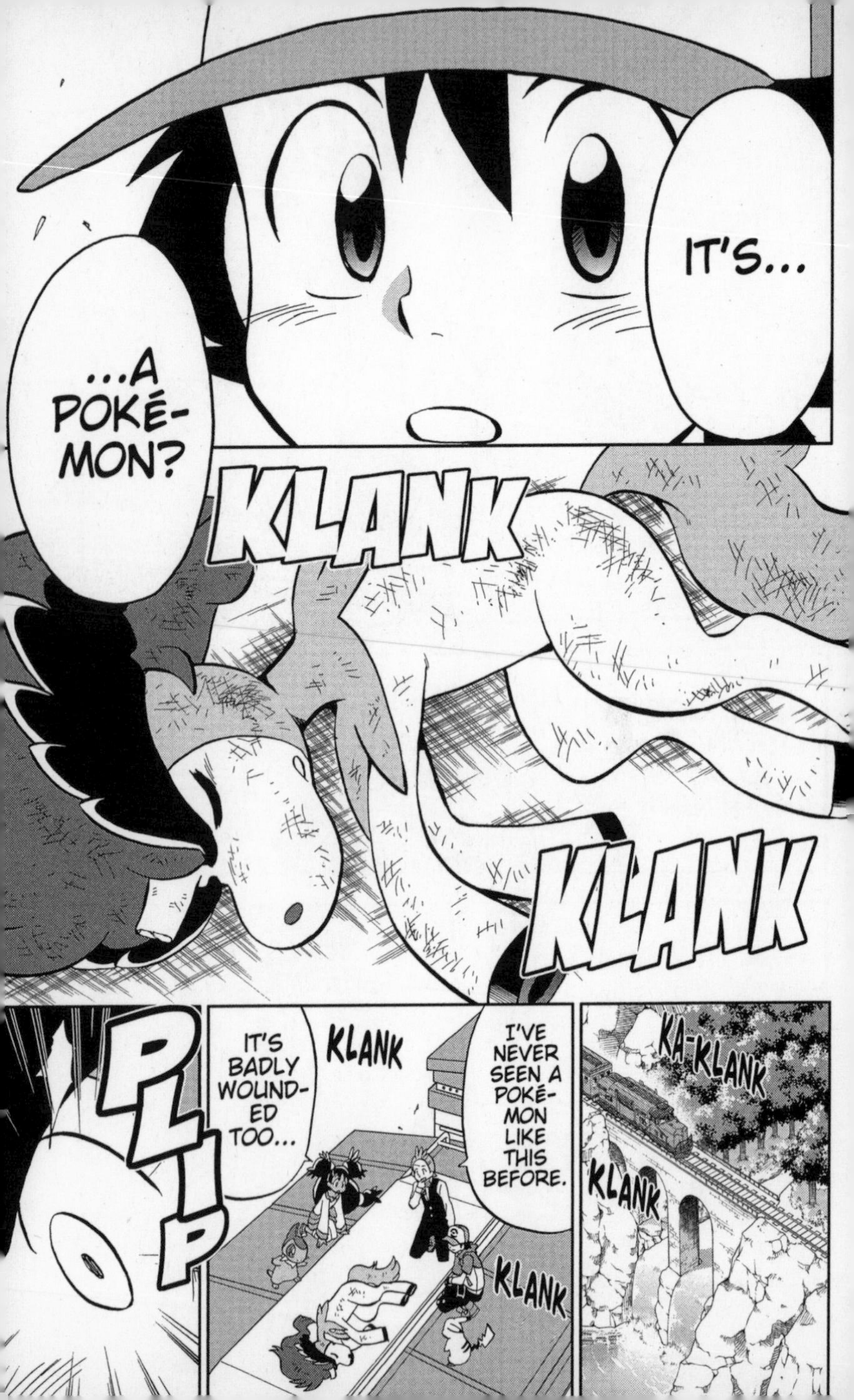
IT'S...
...A POKÉ-MON?
KLANK
KLANK
KA-KLANK
KLANK
I'VE NEVER SEEN A POKÉ-MON LIKE THIS BEFORE.
KLANK
IT'S BADLY WOUND-ED TOO...
KLANK
PLIP

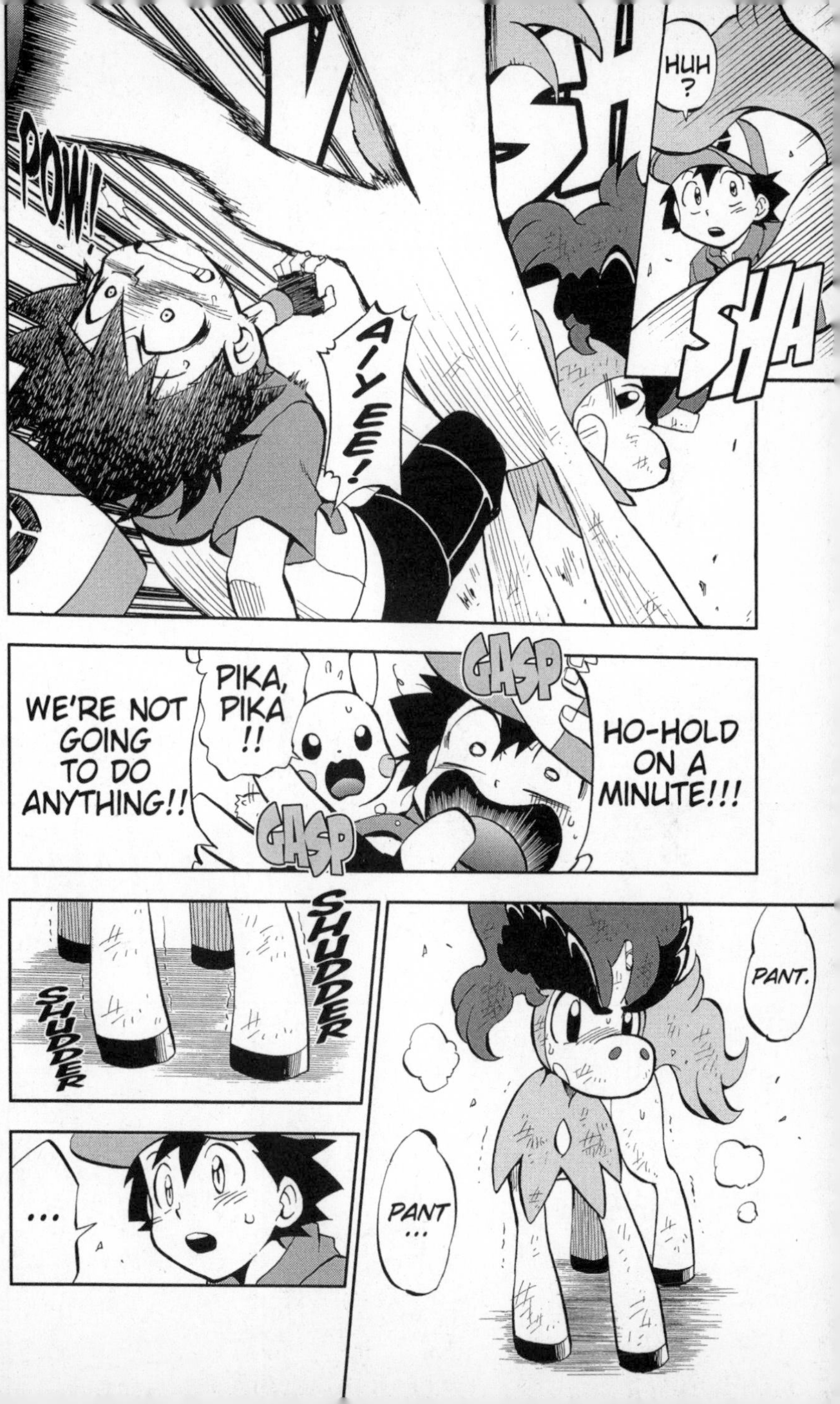
HUH?
SHA
POW!
AIYEEE!
GASP
HO-HOLD ON A MINUTE!!!
PIKA, PIKA!!
WE'RE NOT GOING TO DO ANYTHING!!
GASP
PANT.
PANT...
SHUDDER
SHUDDER
...

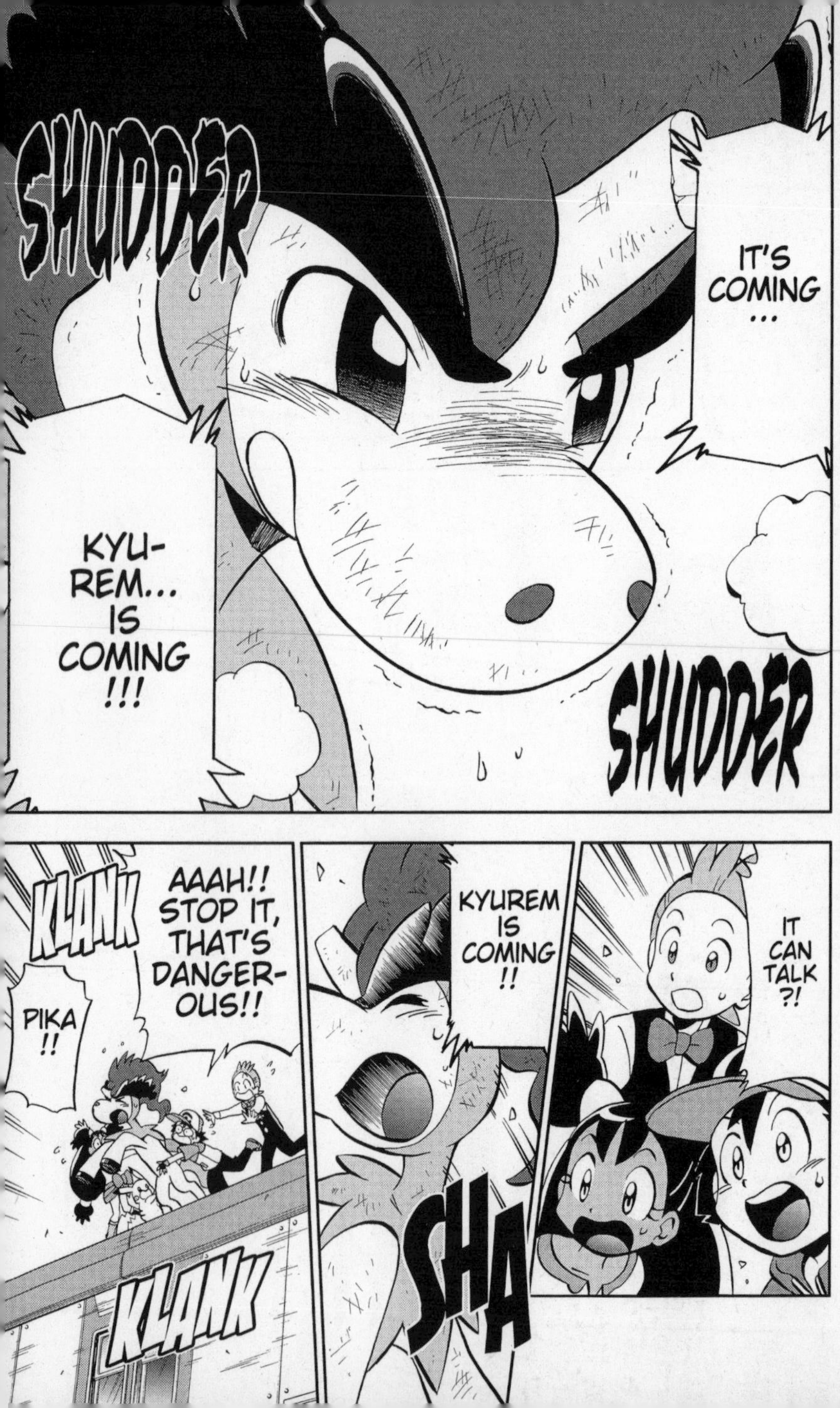
IT'S COMING...
SHUDDER
KYUREM... IS COMING!!!
SHUDDER
IT CAN TALK?!
KYUREM IS COMING!!
SHA
AAAH!! STOP IT, THAT'S DANGEROUS!!
KLANK
PIKA!!
KLANK

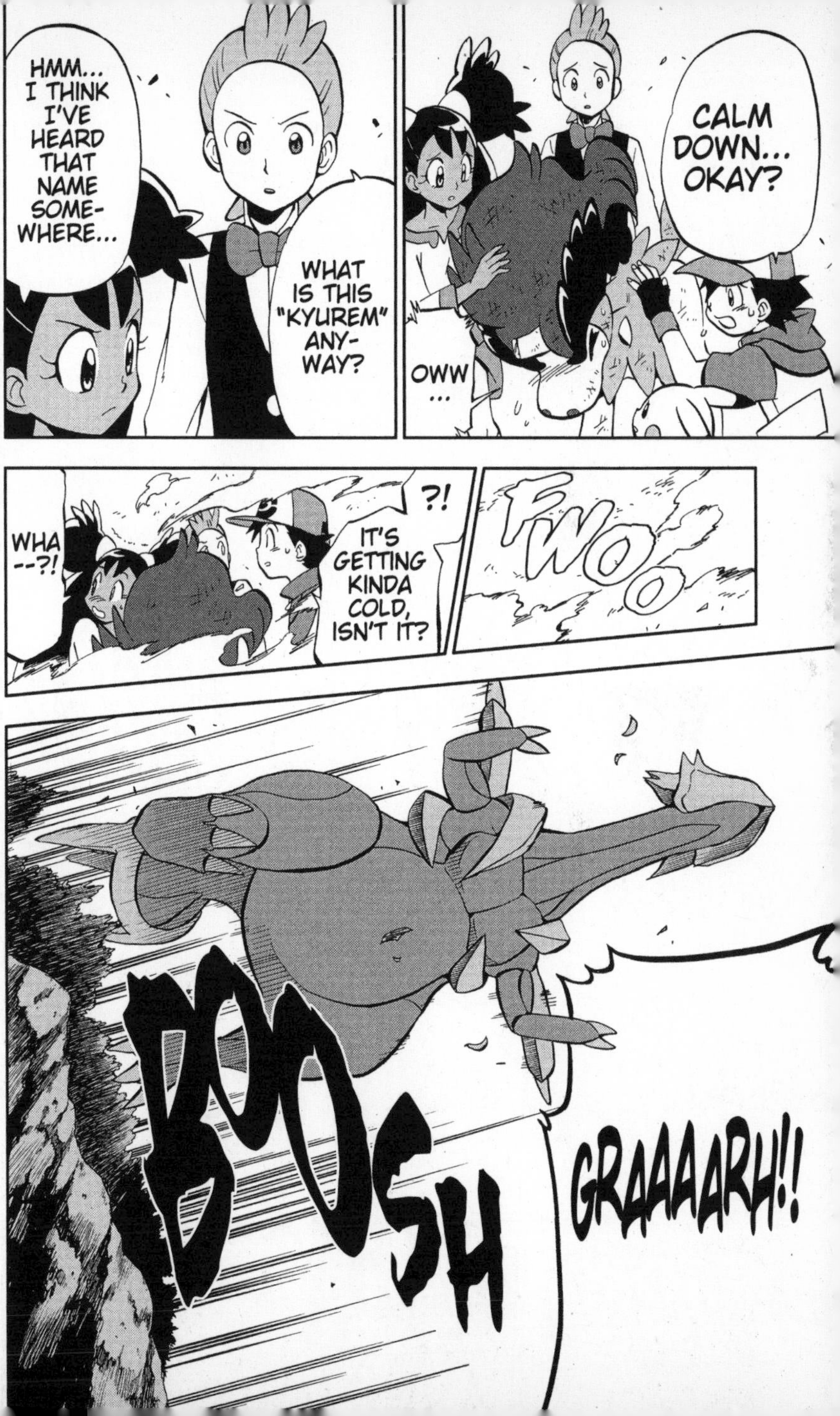
CALM DOWN... OKAY?
OWW ...
WHAT IS THIS "KYUREM" ANYWAY?
HMM... I THINK I'VE HEARD THAT NAME SOMEWHERE...
FWOO
?!
IT'S GETTING KINDA COLD, ISN'T IT?
WHA--?!
GRAAAARH!!
BOOSH

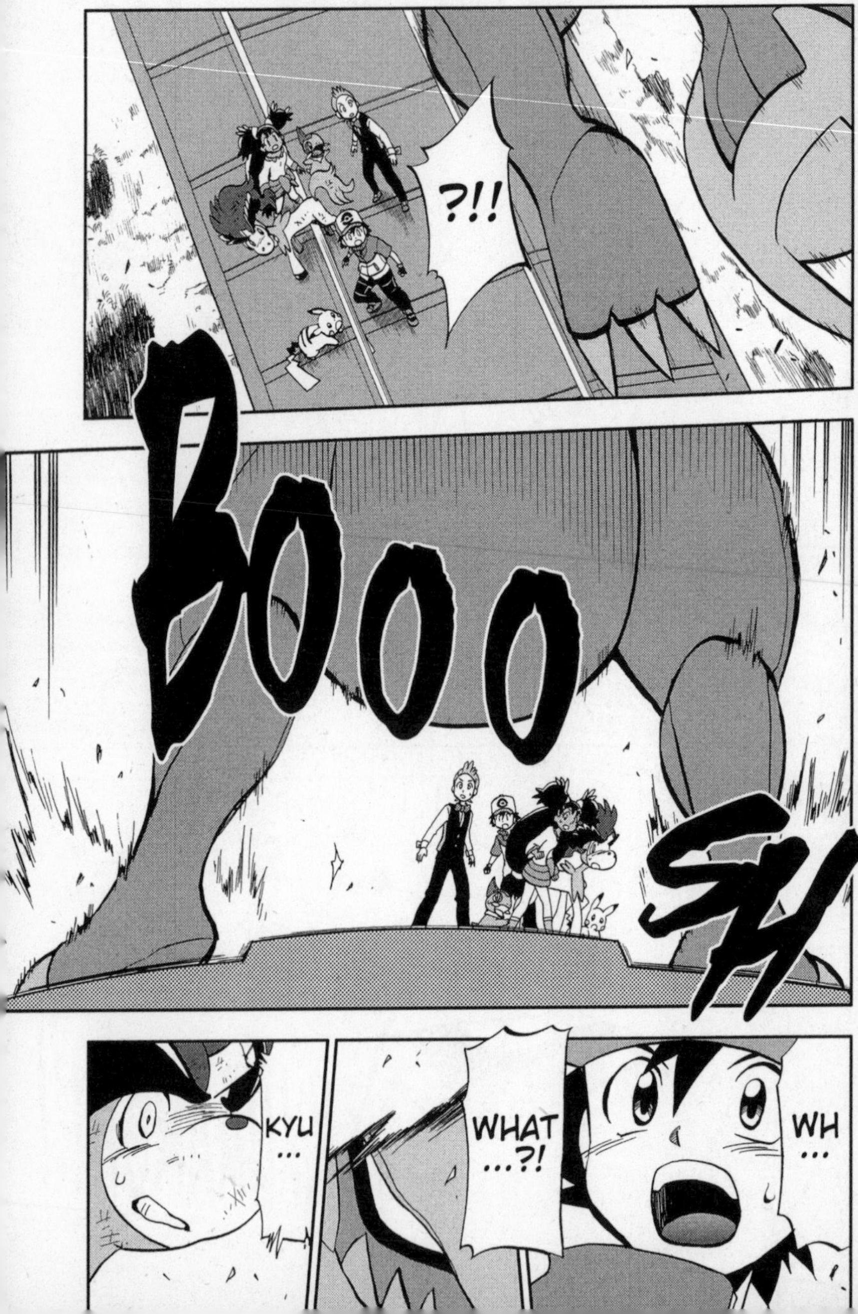
?!!
BOOOOSH
WH...
WHAT...?!
KYU...

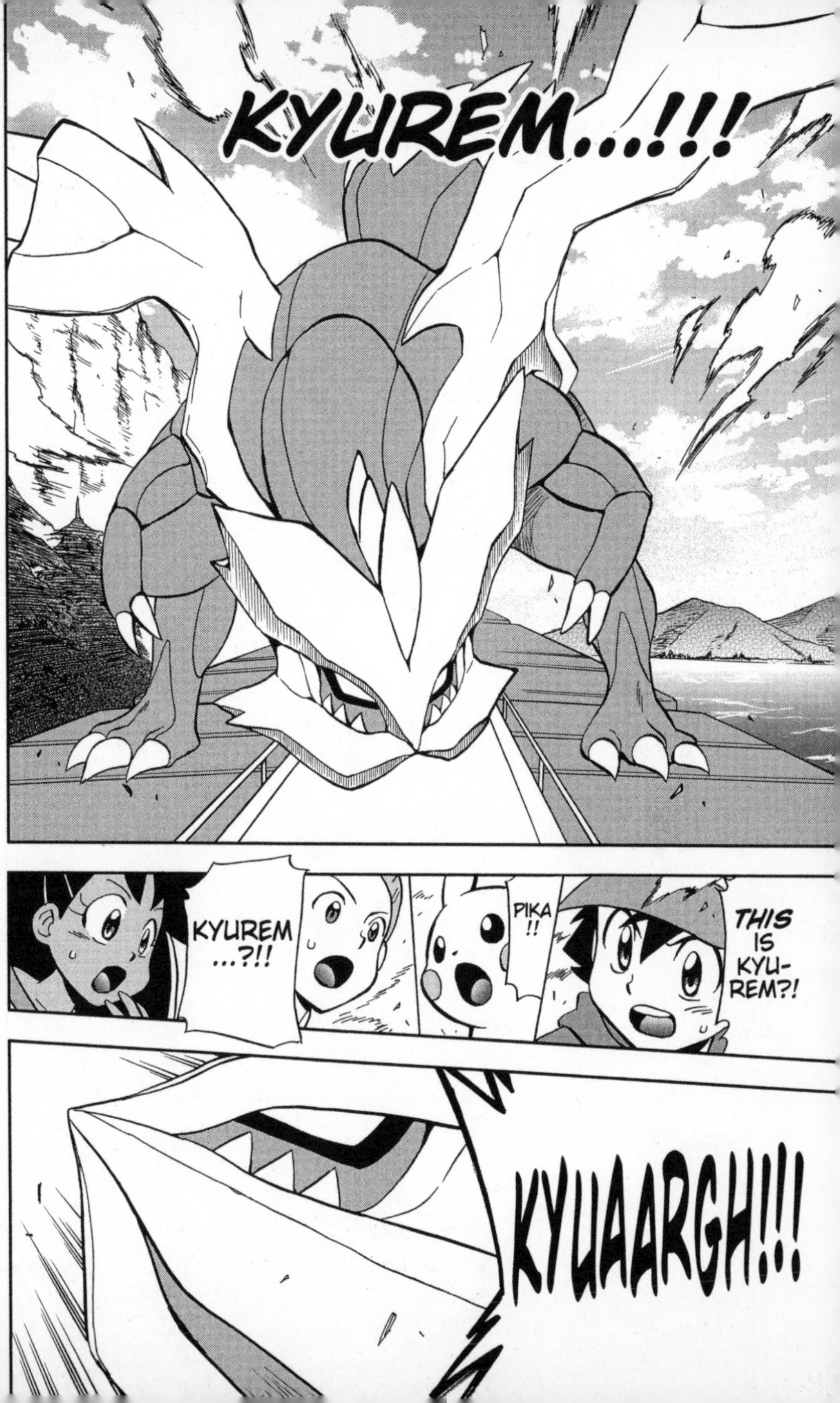
KYUREM...!!!
THIS IS KYU-REM?!
PIKA!!
KYUREM...?!!
KYUAARGH!!!

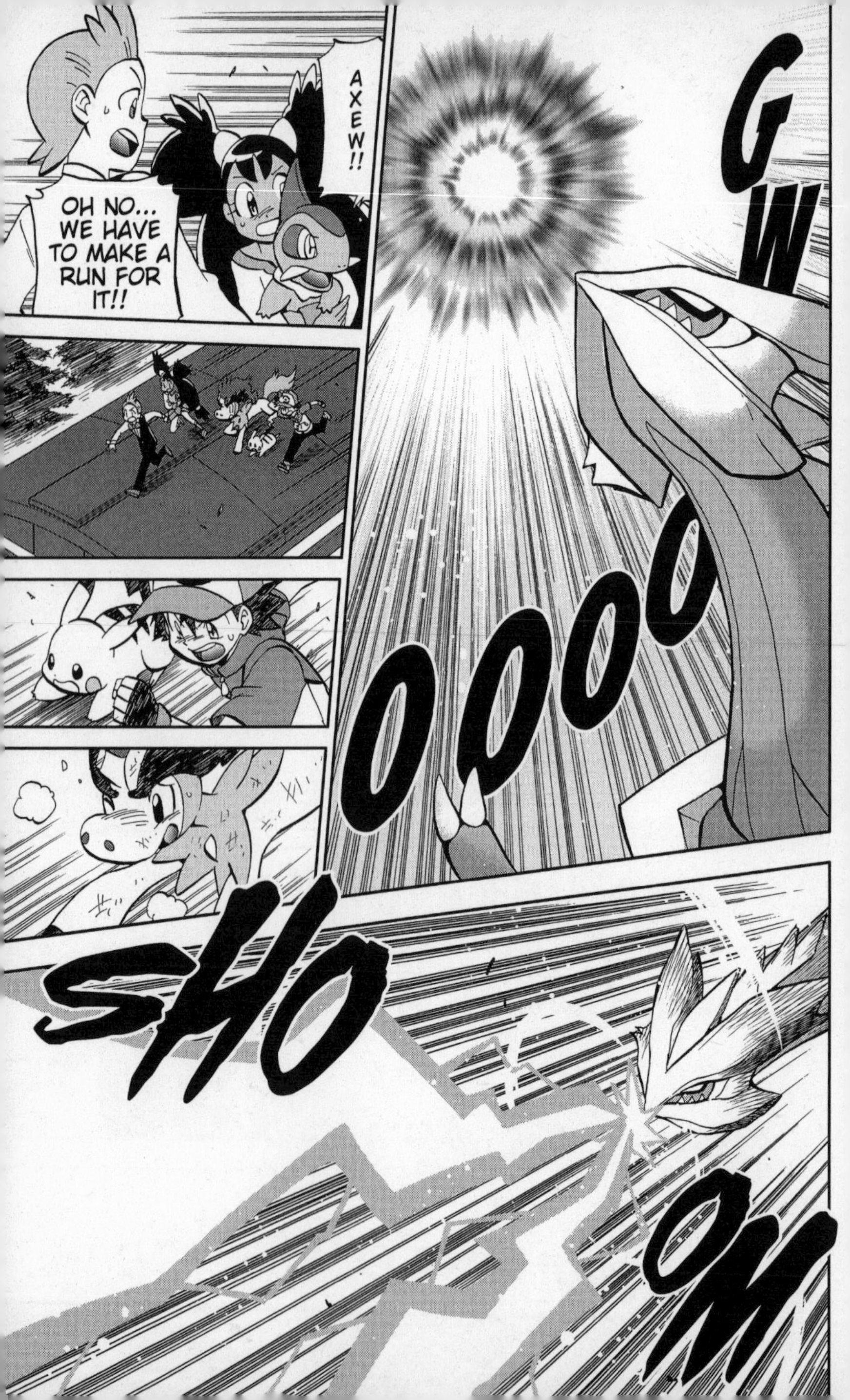
GWOOOOO
AXEW!!
OH NO... WE HAVE TO MAKE A RUN FOR IT!!
SHOOM

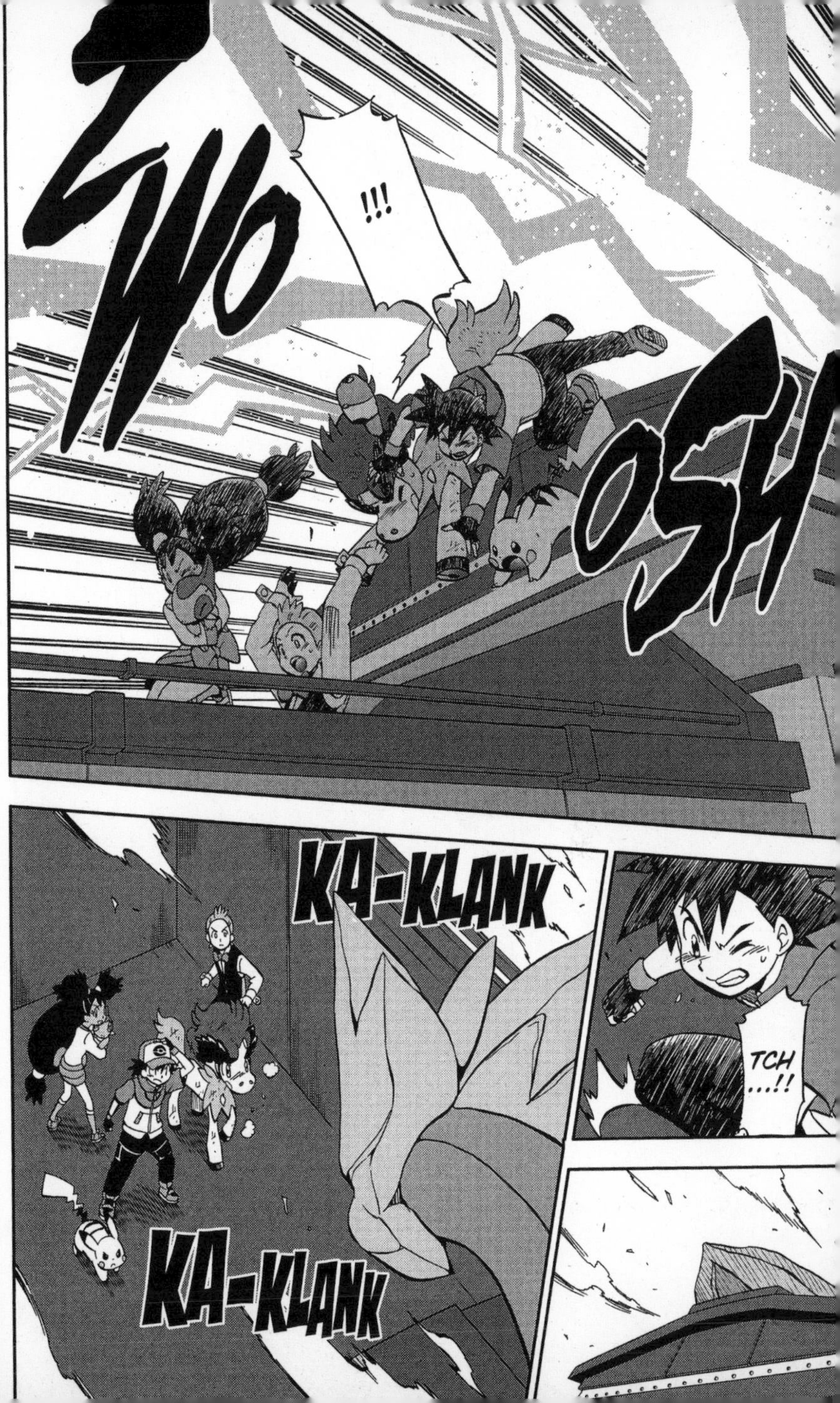
SWO
!!!
OSH
TCH ...!!
KA-KLANK
KA-KLANK

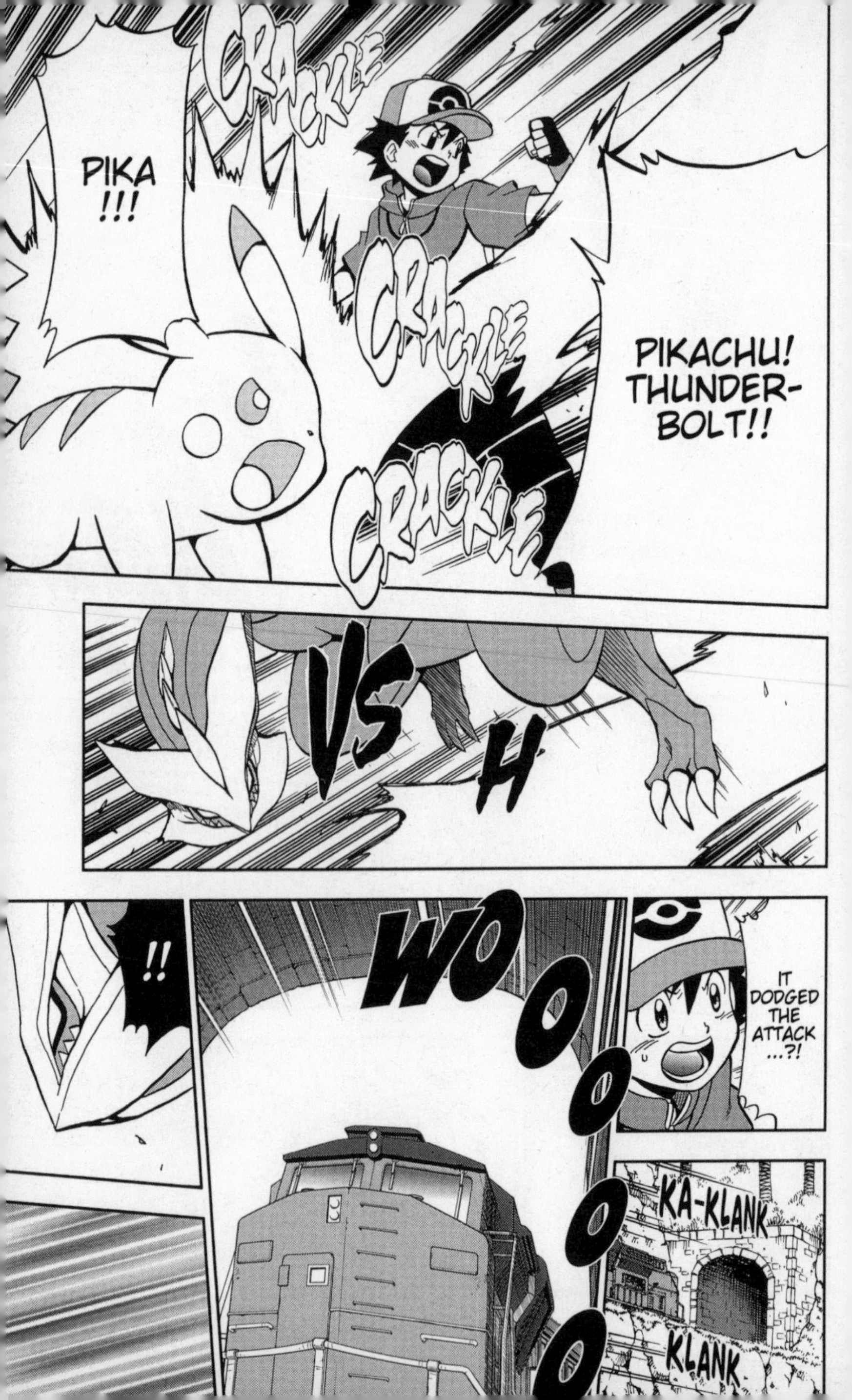
PIKACHU! THUNDER-BOLT!!
CRACKLE
CRACKLE
CRACKLE
PIKA !!!
VSH
IT DODGED THE ATTACK ...?!
KA-KLANK
KLANK
WOOOOOOO
!!

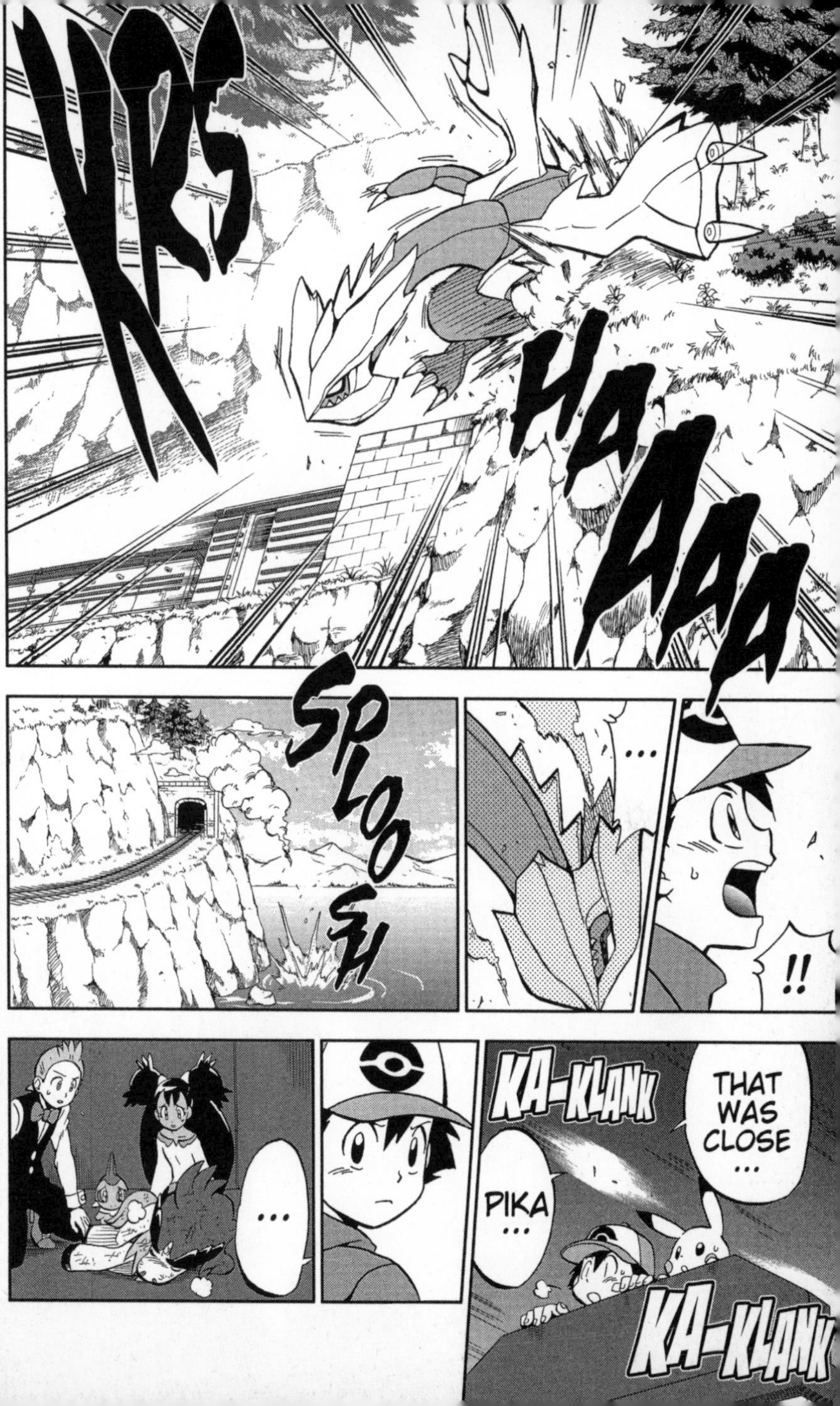
HAAAA
...
!!
SPLOOSH
THAT WAS CLOSE ...
KA-KLANK
PIKA ...
KA-KLANK
...

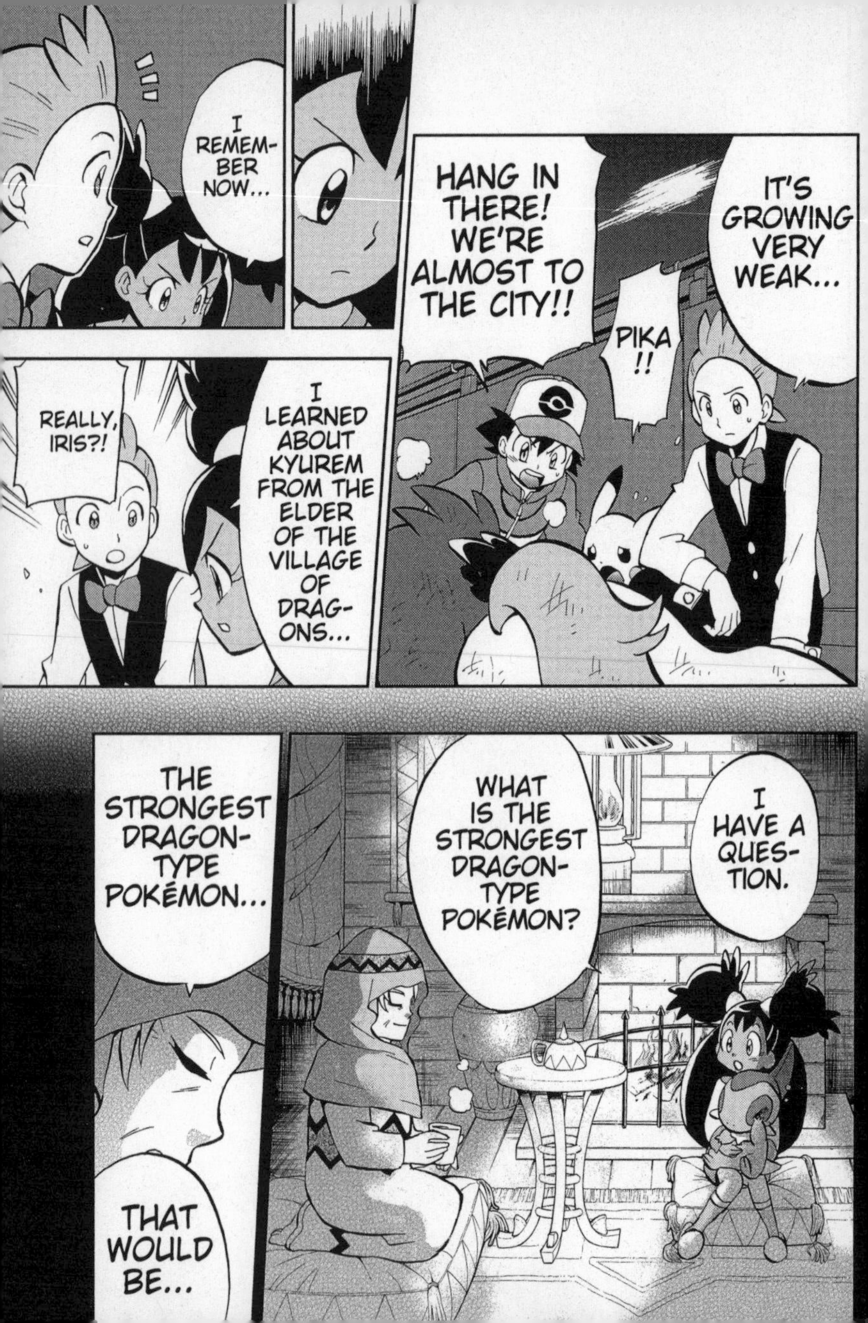
IT'S GROWING VERY WEAK...
HANG IN THERE! WE'RE ALMOST TO THE CITY!!
PIKA !!
I REMEMBER NOW...
I LEARNED ABOUT KYUREM FROM THE ELDER OF THE VILLAGE OF DRAGONS...
REALLY, IRIS?!
I HAVE A QUESTION.
WHAT IS THE STRONGEST DRAGON-TYPE POKÉMON?
THE STRONGEST DRAGON-TYPE POKÉMON...
THAT WOULD BE...

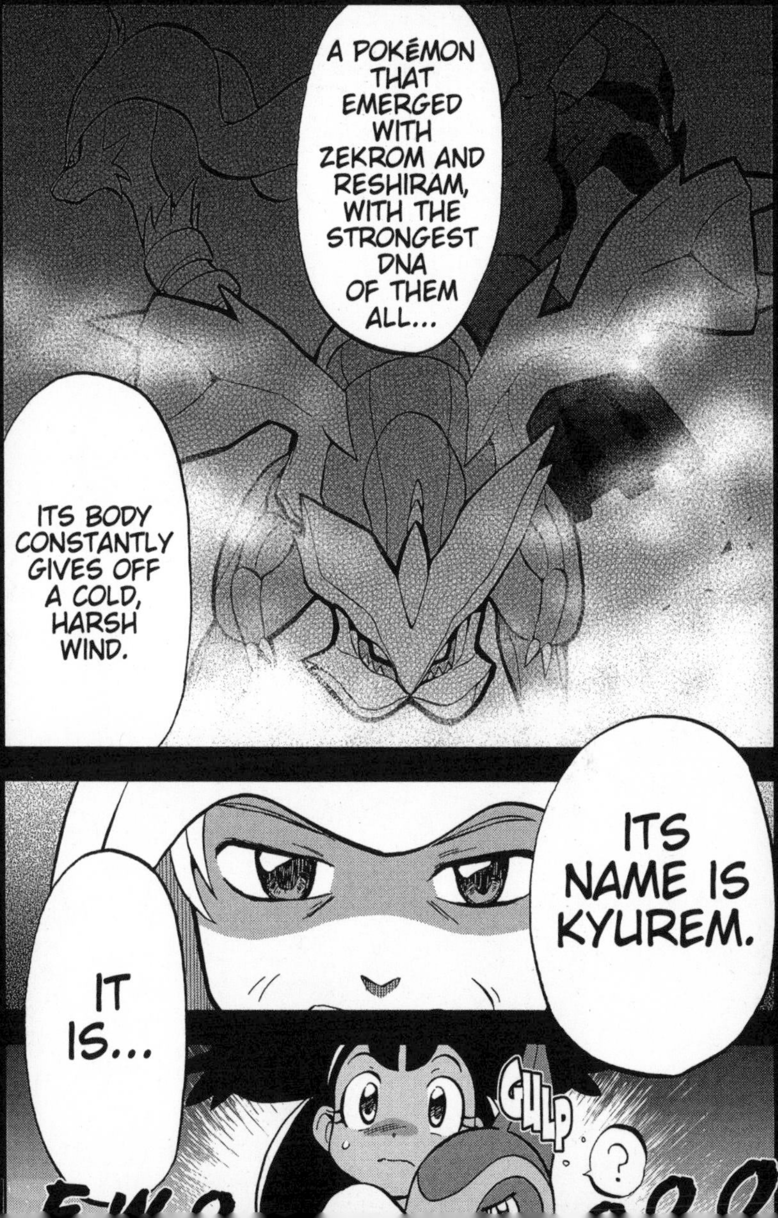
A POKÉMON THAT EMERGED WITH ZEKROM AND RESHIRAM, WITH THE STRONGEST DNA OF THEM ALL...
ITS BODY CONSTANTLY GIVES OFF A COLD, HARSH WIND.
ITS NAME IS KYUREM.
IT IS...
GULP
?

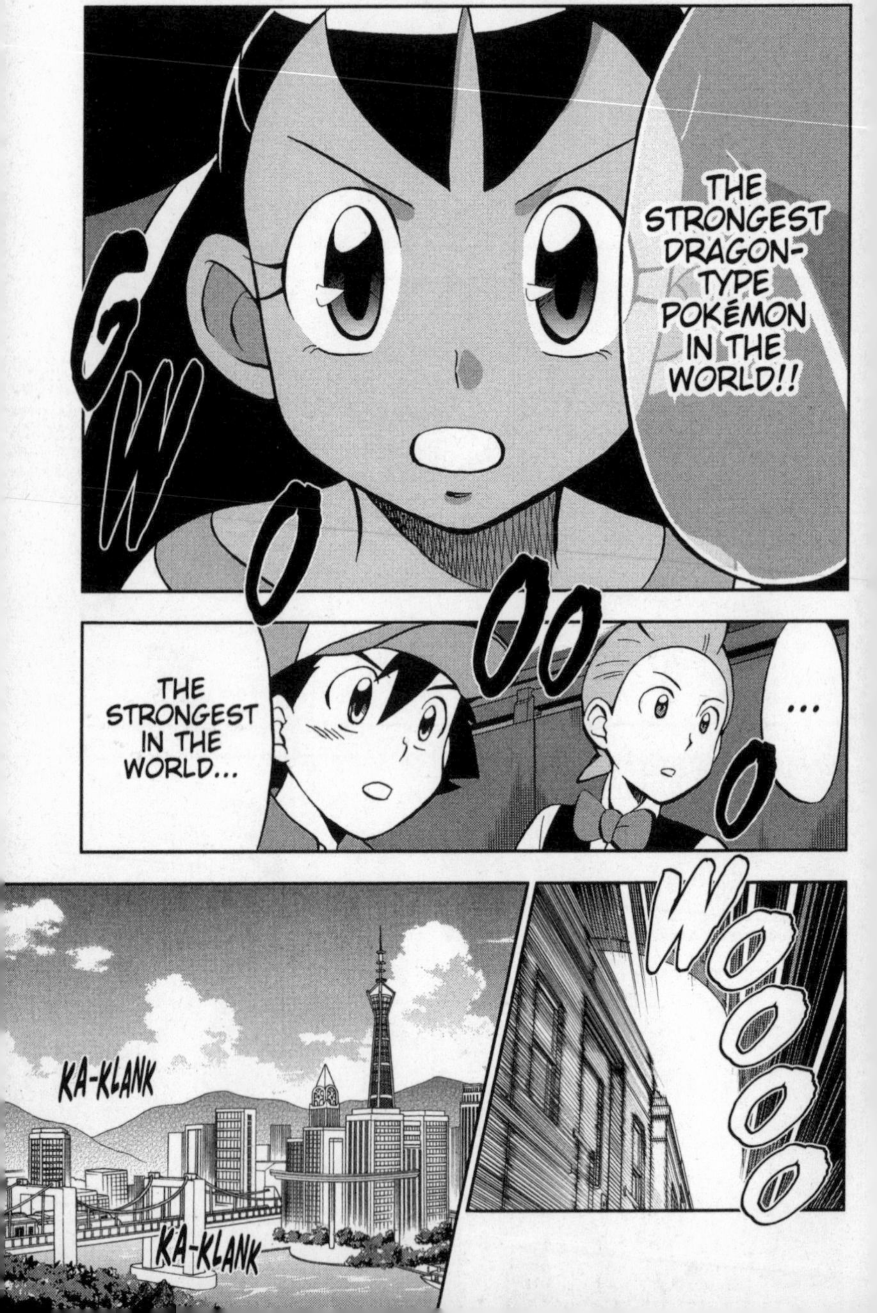
THE STRONGEST DRAGON-TYPE POKÉMON IN THE WORLD!!
GWOOOOO
...
THE STRONGEST IN THE WORLD...
WOOOOO
KA-KLANK
KA-KLANK

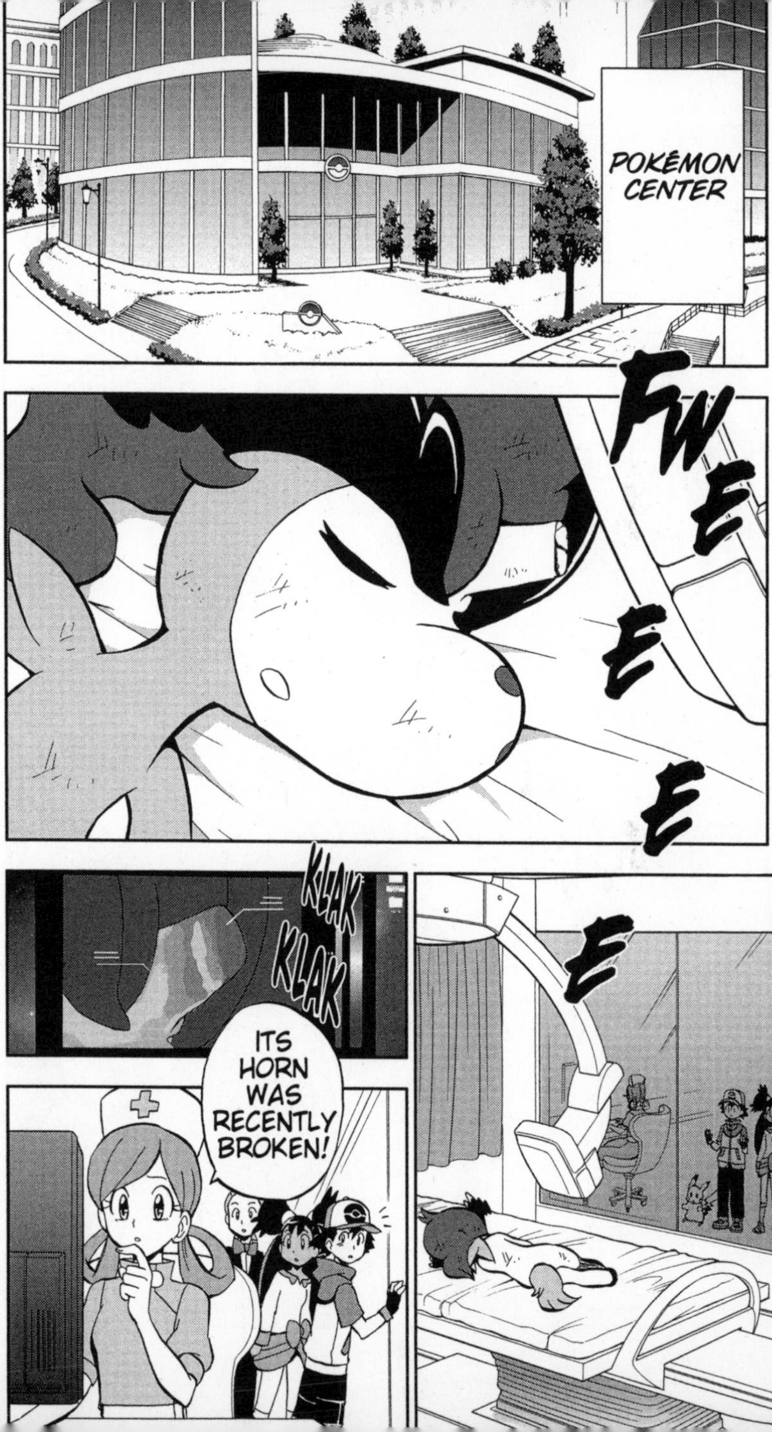
POKéMON CENTER
FWEEEEE
KLAK KLAK
ITS HORN WAS RECENTLY BROKEN!

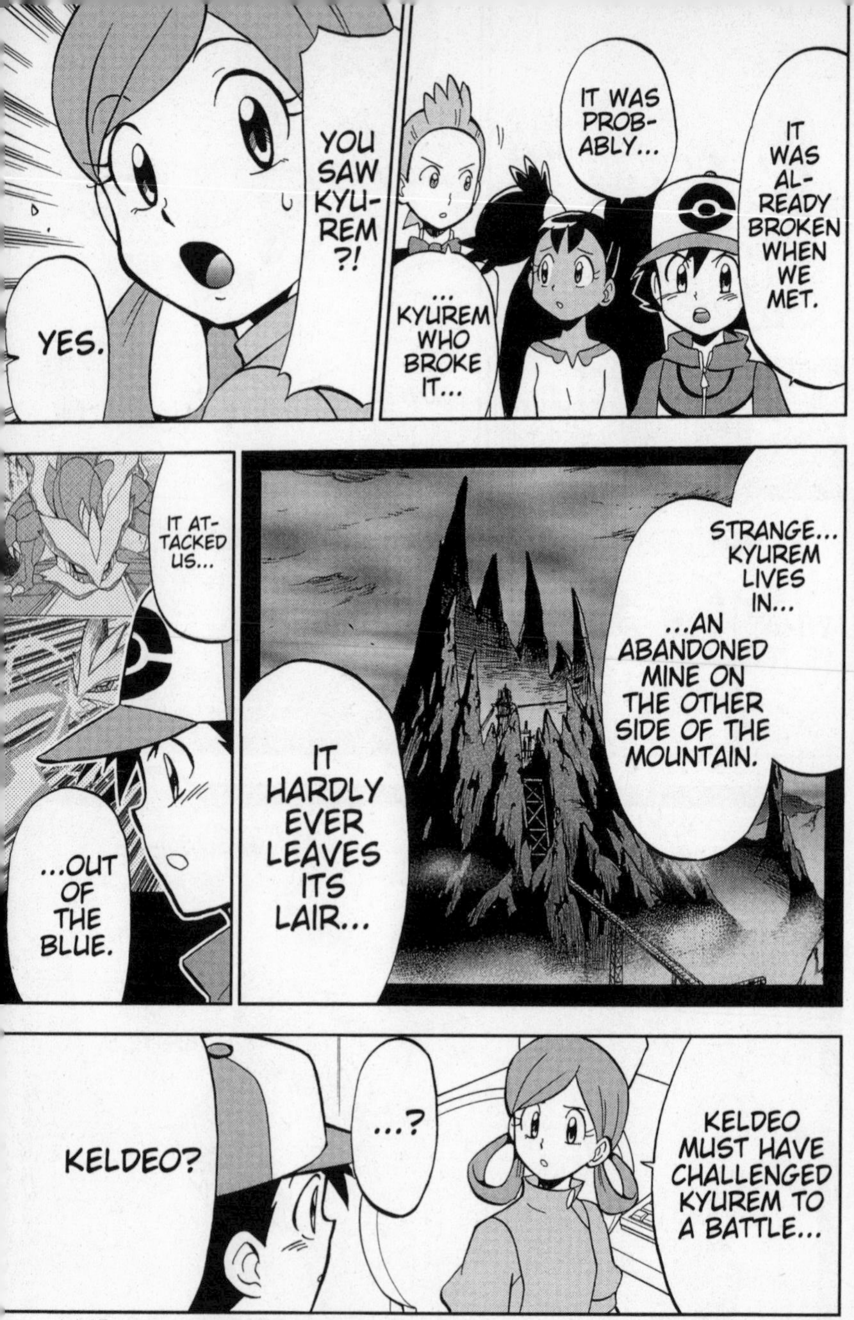
IT WAS ALREADY BROKEN WHEN WE MET.
IT WAS PROBABLY...
...KYUREM WHO BROKE IT...
YOU SAW KYUREM?!
YES.
STRANGE... KYUREM LIVES IN...
...AN ABANDONED MINE ON THE OTHER SIDE OF THE MOUNTAIN.
IT HARDLY EVER LEAVES ITS LAIR...
IT ATTACKED US...
...OUT OF THE BLUE.
KELDEO MUST HAVE CHALLENGED KYUREM TO A BATTLE...
...?
KELDEO?

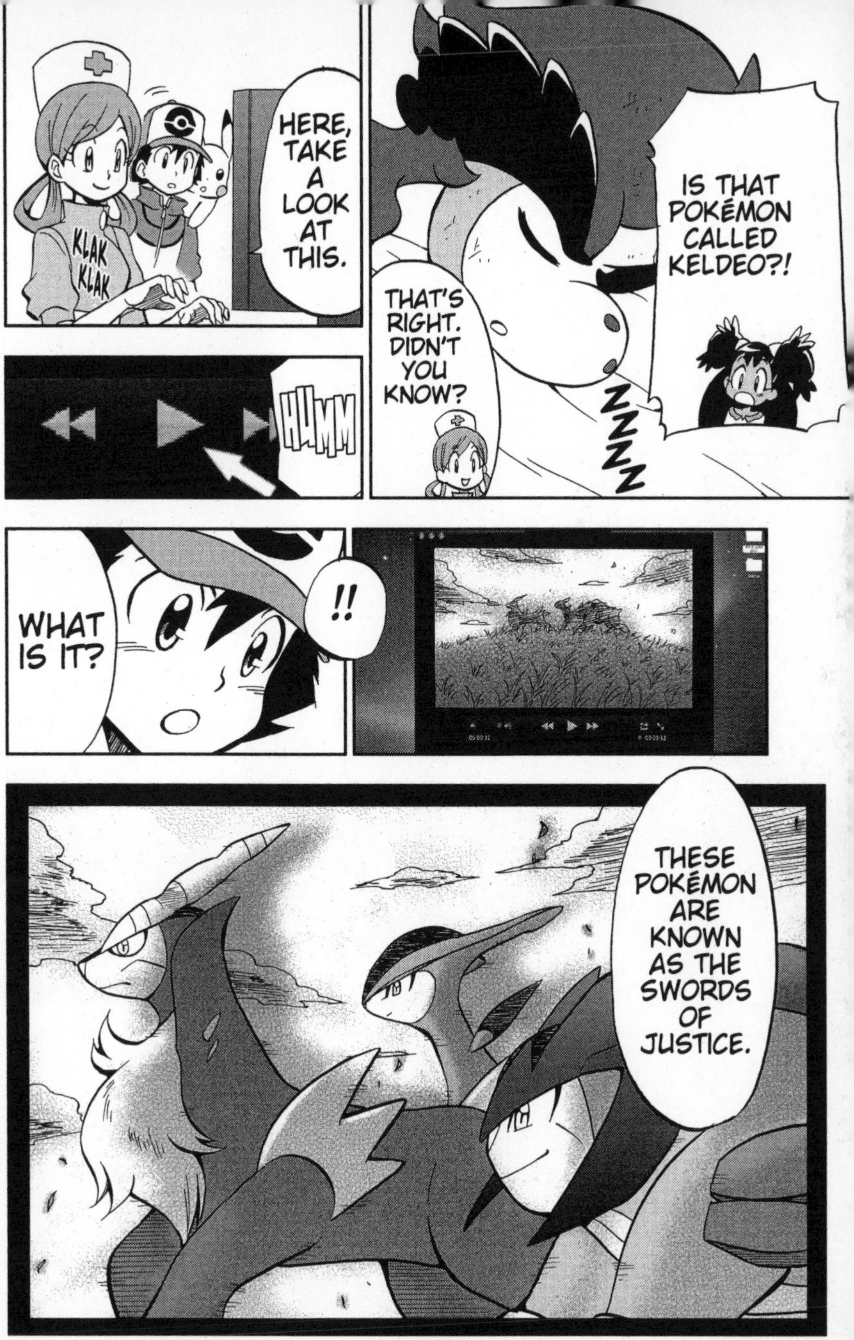
IS THAT POKÉMON CALLED KELDEO?!
THAT'S RIGHT. DIDN'T YOU KNOW?
ZZZZ
HERE, TAKE A LOOK AT THIS.
KLAK KLAK
HUMM
!!
WHAT IS IT?
THESE POKÉMON ARE KNOWN AS THE SWORDS OF JUSTICE.

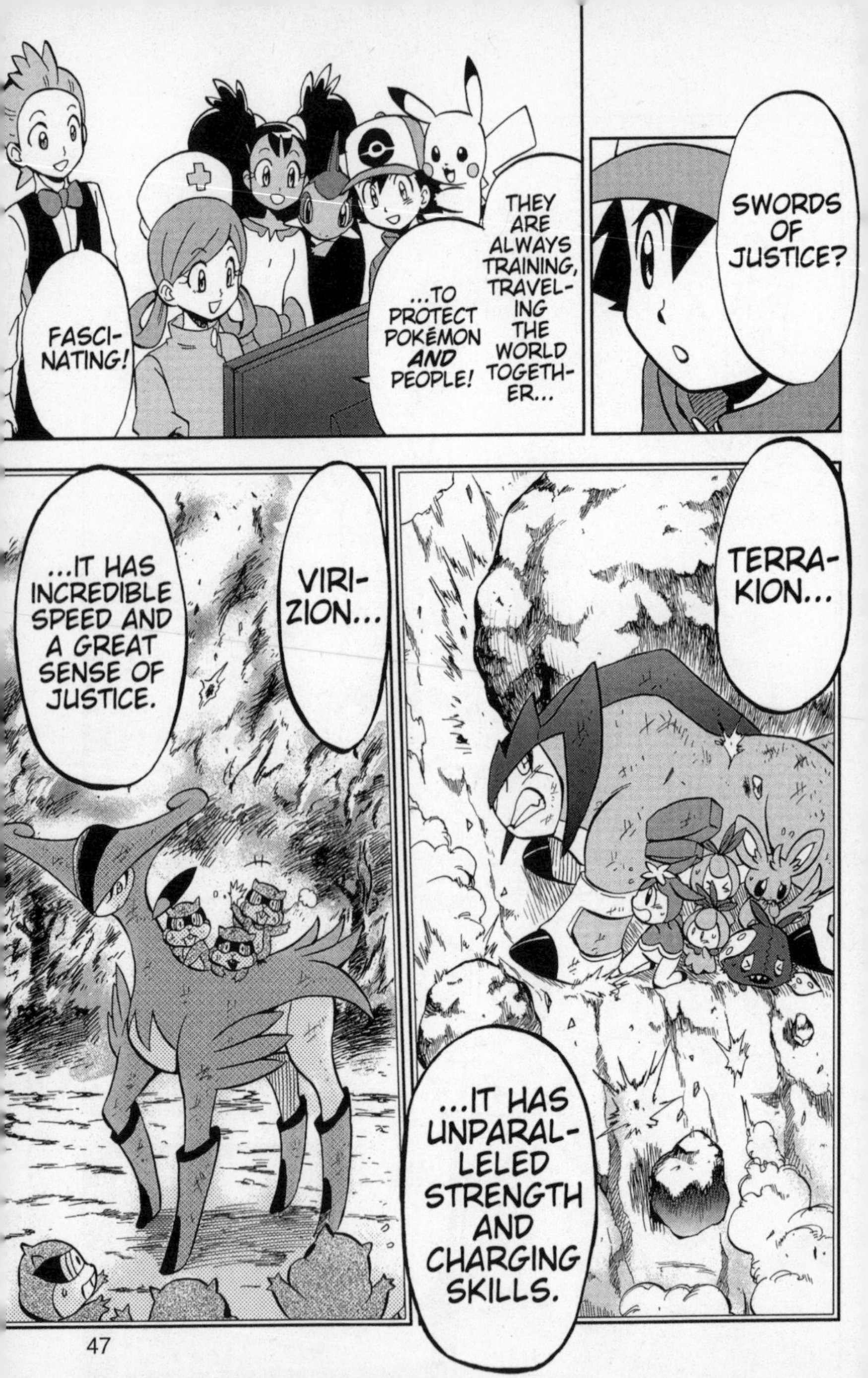
SWORDS OF JUSTICE?
THEY ARE ALWAYS TRAINING, TRAVEL-ING THE WORLD TOGETH-ER...
...TO PROTECT POKÉMON **AND** PEOPLE!
FASCI-NATING!
TERRA-KION...
...IT HAS UNPARAL-LELED STRENGTH AND CHARGING SKILLS.
VIRI-ZION...
...IT HAS INCREDIBLE SPEED AND A GREAT SENSE OF JUSTICE.

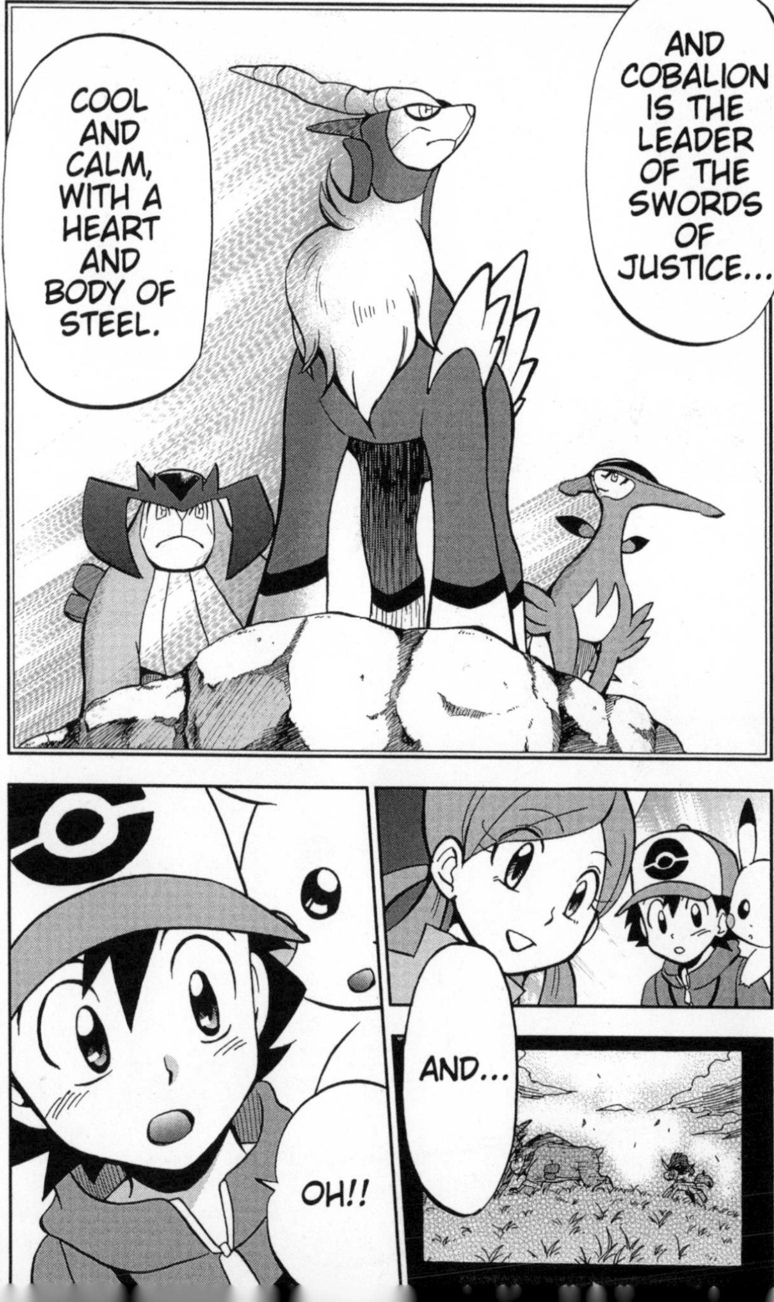
AND COBALION IS THE LEADER OF THE SWORDS OF JUSTICE...
COOL AND CALM, WITH A HEART AND BODY OF STEEL.
AND...
OH!!

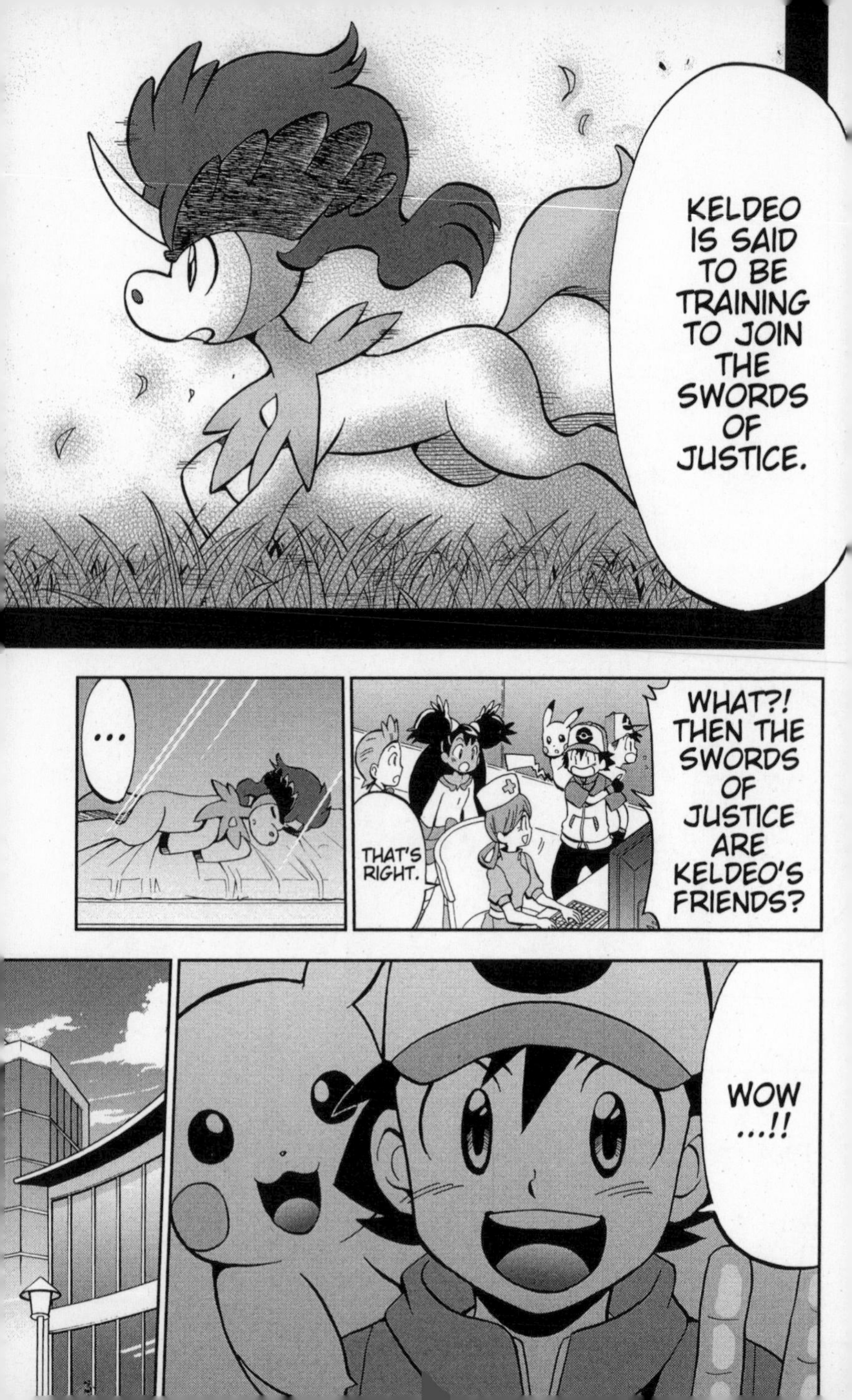
KELDEO IS SAID TO BE TRAINING TO JOIN THE SWORDS OF JUSTICE.
WHAT?! THEN THE SWORDS OF JUSTICE ARE KELDEO'S FRIENDS?
THAT'S RIGHT.
...
WOW ...!!

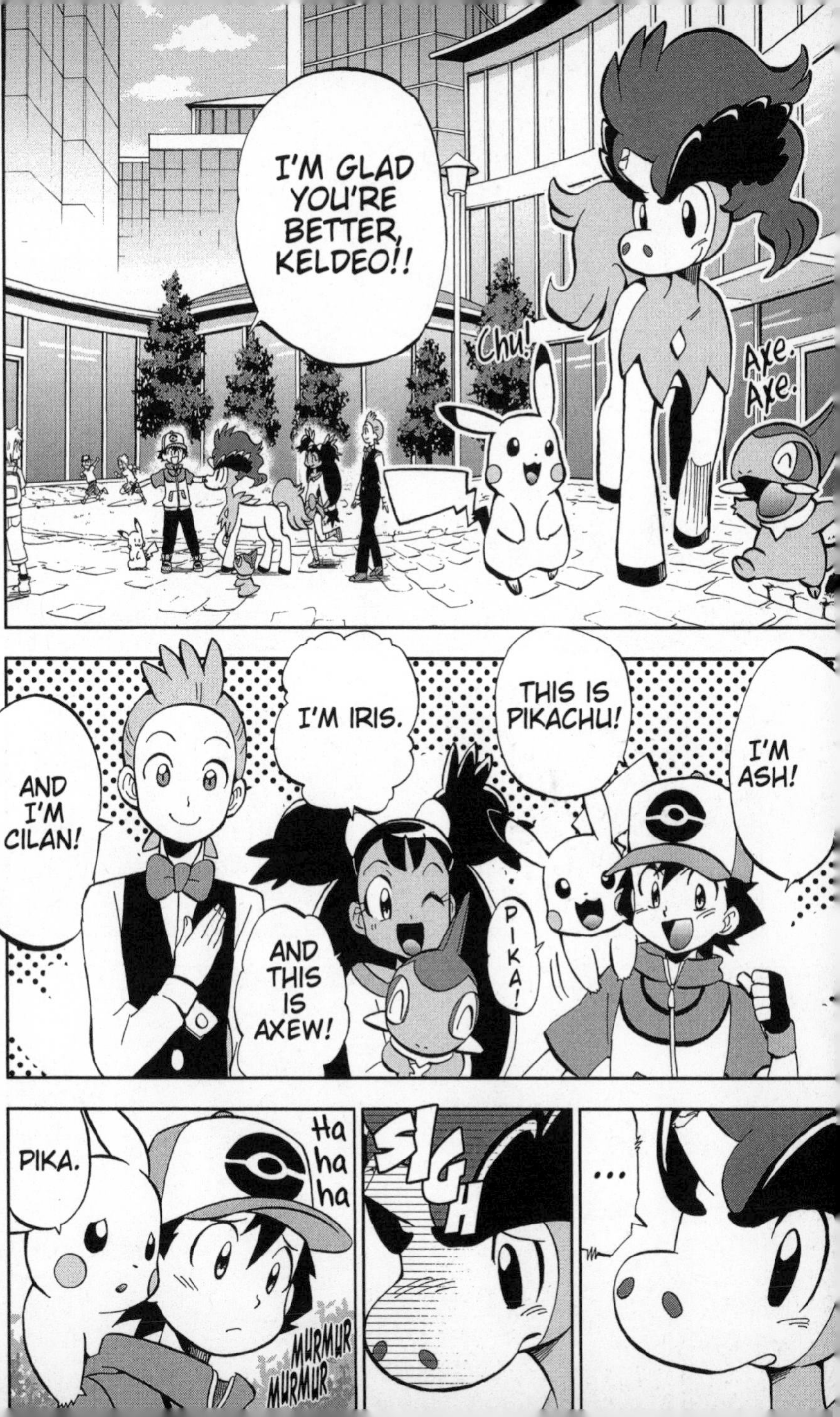
I'M GLAD YOU'RE BETTER, KELDEO!!
Axe. Axe.
Chu!
I'M ASH!
THIS IS PIKACHU!
PIKA!
I'M IRIS.
AND THIS IS AXEW!
AND I'M CILAN!
...
SIGH
Ha ha ha
PIKA.
MURMUR MURMUR

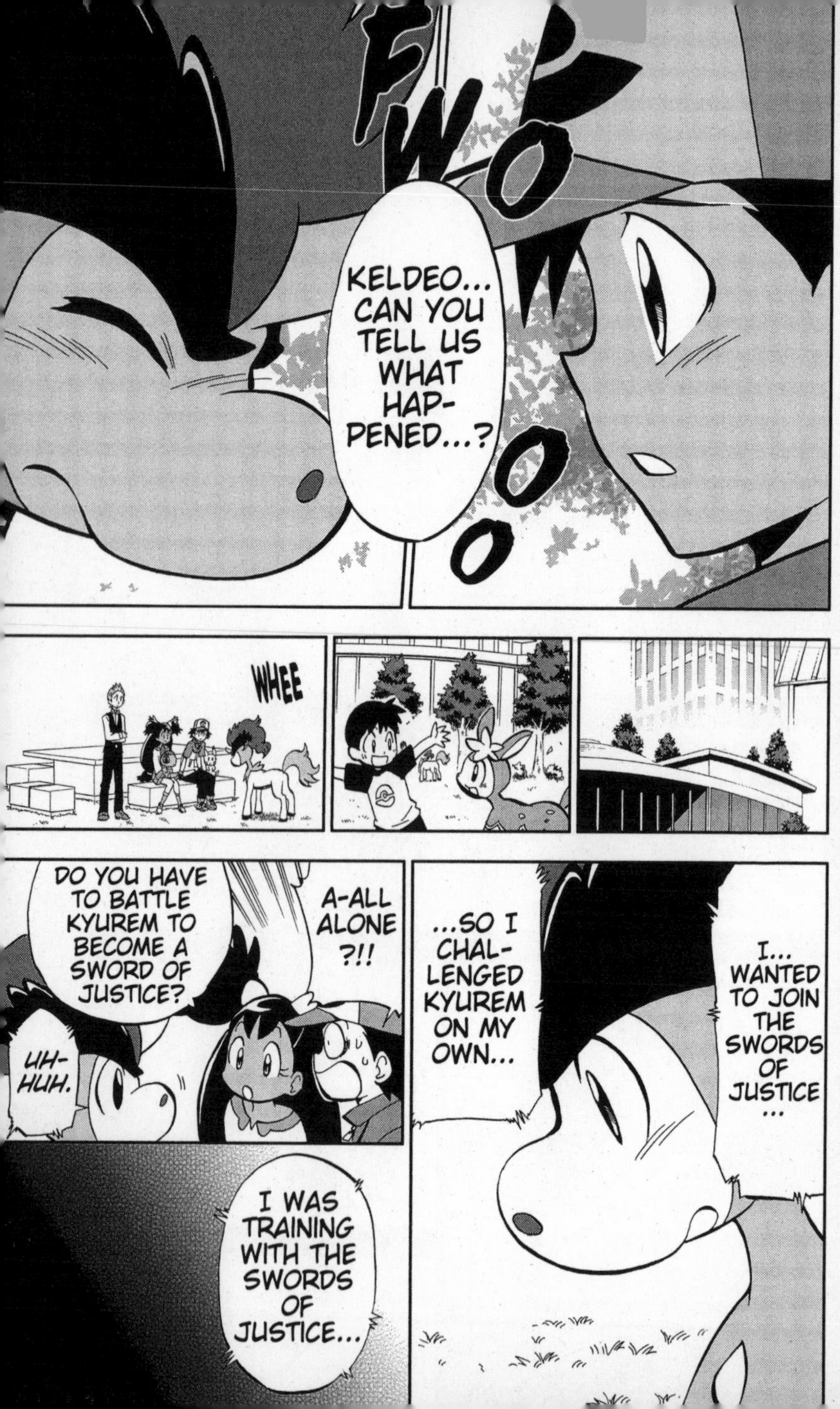
FWOOO
KELDEO... CAN YOU TELL US WHAT HAPPENED...?
WHEE
I... WANTED TO JOIN THE SWORDS OF JUSTICE...
...SO I CHALLENGED KYUREM ON MY OWN...
A-ALL ALONE?!!
DO YOU HAVE TO BATTLE KYUREM TO BECOME A SWORD OF JUSTICE?
UH-HUH.
I WAS TRAINING WITH THE SWORDS OF JUSTICE...

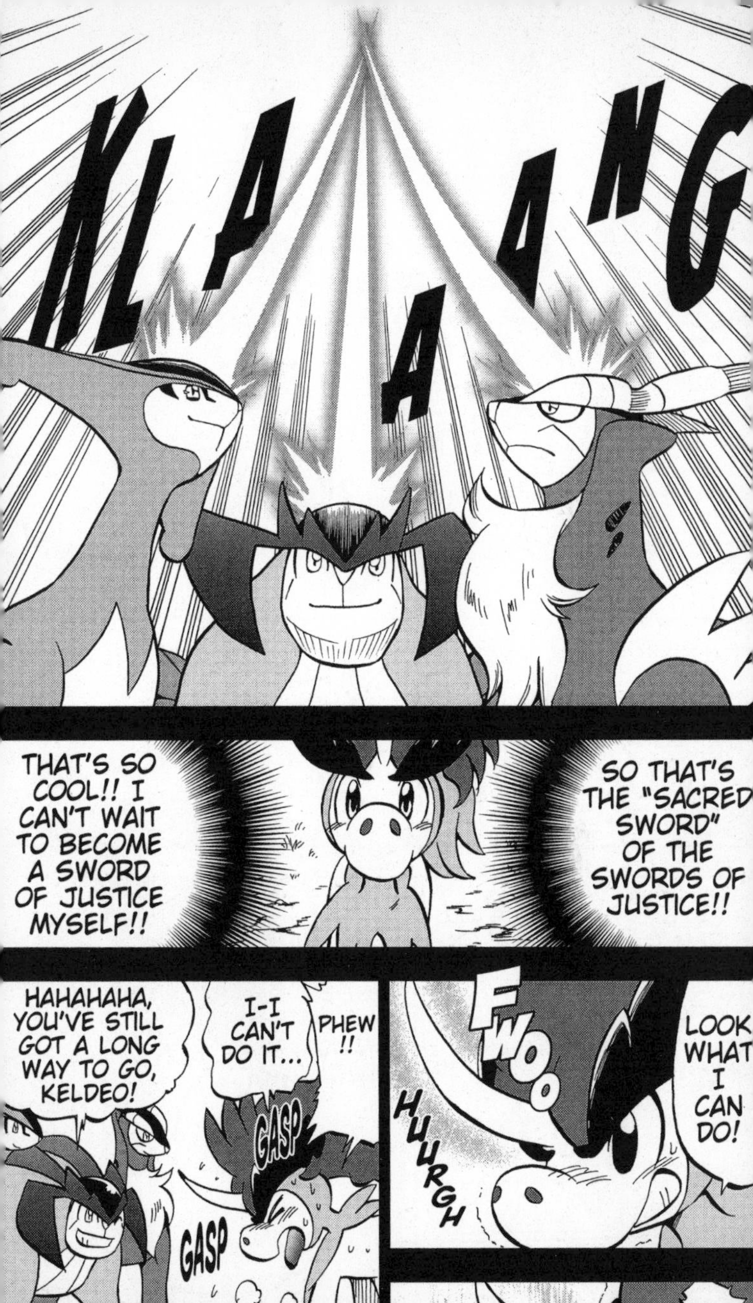
KLPAANG
SO THAT'S THE "SACRED SWORD" OF THE SWORDS OF JUSTICE!!
THAT'S SO COOL!! I CAN'T WAIT TO BECOME A SWORD OF JUSTICE MYSELF!!
LOOK WHAT I CAN DO!
FWOO
HUURGH
PHEW!!
I-I CAN'T DO IT...
HAHAHAHA, YOU'VE STILL GOT A LONG WAY TO GO, KELDEO!
GASP
GASP

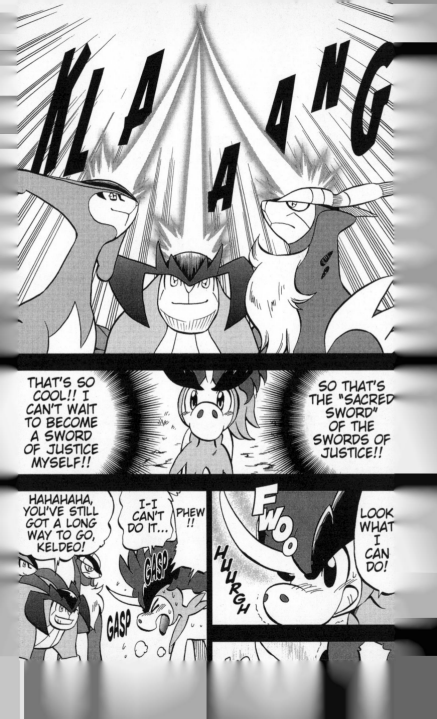

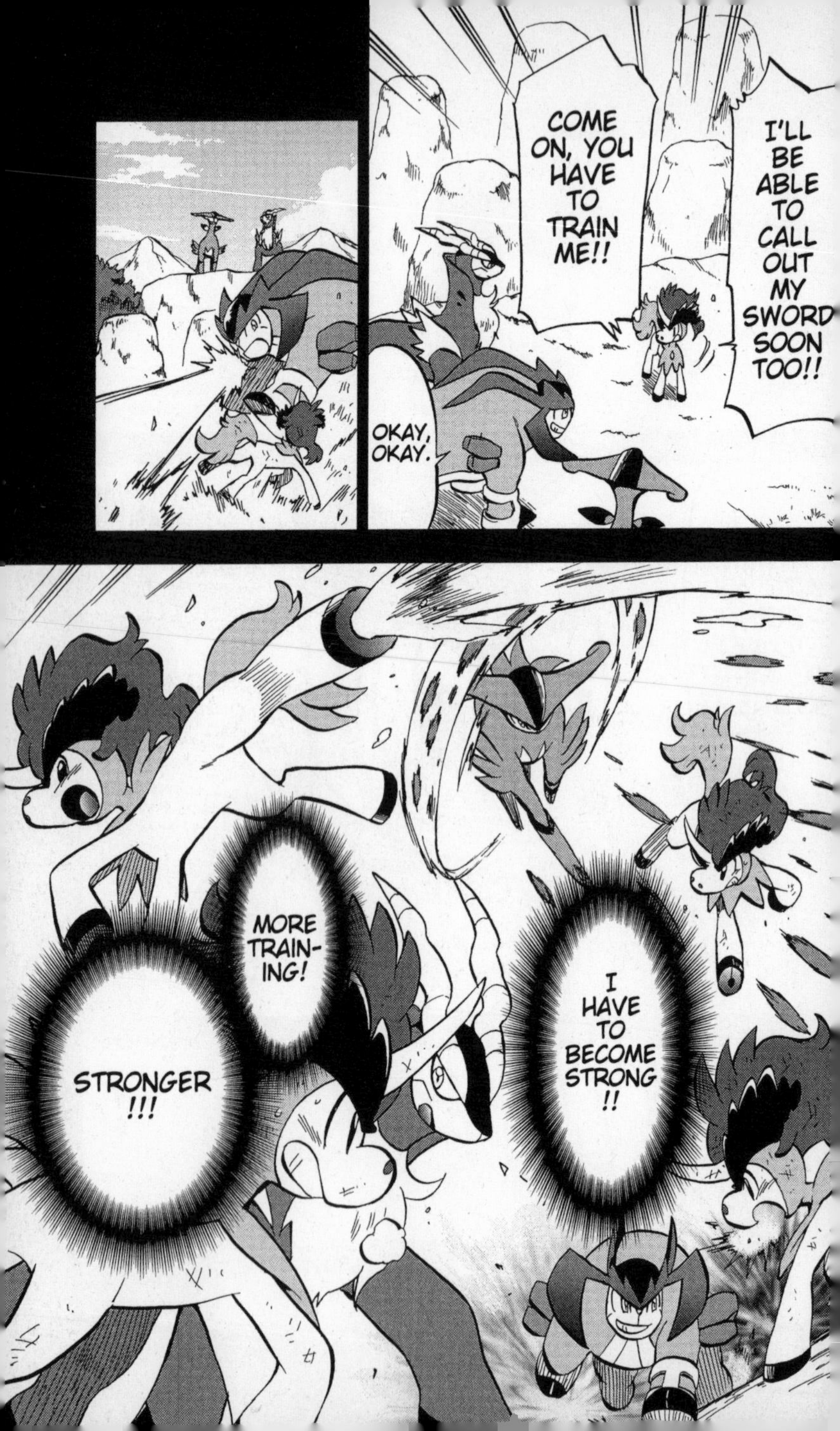
I'LL BE ABLE TO CALL OUT MY SWORD SOON TOO!!
COME ON, YOU HAVE TO TRAIN ME!!
OKAY, OKAY.
I HAVE TO BECOME STRONG!!
MORE TRAIN-ING!
STRONGER!!!

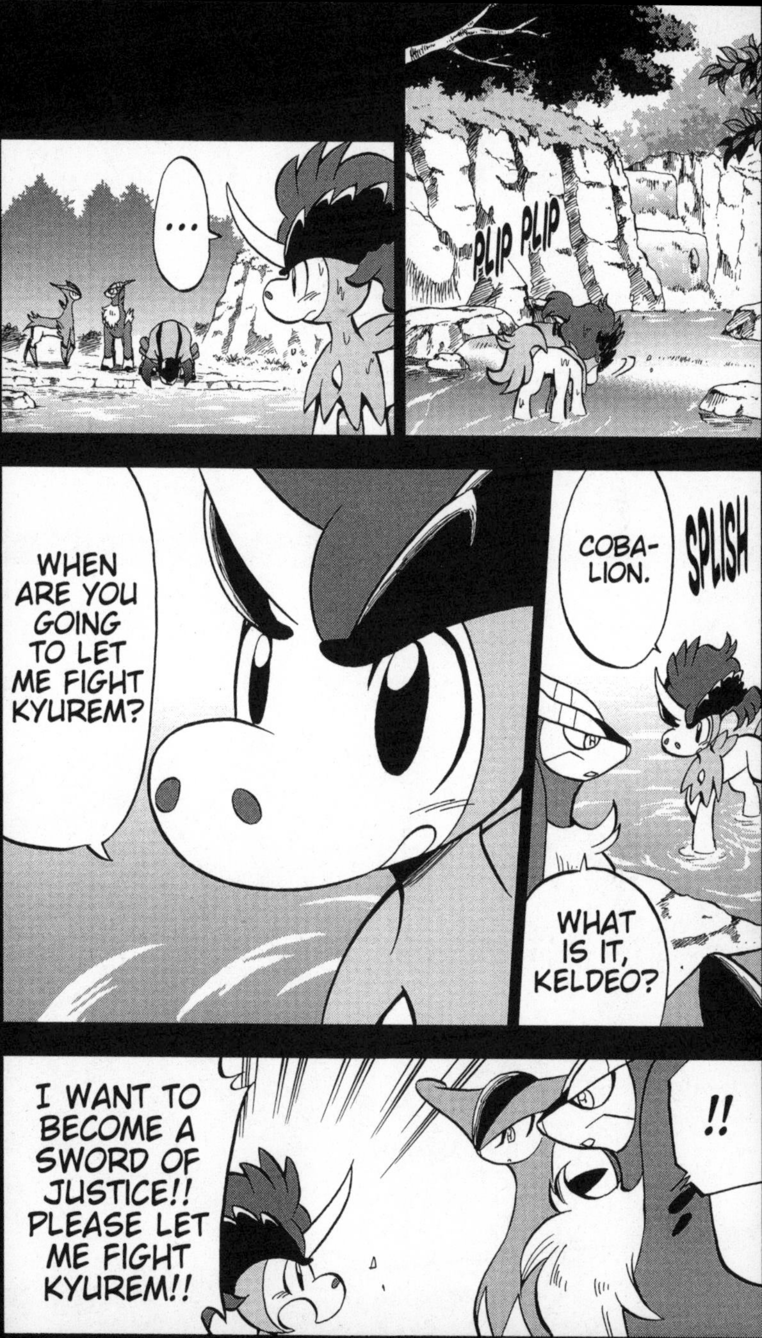
PLIP PLIP
...
COBA-LION.
SPLISH
WHAT IS IT, KELDEO?
WHEN ARE YOU GOING TO LET ME FIGHT KYUREM?
!!
I WANT TO BECOME A SWORD OF JUSTICE!! PLEASE LET ME FIGHT KYUREM!!

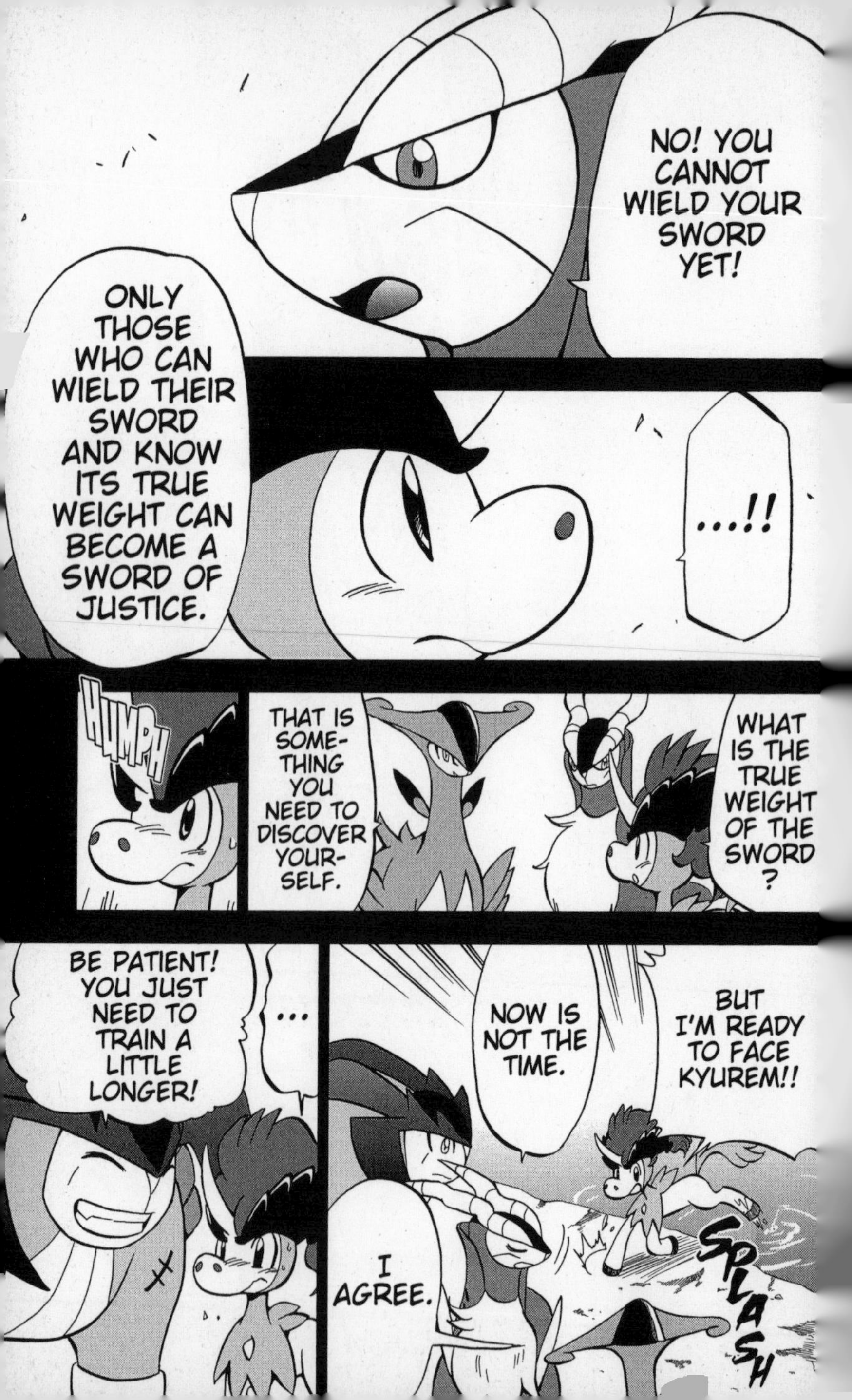
NO! YOU CANNOT WIELD YOUR SWORD YET!
ONLY THOSE WHO CAN WIELD THEIR SWORD AND KNOW ITS TRUE WEIGHT CAN BECOME A SWORD OF JUSTICE.
...!!
WHAT IS THE TRUE WEIGHT OF THE SWORD ?
THAT IS SOME-THING YOU NEED TO DISCOVER YOUR-SELF.
HUMPH
BUT I'M READY TO FACE KYUREM!!
NOW IS NOT THE TIME.
I AGREE.
SPLASH
...
BE PATIENT! YOU JUST NEED TO TRAIN A LITTLE LONGER!

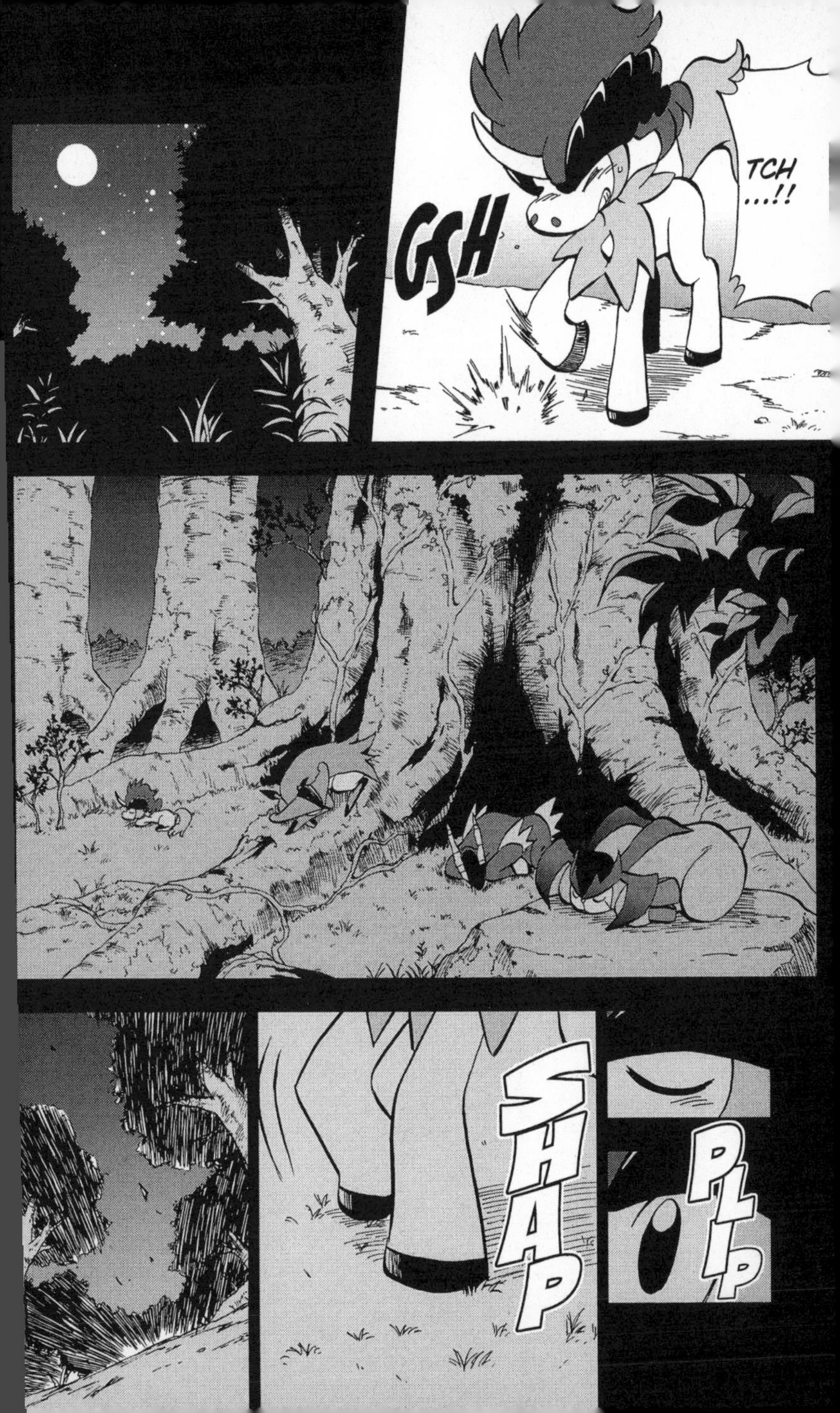
TCH ...!!
GSH
PLIP
SHAP

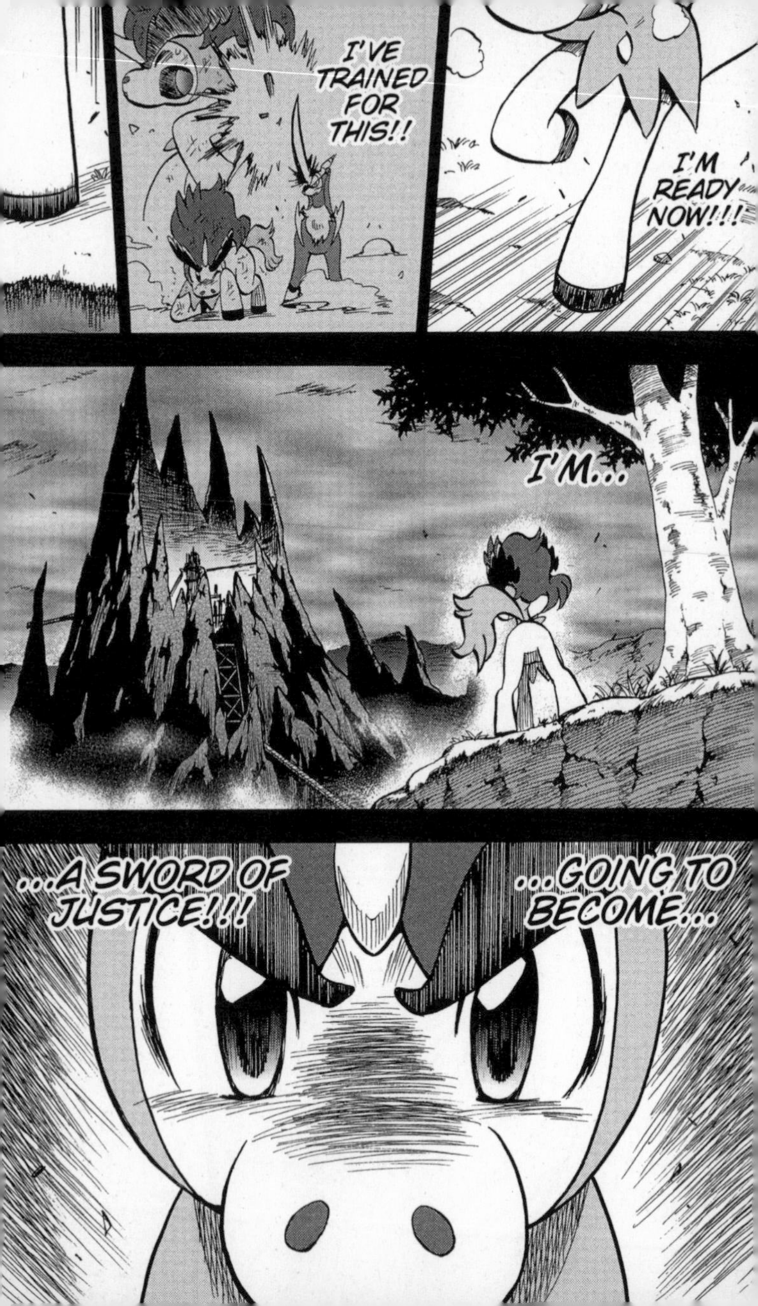
I'M READY NOW!!!
I'VE TRAINED FOR THIS!!
I'M...
...GOING TO BECOME...
...A SWORD OF JUSTICE!!!

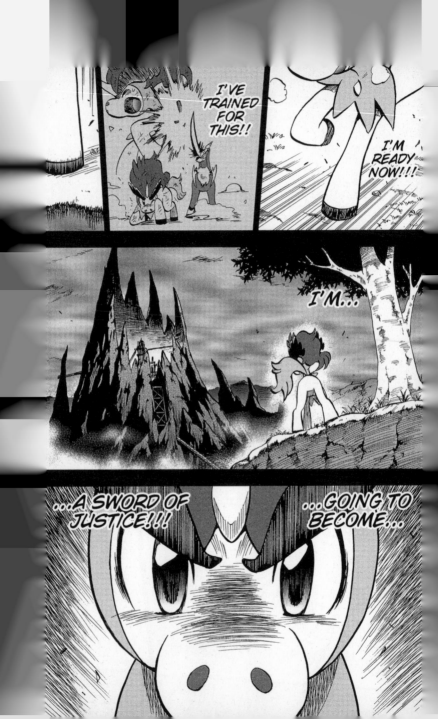

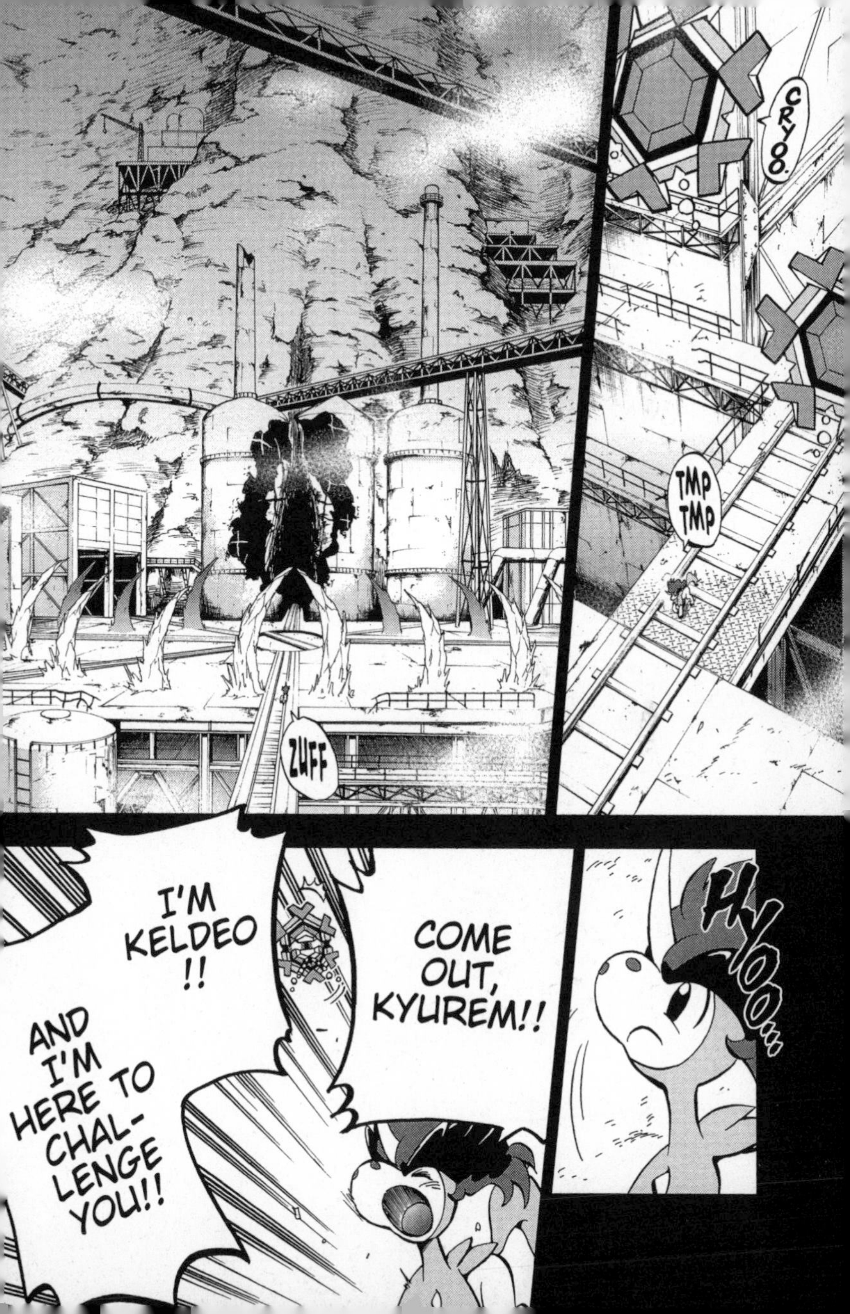
CRYOO.
TMP TMP
ZUFF
HYOO...
COME OUT, KYUREM!!
I'M KELDEO!!
AND I'M HERE TO CHAL-LENGE YOU!!

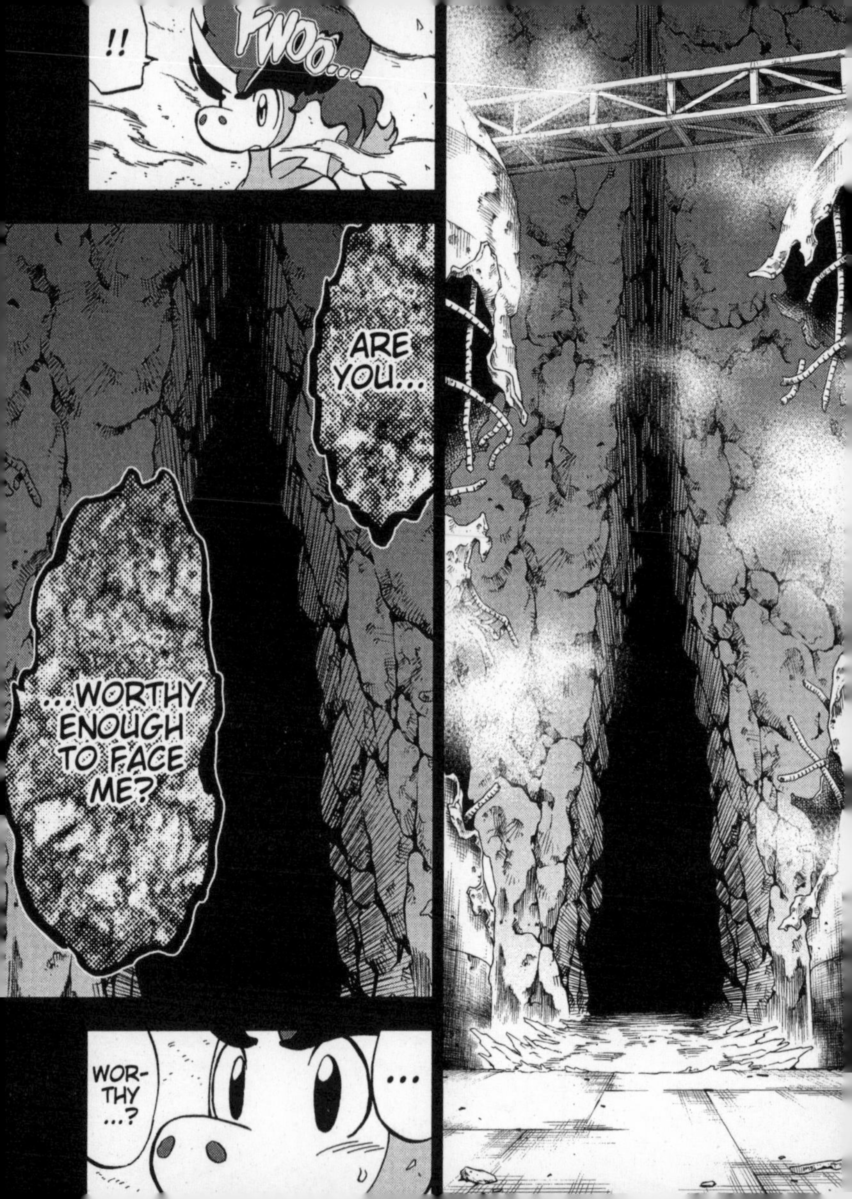
FWOO...
!!
ARE YOU...
...WORTHY ENOUGH TO FACE ME?
...
WOR-THY...?

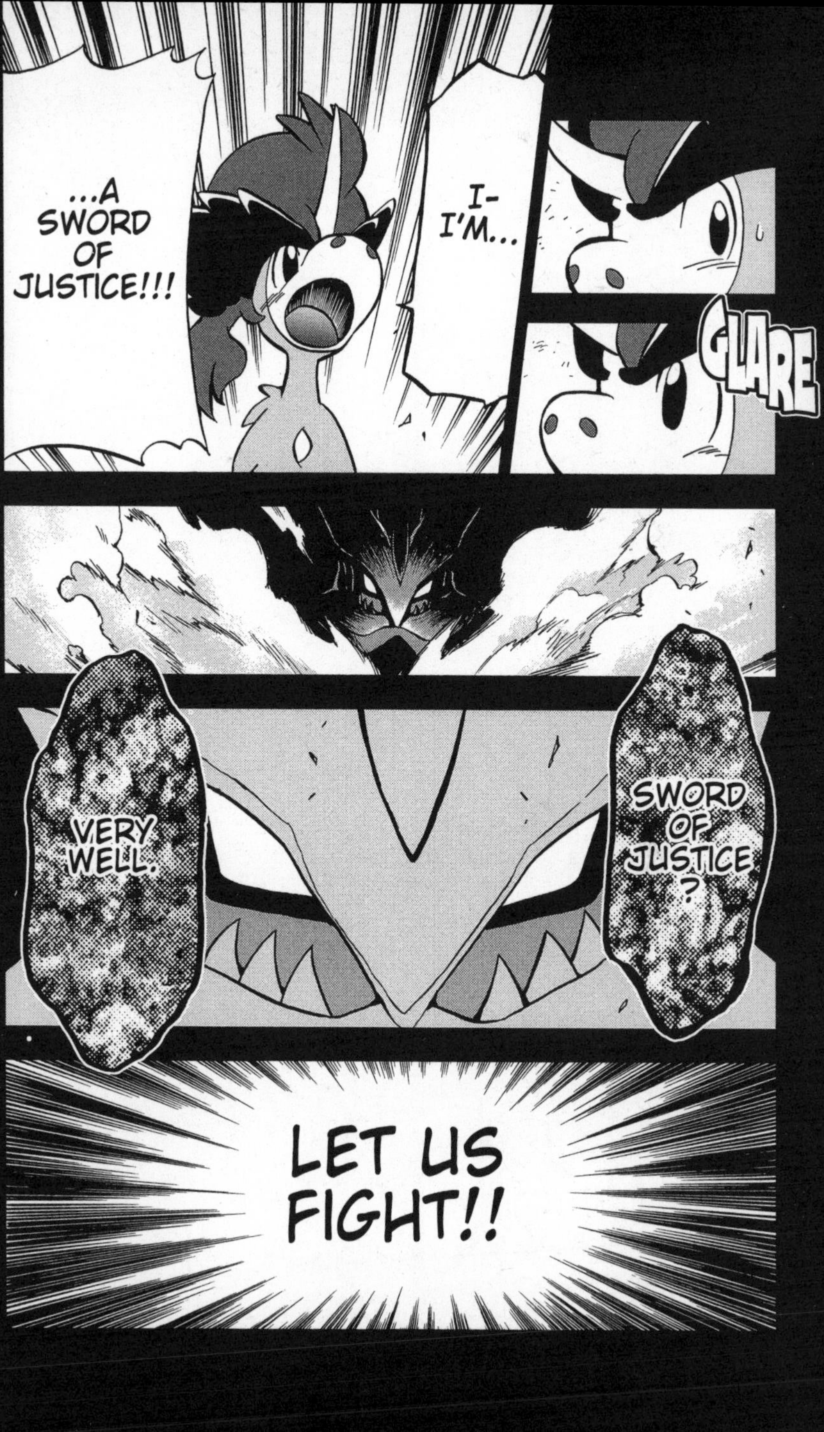
I-
I'M...
GLARE
...A SWORD OF JUSTICE!!!
SWORD OF JUSTICE?
VERY WELL.
LET US FIGHT!!

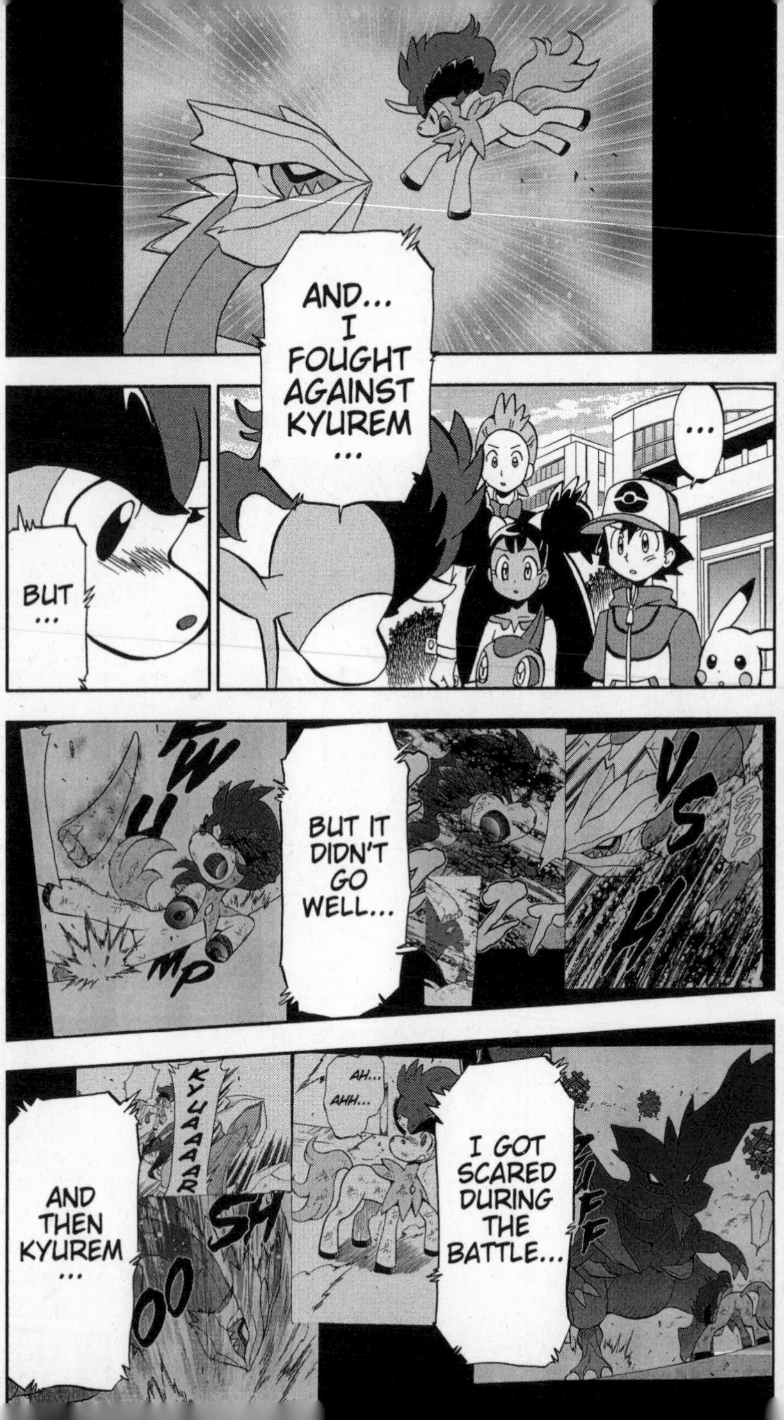
AND... I FOUGHT AGAINST KYUREM...
...
BUT...
BUT IT DIDN'T GO WELL...
I GOT SCARED DURING THE BATTLE...
AH... AHH...
!
KYUAAAAAR
AND THEN KYUREM...

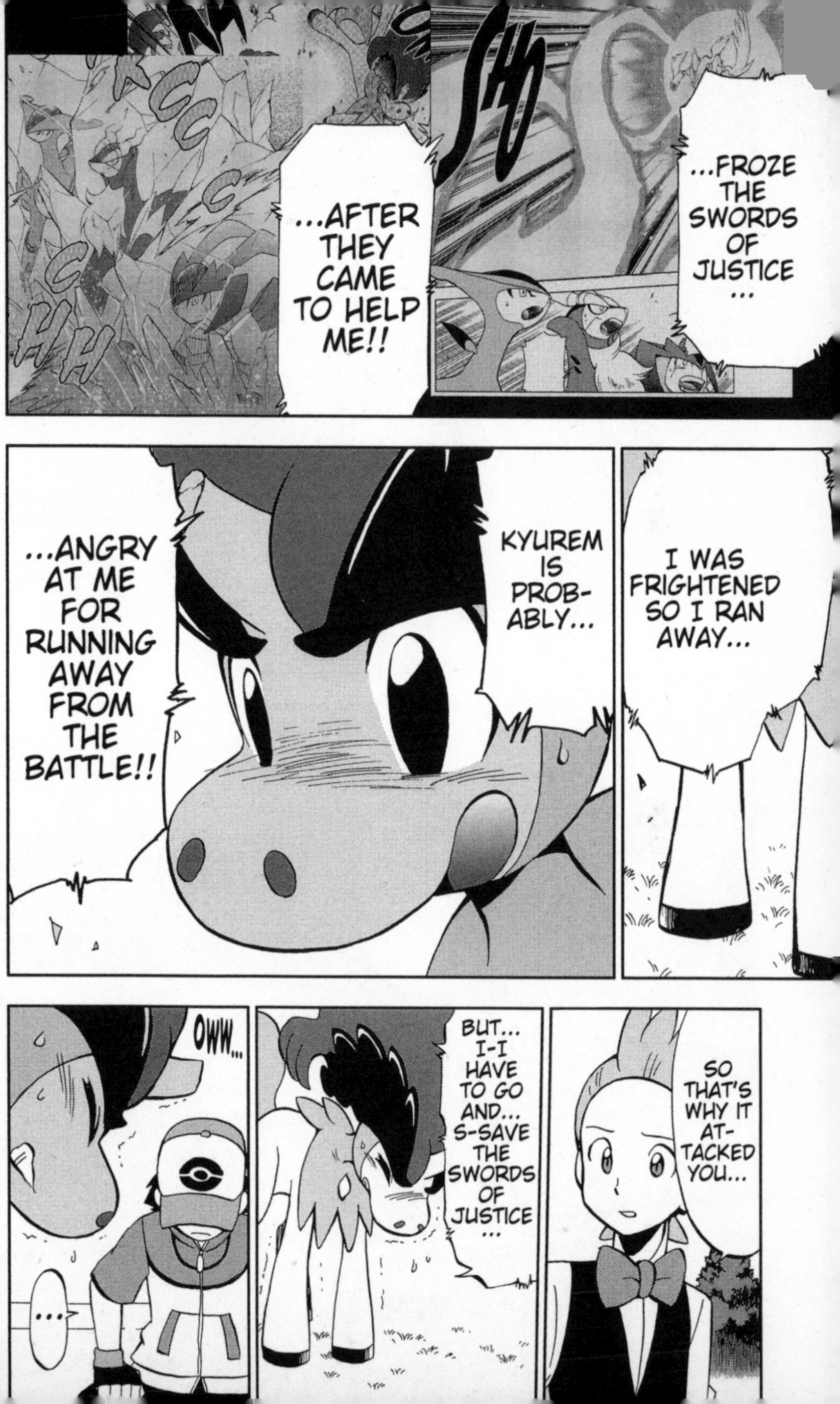
...FROZE THE SWORDS OF JUSTICE...
...AFTER THEY CAME TO HELP ME!!
I WAS FRIGHTENED SO I RAN AWAY...
KYUREM IS PROB-ABLY...
...ANGRY AT ME FOR RUNNING AWAY FROM THE BATTLE!!
SO THAT'S WHY IT AT-TACKED YOU...
BUT... I-I HAVE TO GO AND... S-SAVE THE SWORDS OF JUSTICE...
OWW...
...

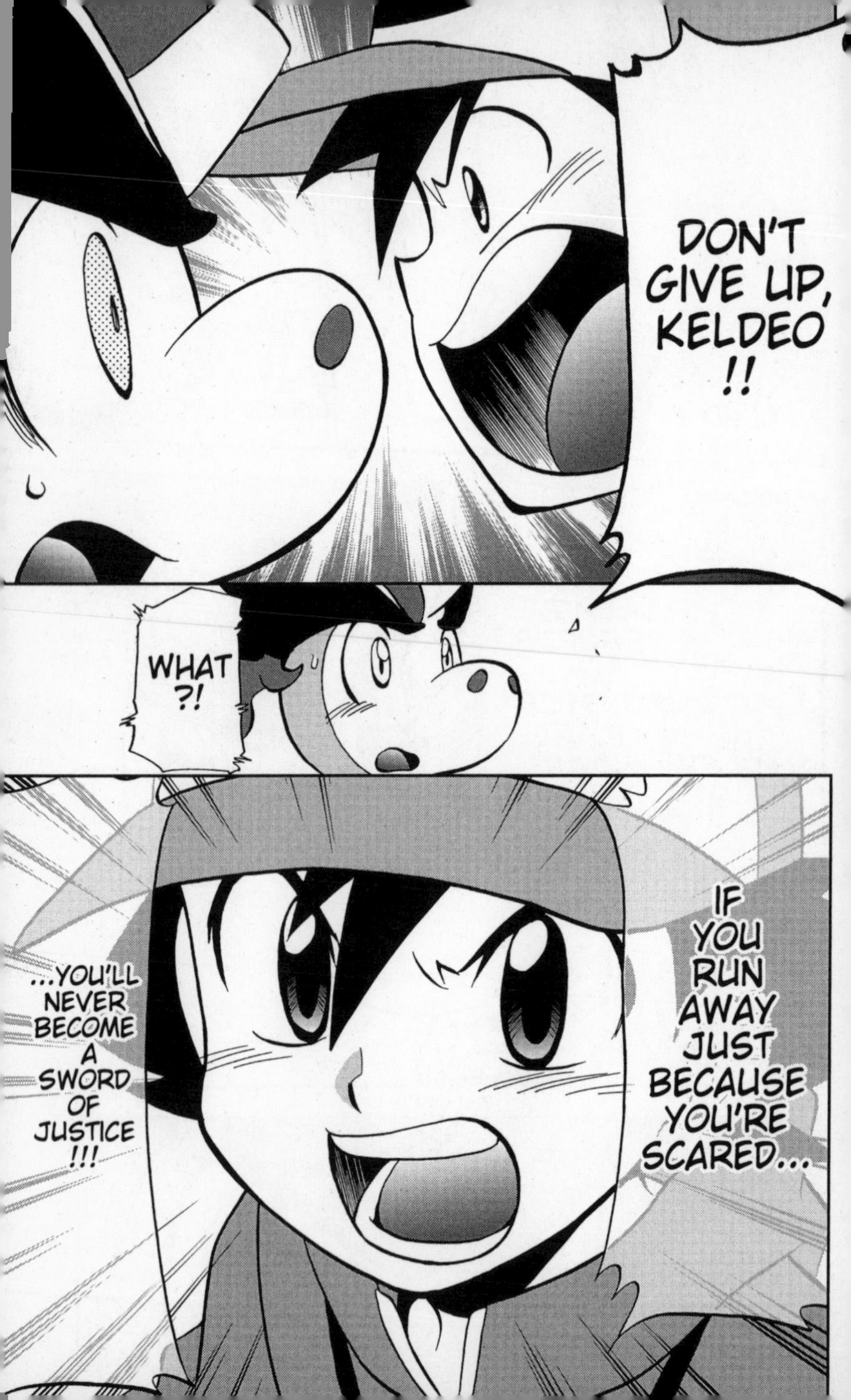
DON'T GIVE UP, KELDEO !!
WHAT ?!
IF YOU RUN AWAY JUST BECAUSE YOU'RE SCARED...
...YOU'LL NEVER BECOME A SWORD OF JUSTICE !!!

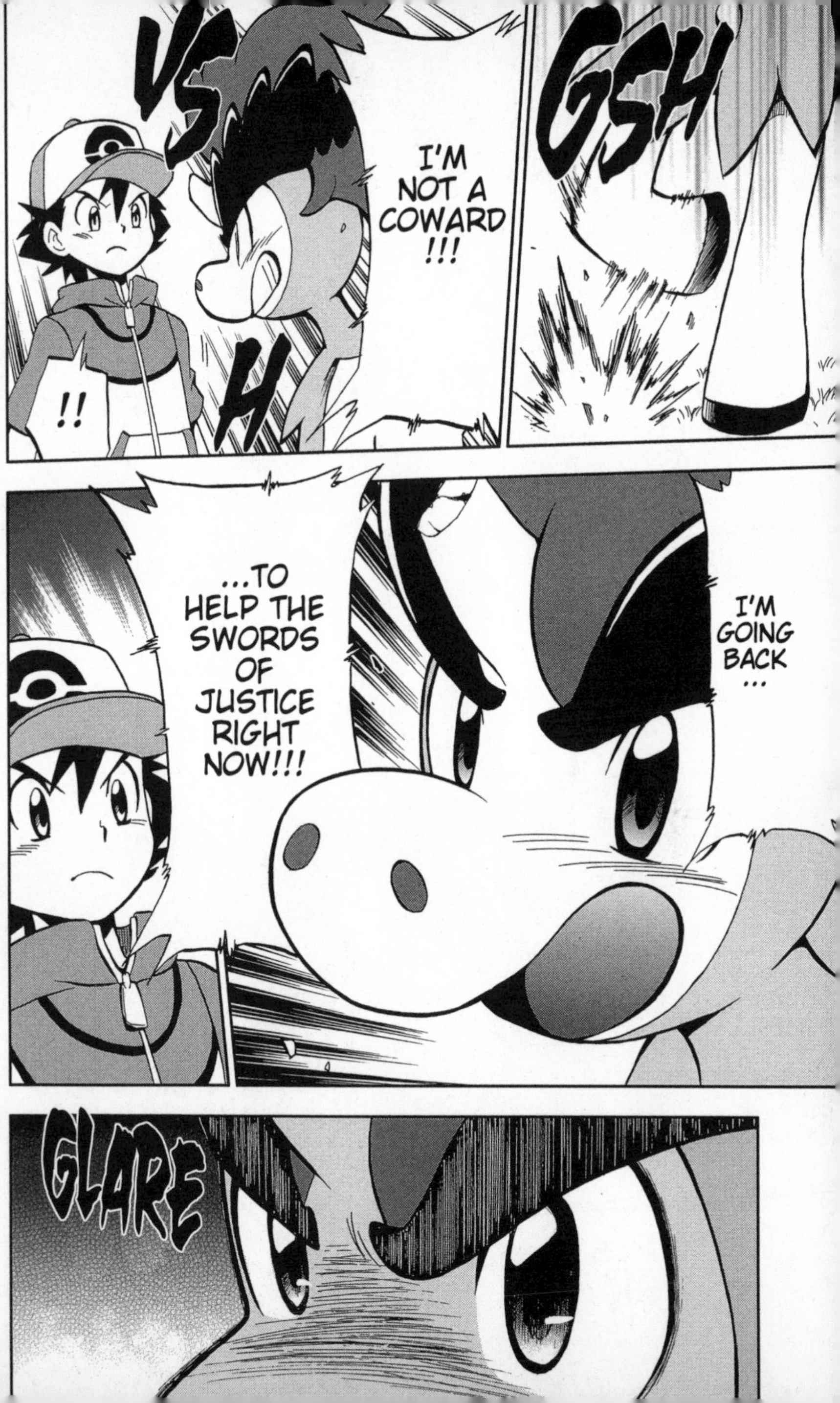
GSH
I'M NOT A COWARD!!!
VS
H
!!
I'M GOING BACK...
...TO HELP THE SWORDS OF JUSTICE RIGHT NOW!!!
GLARE

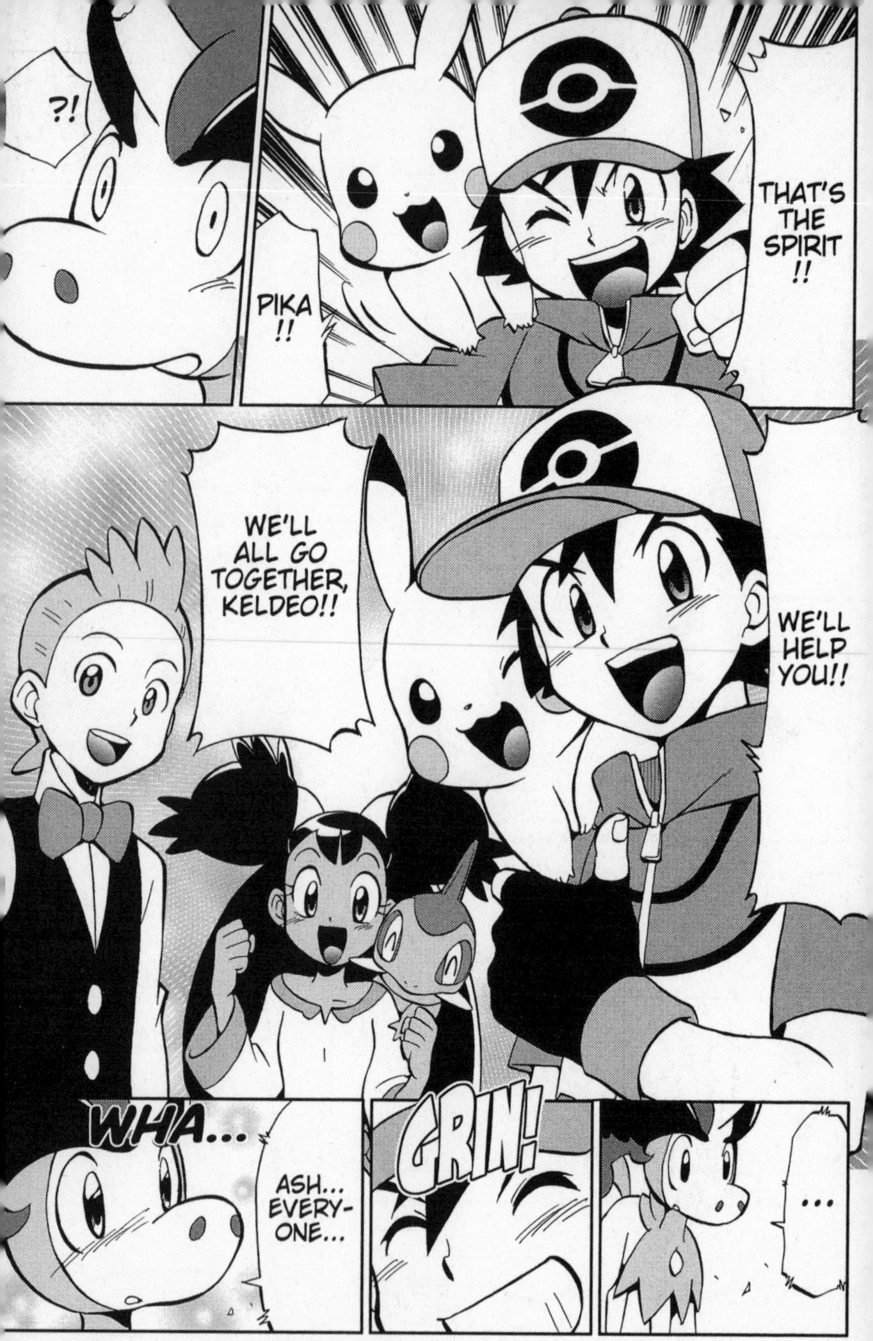
THAT'S THE SPIRIT!!
PIKA!!
?!
WE'LL HELP YOU!!
WE'LL ALL GO TOGETHER, KELDEO!!
...
GRIN!
WHA...
ASH... EVERYONE...

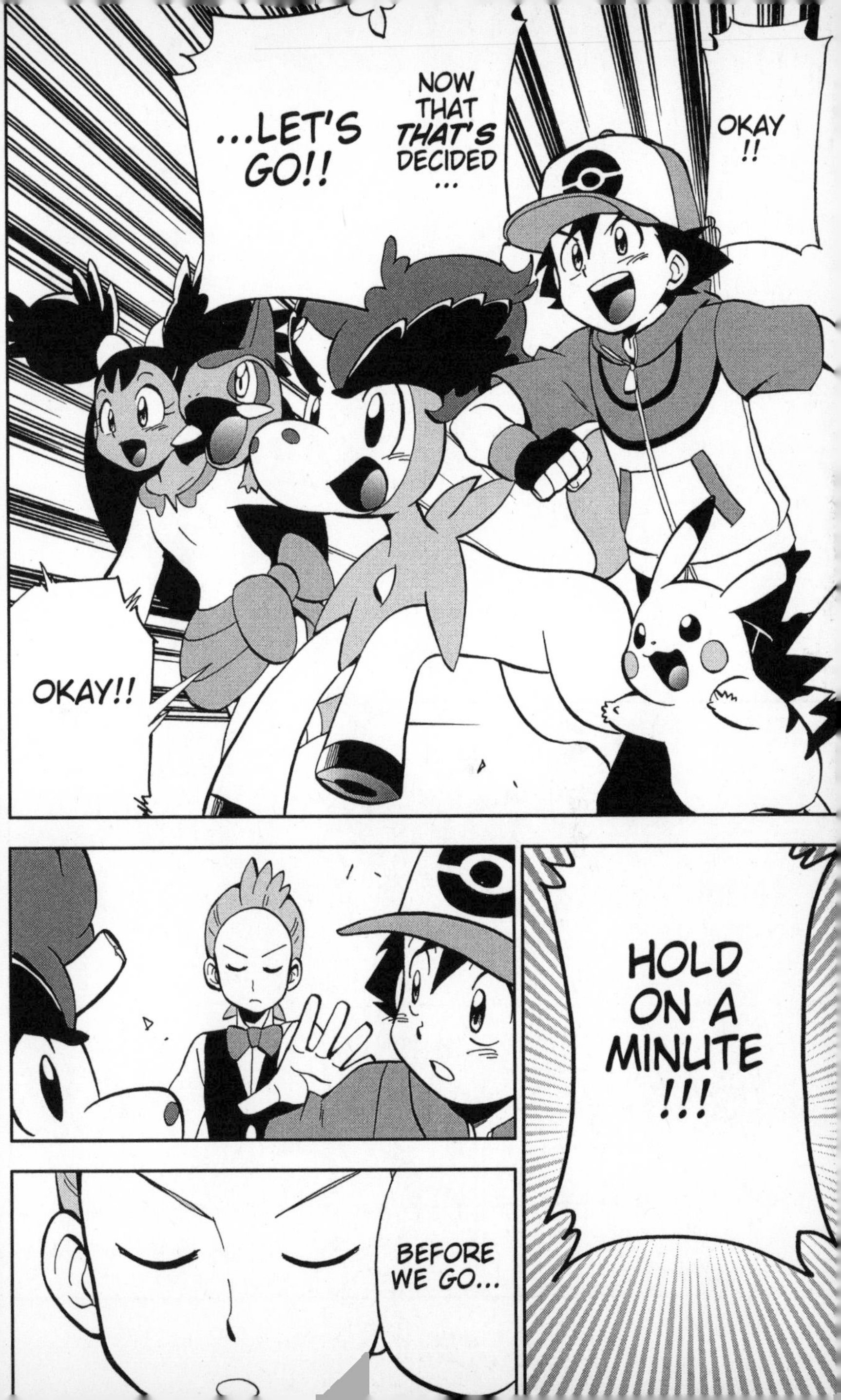
OKAY !!
NOW THAT THAT'S DECIDED ...
...LET'S GO!!
OKAY!!
HOLD ON A MINUTE !!!
BEFORE WE GO...

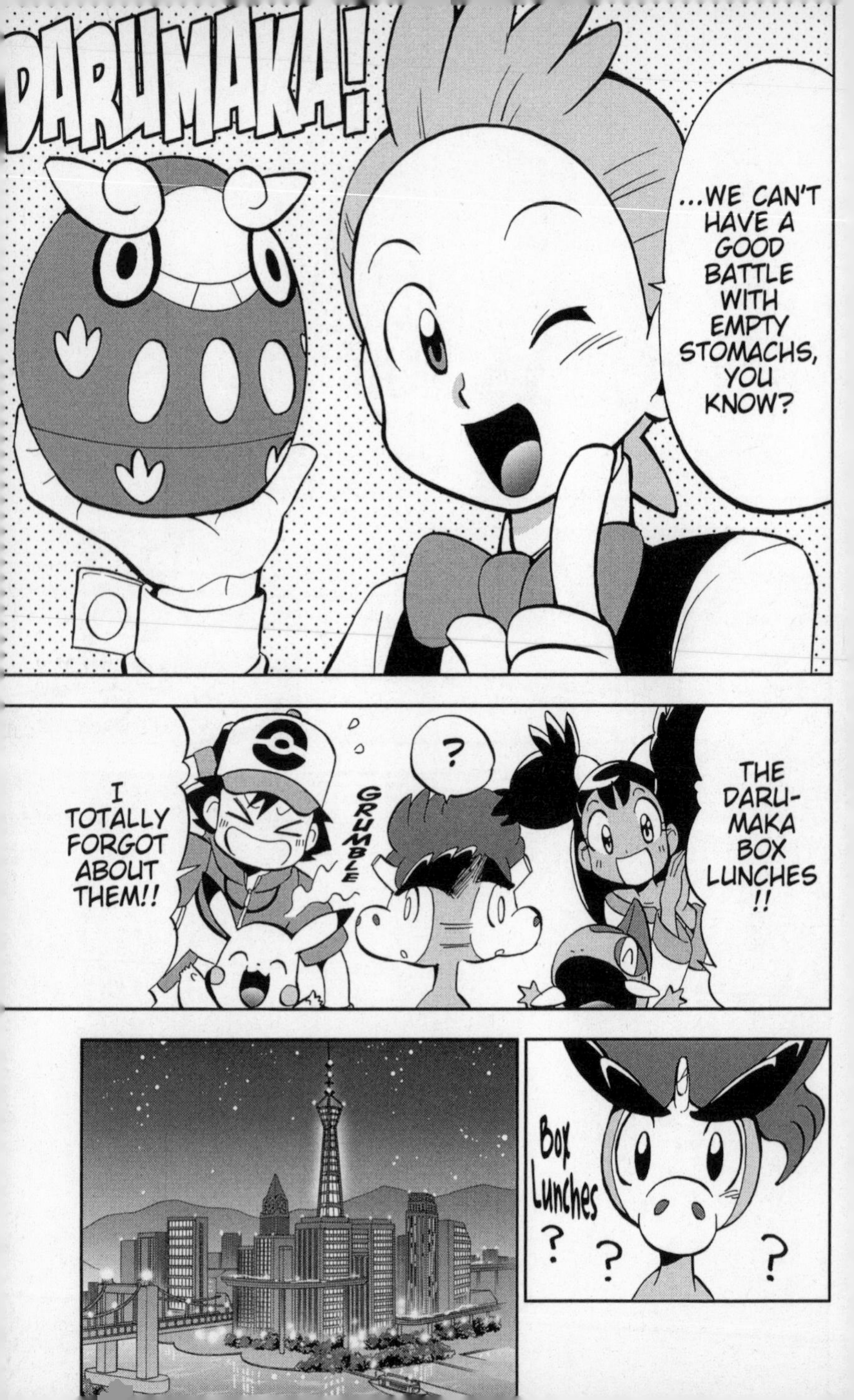
DARUMAKA!
...WE CAN'T HAVE A GOOD BATTLE WITH EMPTY STOMACHS, YOU KNOW?
THE DARU-MAKA BOX LUNCHES !!
?
GRUMBLE
I TOTALLY FORGOT ABOUT THEM!!
Box Lunches ?
? ?

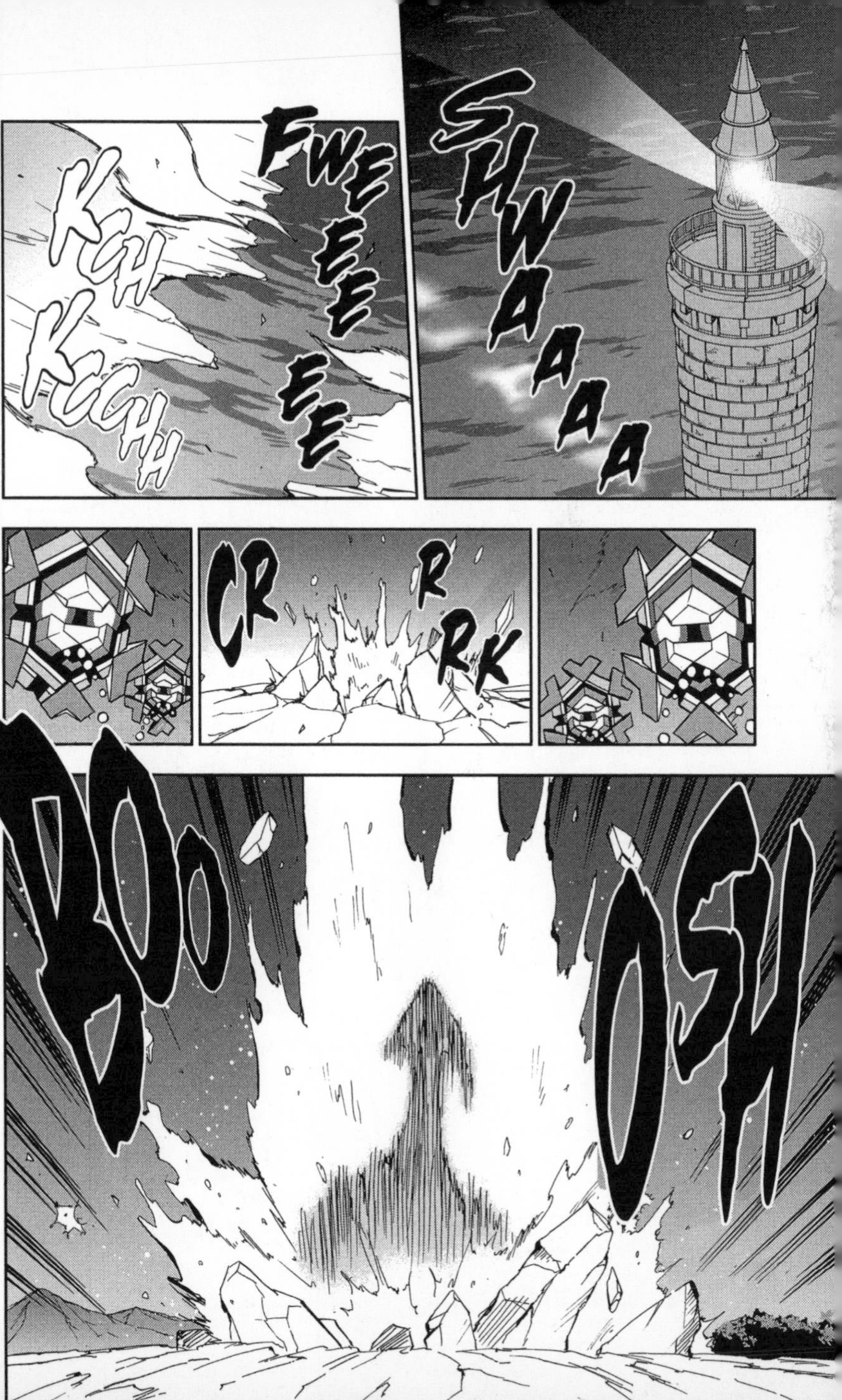
SHWAAAAA
FWEEEEE
KCH KCCHH
CR RRK
BOOOSH

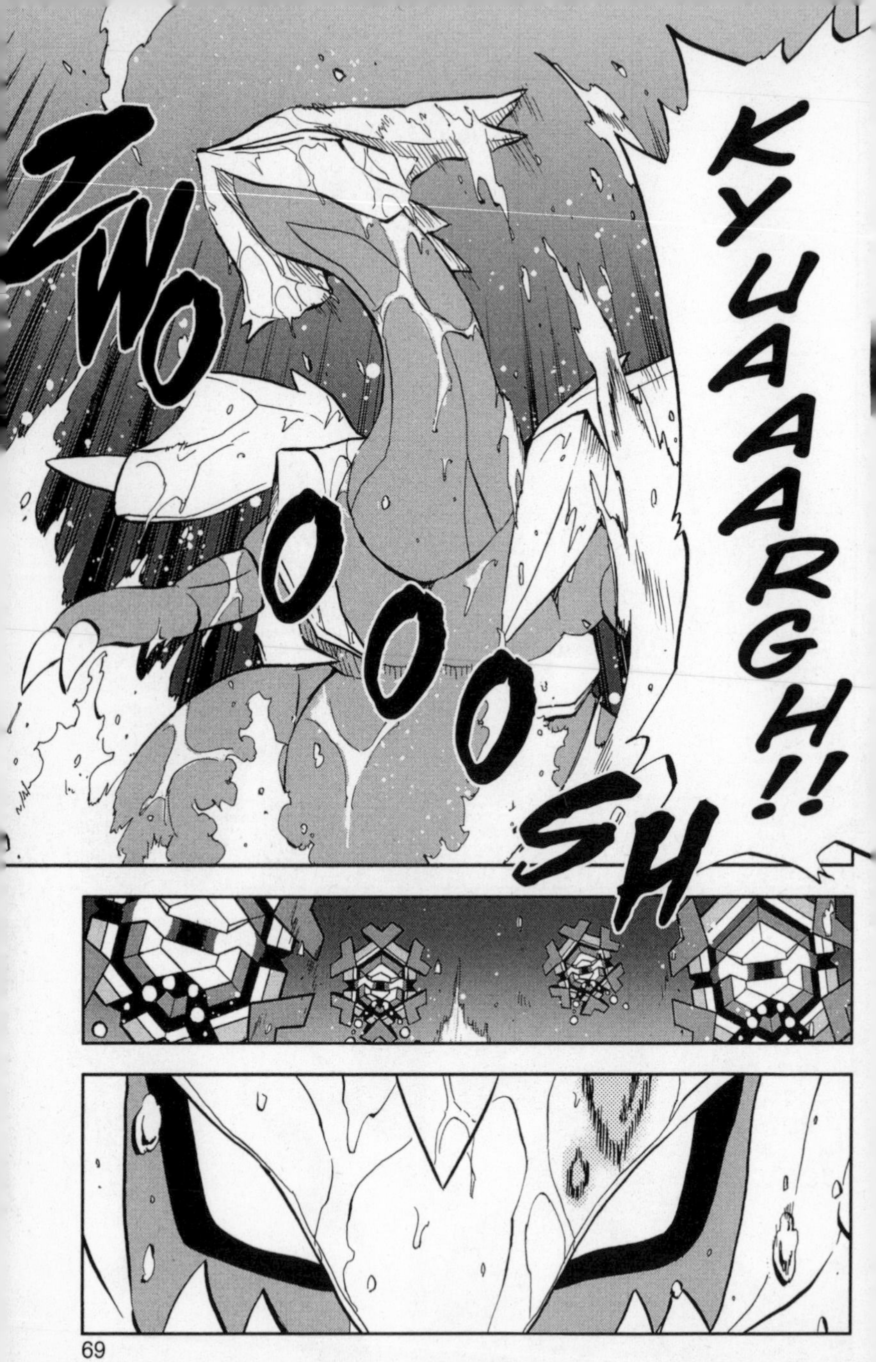
KYUAAARGH!!
ZWOOOOSH

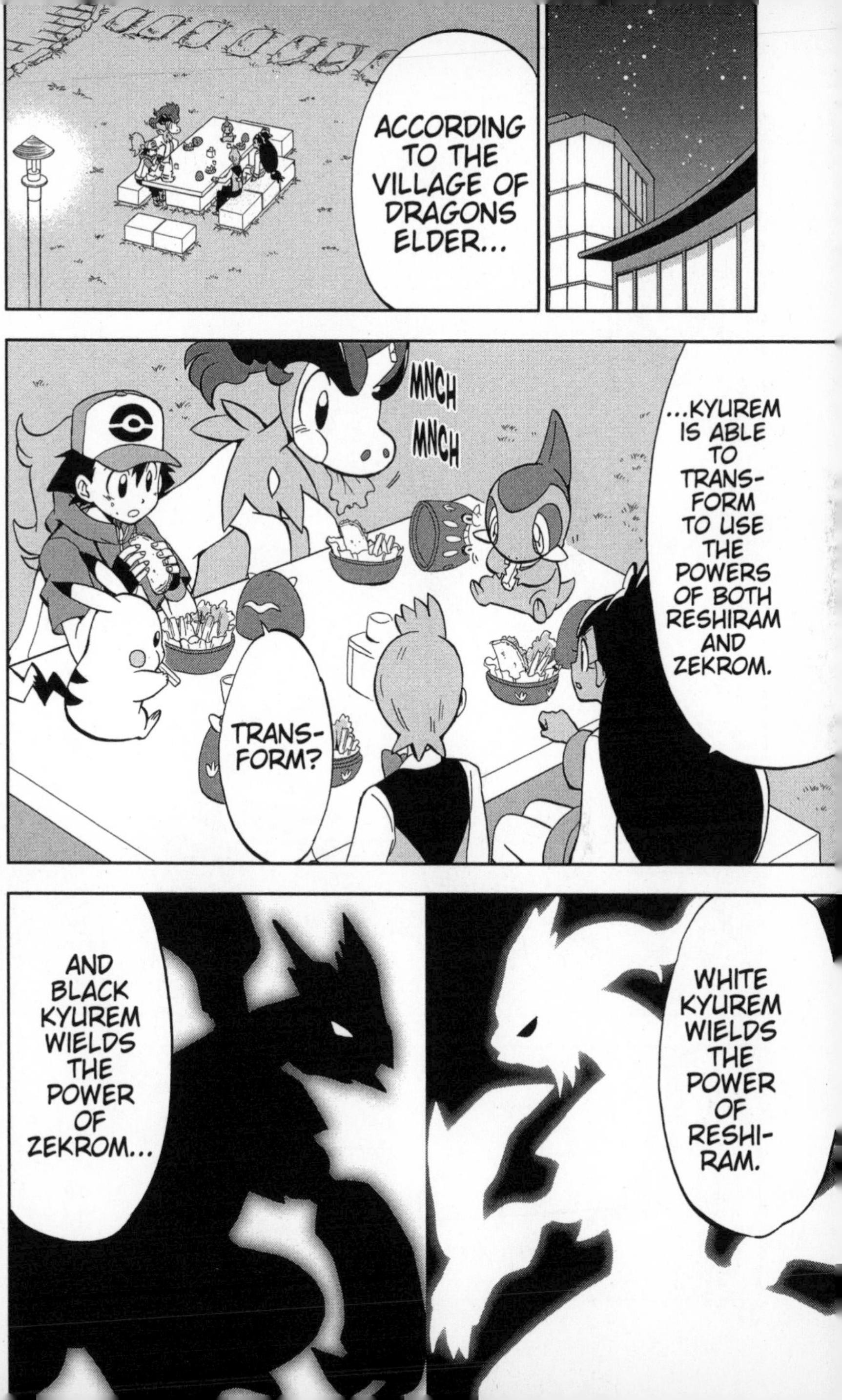
ACCORDING TO THE VILLAGE OF DRAGONS ELDER...
...KYUREM IS ABLE TO TRANS-FORM TO USE THE POWERS OF BOTH RESHIRAM AND ZEKROM.
MNCH MNCH
TRANS-FORM?
WHITE KYUREM WIELDS THE POWER OF RESHI-RAM.
AND BLACK KYUREM WIELDS THE POWER OF ZEKROM...

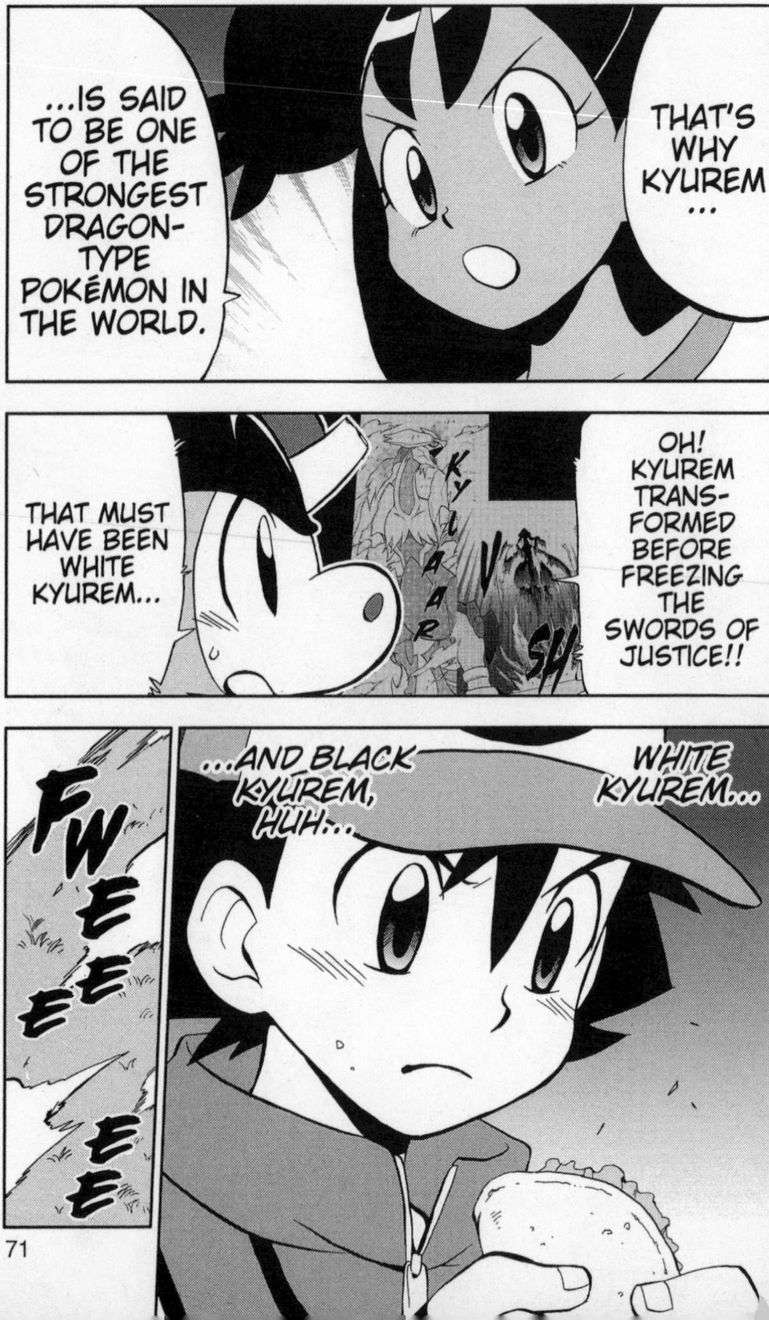
THAT'S WHY KYUREM...
...IS SAID TO BE ONE OF THE STRONGEST DRAGON-TYPE POKÉMON IN THE WORLD.
OH! KYUREM TRANSFORMED BEFORE FREEZING THE SWORDS OF JUSTICE!!
KYUAAR
VSH
THAT MUST HAVE BEEN WHITE KYUREM...
WHITE KYUREM...
...AND BLACK KYUREM, HUH...
FWEEEEEE

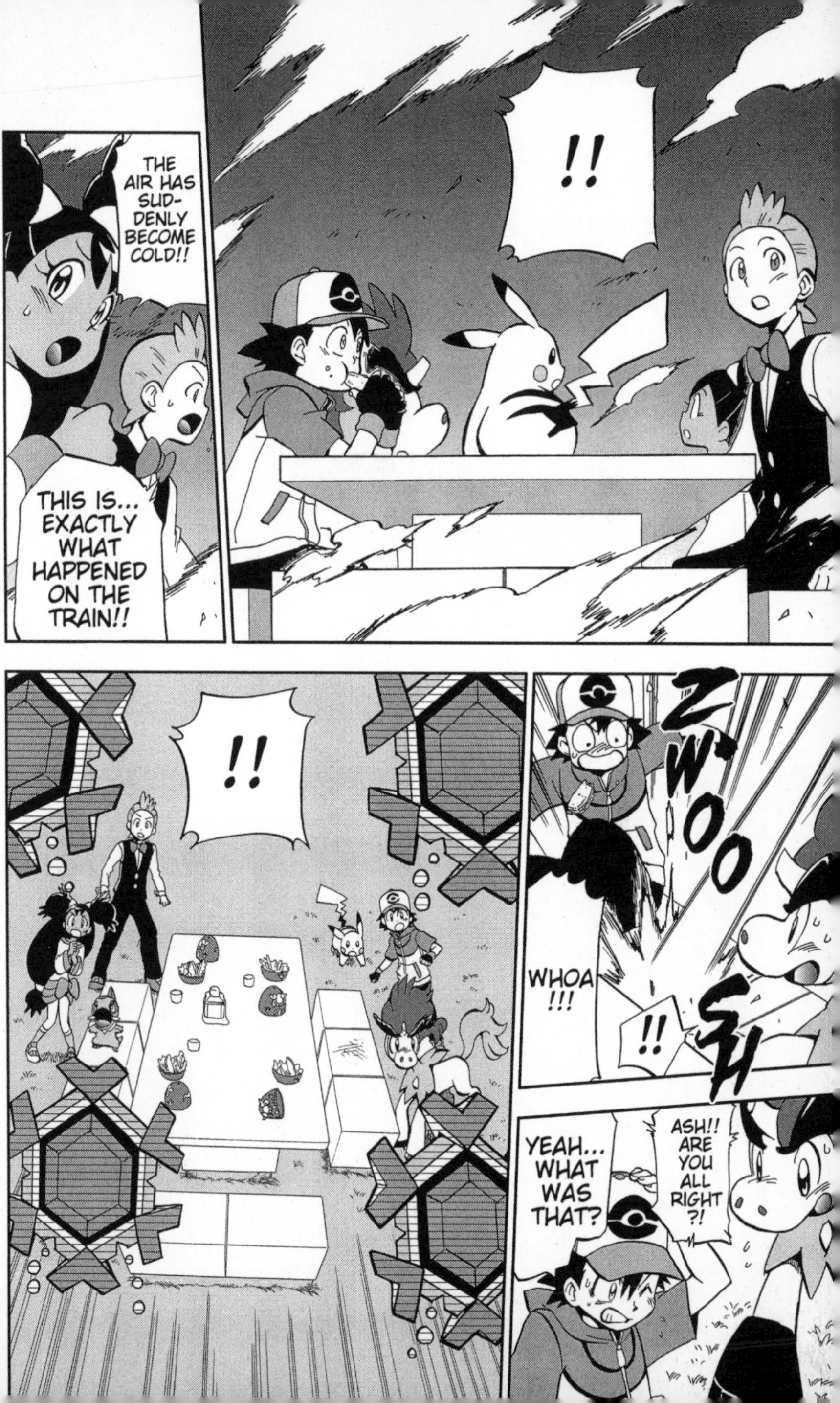
!!
THE AIR HAS SUD-DENLY BECOME COLD!!
THIS IS... EXACTLY WHAT HAPPENED ON THE TRAIN!!
ZWOOSH
WHOA!!!
!!
ASH!! ARE YOU ALL RIGHT?!
YEAH... WHAT WAS THAT?
!!

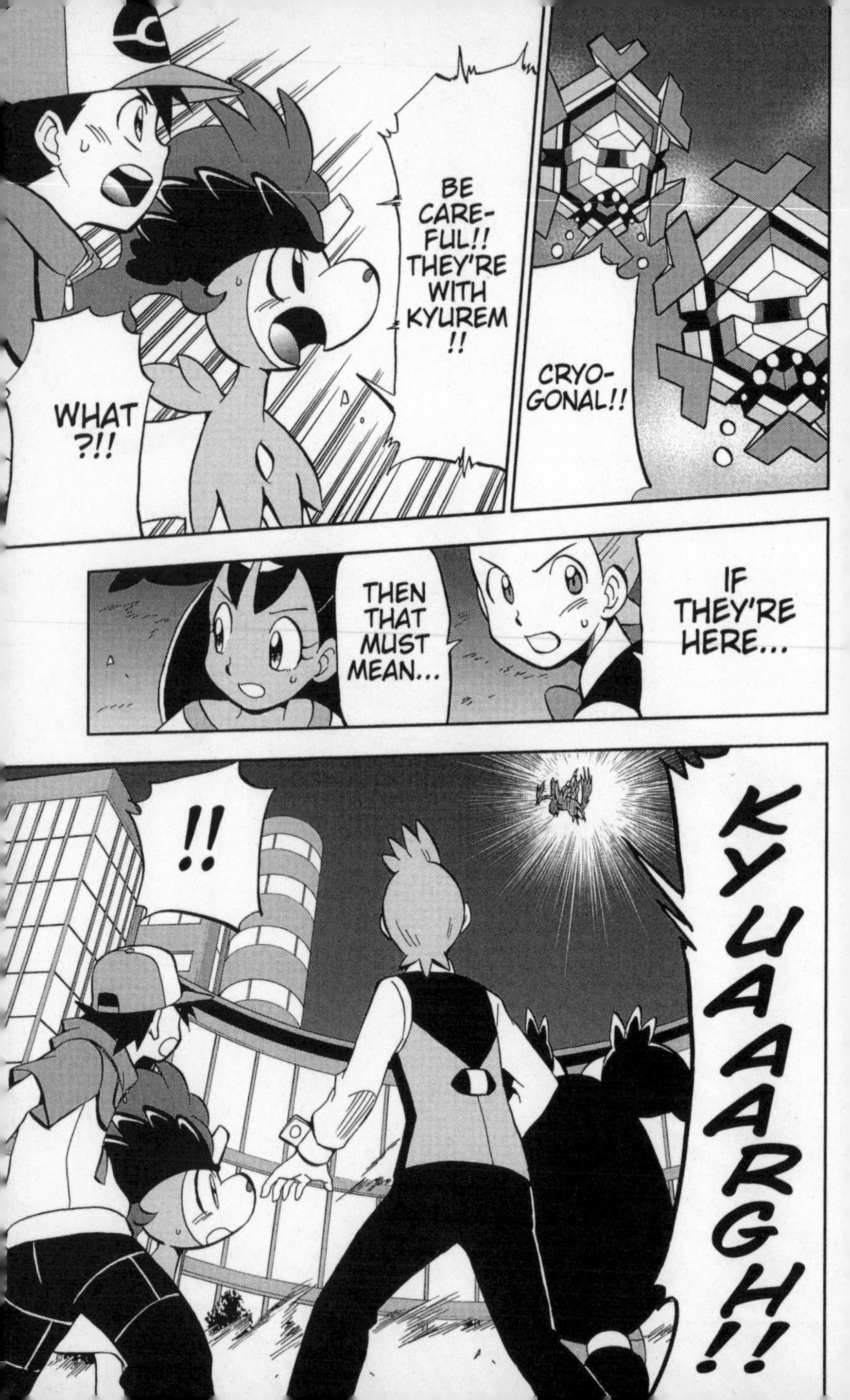
CRYO-GONAL!!
BE CARE-FUL!! THEY'RE WITH KYUREM!!
WHAT?!!
IF THEY'RE HERE...
THEN THAT MUST MEAN...
KYUAAAARGH!!
!!

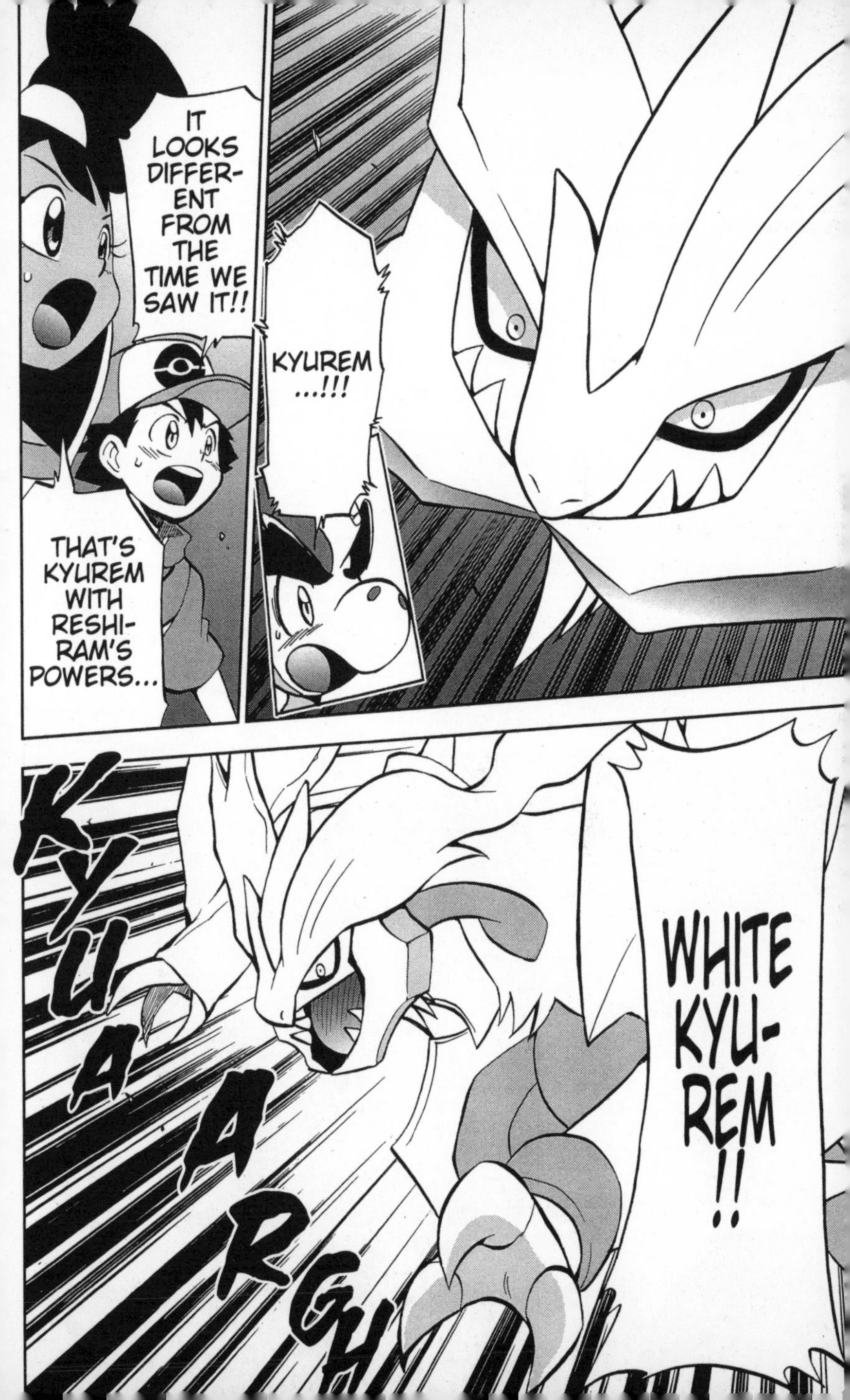
KYUREM ...!!!
IT LOOKS DIFFERENT FROM THE TIME WE SAW IT!!
THAT'S KYUREM WITH RESHIRAM'S POWERS...
WHITE KYUREM!!
KYUAAARGH

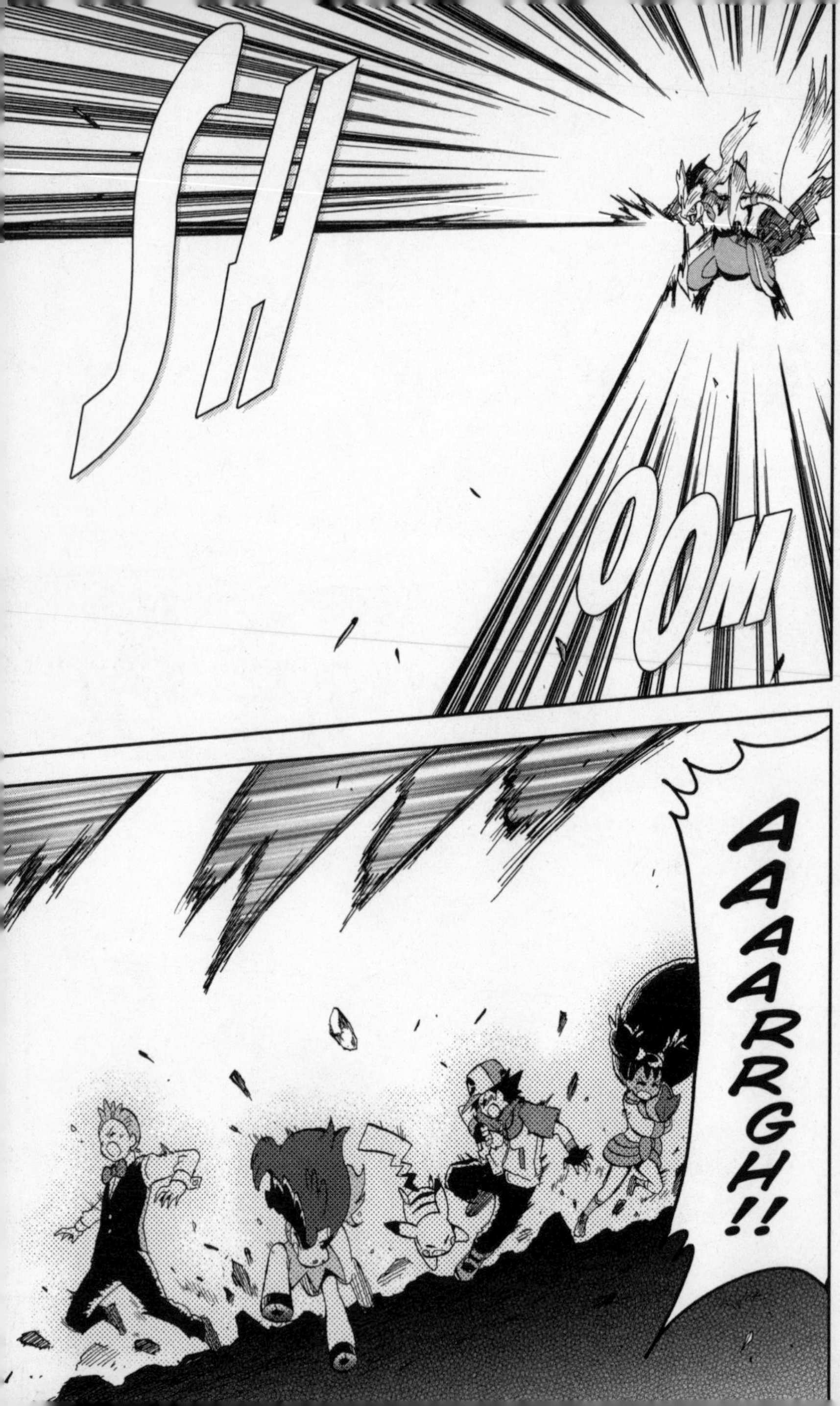
SH
OOM
AAAARRGH!!

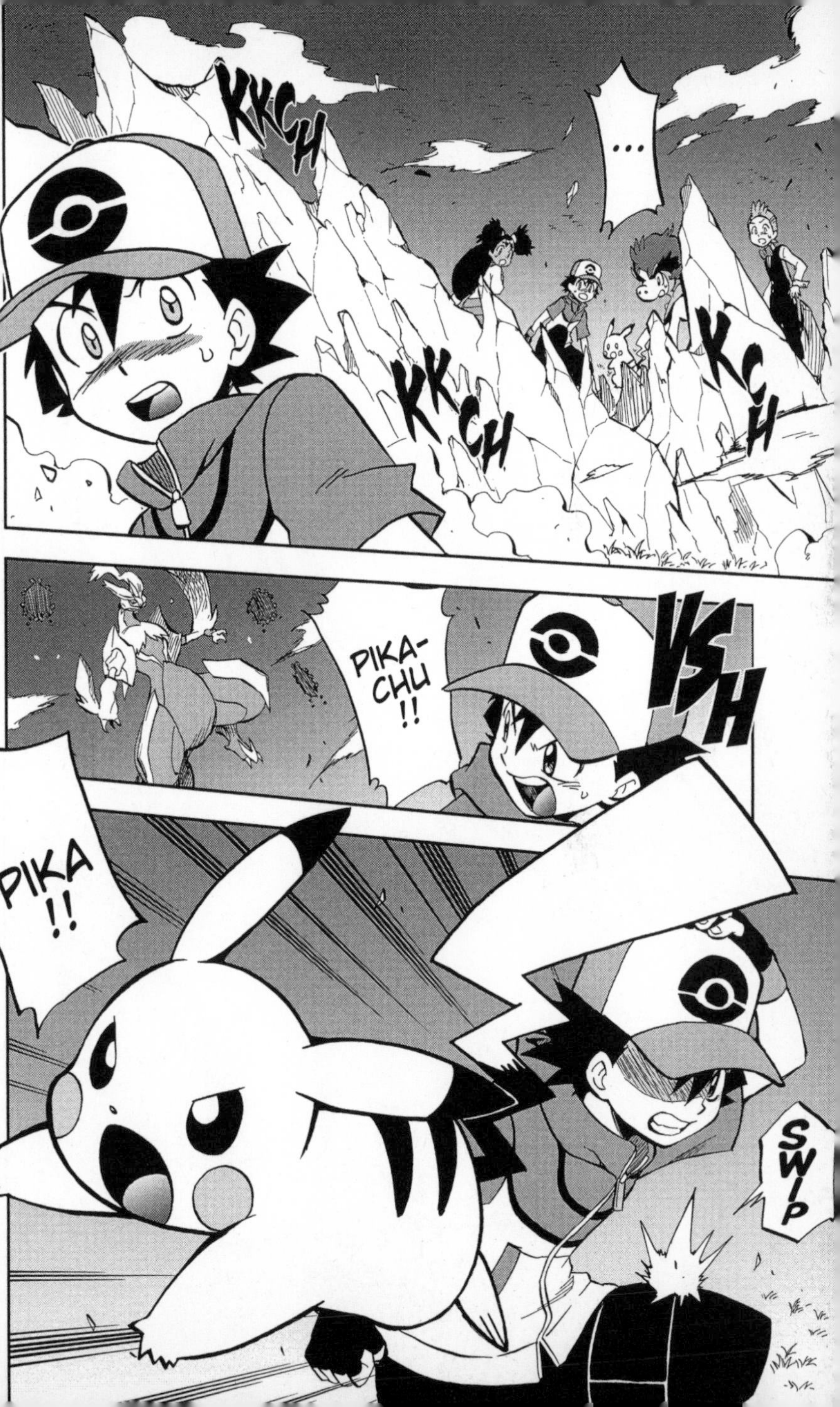
...
KCH
KKCH
KKCH
VSH
PIKA-CHU!!
PIKA!!
SWIP

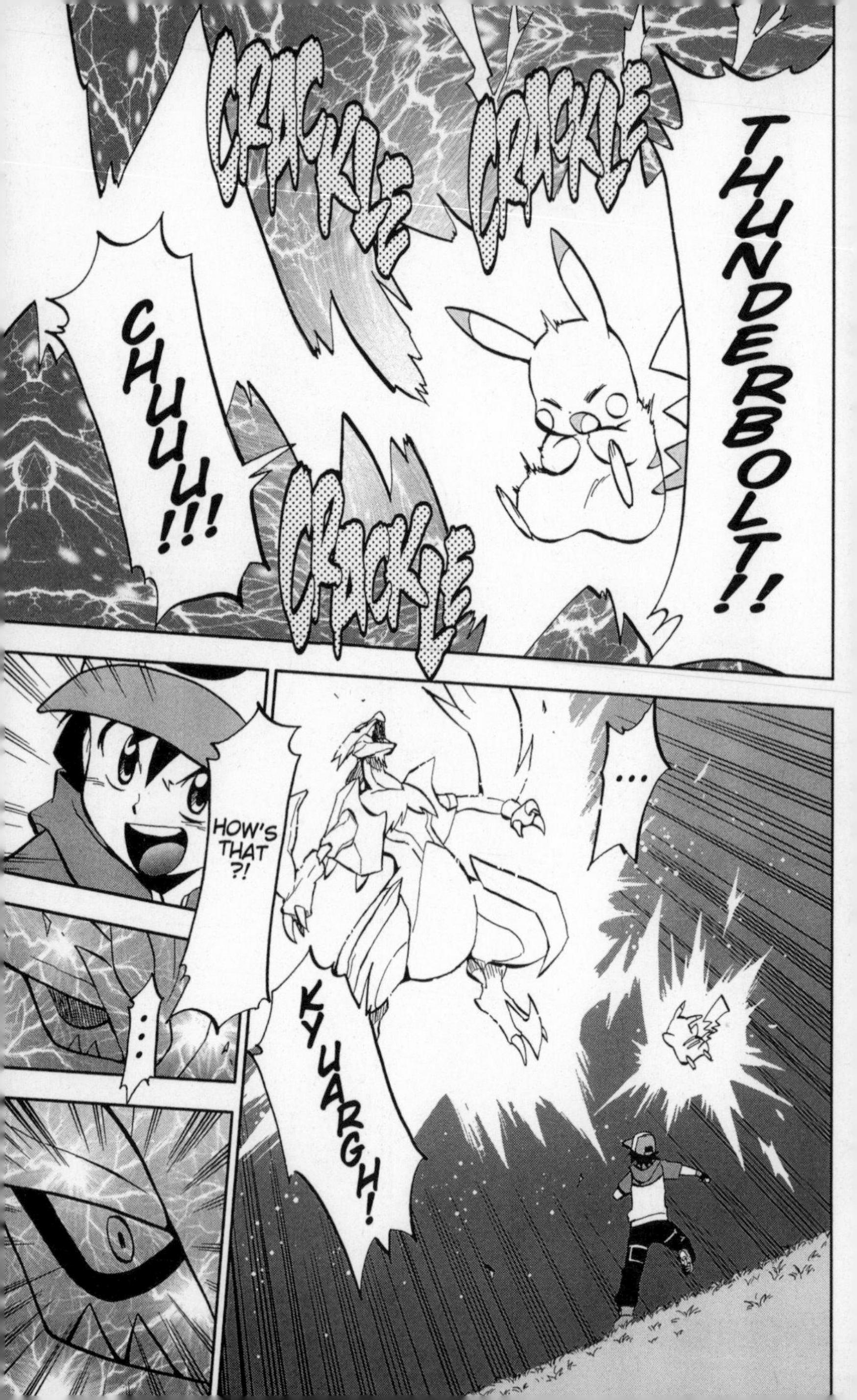
THUNDERBOLT!!
CRACKLE
CRACKLE
CRACKLE
CHUUUU!!!
...
KYUARGH!
HOW'S THAT ?!
...

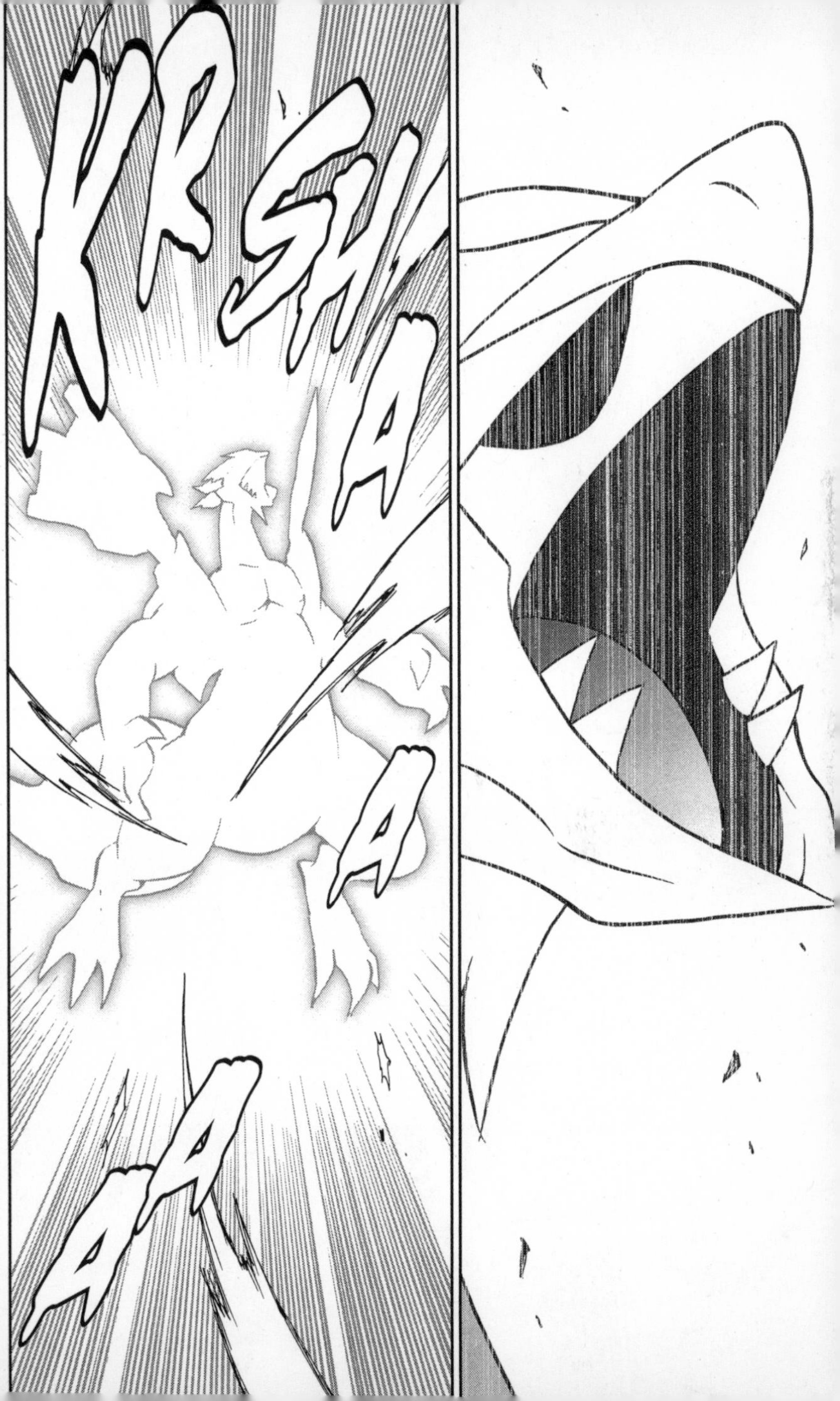
KRSHAAAA

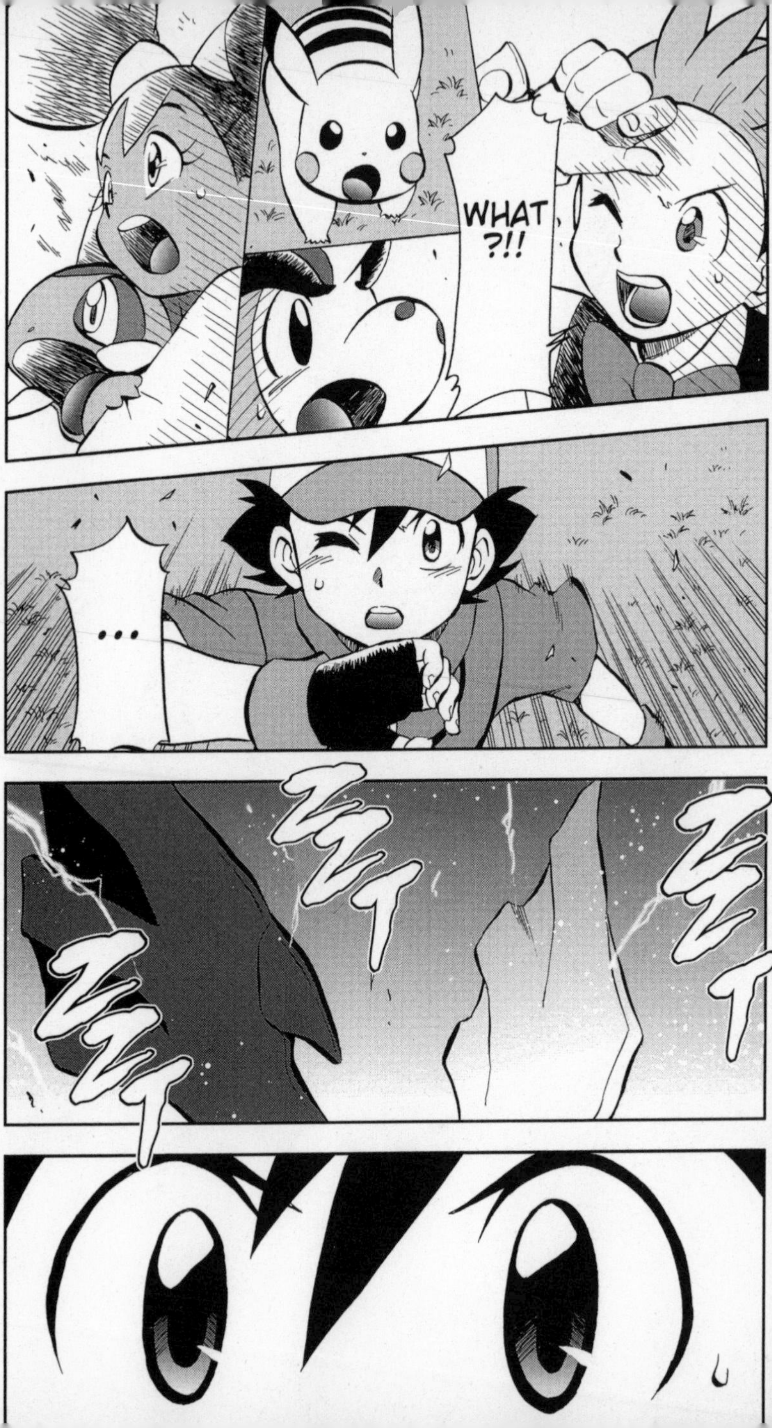
WHAT ?!!
...
ZZZT
ZZZT
ZZZT

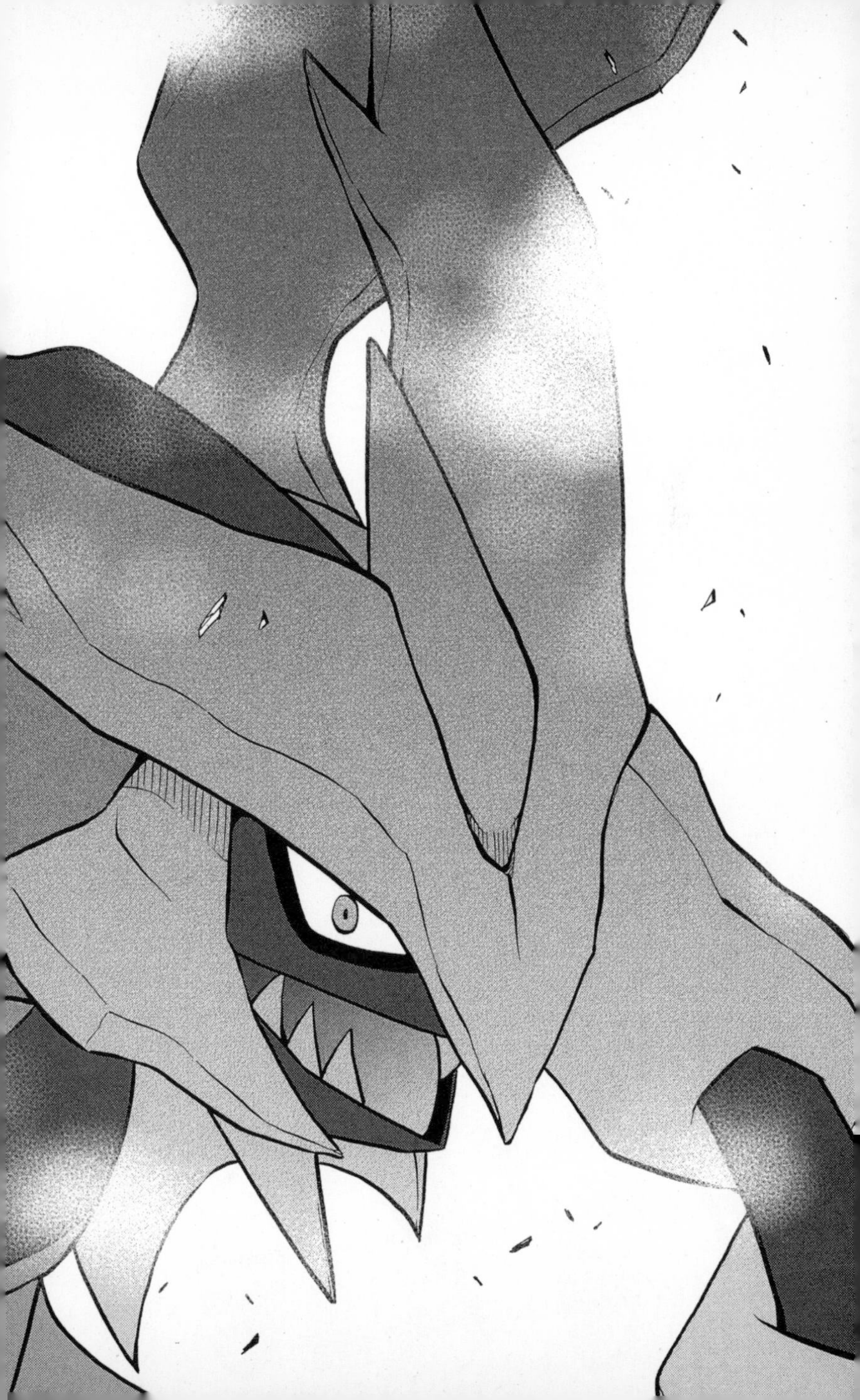

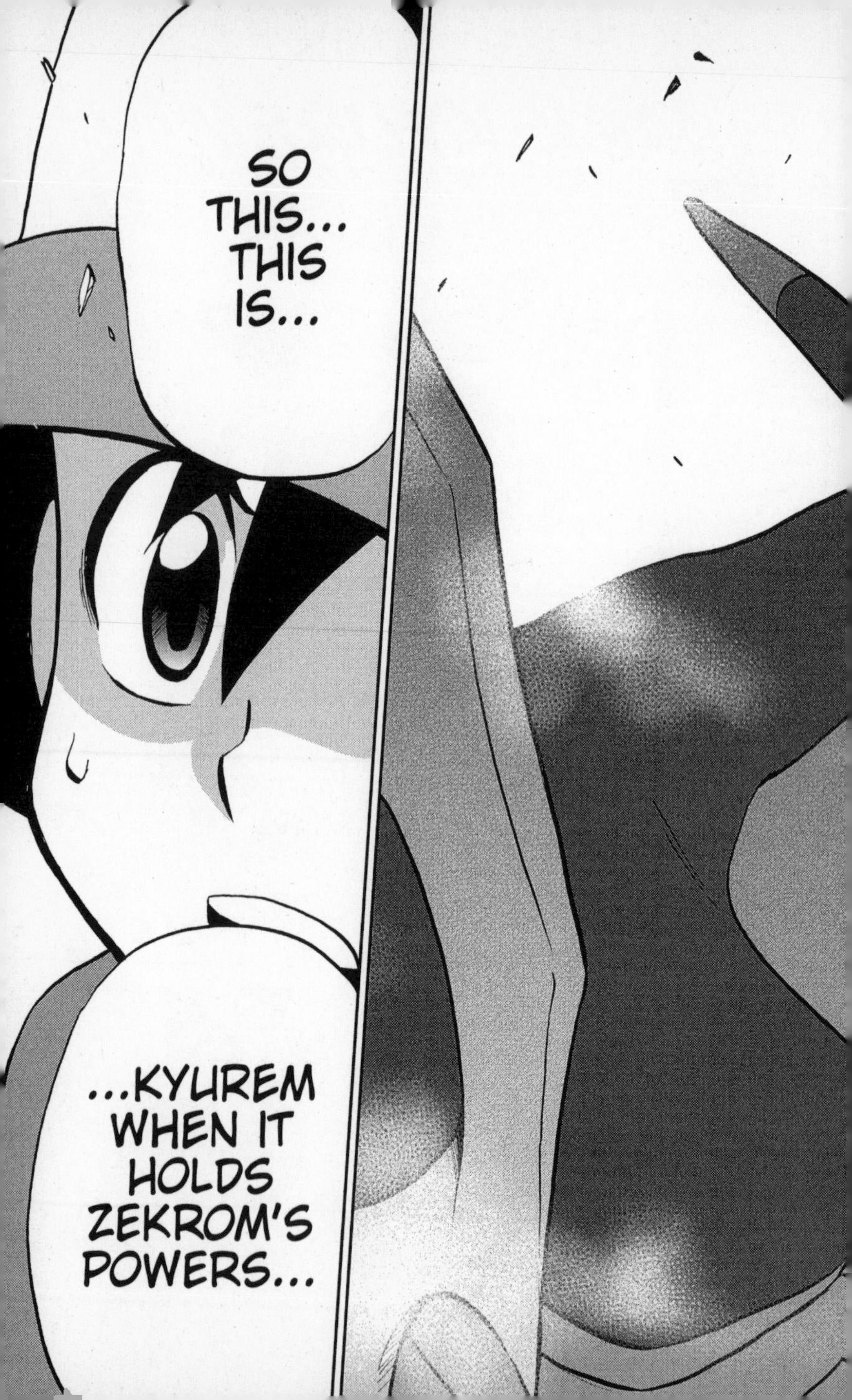
SO THIS... THIS IS...
...KYUREM WHEN IT HOLDS ZEKROM'S POWERS...

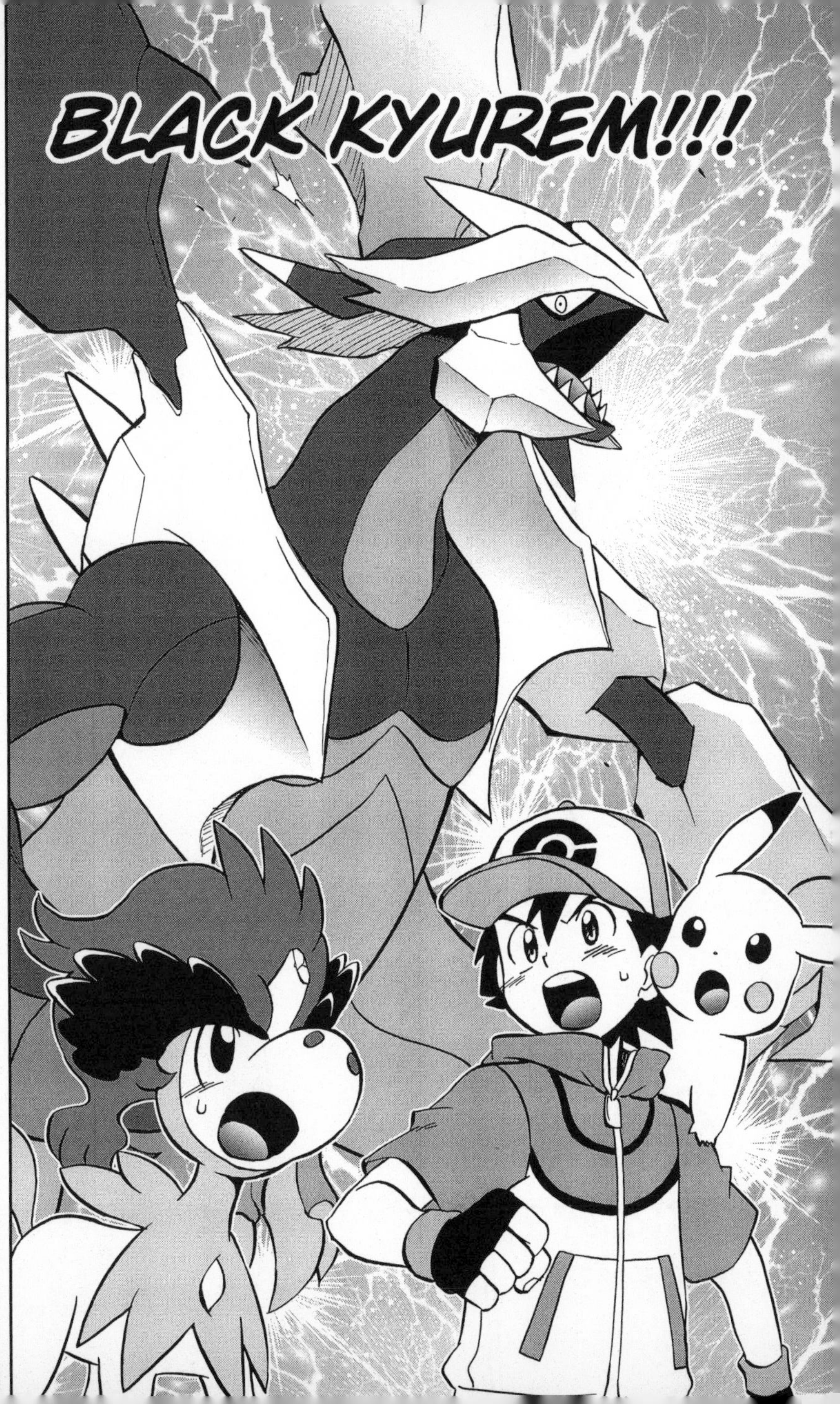
BLACK KYUREM!!!

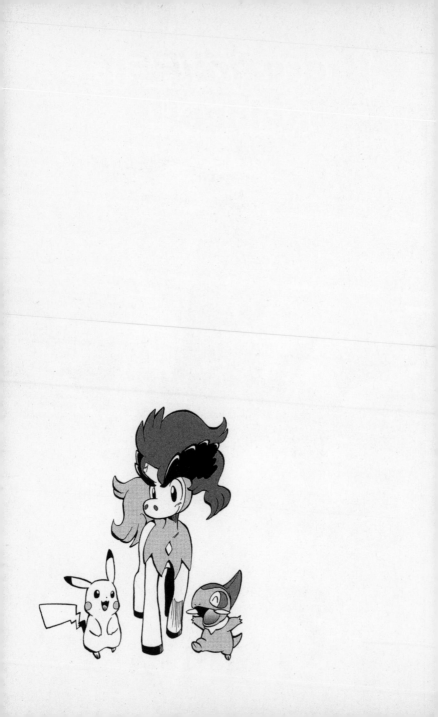

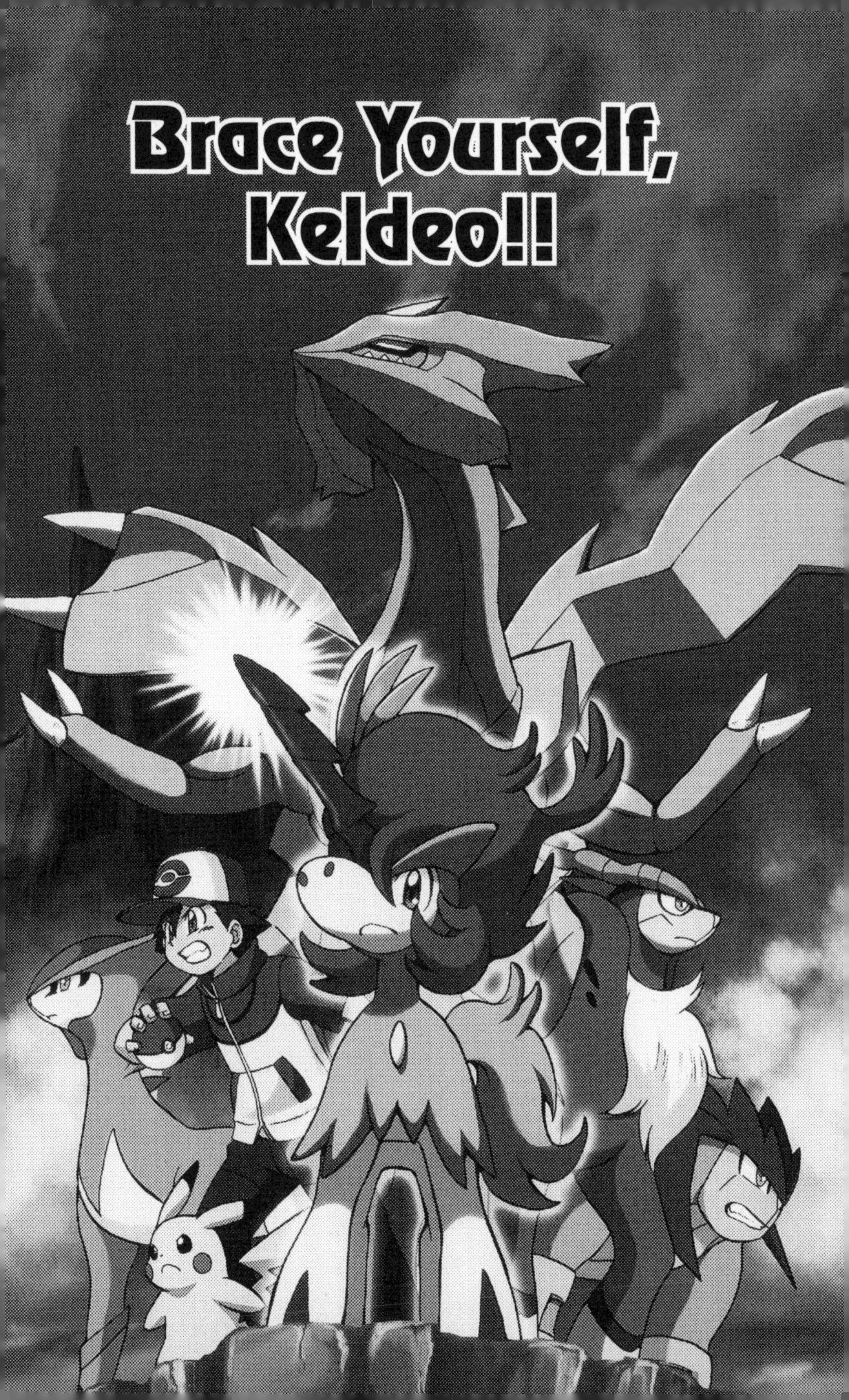
Brace Yourself, Keldeo!!

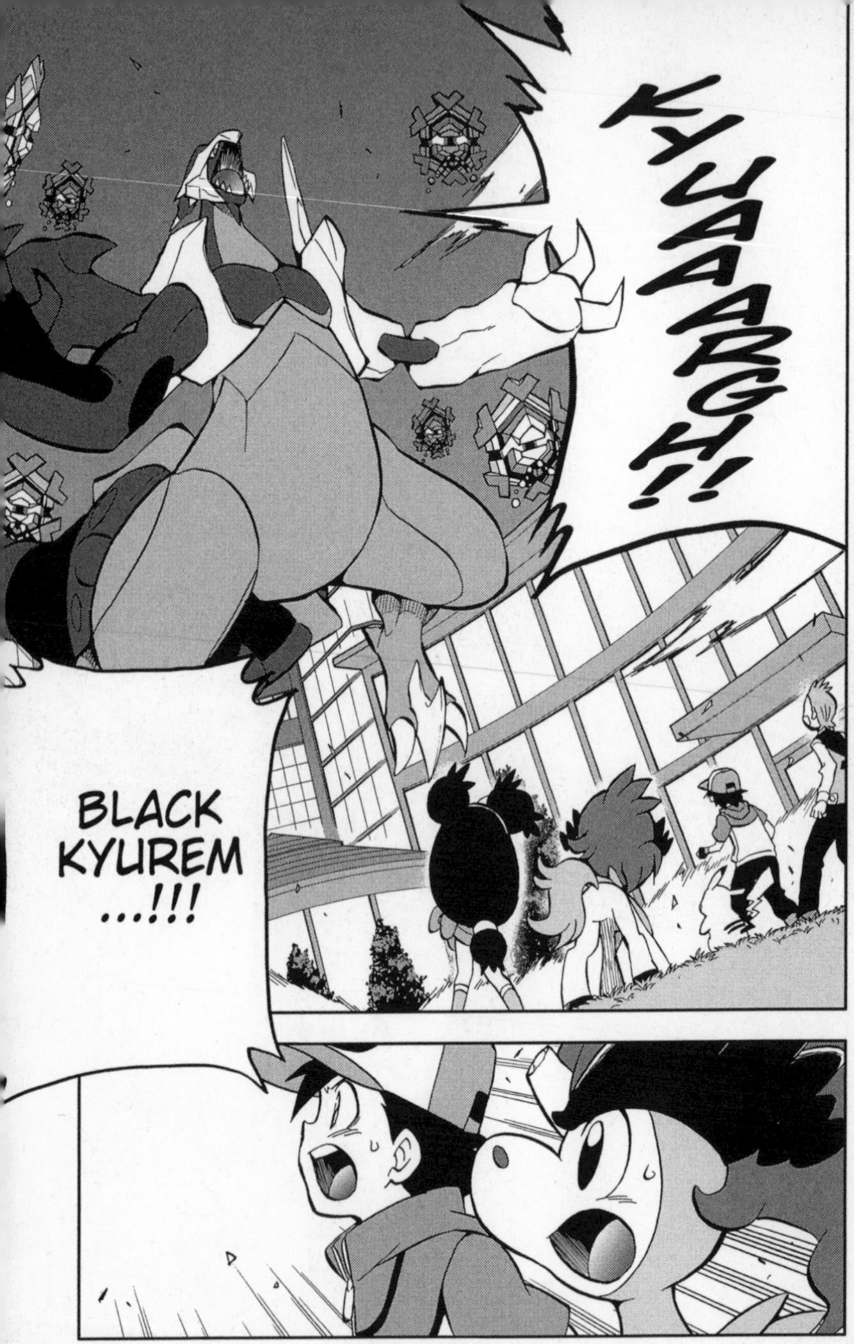
KYUAAARGH!!
BLACK KYUREM ...!!!

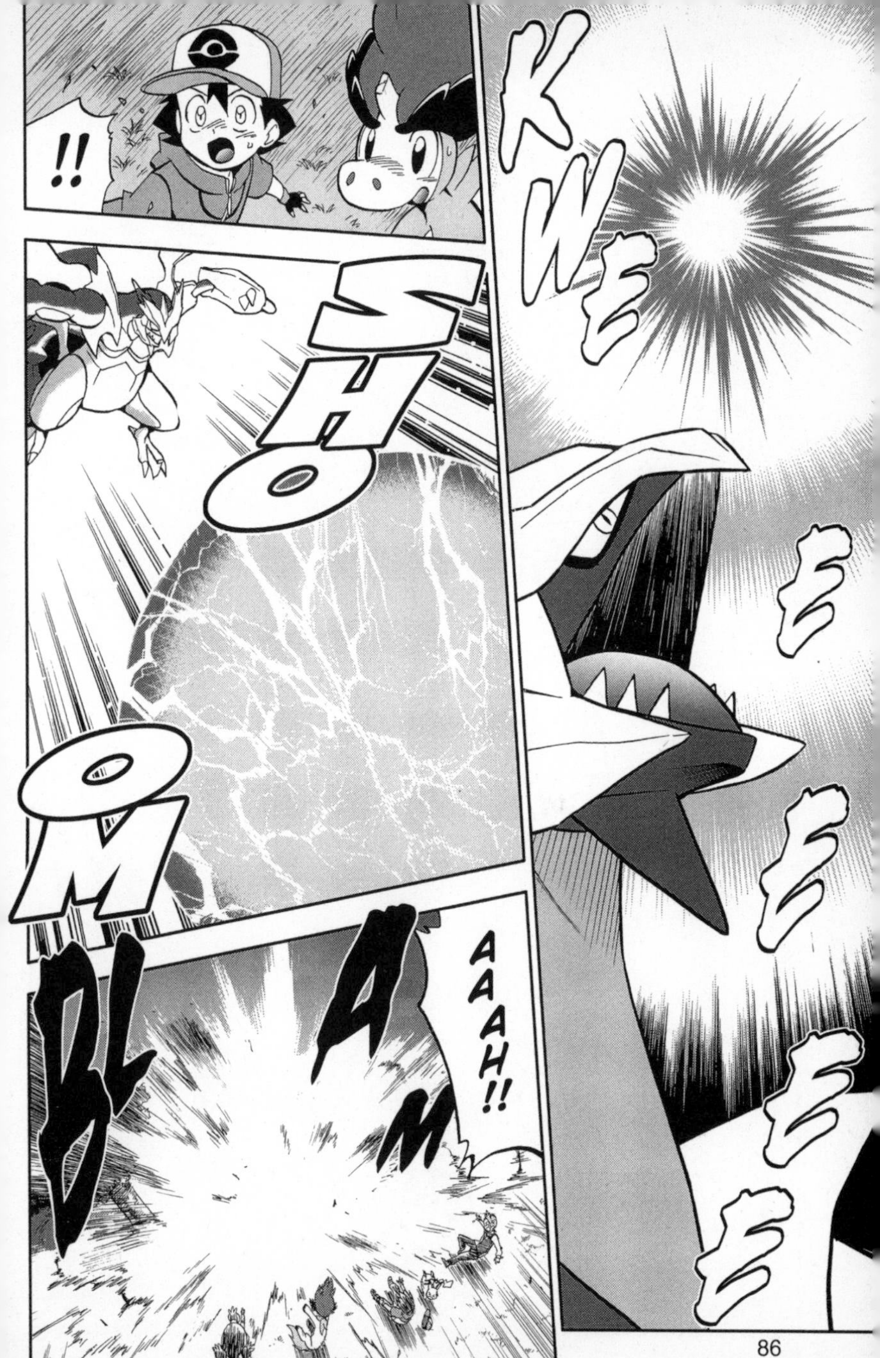
KWEEEEEE
!!
SHOOM
BLAM
AAAAH!!

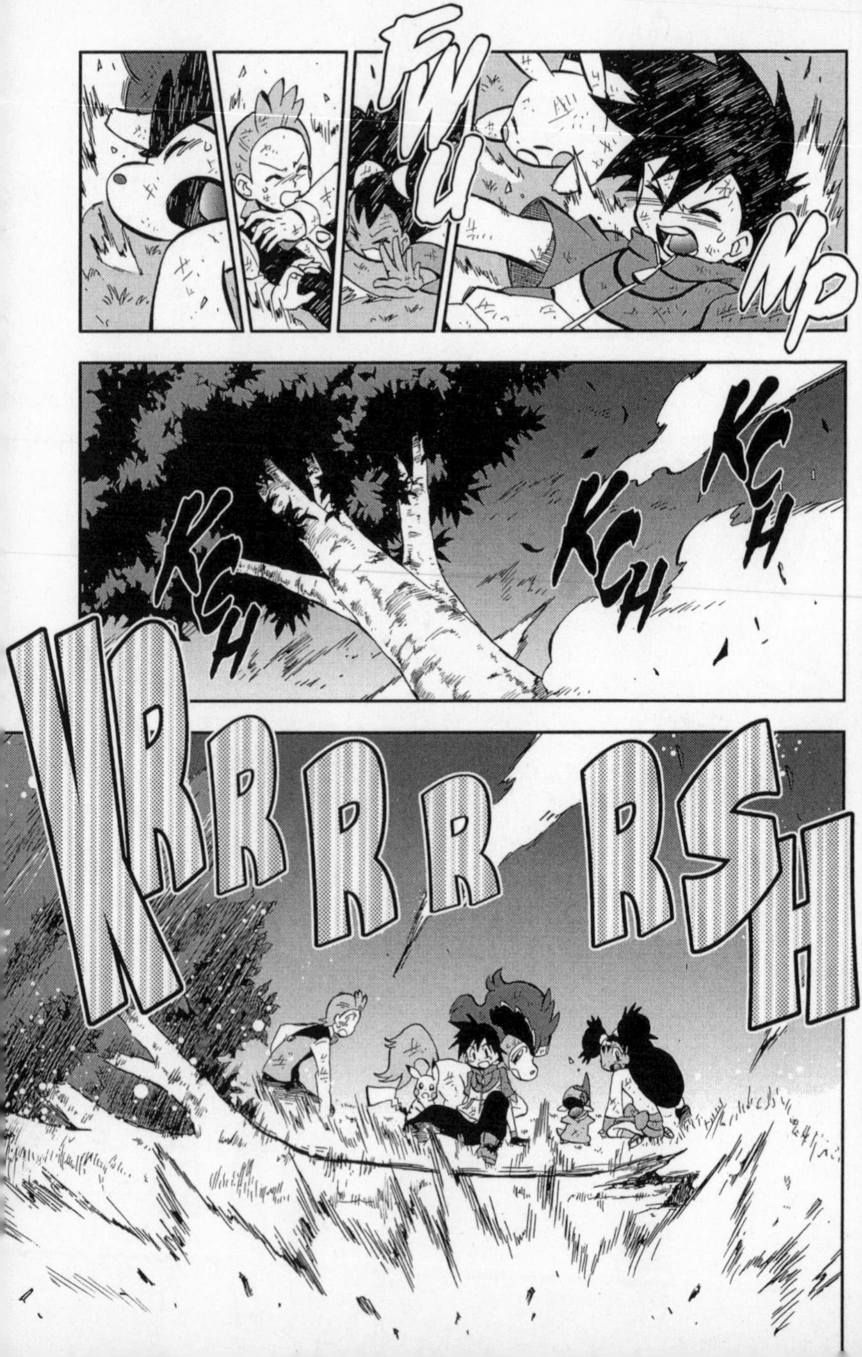
FWUMP
KCH
KCH
KCH
KRRRRRSH

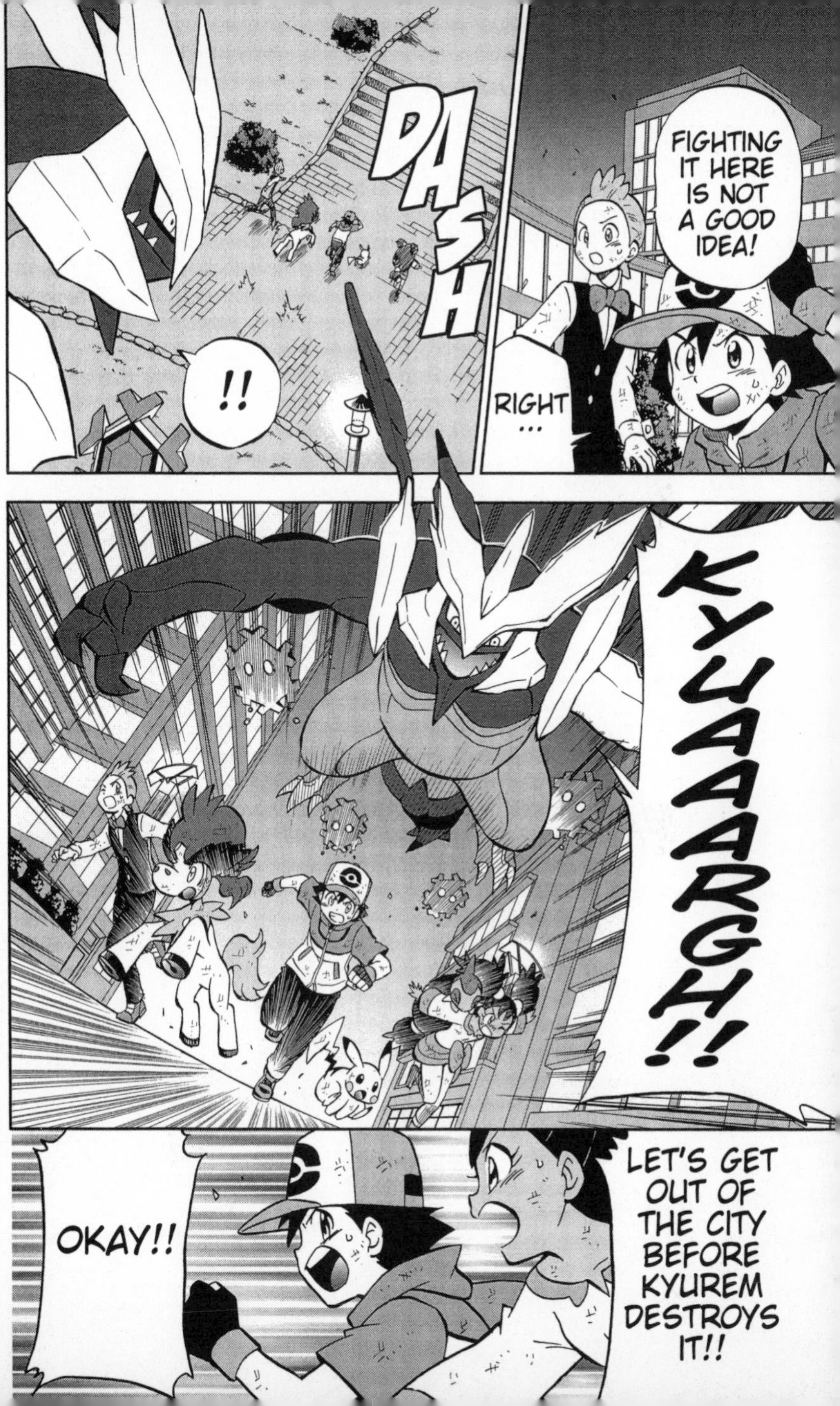
FIGHTING IT HERE IS NOT A GOOD IDEA!
RIGHT...
DASH
!!
KYUAAARGH!!
LET'S GET OUT OF THE CITY BEFORE KYUREM DESTROYS IT!!
OKAY!!

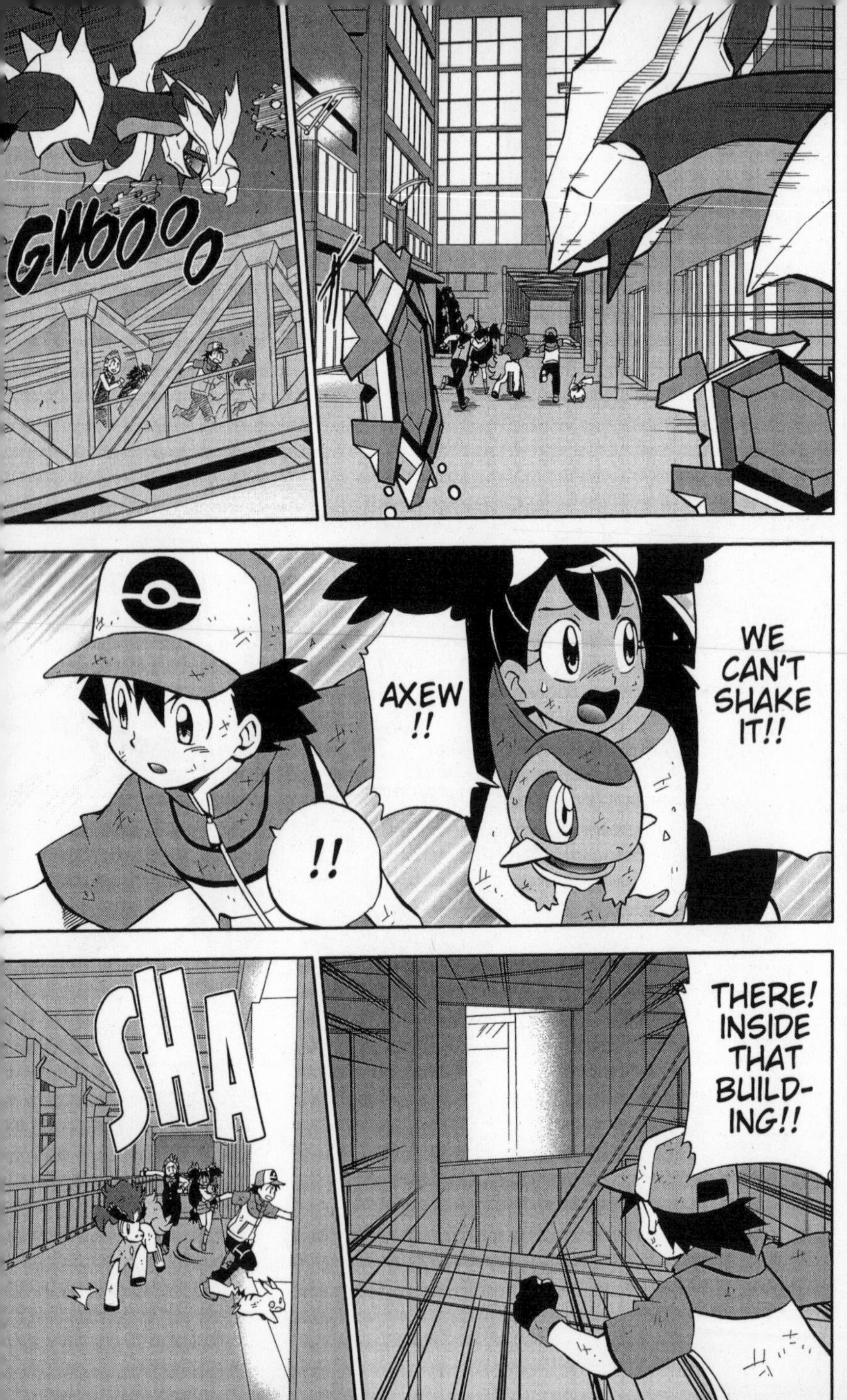
GWOOOO
WE CAN'T SHAKE IT!!
AXEW!!
!!
THERE! INSIDE THAT BUILD-ING!!
SHA

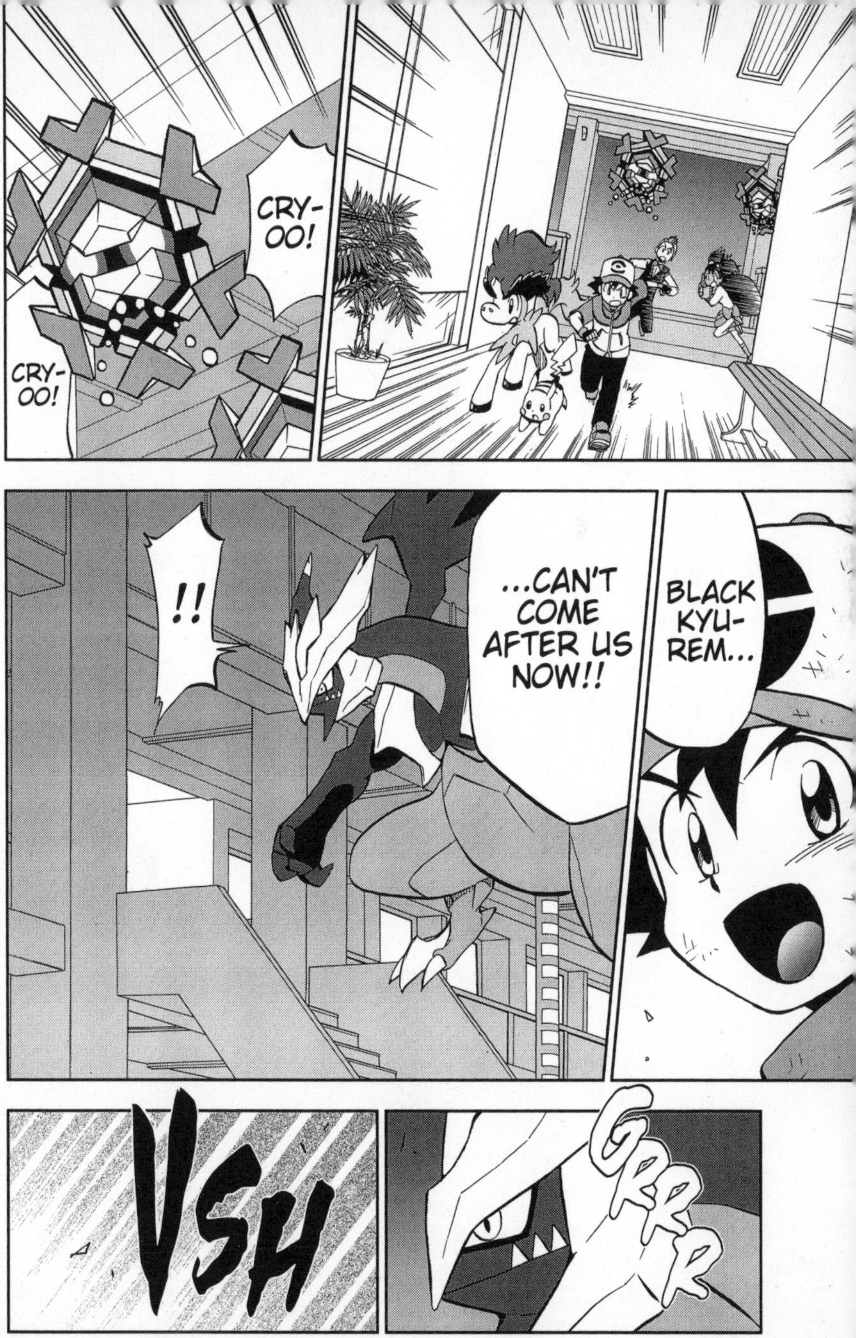
CRY-OO!
CRY-OO!
BLACK KYU-REM...
...CAN'T COME AFTER US NOW!!
!!
GRRR
VSH

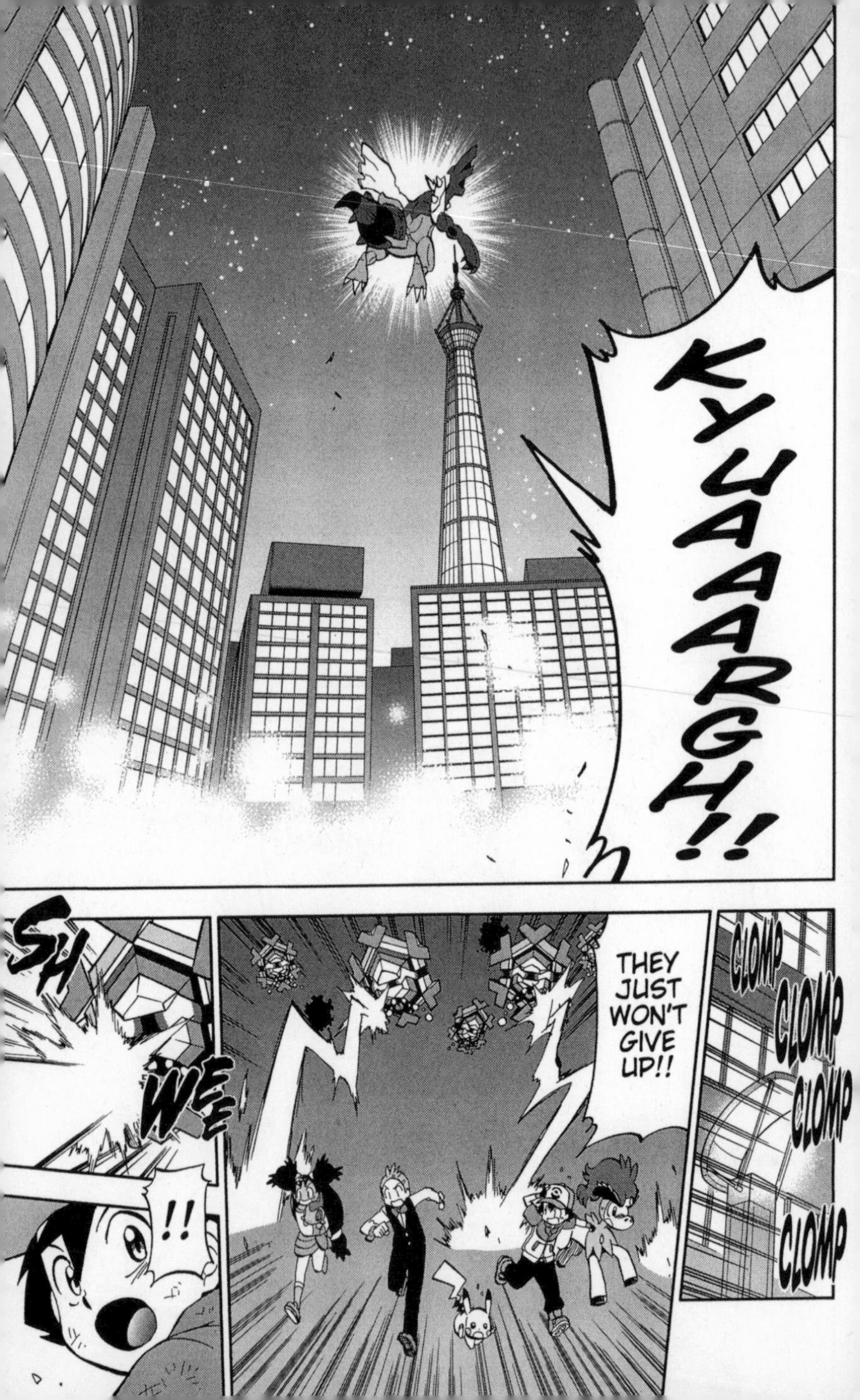
KYUAAARGH!!
CLOMP
CLOMP
CLOMP
CLOMP
THEY JUST WON'T GIVE UP!!
SHWEE
!!

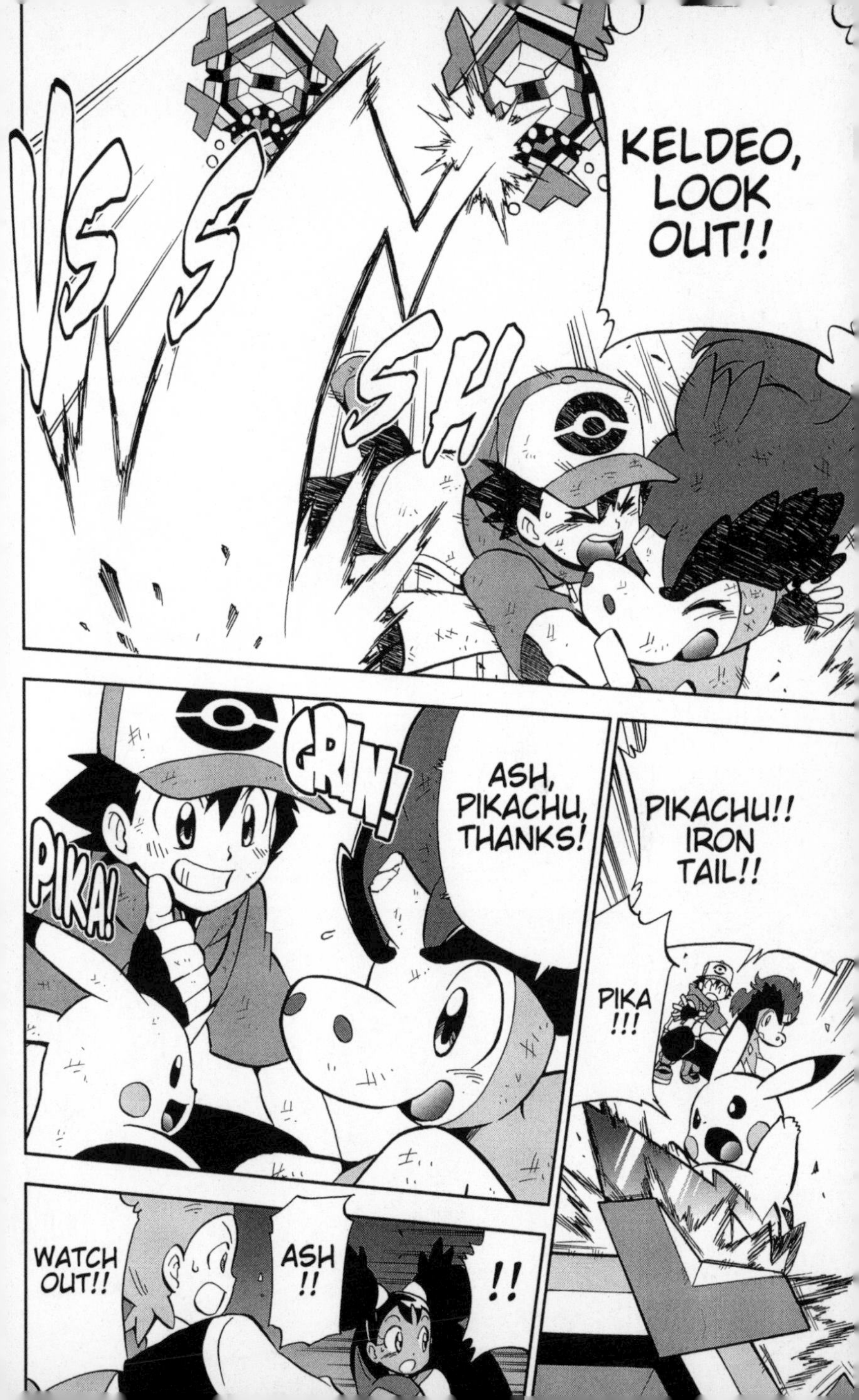
KELDEO, LOOK OUT!!
VSSSH
PIKACHU!! IRON TAIL!!
PIKA !!!
ASH, PIKACHU, THANKS!
GRIN!
PIKA!
!!
ASH !!
WATCH OUT!!

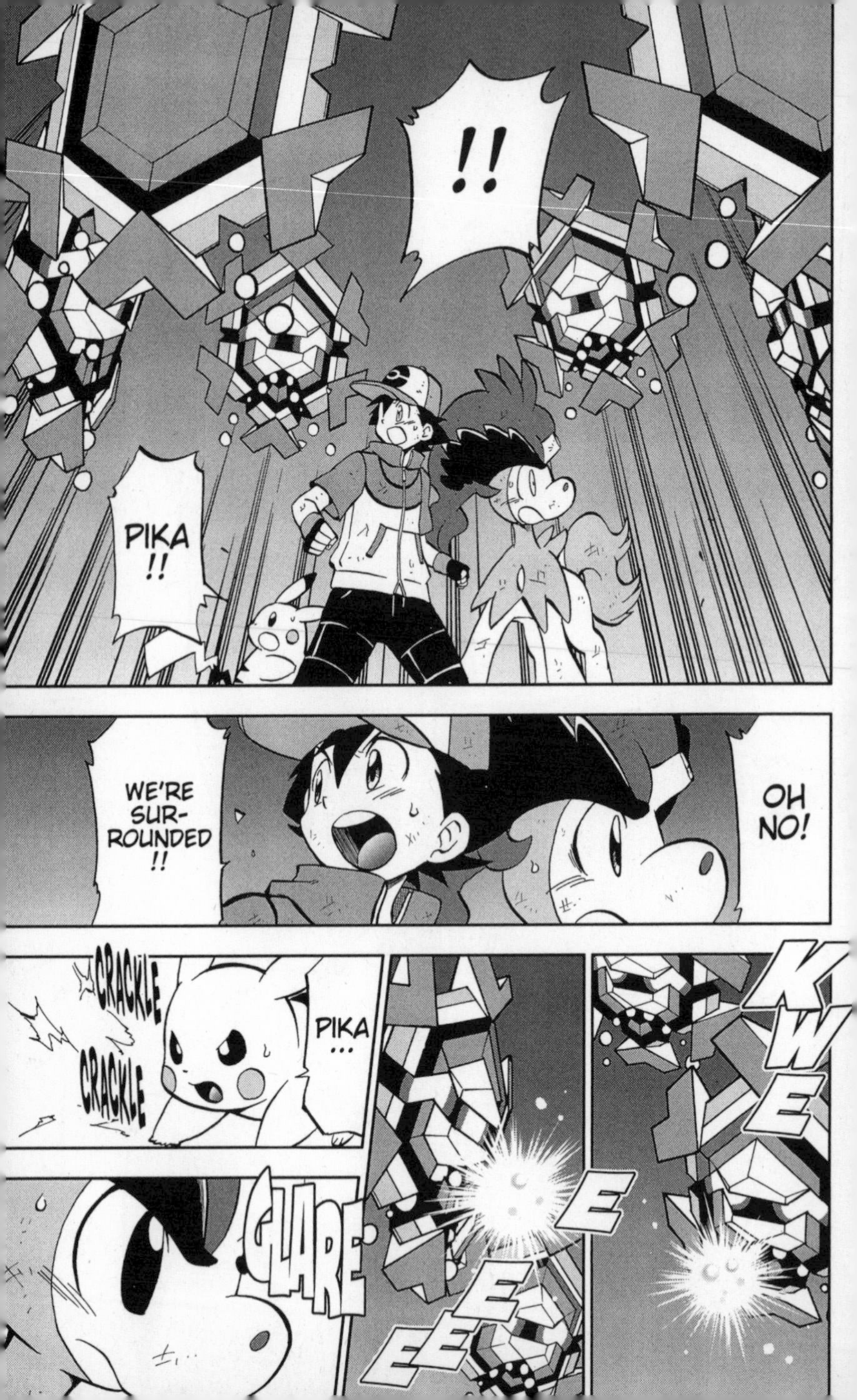
!!
PIKA !!
OH NO!
WE'RE SUR-ROUNDED !!
KWEEEEEE
PIKA ...
CRACKLE
CRACKLE
GLARE

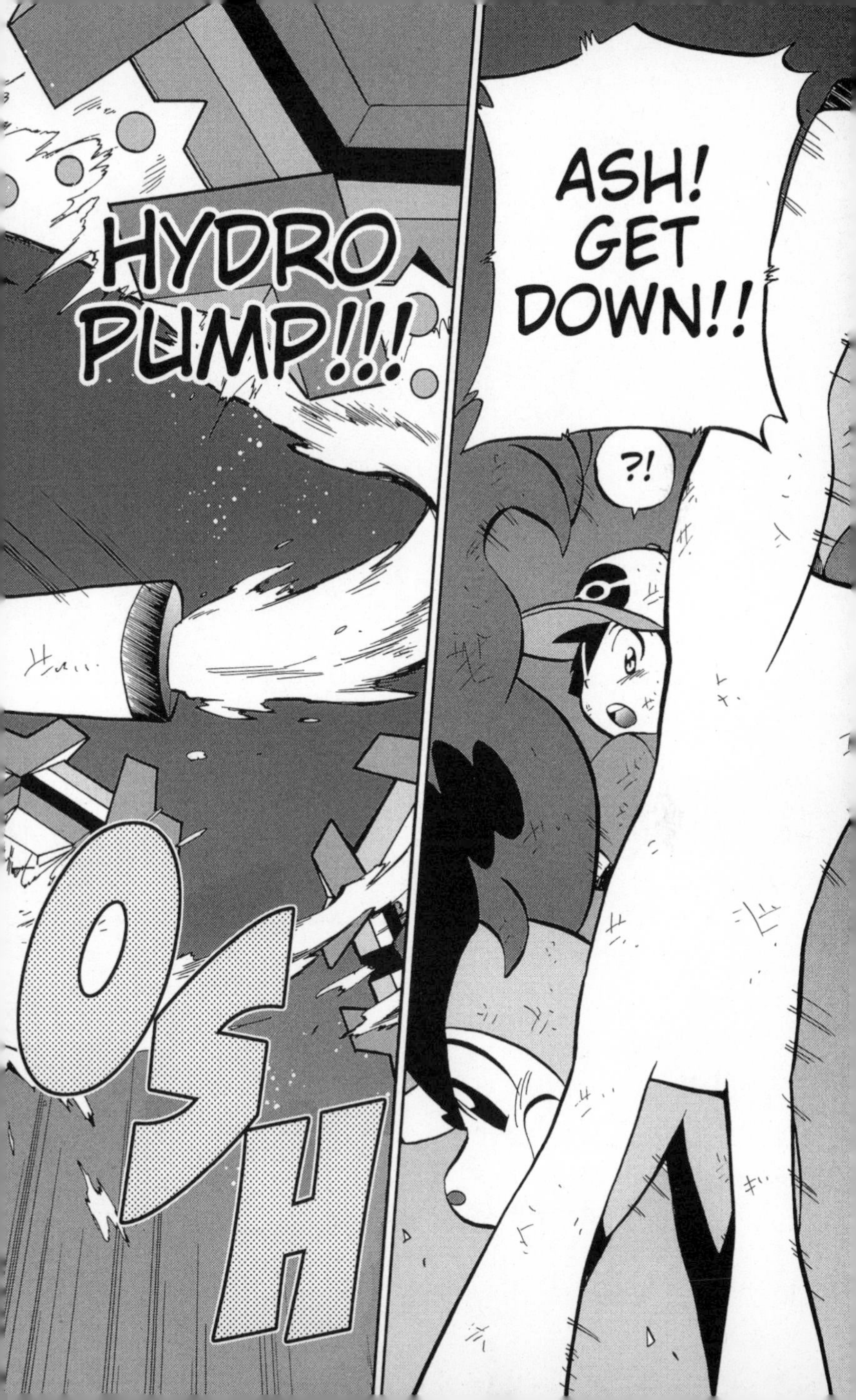
ASH! GET DOWN!!
?!
HYDRO PUMP!!!
OSH

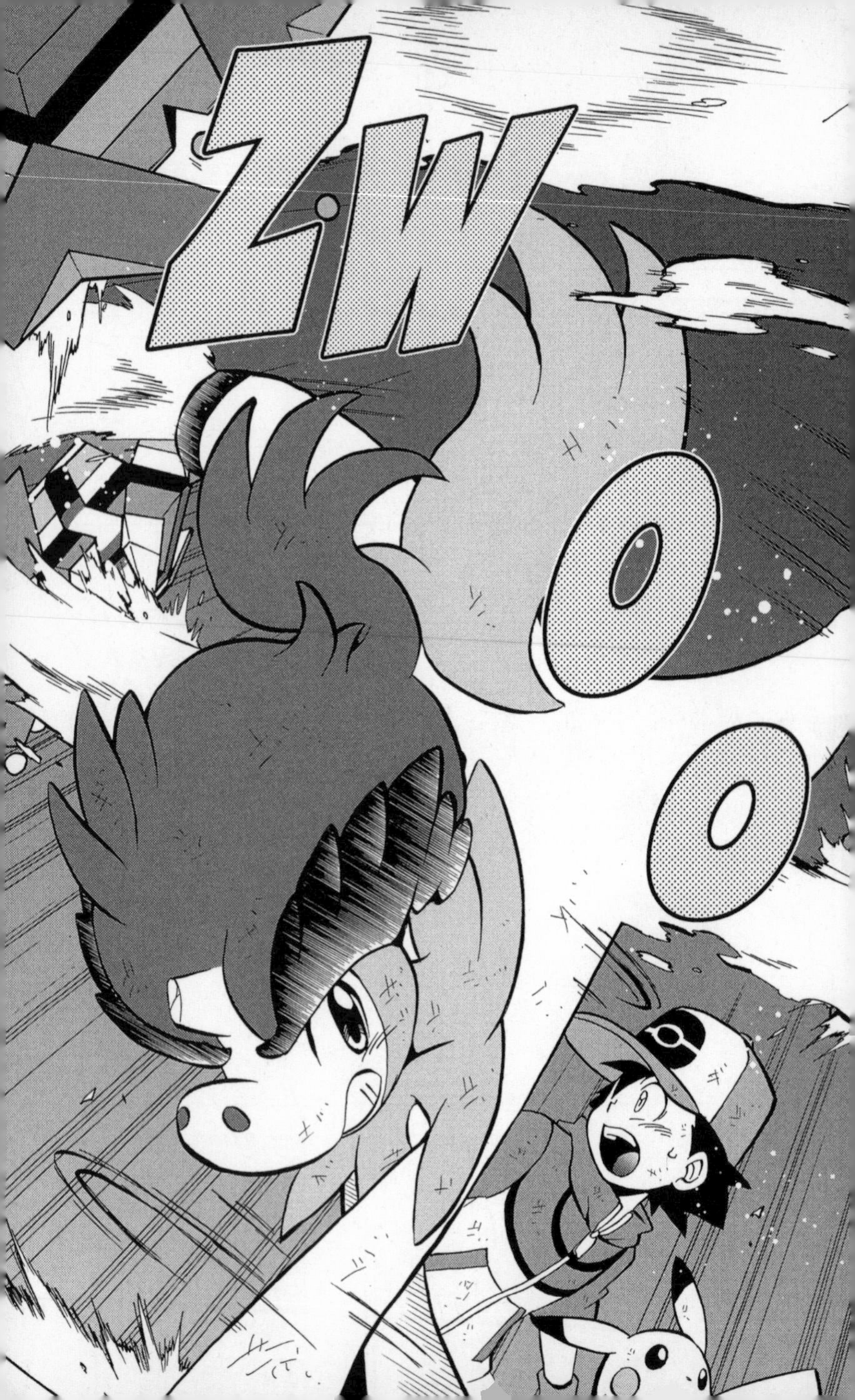
ZWOOO

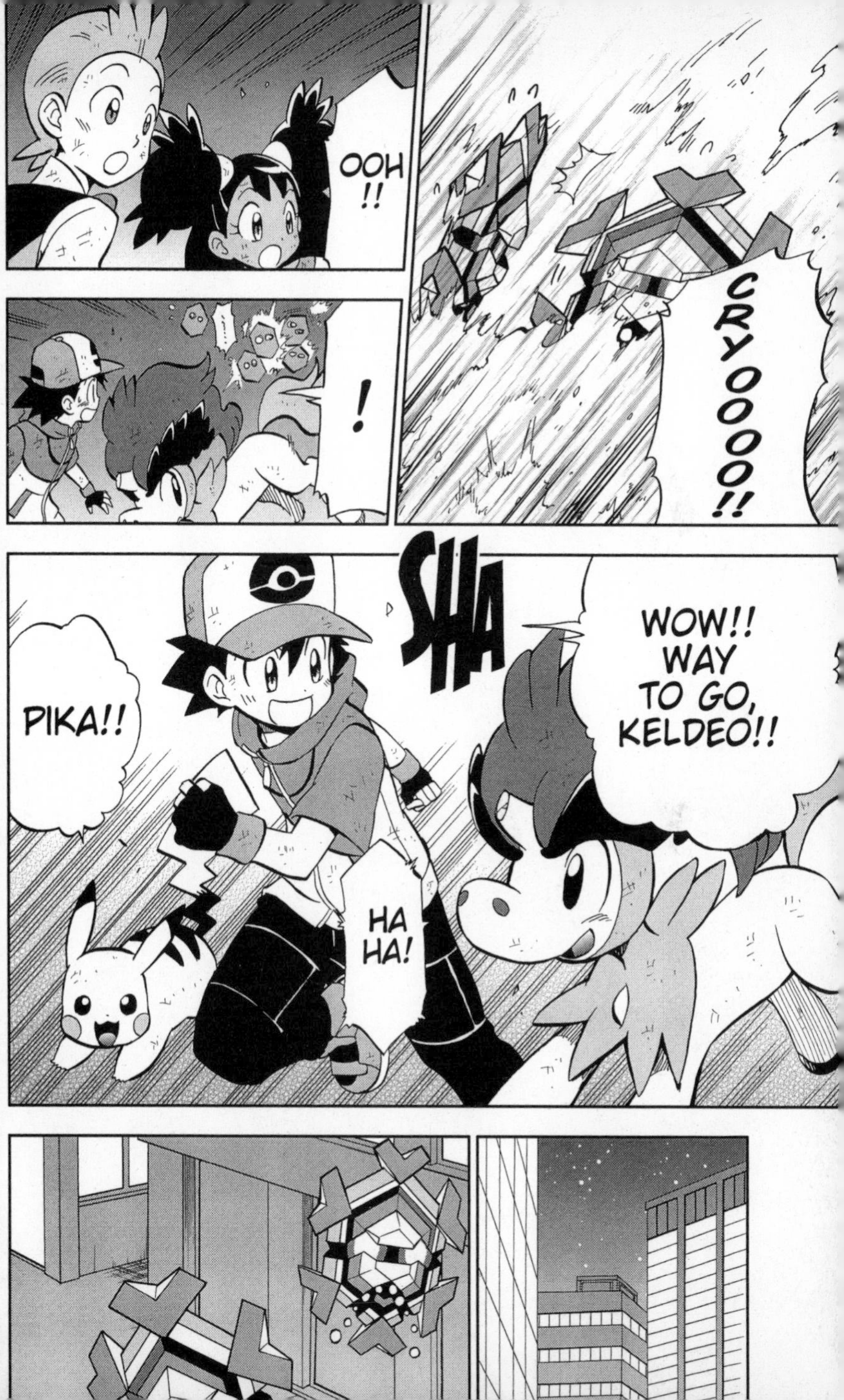
CRYOOOOO!!
OOH!!
!
SHA
WOW!! WAY TO GO, KELDEO!!
HA HA!
PIKA!!

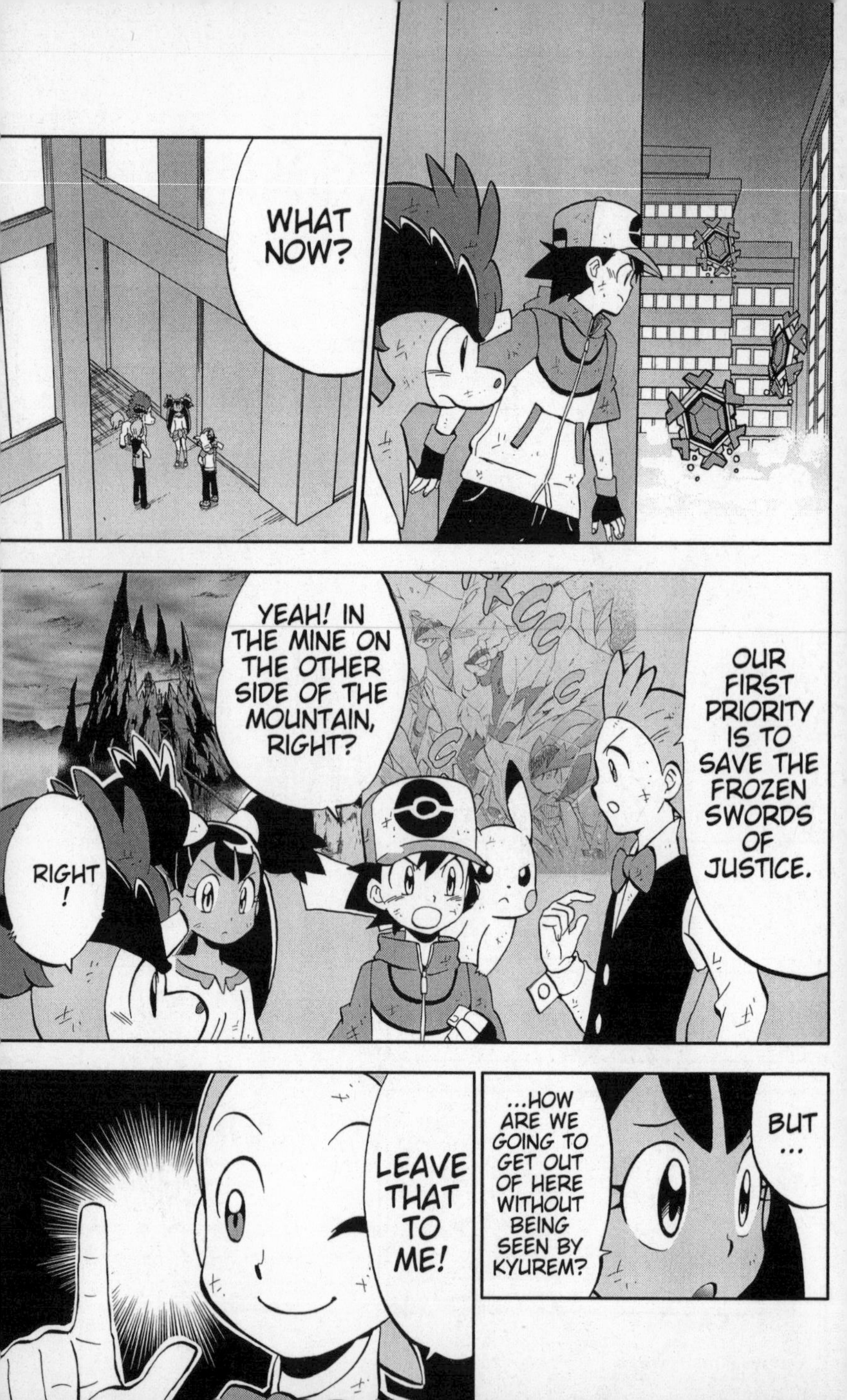
WHAT NOW?
OUR FIRST PRIORITY IS TO SAVE THE FROZEN SWORDS OF JUSTICE.
YEAH! IN THE MINE ON THE OTHER SIDE OF THE MOUNTAIN, RIGHT?
RIGHT!
BUT...
...HOW ARE WE GOING TO GET OUT OF HERE WITHOUT BEING SEEN BY KYUREM?
LEAVE THAT TO ME!

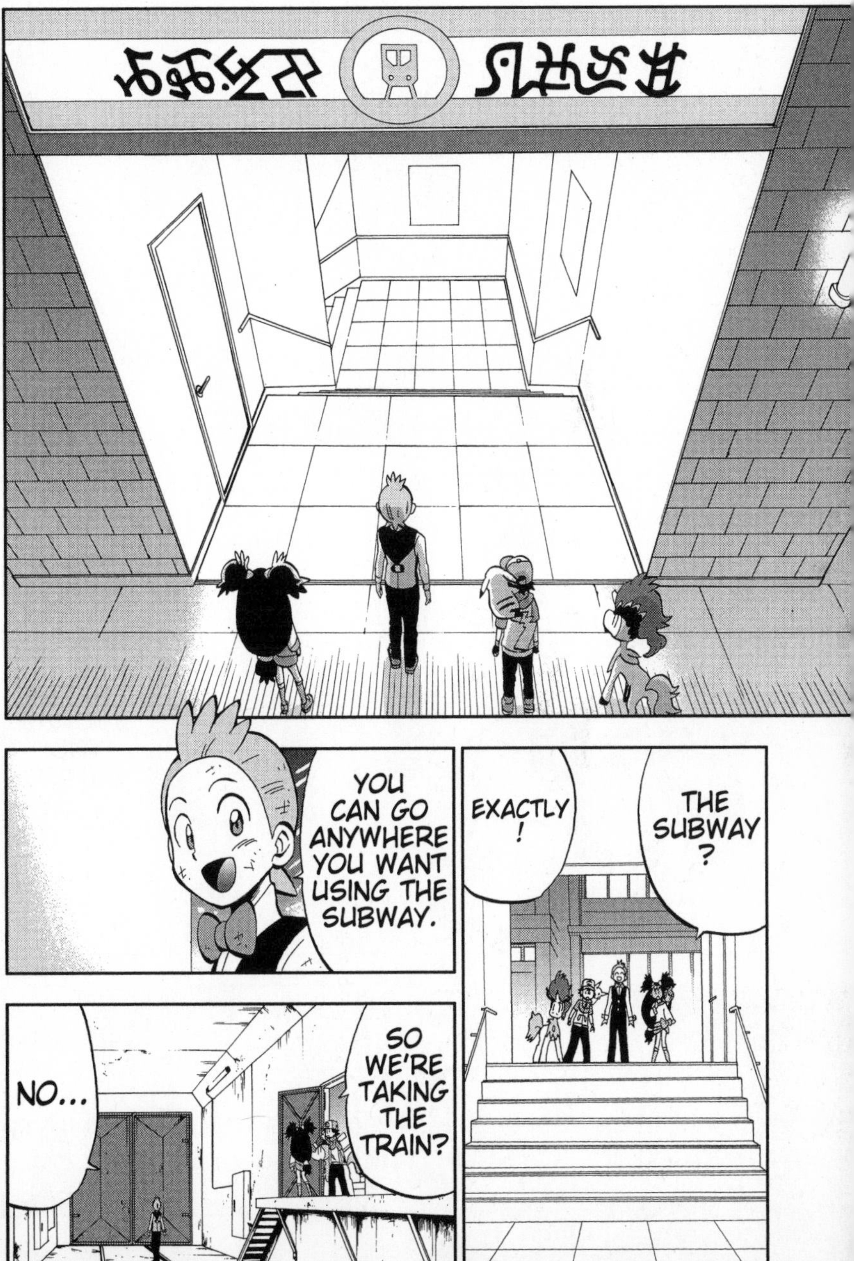
THE SUBWAY?
EXACTLY!
YOU CAN GO ANYWHERE YOU WANT USING THE SUBWAY.
SO WE'RE TAKING THE TRAIN?
NO...

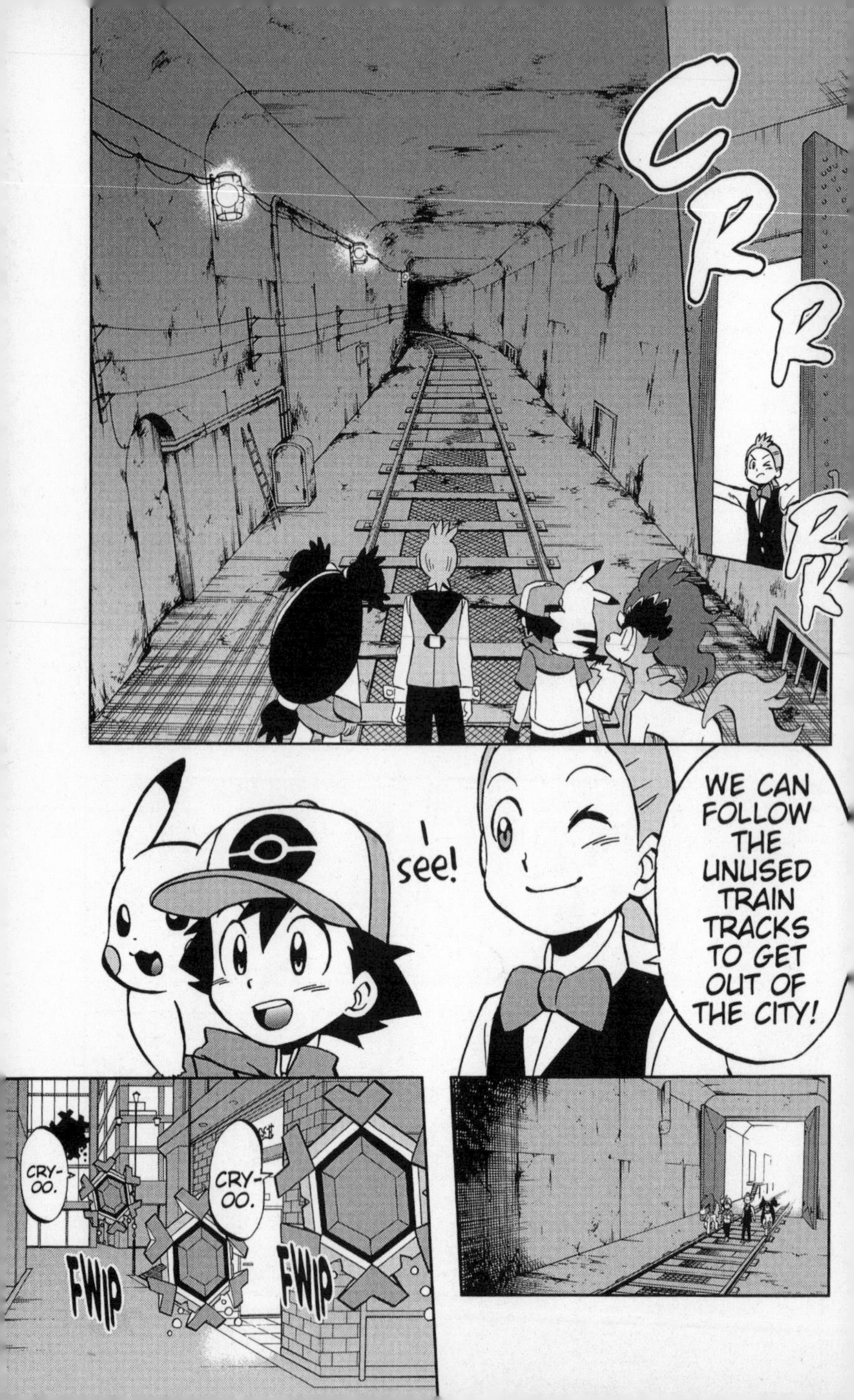
CRRRR
WE CAN FOLLOW THE UNUSED TRAIN TRACKS TO GET OUT OF THE CITY!
I see!
CRY-OO.
CRY-OO.
FWIP
FWIP

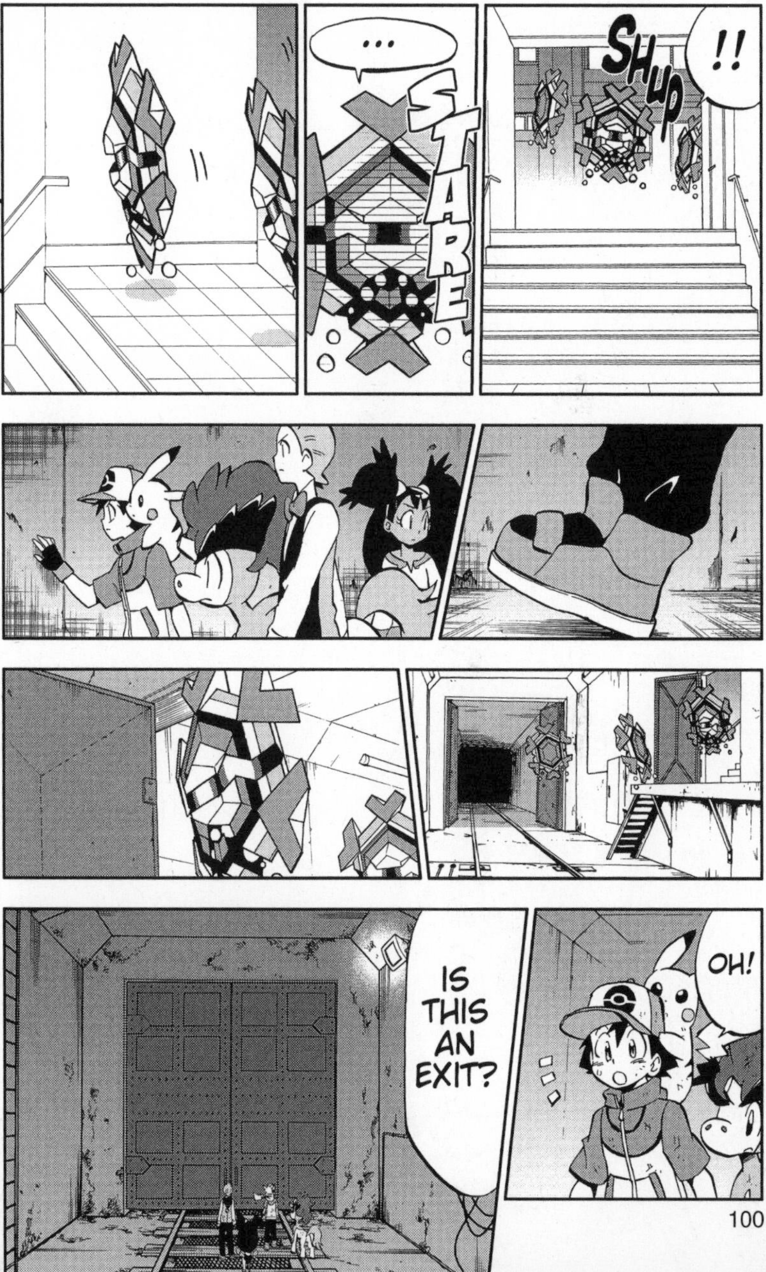

!!
SHUP
...
STARE
OH!
IS THIS AN EXIT?

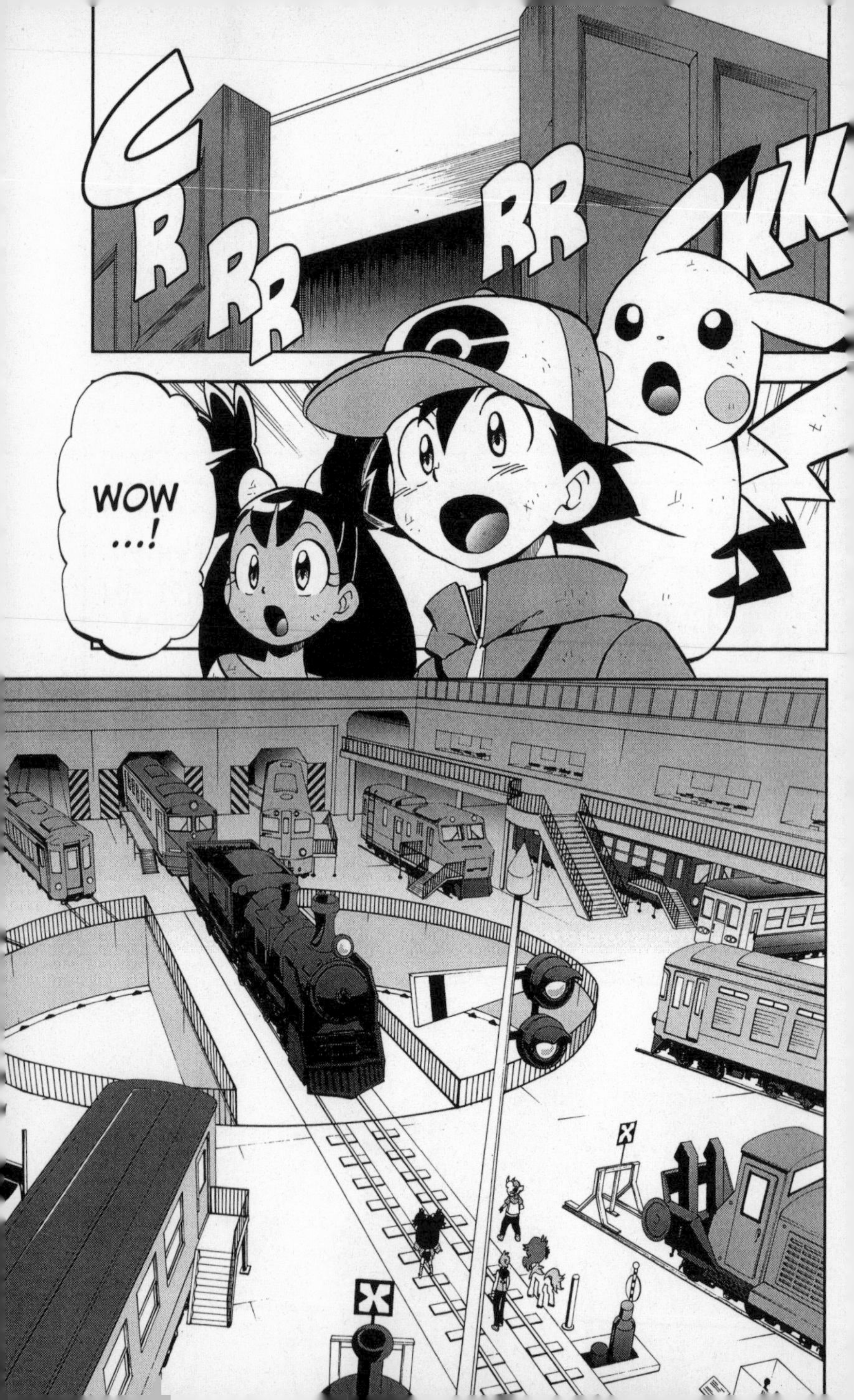
CRRRRRKK
WOW ...!

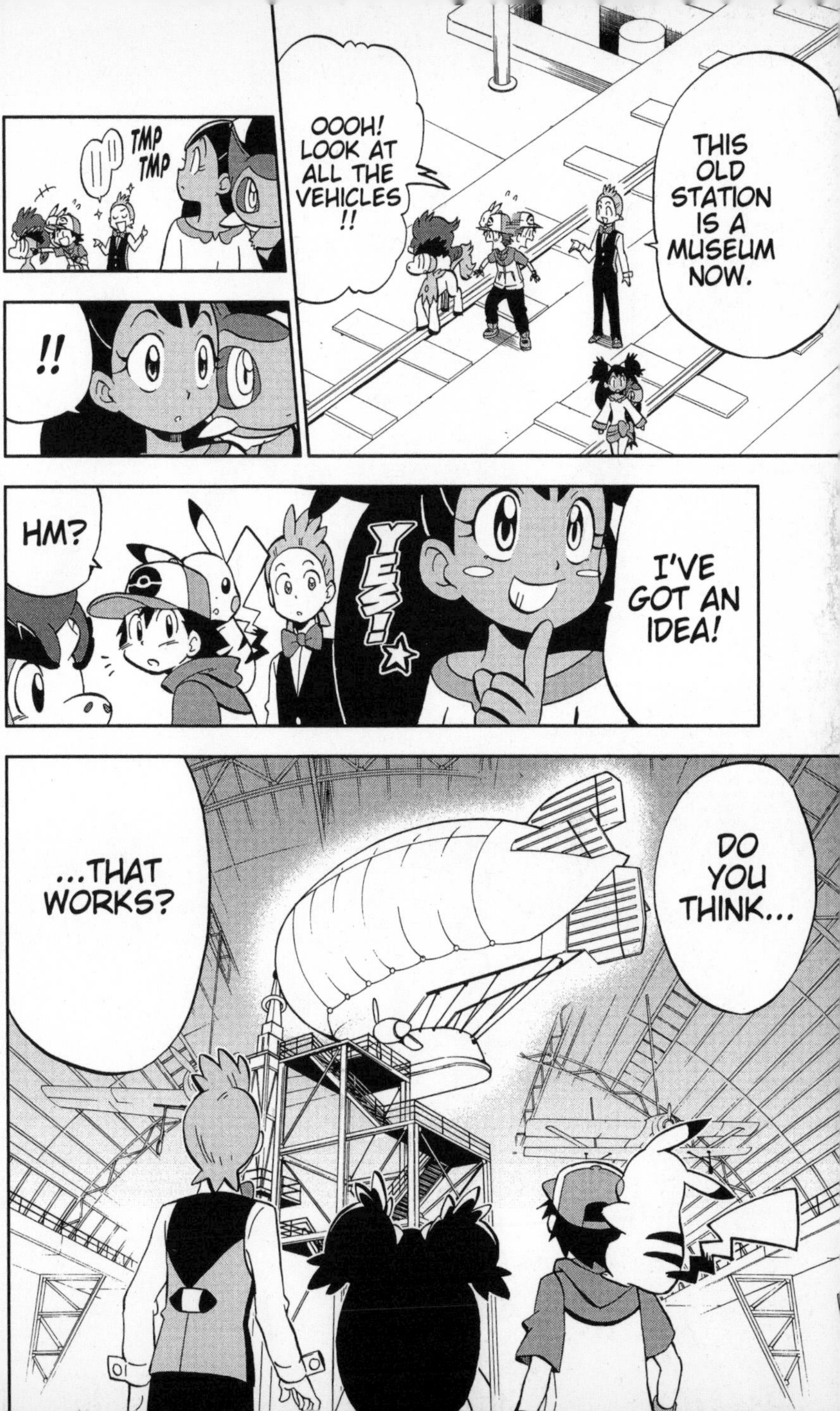
THIS OLD STATION IS A MUSEUM NOW.
OOOH! LOOK AT ALL THE VEHICLES!!
TMP TMP
!!
!!
I'VE GOT AN IDEA!
YES!
HM?
DO YOU THINK...
...THAT WORKS?

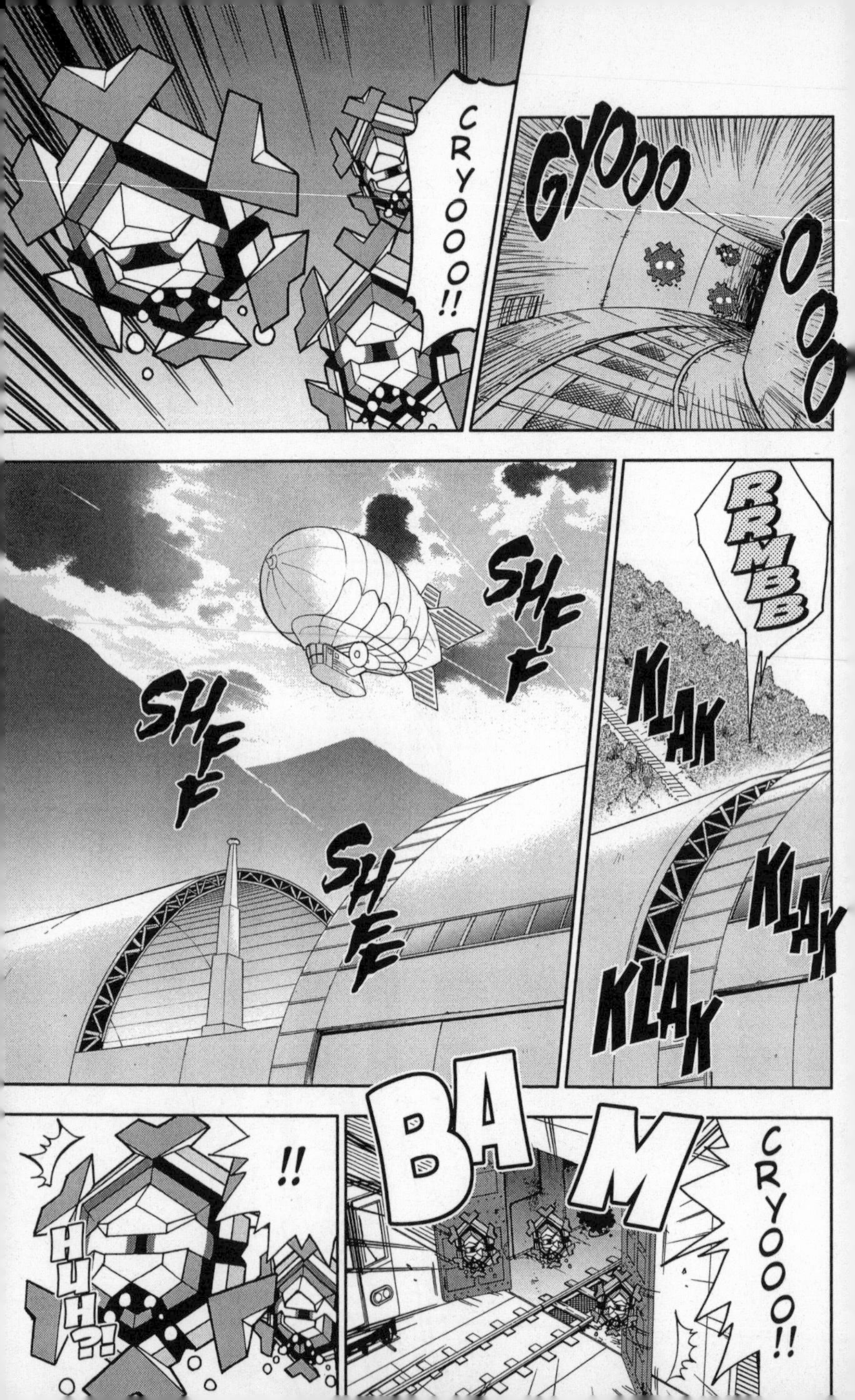
GYOOOOOOO
CRYOOOO!!
RRMBB
KLAK
KLAK
KLAK
SHFF
SHFF
SHFF
BAM
CRYOOOO!!
!!
HUH?!

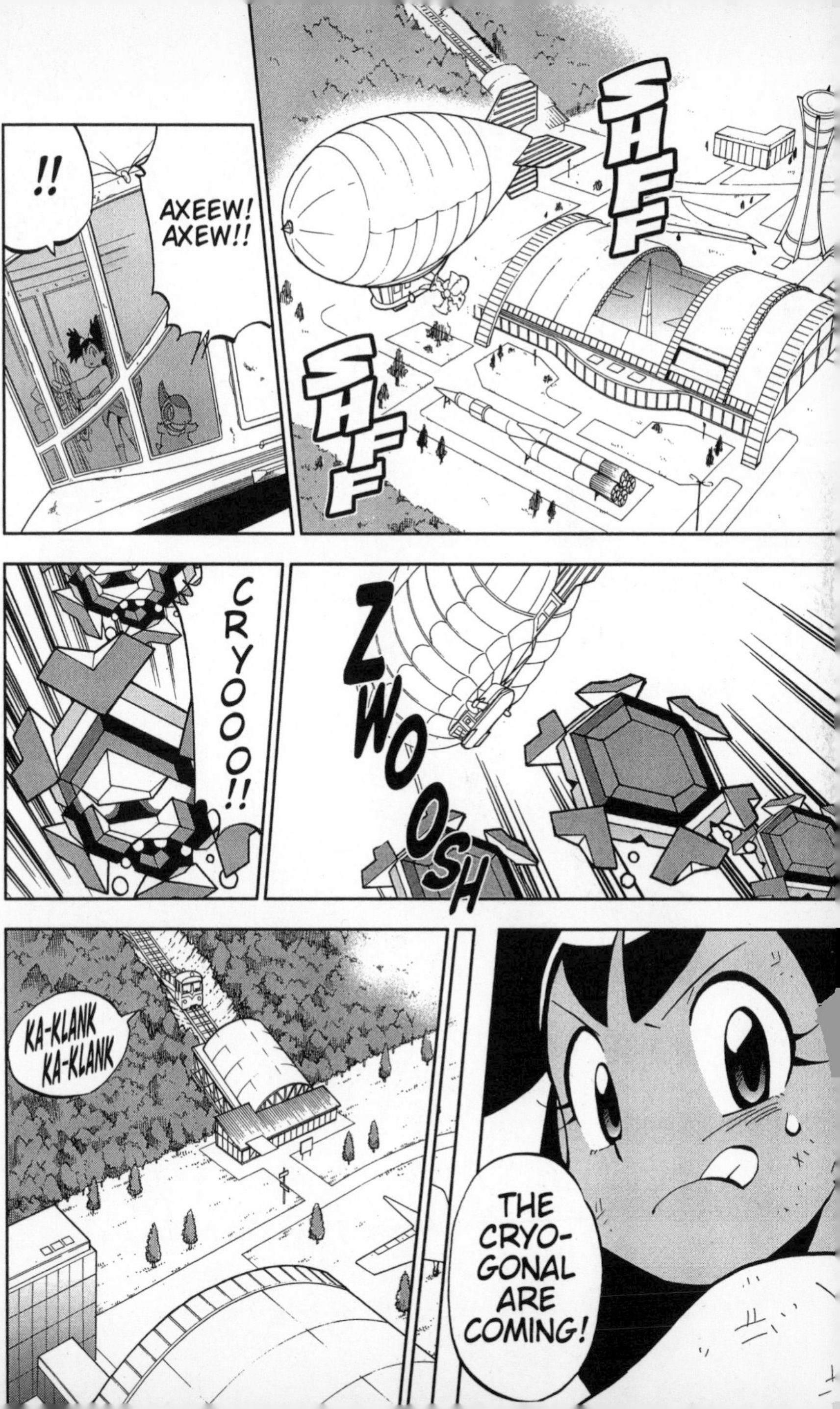
SHFF
SHFF
!!
AXEEW! AXEW!!
ZWOOOSH
CRYOOOO!!
THE CRYO-GONAL ARE COMING!
KA-KLANK KA-KLANK

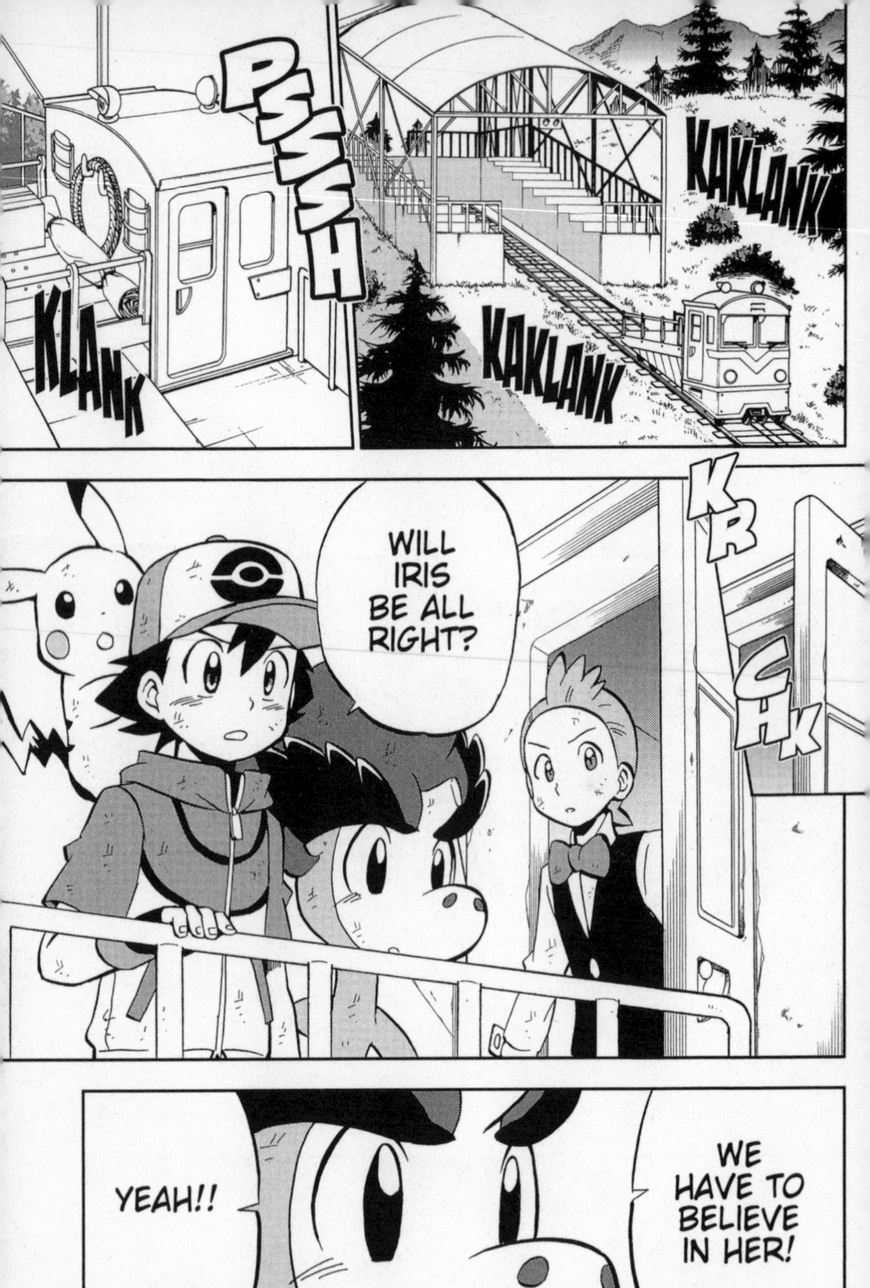
KAKLANK
KAKLANK
PSSSH
KLANK
KRCHK
WILL IRIS BE ALL RIGHT?
WE HAVE TO BELIEVE IN HER!
YEAH!!

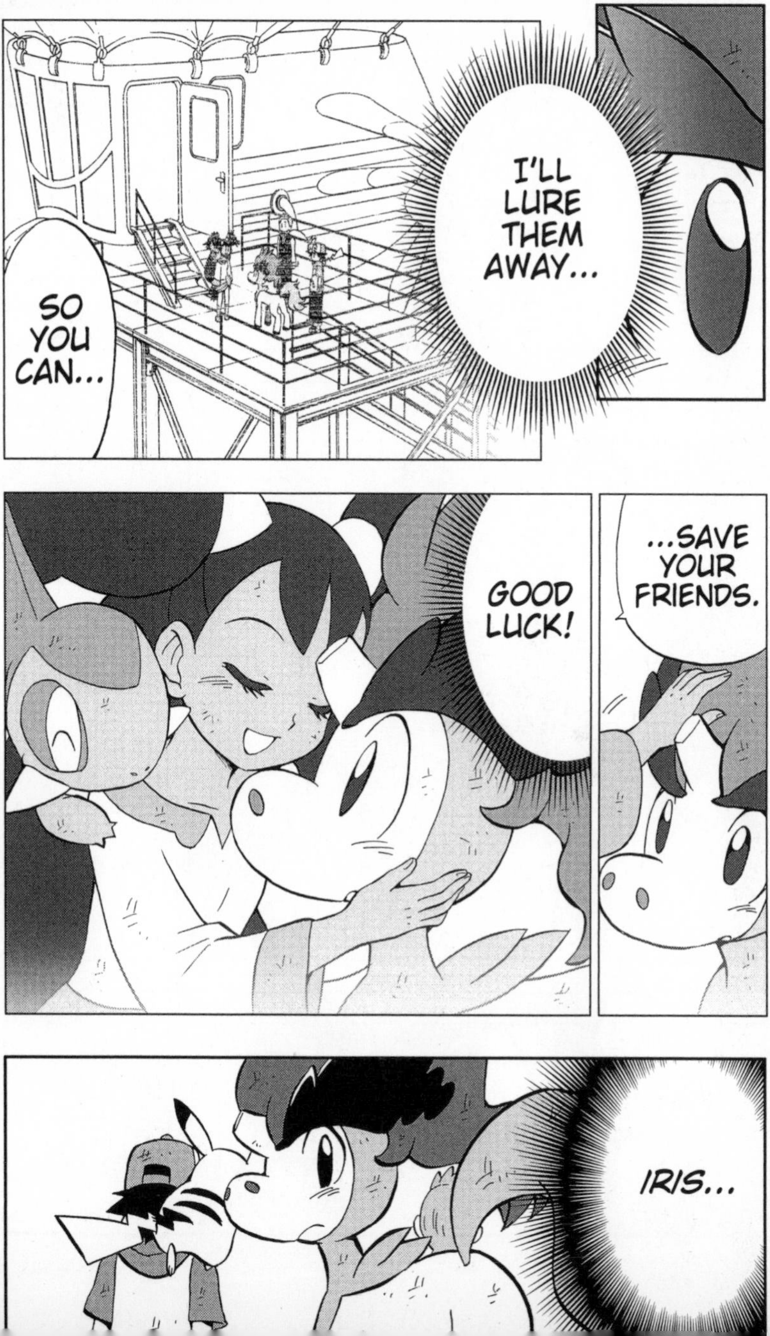
I'LL LURE THEM AWAY...
SO YOU CAN...
...SAVE YOUR FRIENDS.
GOOD LUCK!
IRIS...

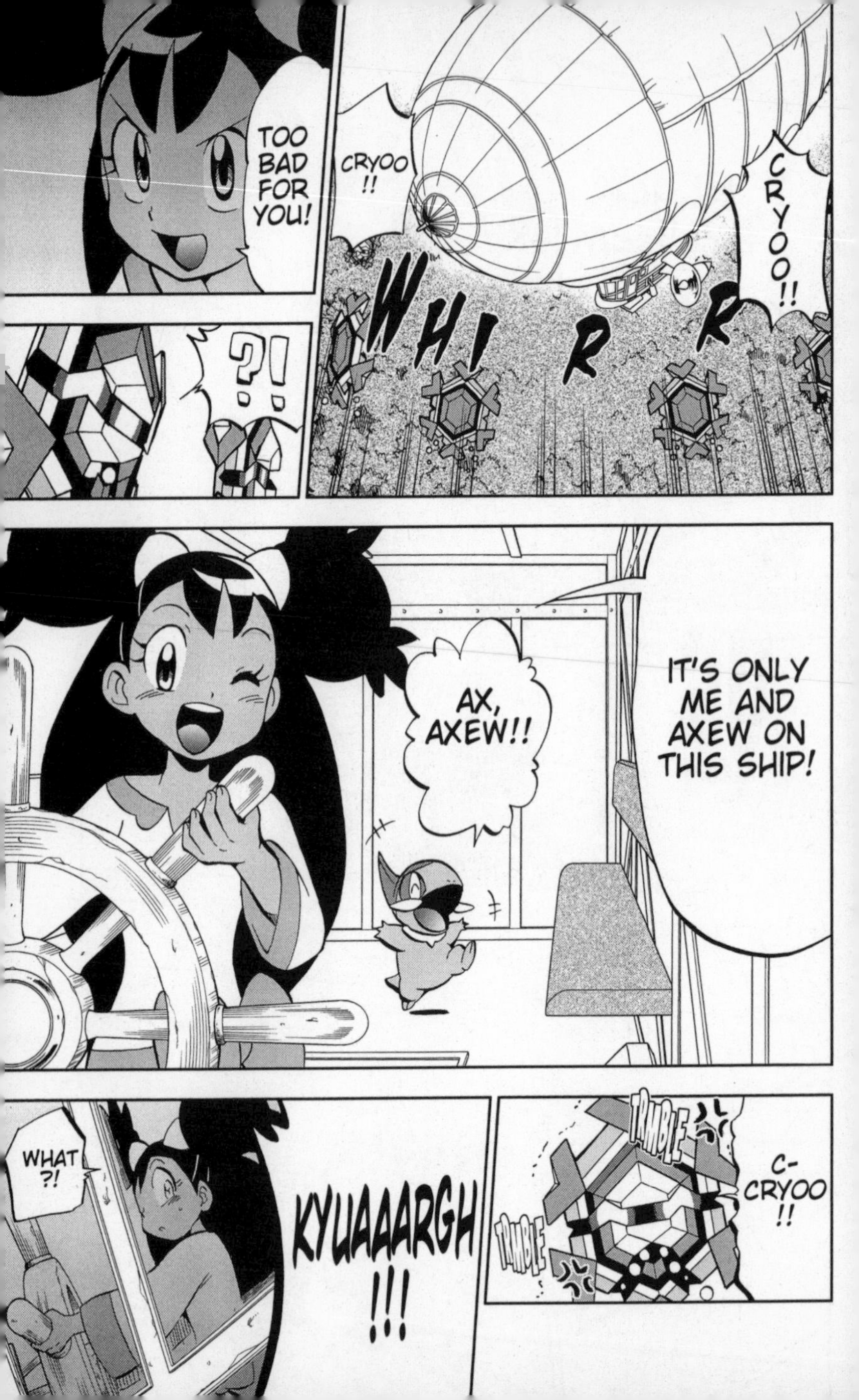
CRYOO!!
CRYOO!!
WHIRR
TOO BAD FOR YOU!
?!
IT'S ONLY ME AND AXEW ON THIS SHIP!
AX, AXEW!!
TRMBLE
C-CRYOO!!
TRMBLE
KYUAAARGH!!!
WHAT?!

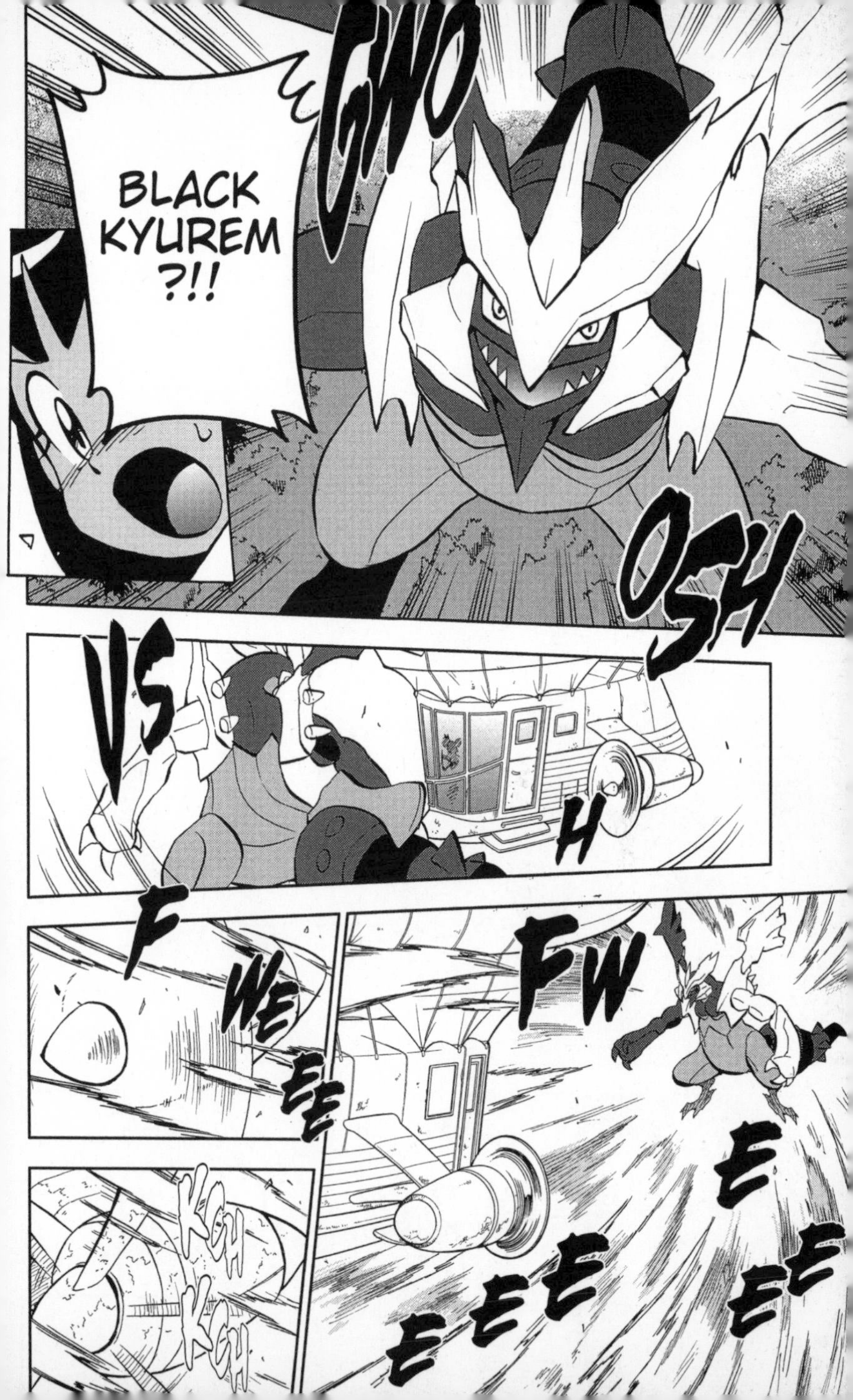
GWO
BLACK KYUREM ?!!
OSH
VS
H
FW
E
EE
EE
E
E
E
E
F
WE
EE
KCH
KCH

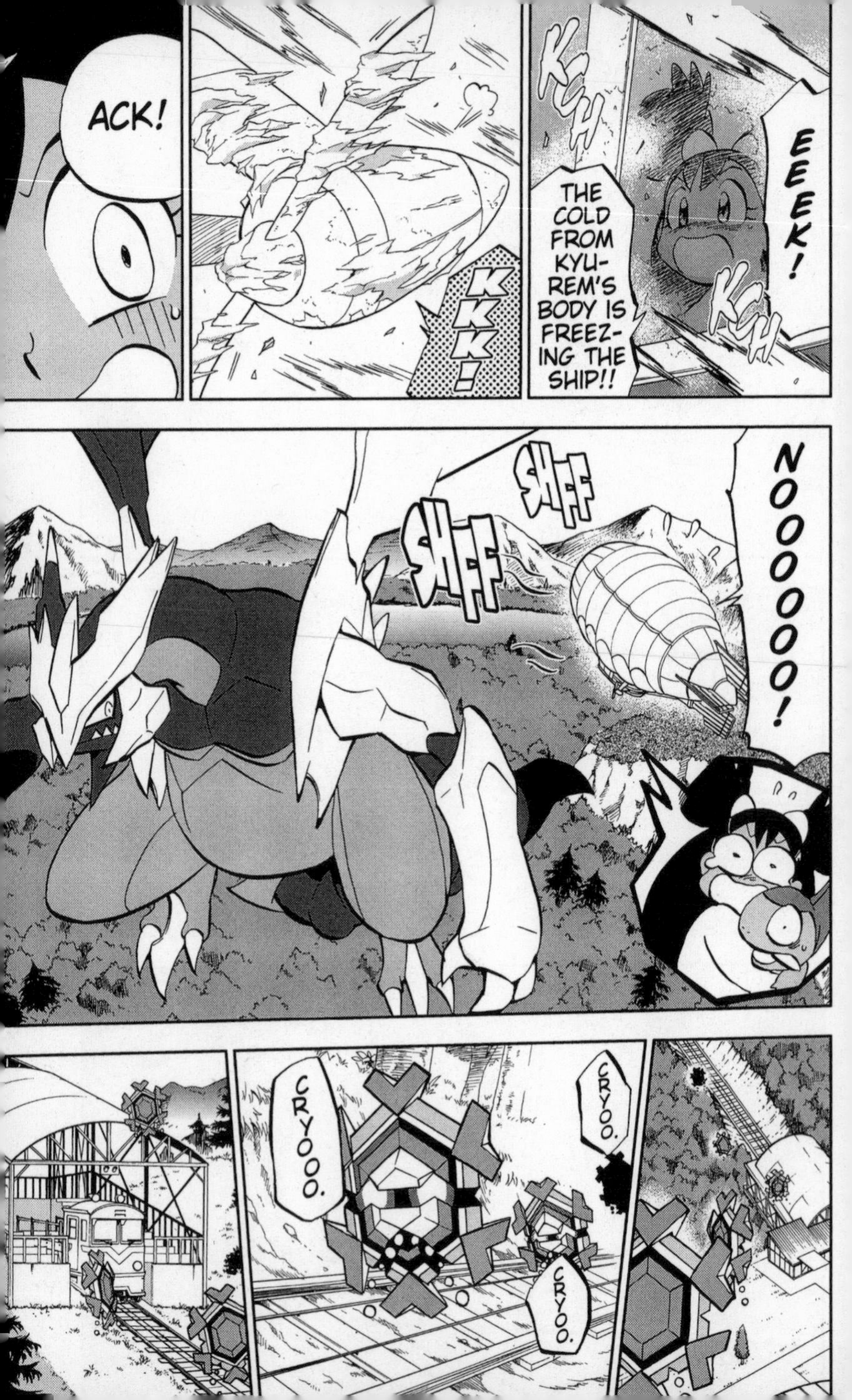
EEEEK!
KCH
KCH
THE COLD FROM KYU-REM'S BODY IS FREEZ-ING THE SHIP!!
KKK!
ACK!
NOOOOOOOO!
SHFF
SHFF
CRYOO.
CRYOOO.
CRYOO.

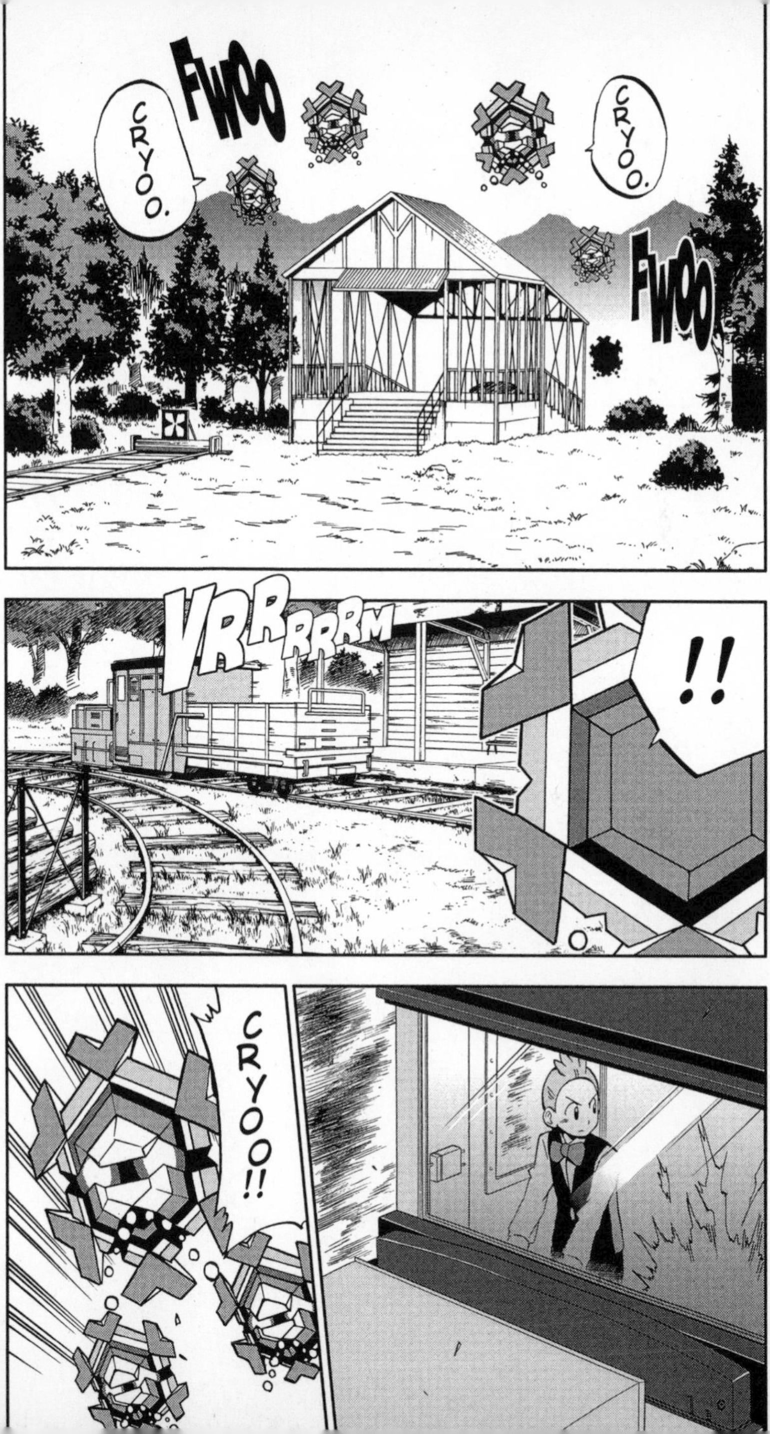
CRYOO.
FWOO
CRYOO.
FWOO
!!
VRRRRRM
CRYOO!!

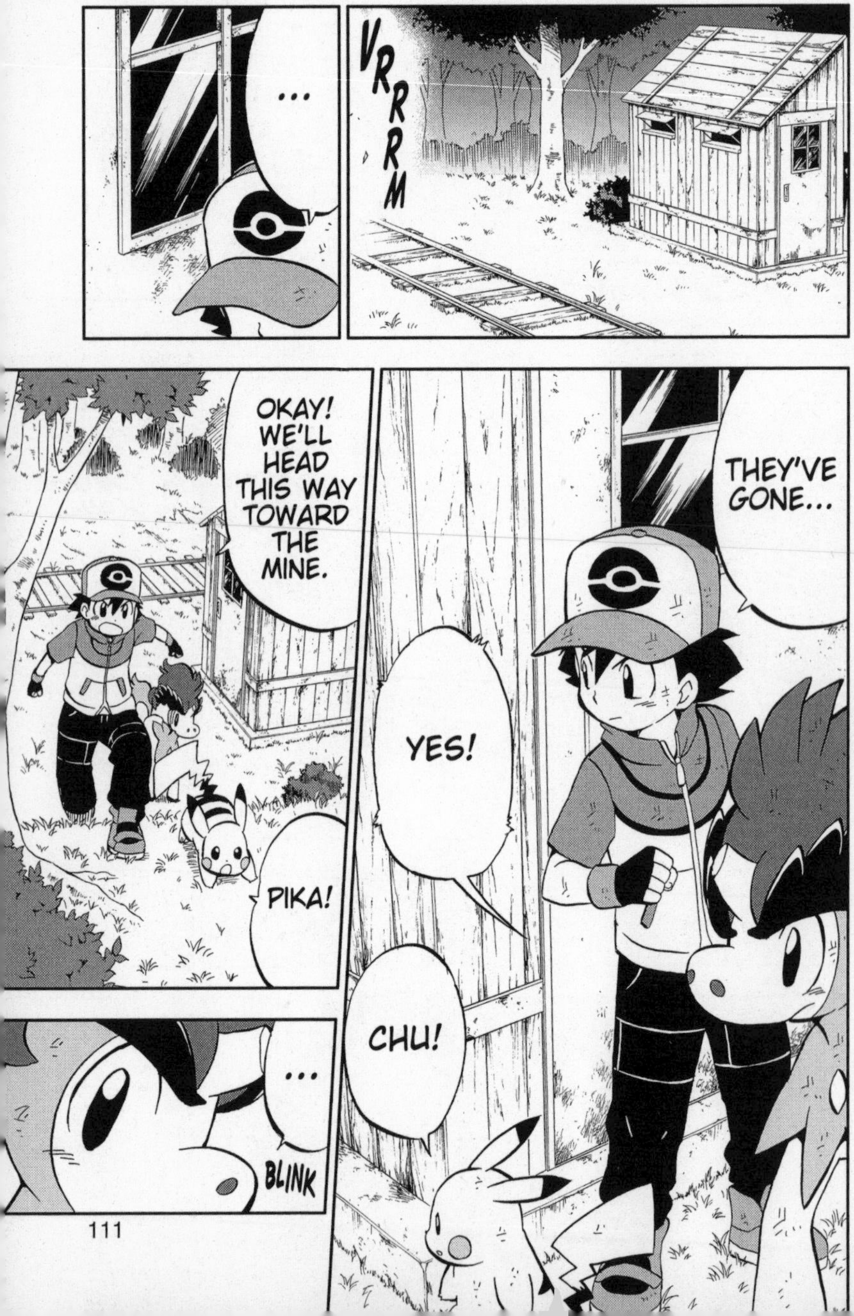
VRRRM
...
THEY'VE GONE...
YES!
CHU!
OKAY! WE'LL HEAD THIS WAY TOWARD THE MINE.
PIKA!
...
BLINK

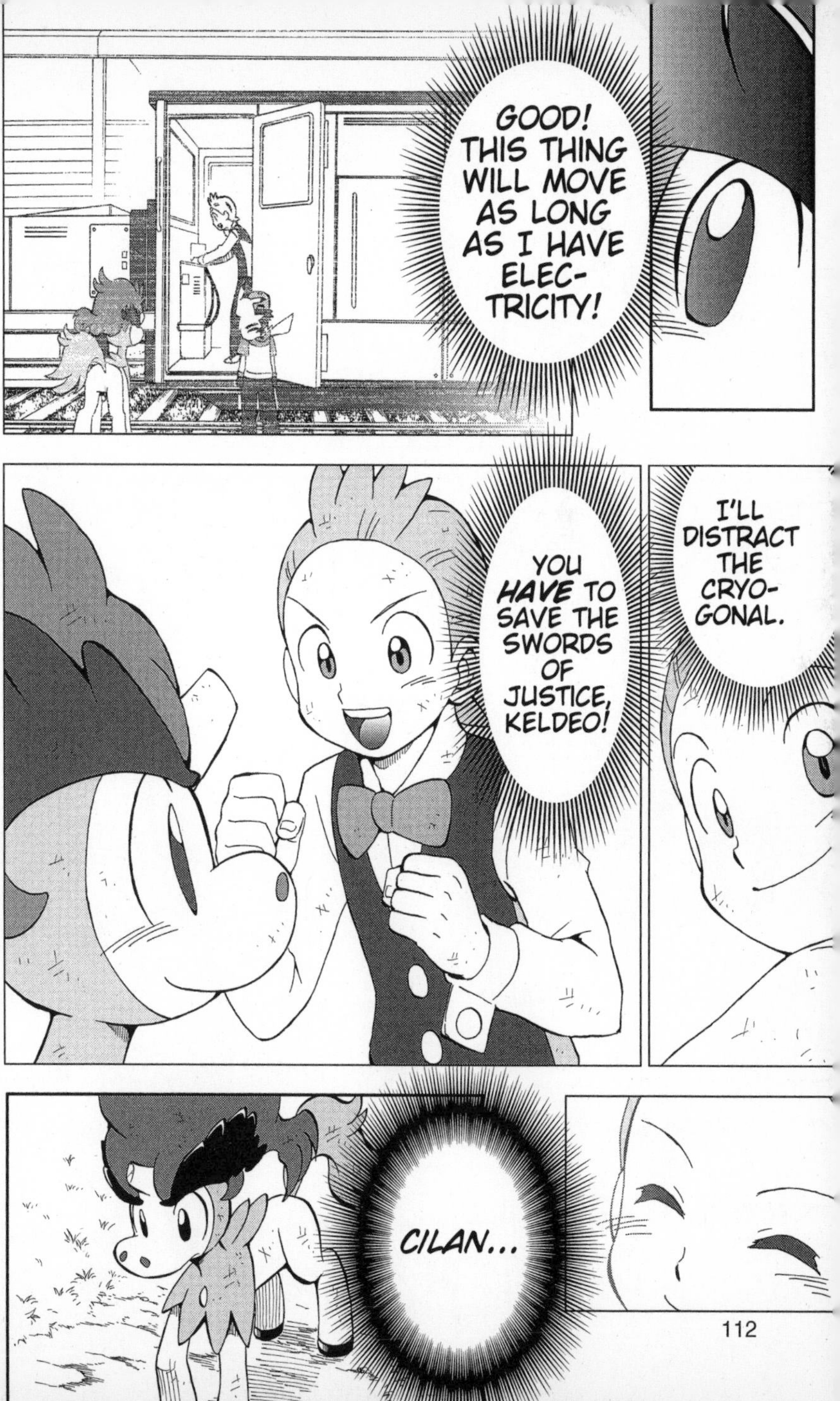
GOOD! THIS THING WILL MOVE AS LONG AS I HAVE ELEC-TRICITY!
I'LL DISTRACT THE CRYO-GONAL.
YOU *HAVE* TO SAVE THE SWORDS OF JUSTICE, KELDEO!
CILAN...

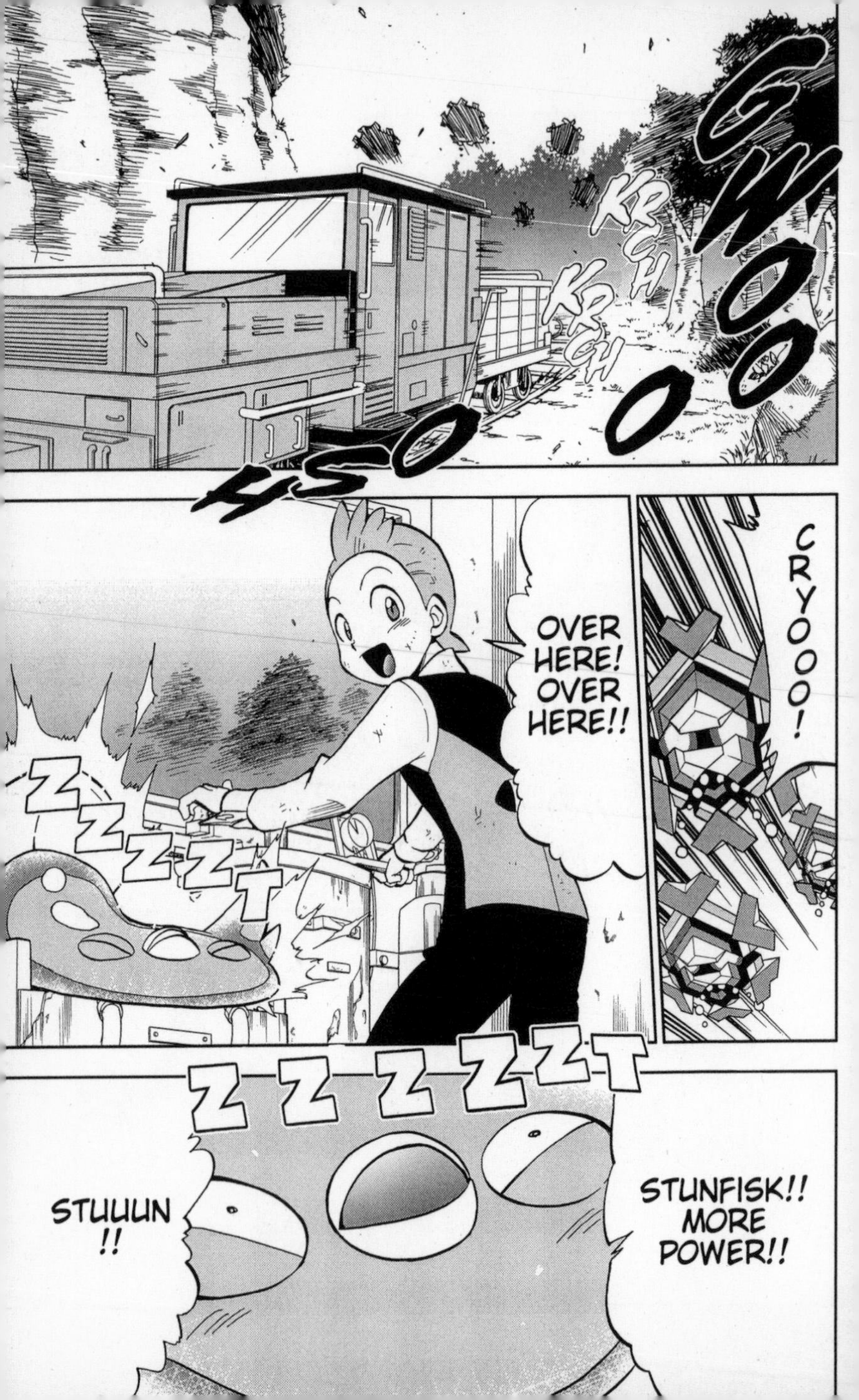
GWOOOO
KRCH
KRCH
SHOO
CRYOOOO!
OVER HERE! OVER HERE!!
ZZZZT
ZZZZZT
STUNFISK!! MORE POWER!!
STUUUN !!

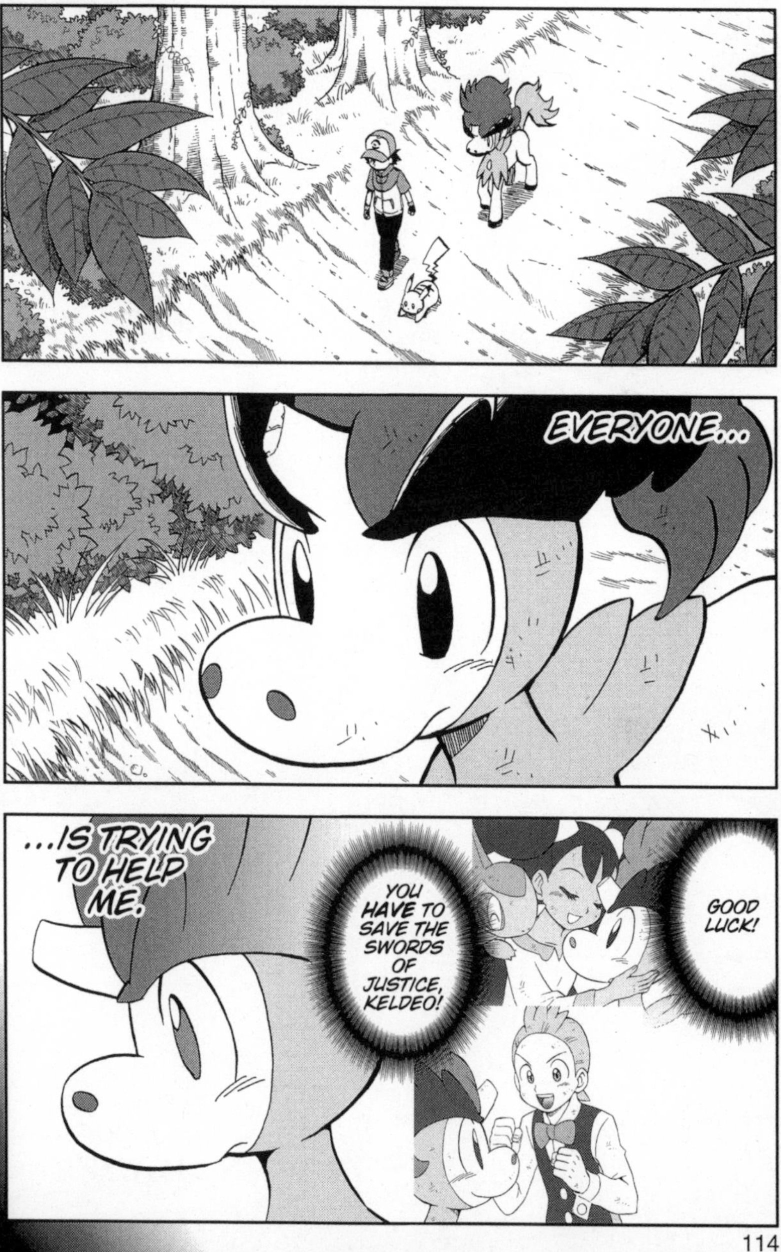
EVERYONE...
GOOD LUCK!
YOU HAVE TO SAVE THE SWORDS OF JUSTICE, KELDEO!
...IS TRYING TO HELP ME.

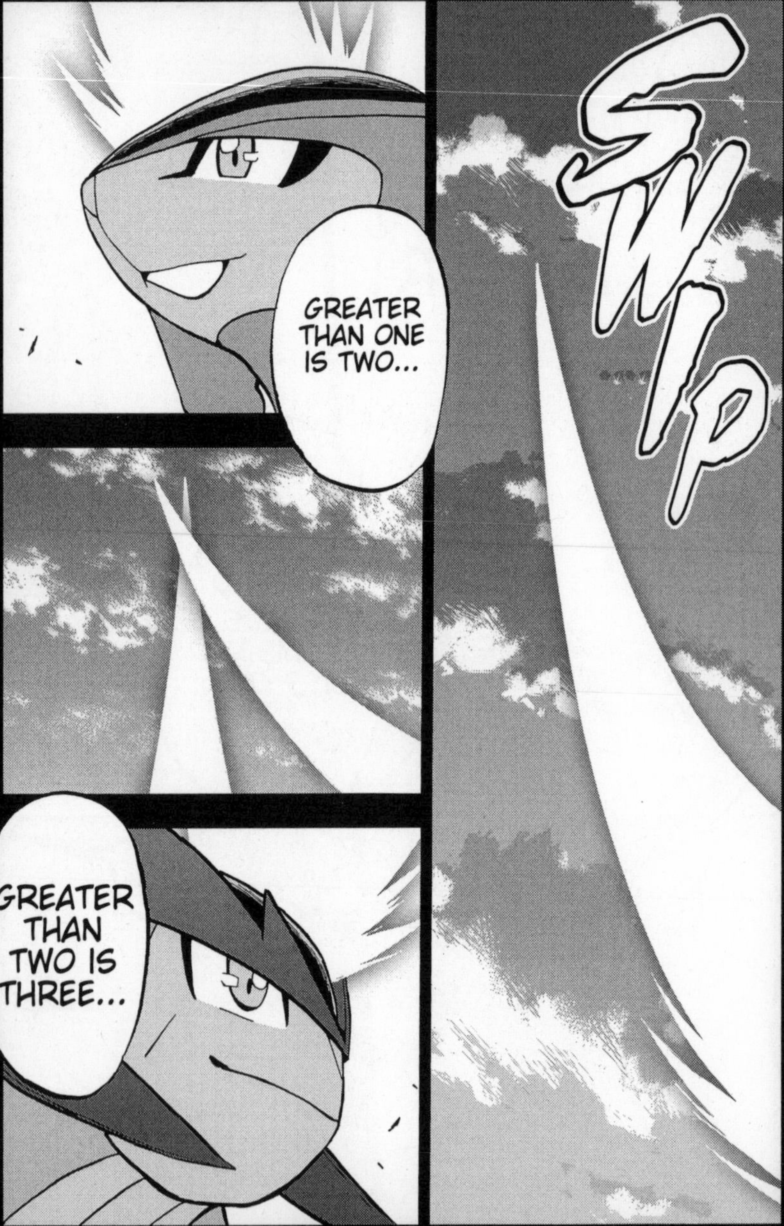
SWIP
GREATER THAN ONE IS TWO...
GREATER THAN TWO IS THREE...

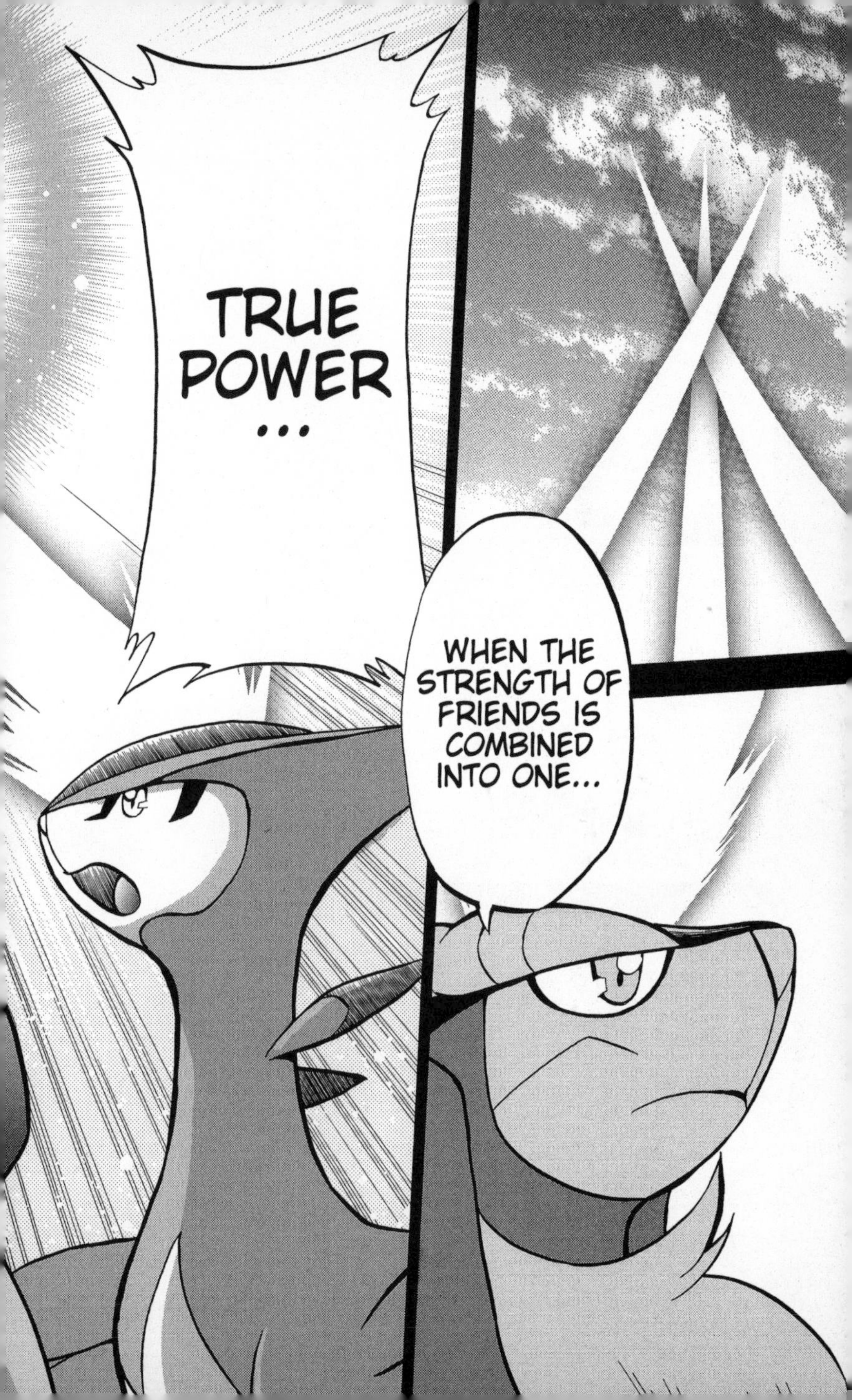
WHEN THE STRENGTH OF FRIENDS IS COMBINED INTO ONE...
TRUE POWER ...

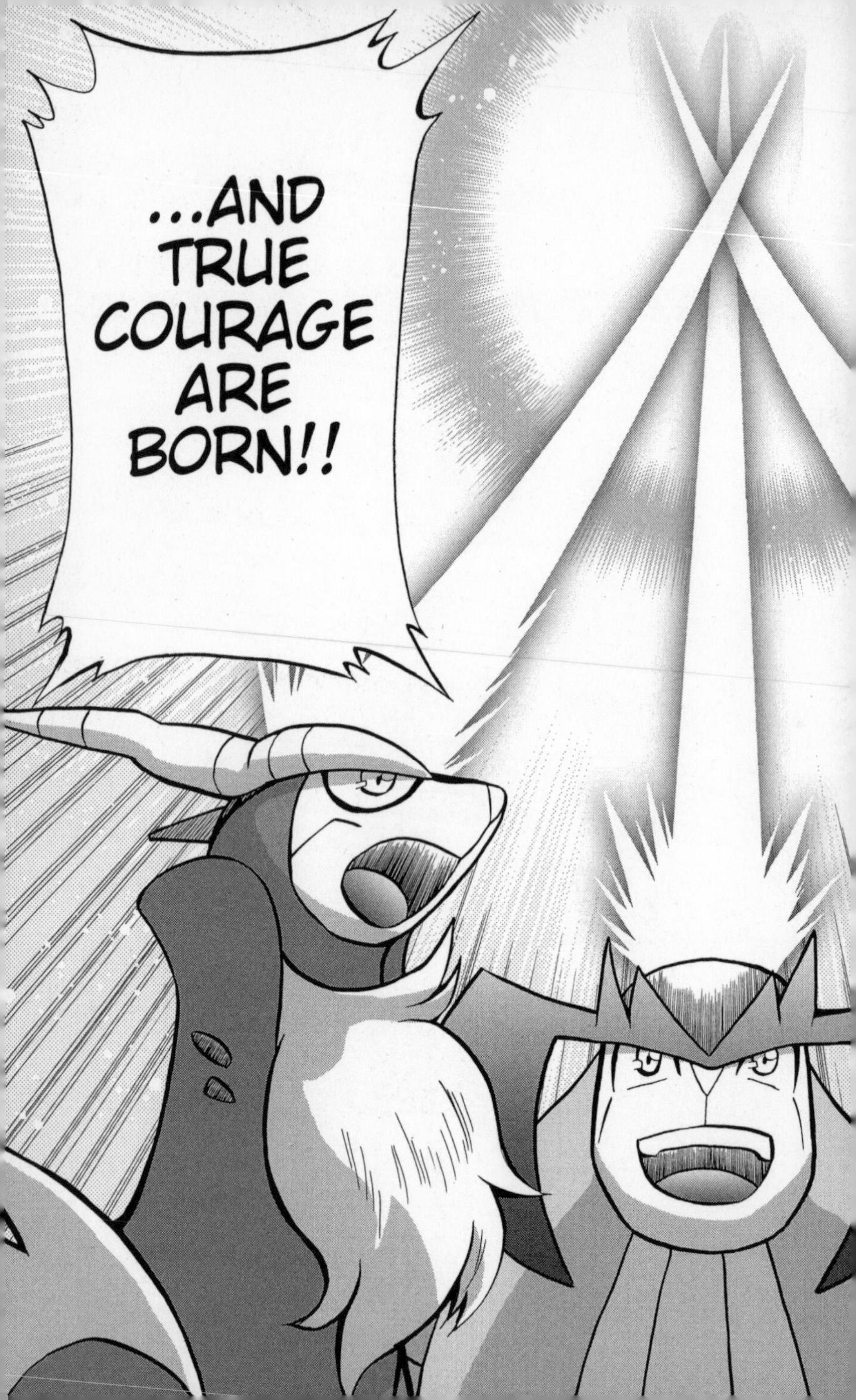
...AND TRUE COURAGE ARE BORN!!

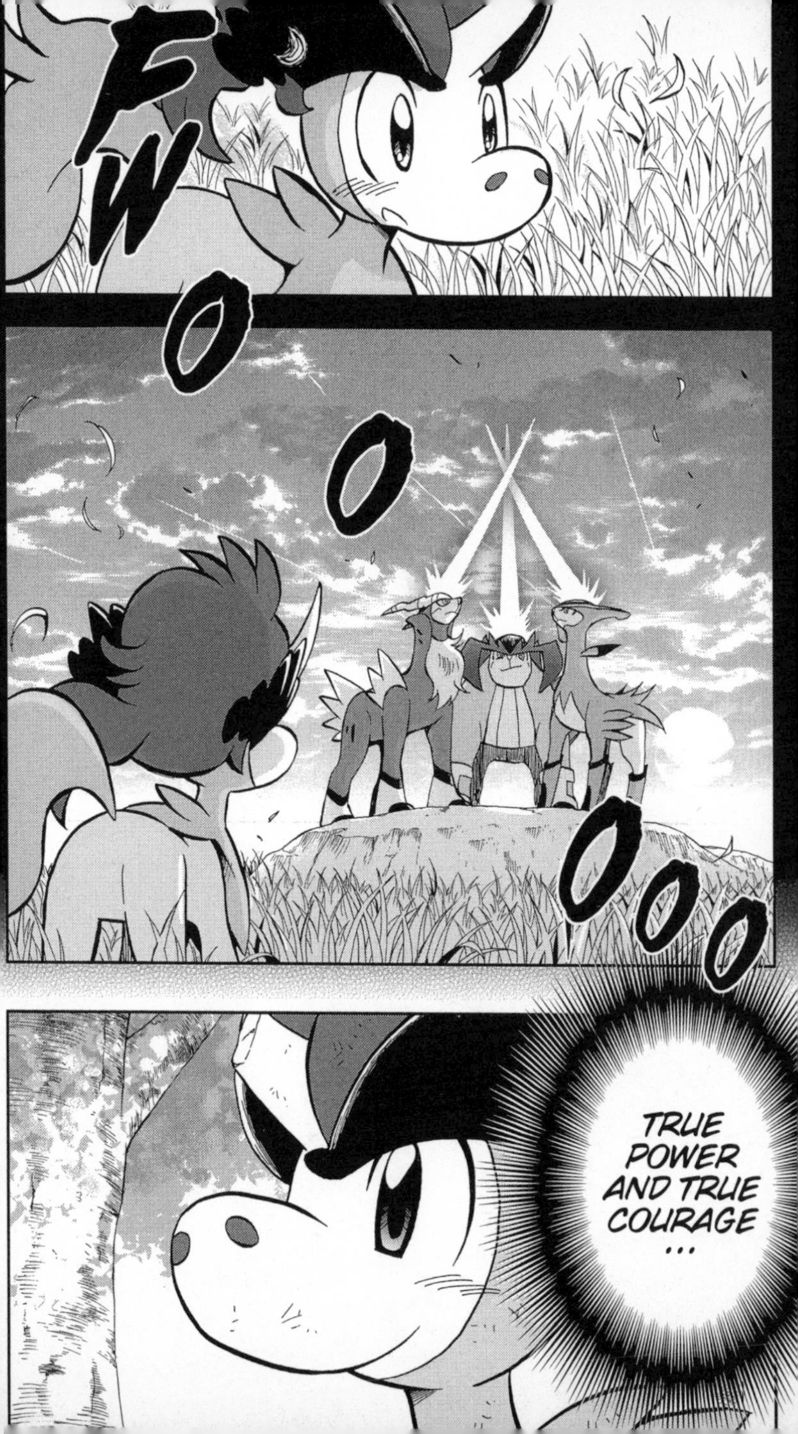
FWOOOOOO
TRUE POWER AND TRUE COURAGE ...

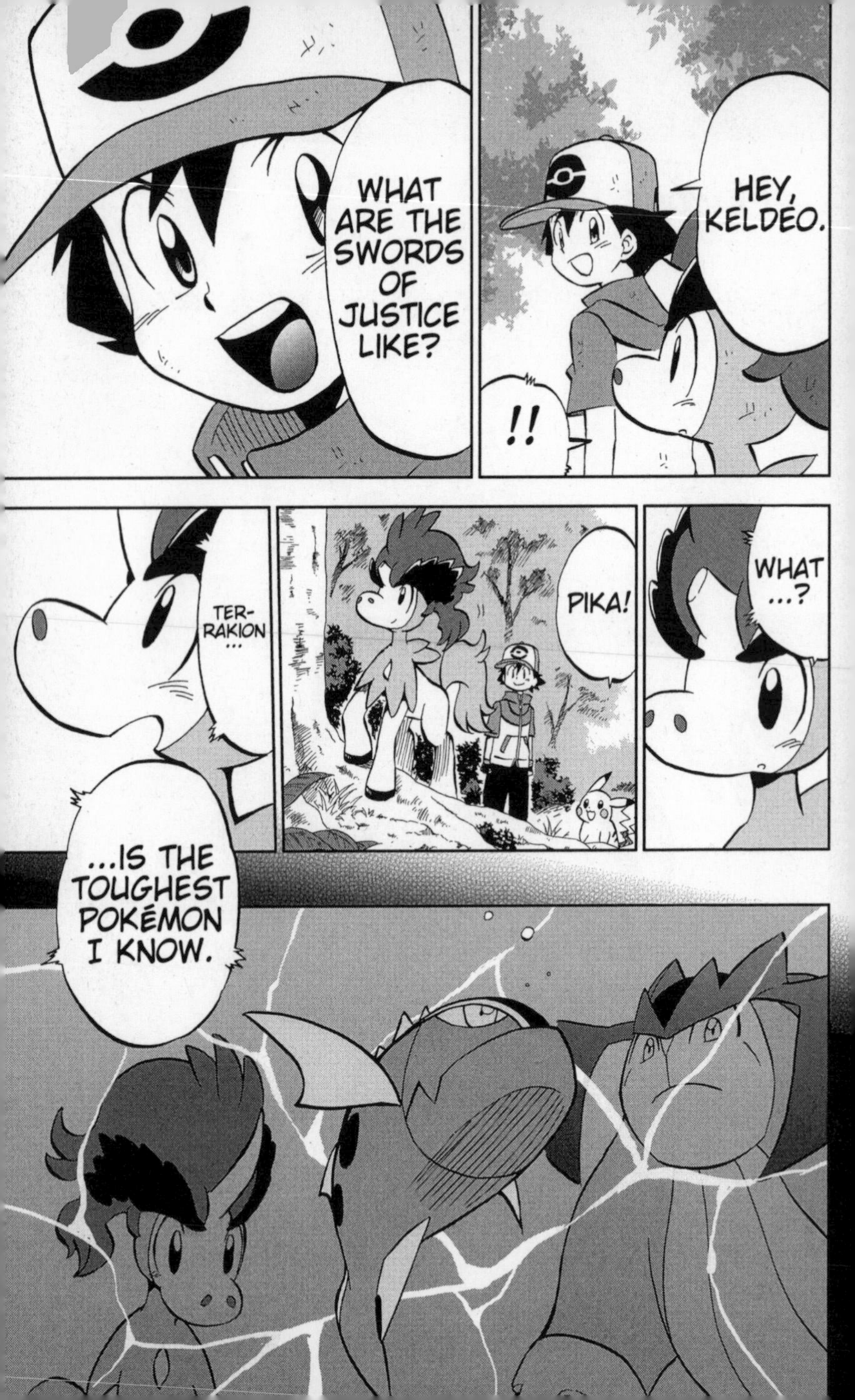
HEY, KELDEO.
!!
WHAT ARE THE SWORDS OF JUSTICE LIKE?
WHAT ...?
PIKA!
TER-RAKION ...
...IS THE TOUGHEST POKÉMON I KNOW.

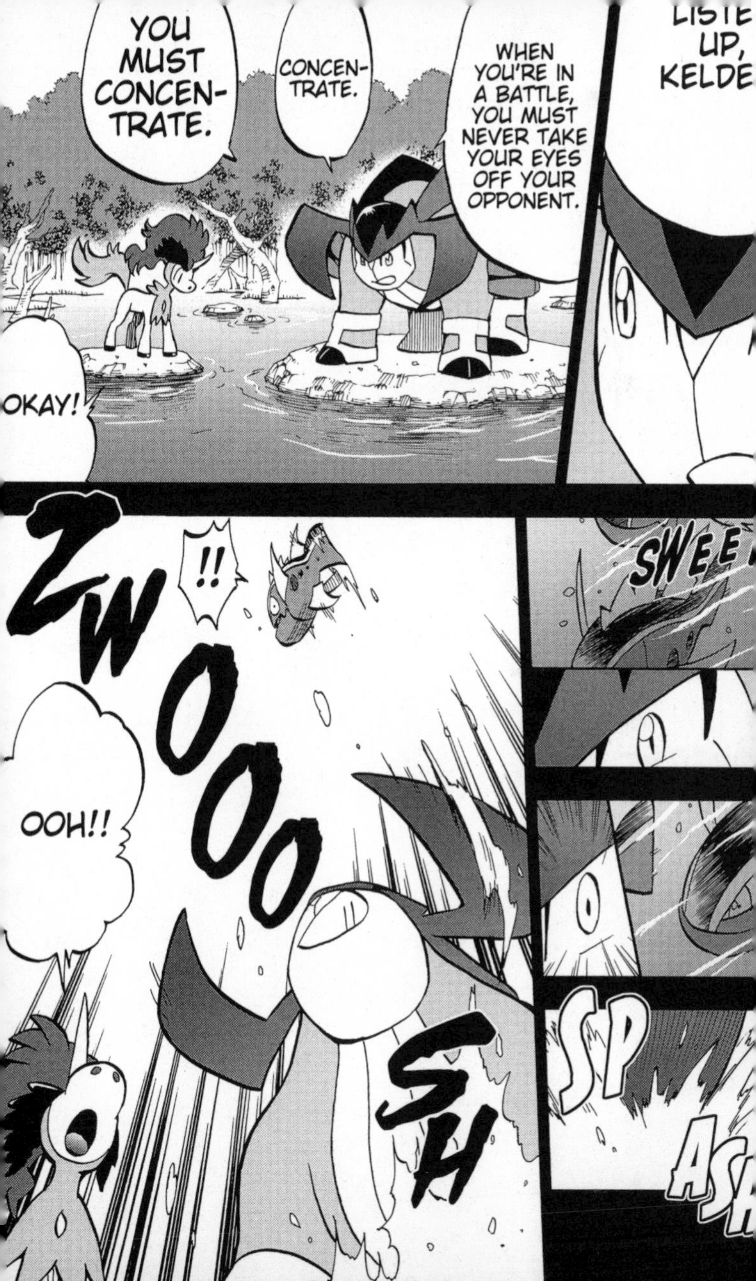
LISTE UP, KELDE
WHEN YOU'RE IN A BATTLE, YOU MUST NEVER TAKE YOUR EYES OFF YOUR OPPONENT.
CONCEN-TRATE.
YOU MUST CONCEN-TRATE.
OKAY!
SWEE
SP
AS
!!
ZWOOOO
SH
OOH!!

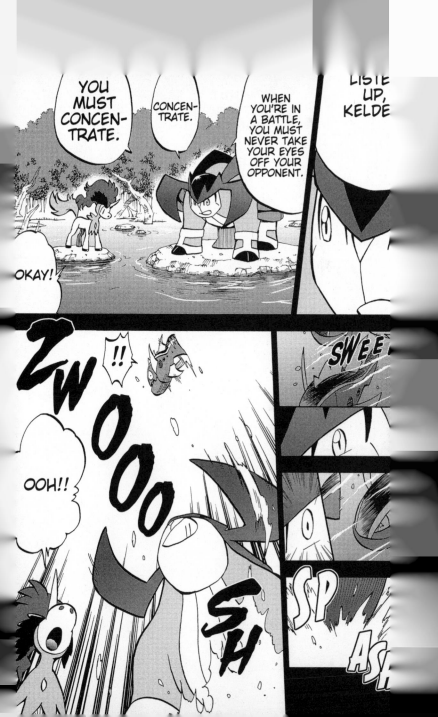

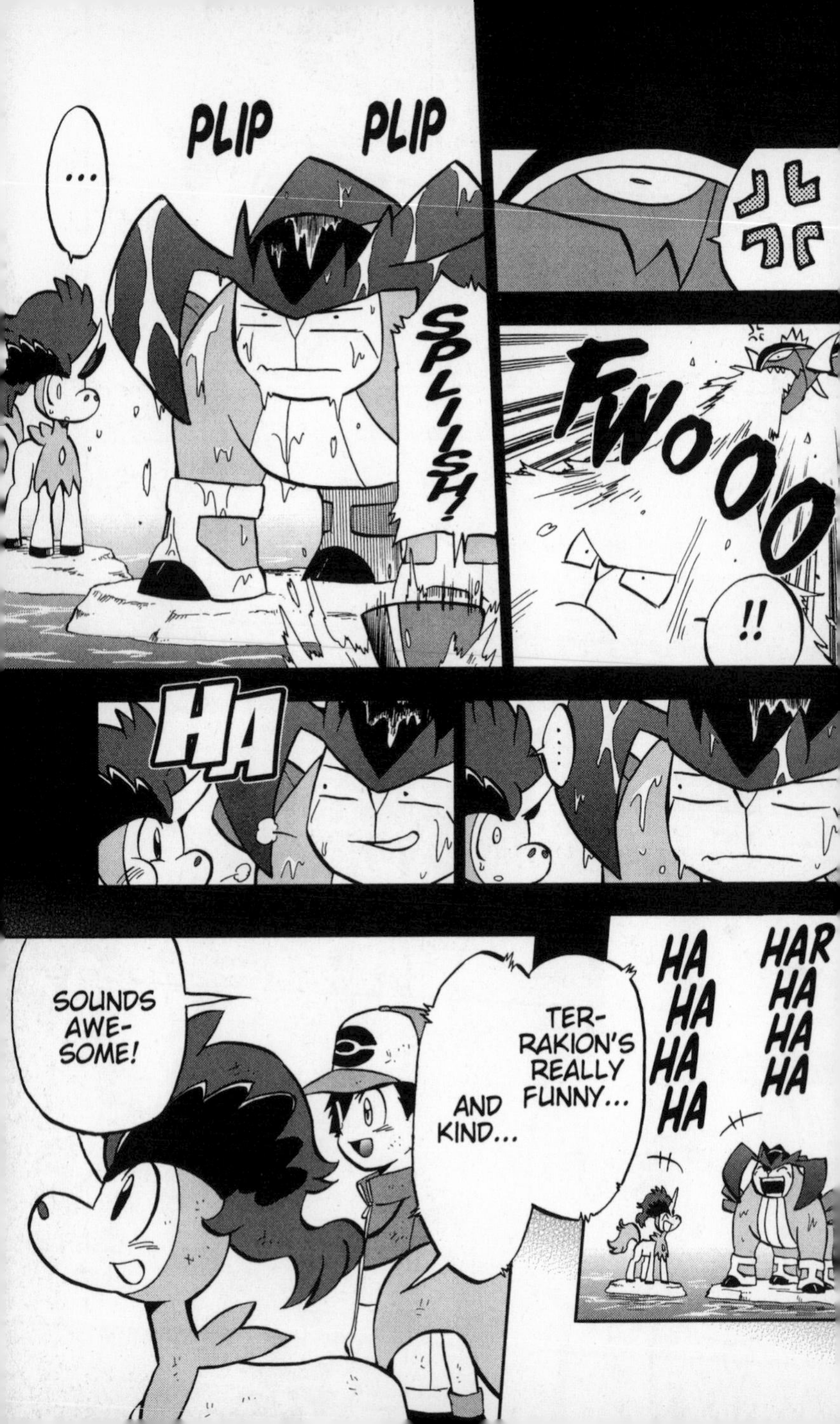
FWOOO
!!
PLIP
PLIP
...
SPLISH!
...
HA
HAR HA HA HA HA
HA HA HA HA HA
TER-RAKION'S REALLY FUNNY...
AND KIND...
SOUNDS AWE-SOME!

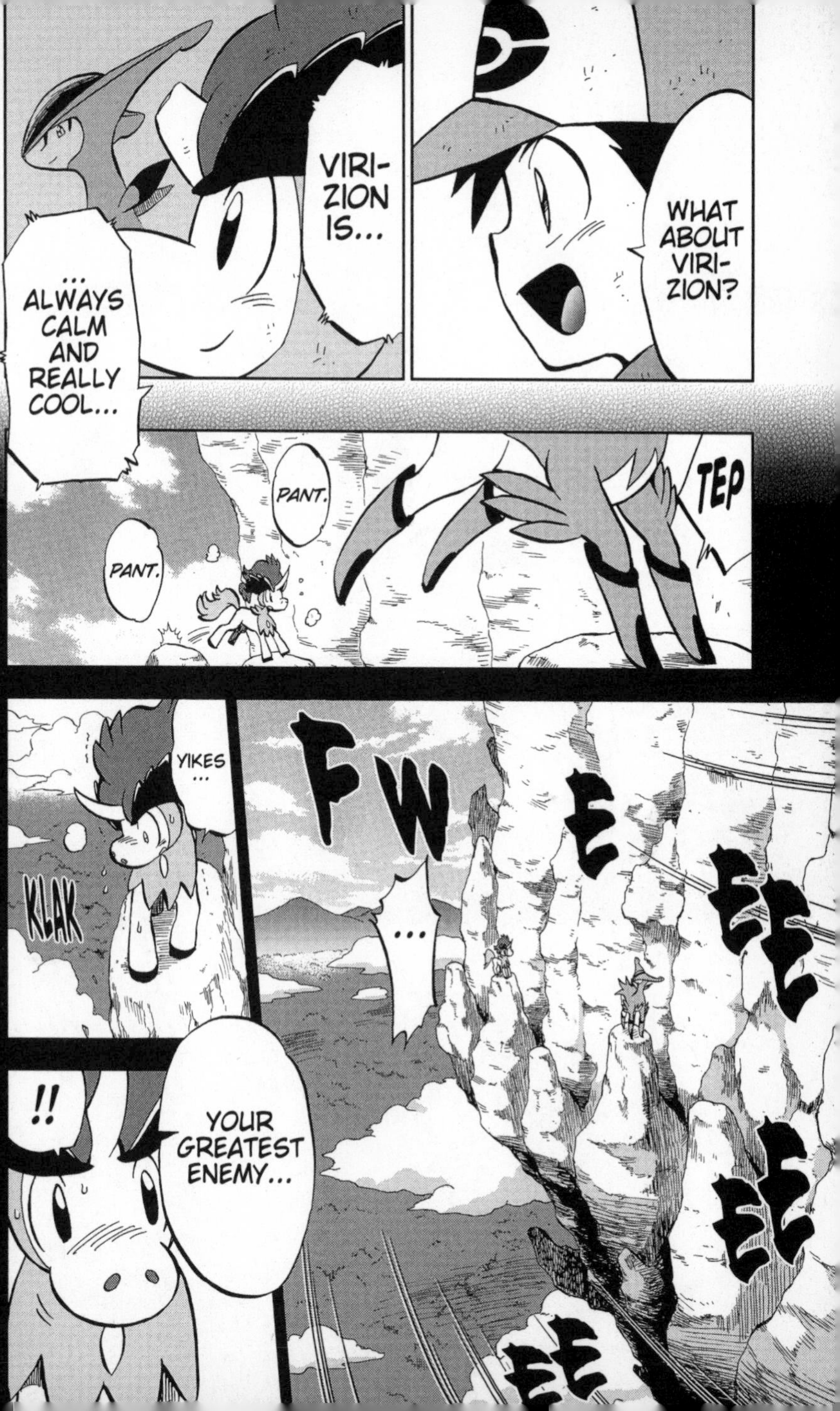
WHAT ABOUT VIRIZION?
VIRIZION IS...
... ALWAYS CALM AND REALLY COOL...
TEP
PANT.
PANT.
FWEEEEEEEEE
...
YIKES...
KLAK
YOUR GREATEST ENEMY...
!!

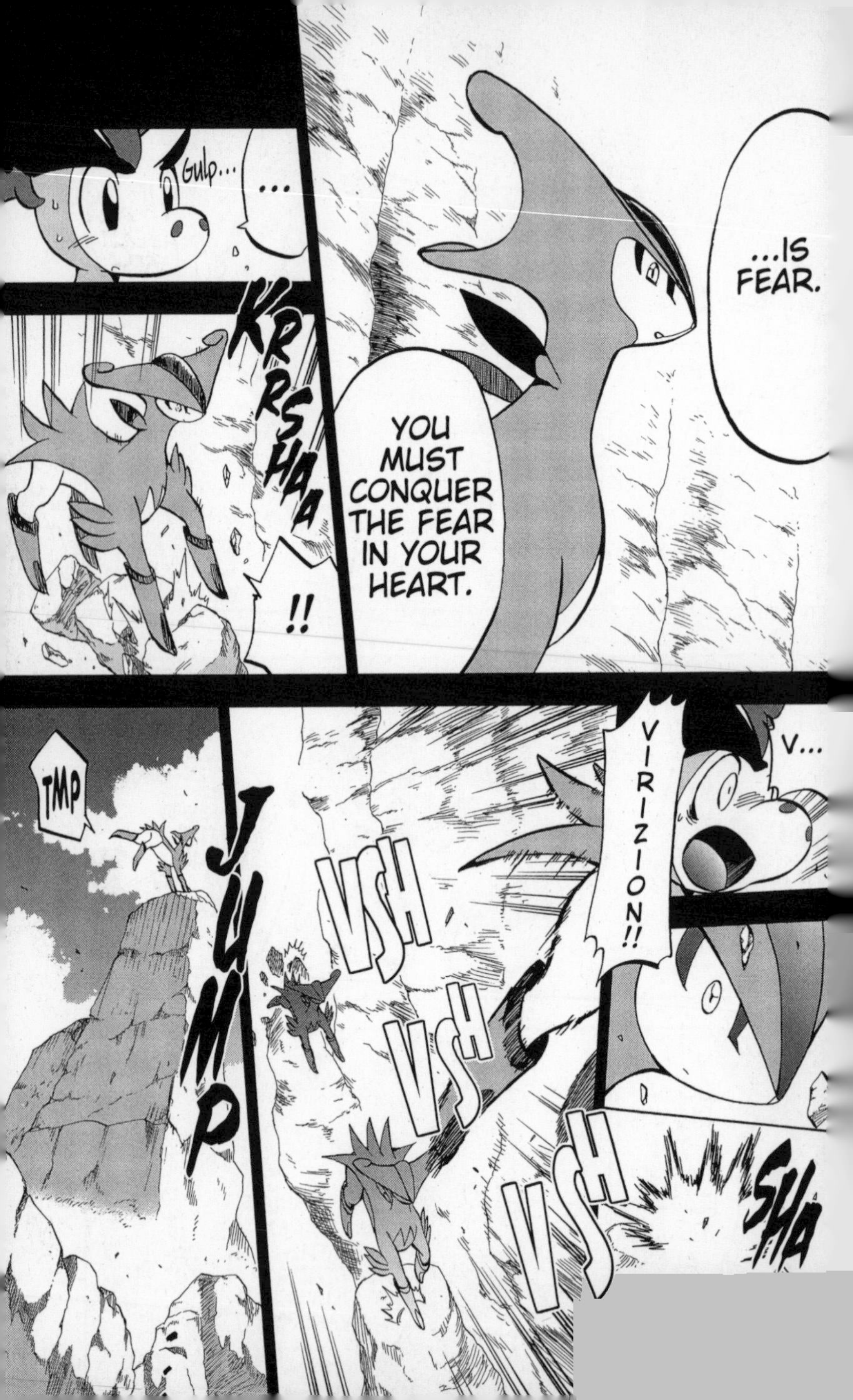
...IS FEAR.
YOU MUST CONQUER THE FEAR IN YOUR HEART.
Gulp...
...
KRRSHAA
!!
V...
VIRIZION!!
SHA
VSH
VSH
VSH
TMP
JUMP

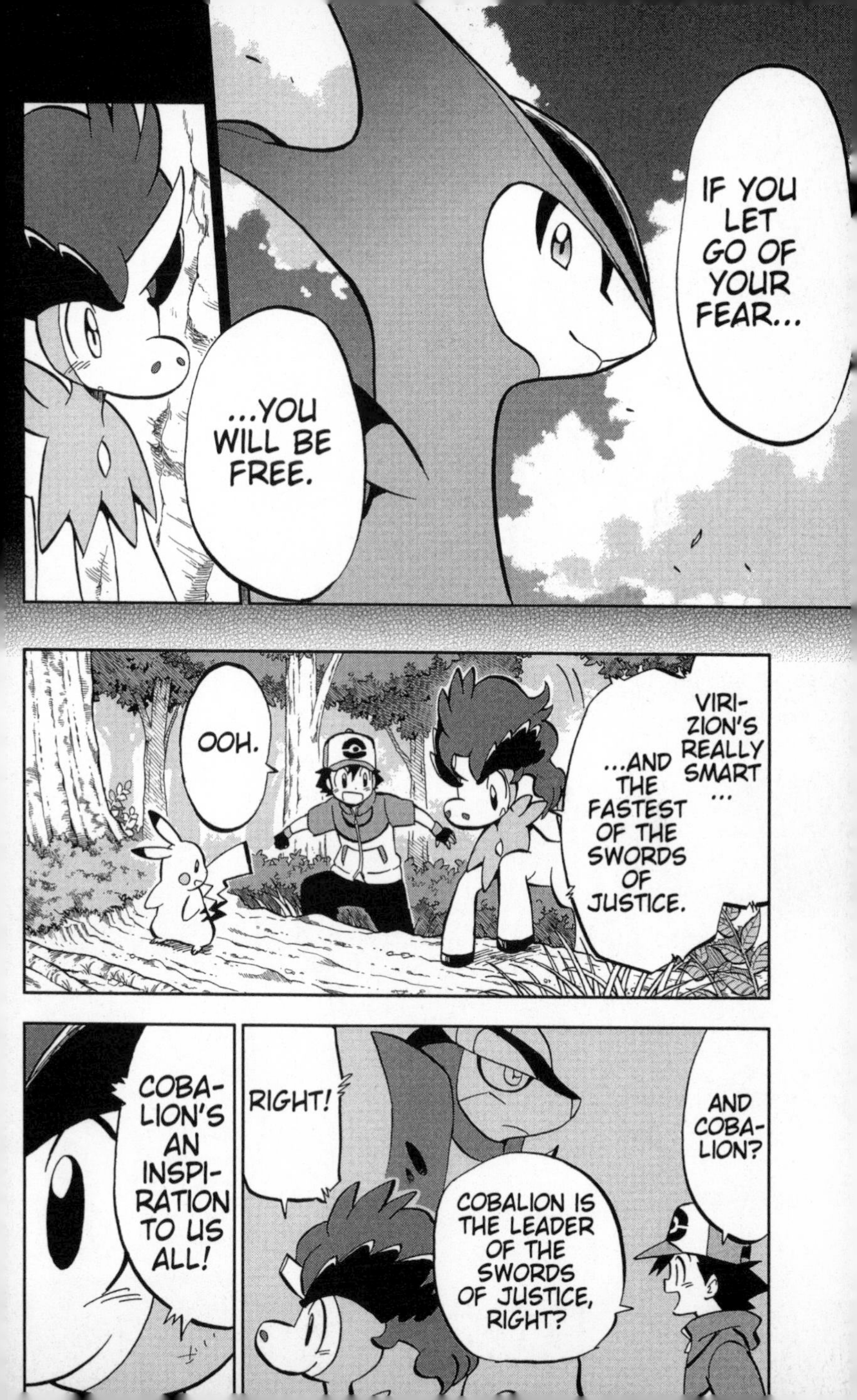
IF YOU LET GO OF YOUR FEAR...
...YOU WILL BE FREE.
VIRIZION'S REALLY SMART ...
...AND THE FASTEST OF THE SWORDS OF JUSTICE.
OOH.
AND COBALION?
COBALION IS THE LEADER OF THE SWORDS OF JUSTICE, RIGHT?
RIGHT!
COBALION'S AN INSPIRATION TO US ALL!

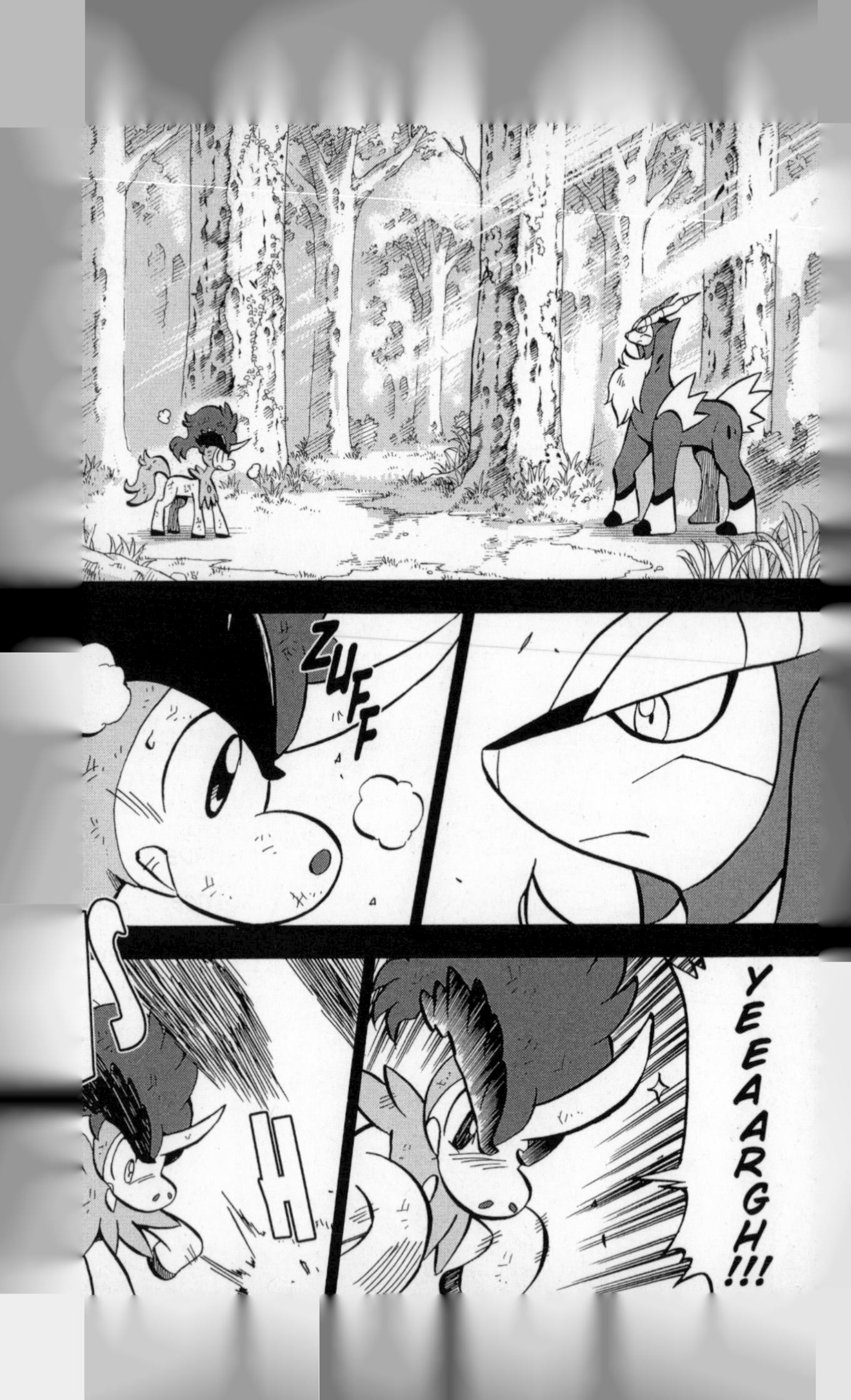

ZUFF
YEEAARGH!!!
H

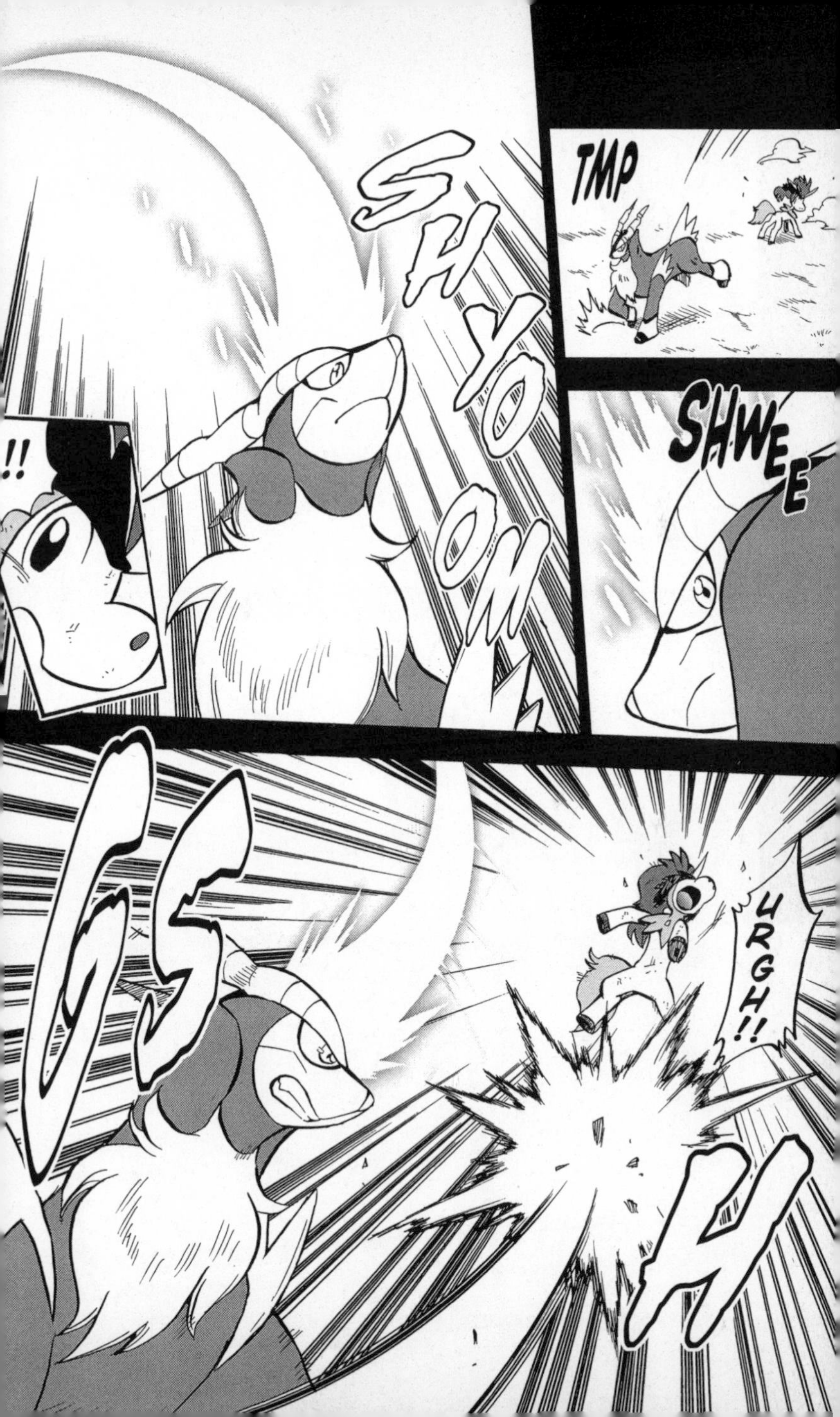
TMP
SHWEE
SHYOOM
!!
URGH!!

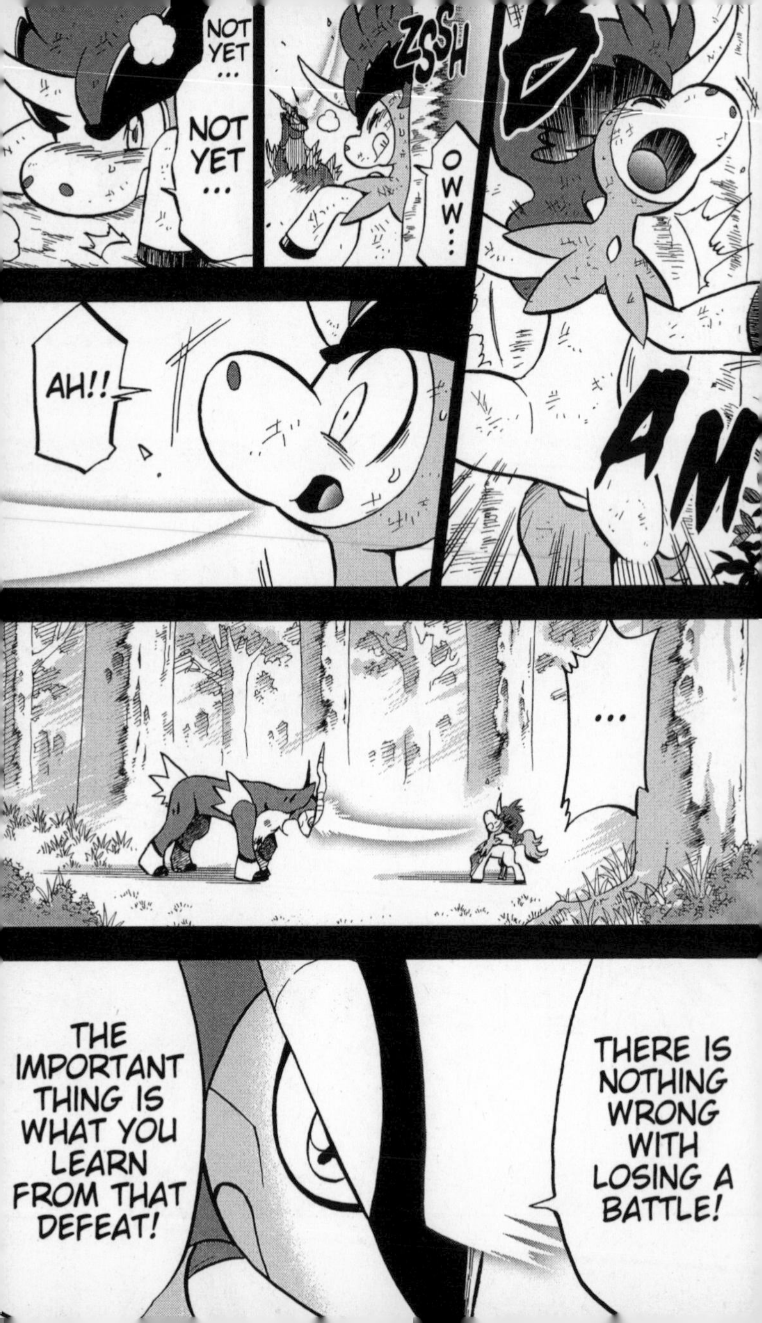
AM
ZSSH
OWW...
NOT YET...
NOT YET...
AH!!
...
THERE IS NOTHING WRONG WITH LOSING A BATTLE!
THE IMPORTANT THING IS WHAT YOU LEARN FROM THAT DEFEAT!

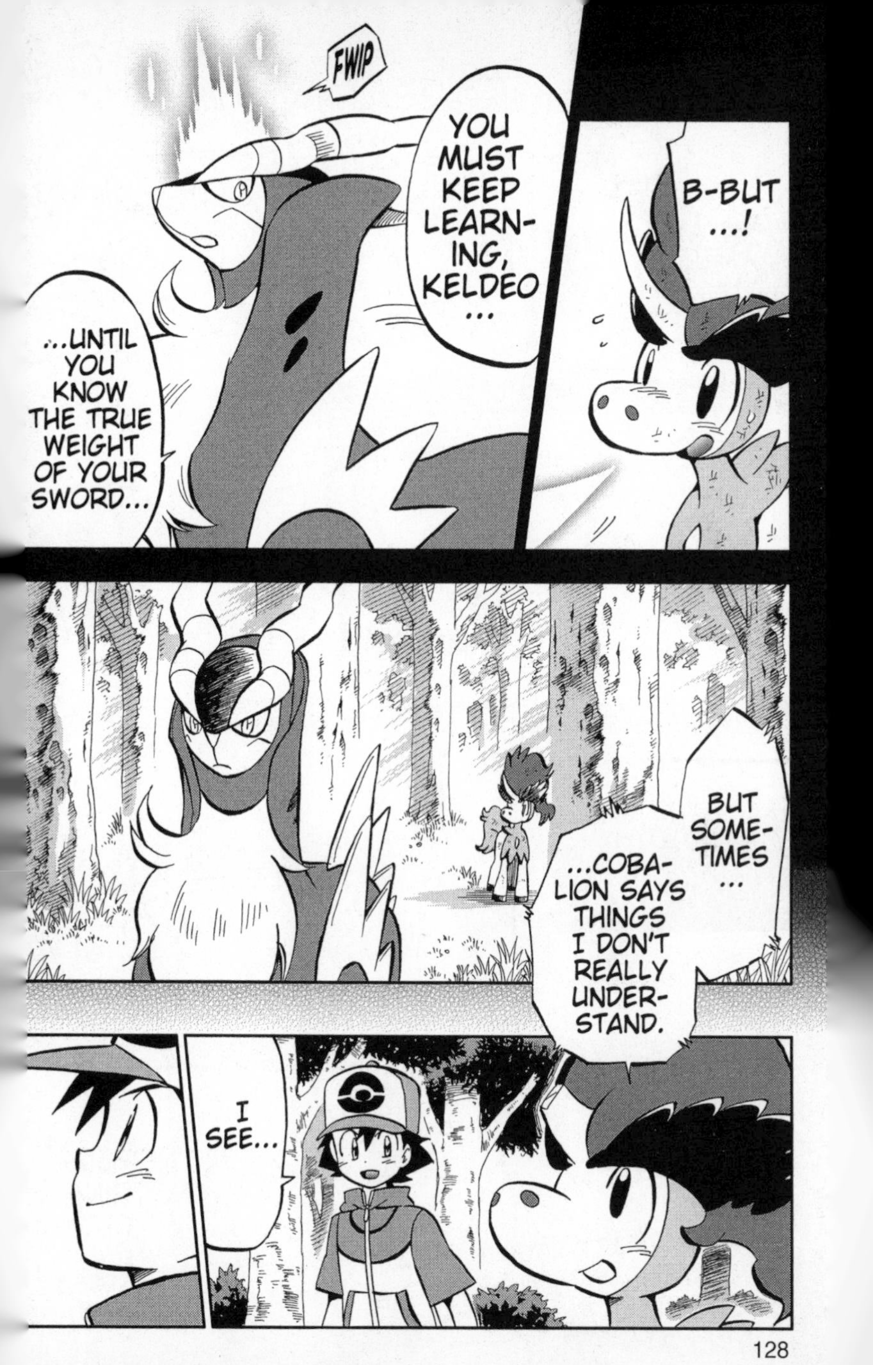
B-BUT ...!
FWIP
YOU MUST KEEP LEARNING, KELDEO ...
...UNTIL YOU KNOW THE TRUE WEIGHT OF YOUR SWORD...
BUT SOMETIMES ...
...COBALION SAYS THINGS I DON'T REALLY UNDERSTAND.
I SEE...

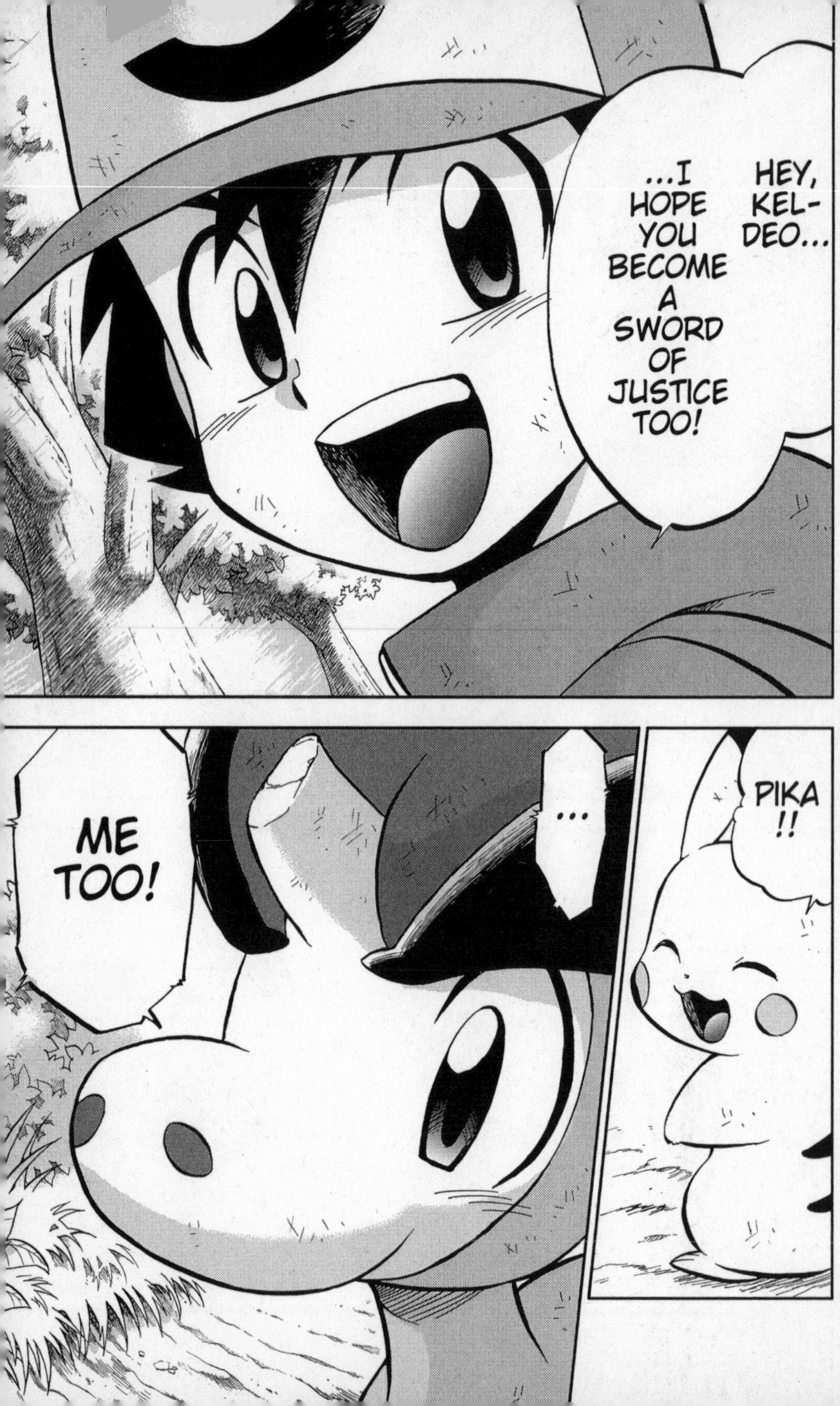
HEY, KEL-DEO...
...I HOPE YOU BECOME A SWORD OF JUSTICE TOO!
PIKA!!
...
ME TOO!

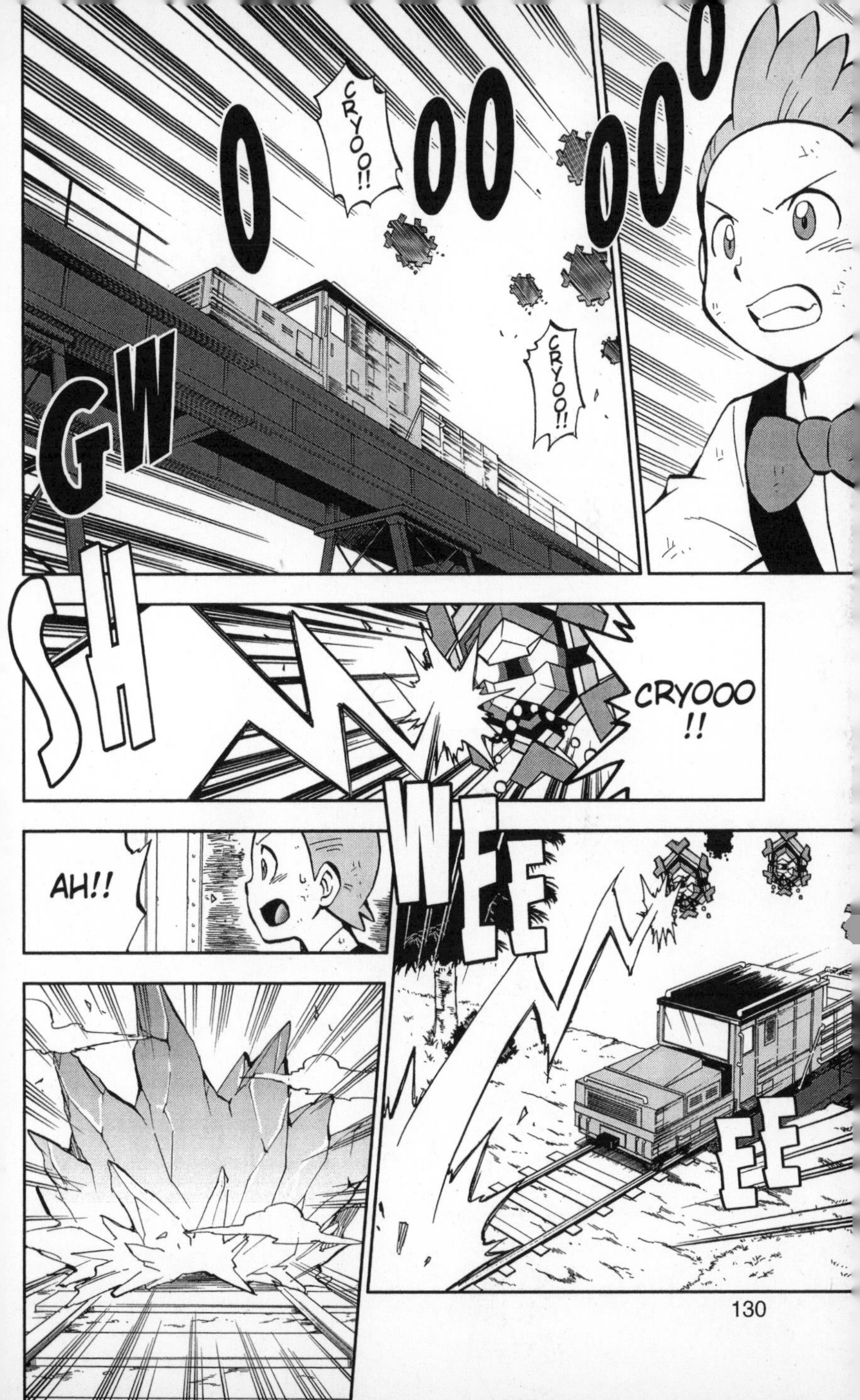
CRYOO!!
CRYOO!!
O OO OOO
GW
SH
CRYOOO!!
WEE
EE
AH!!

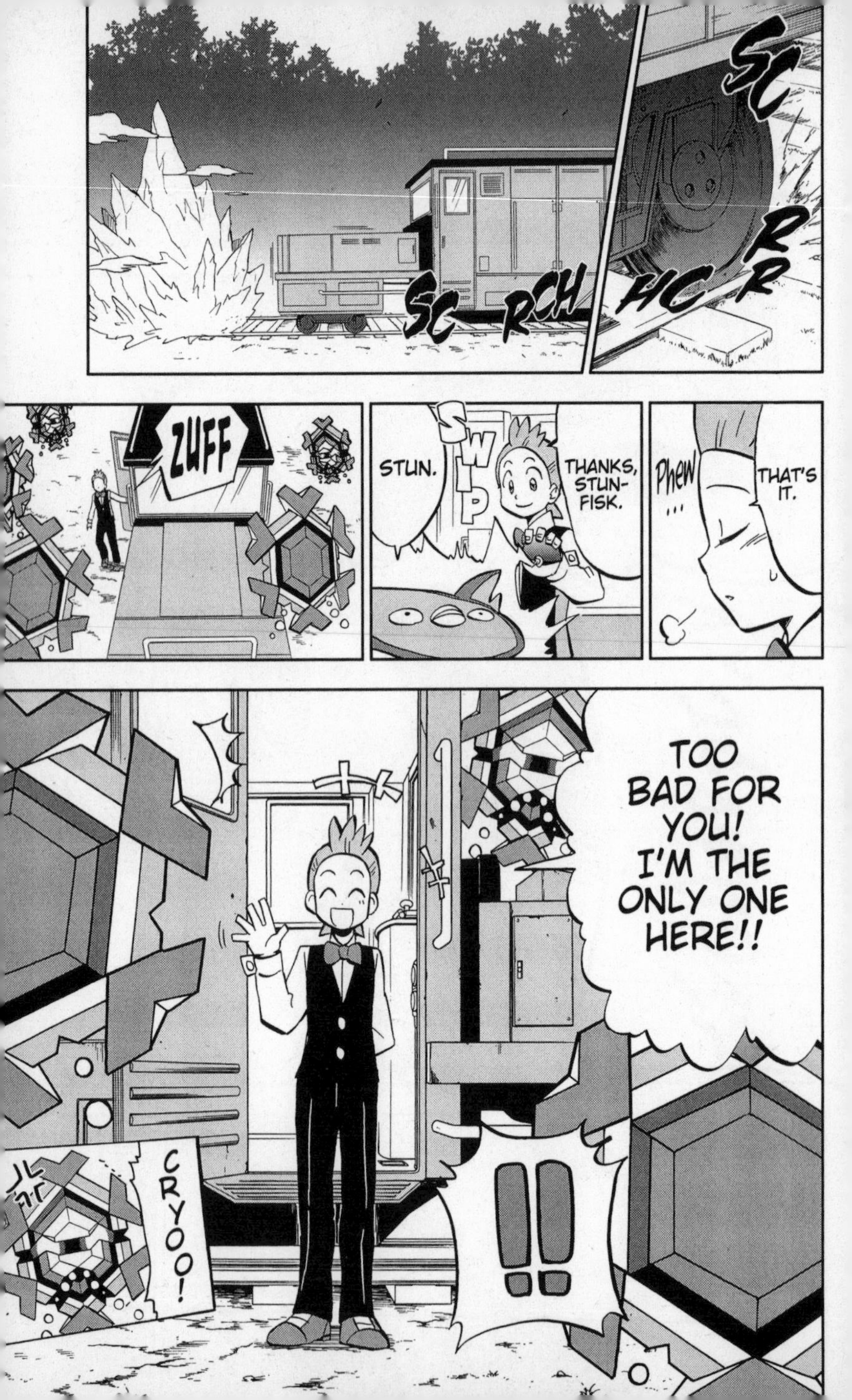
SC R R
HC
SC RCH
THAT'S IT.
Phew...
THANKS, STUN-FISK.
SWIP
STUN.
ZUFF
TOO BAD FOR YOU! I'M THE ONLY ONE HERE!!
!!
CRYOO!

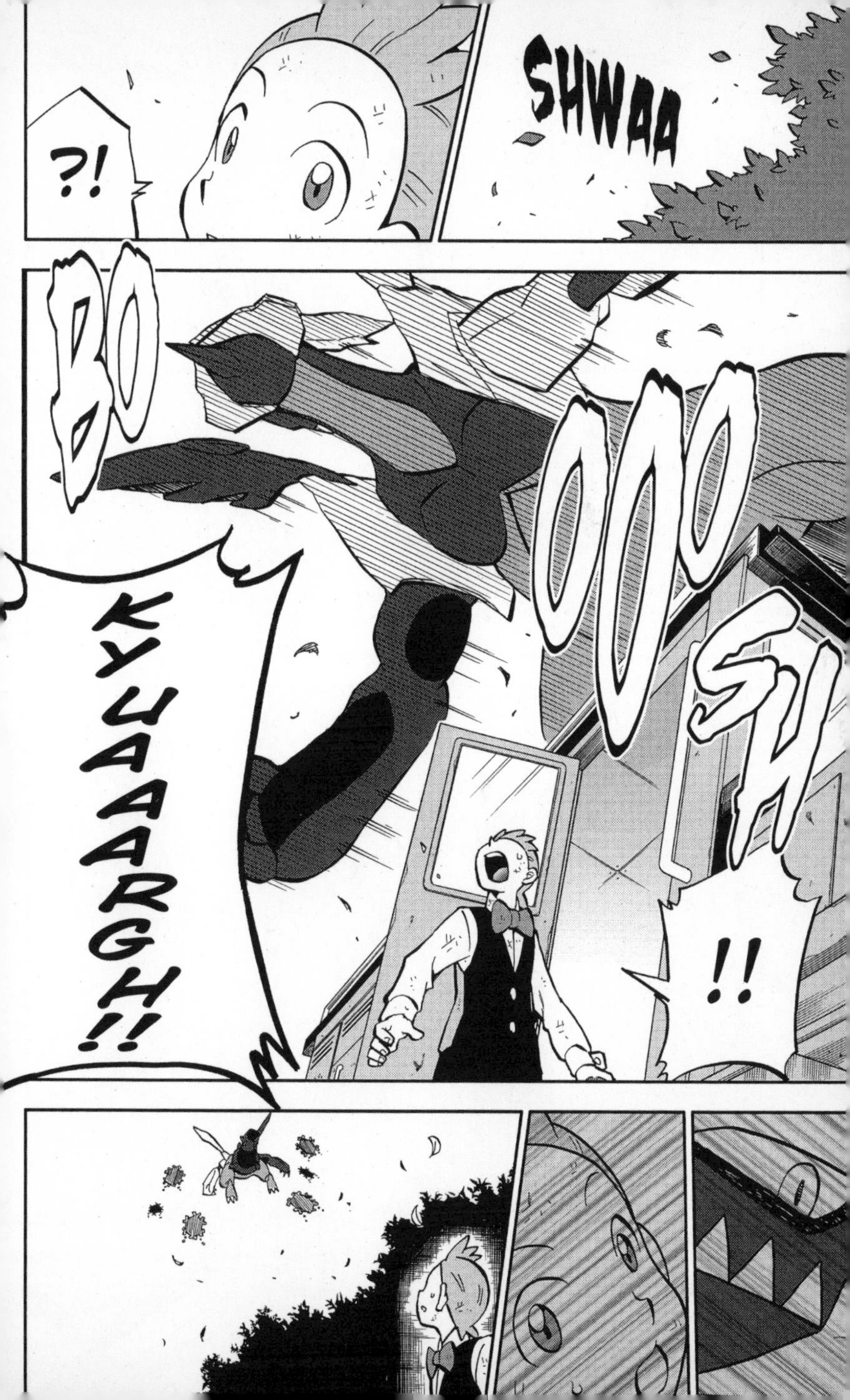
SHWAA
?!
BOOOOSH
!!
KYUAAAARGH!!

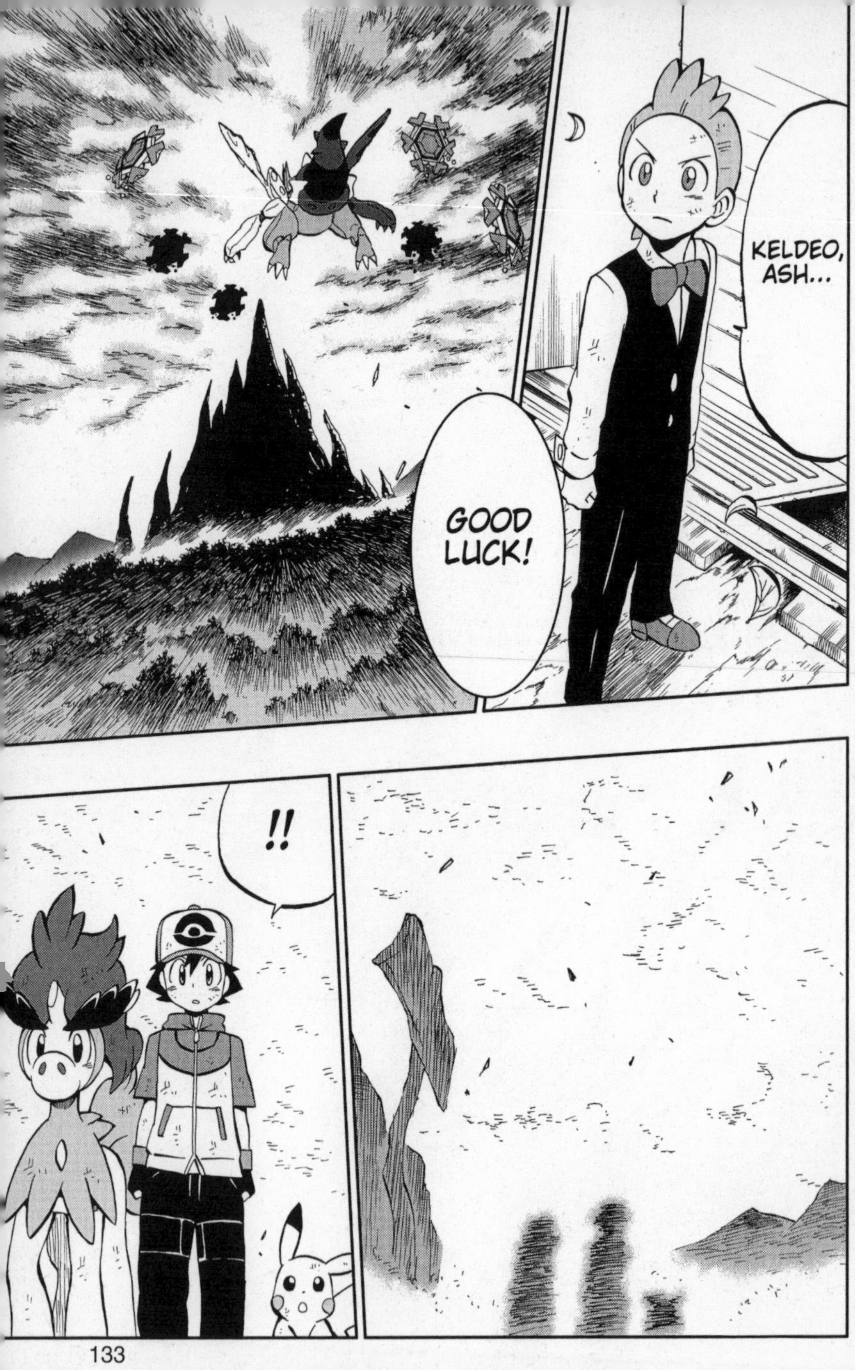
KELDEO, ASH...
GOOD LUCK!
!!

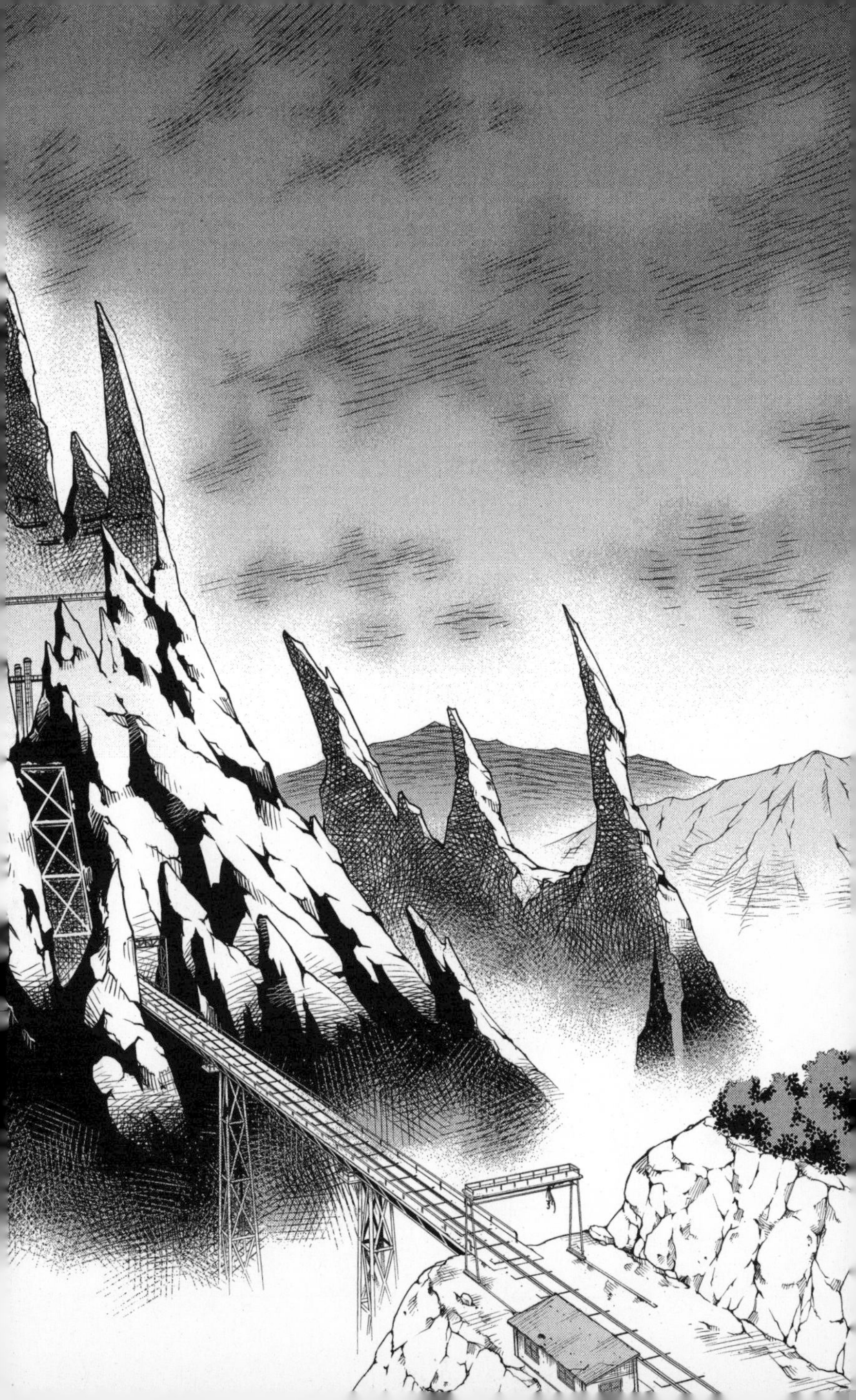

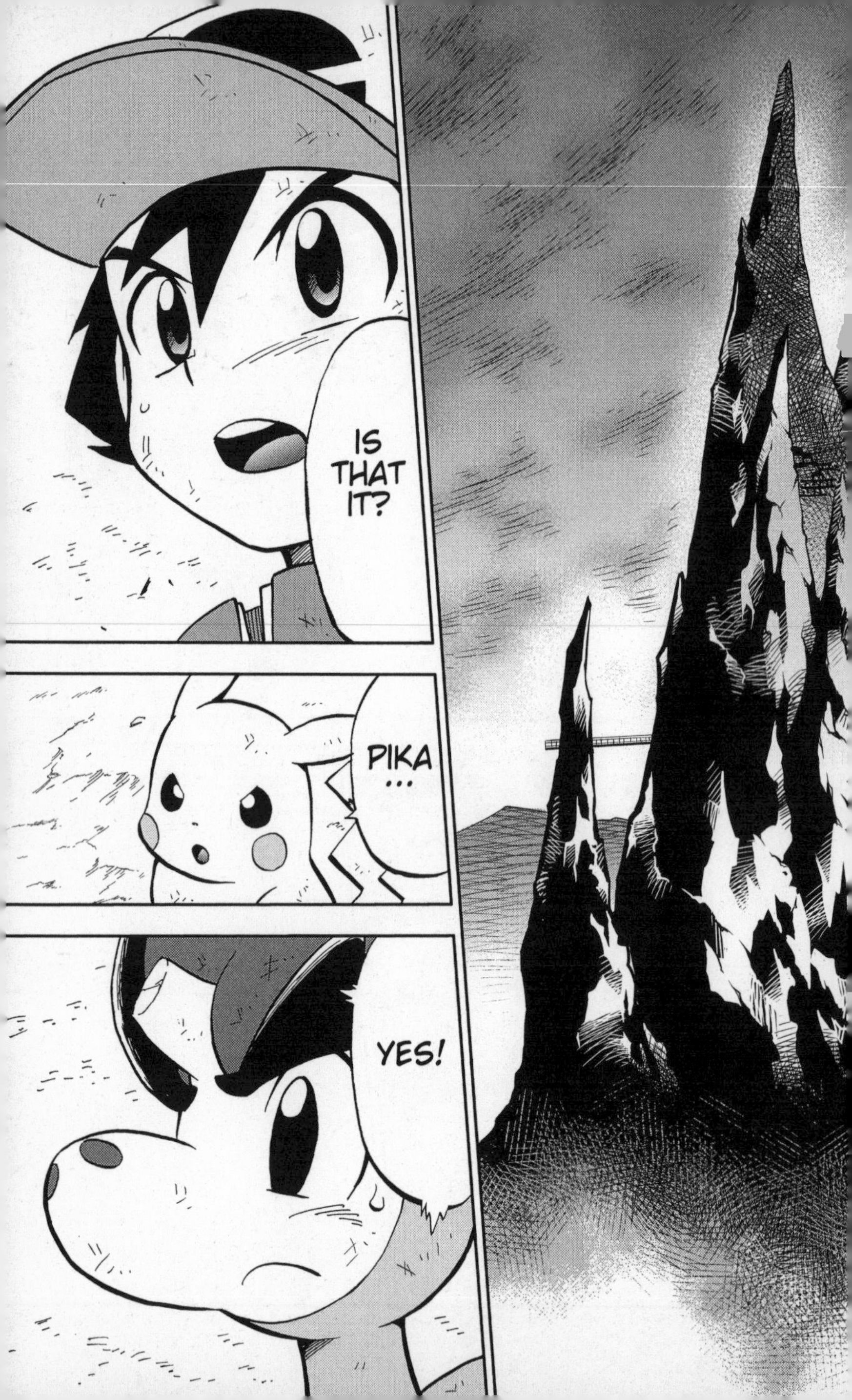
IS THAT IT?
PIKA ...
YES!

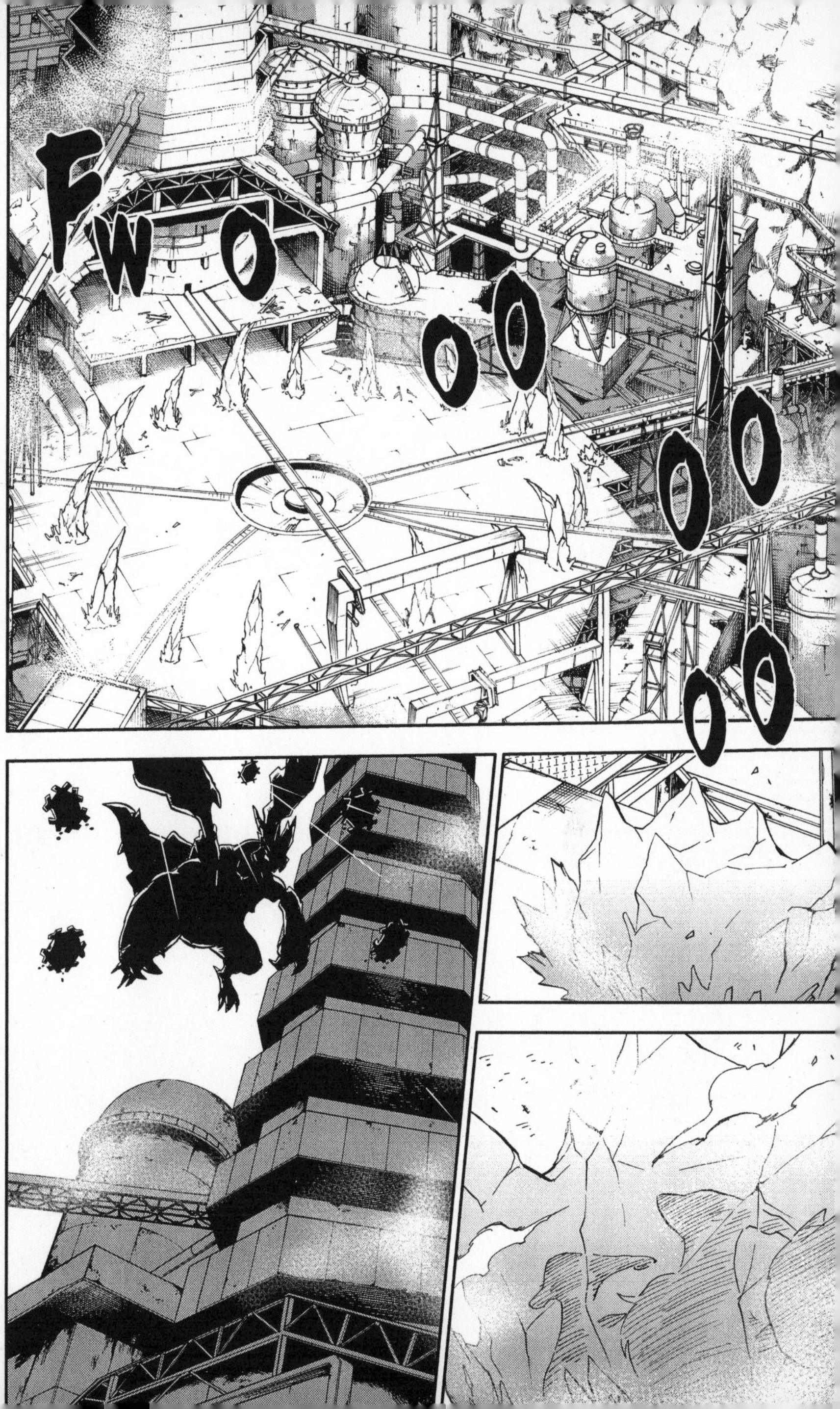
FWOOOOOOOO

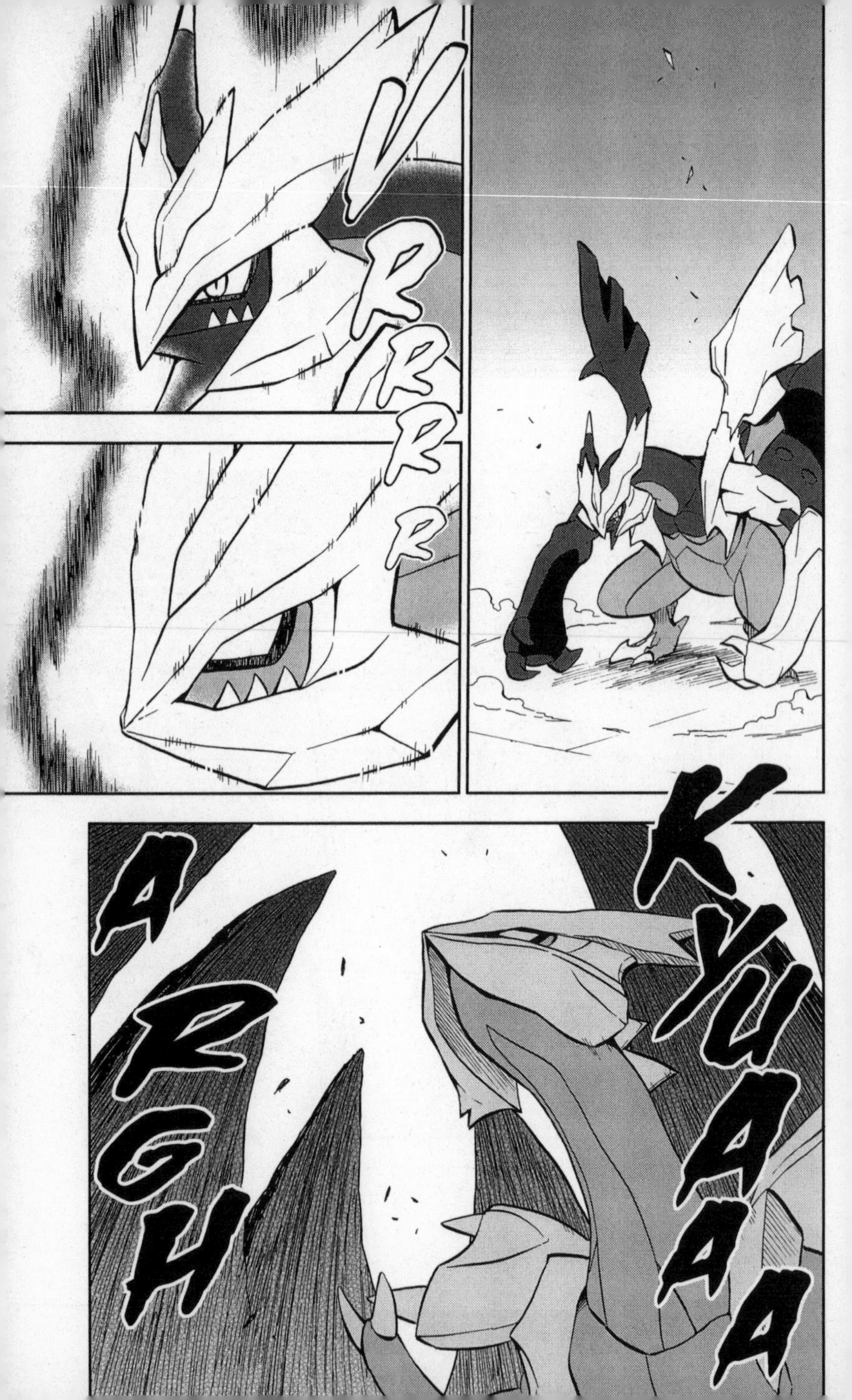
VRRRR
KYUAAA
ARGH

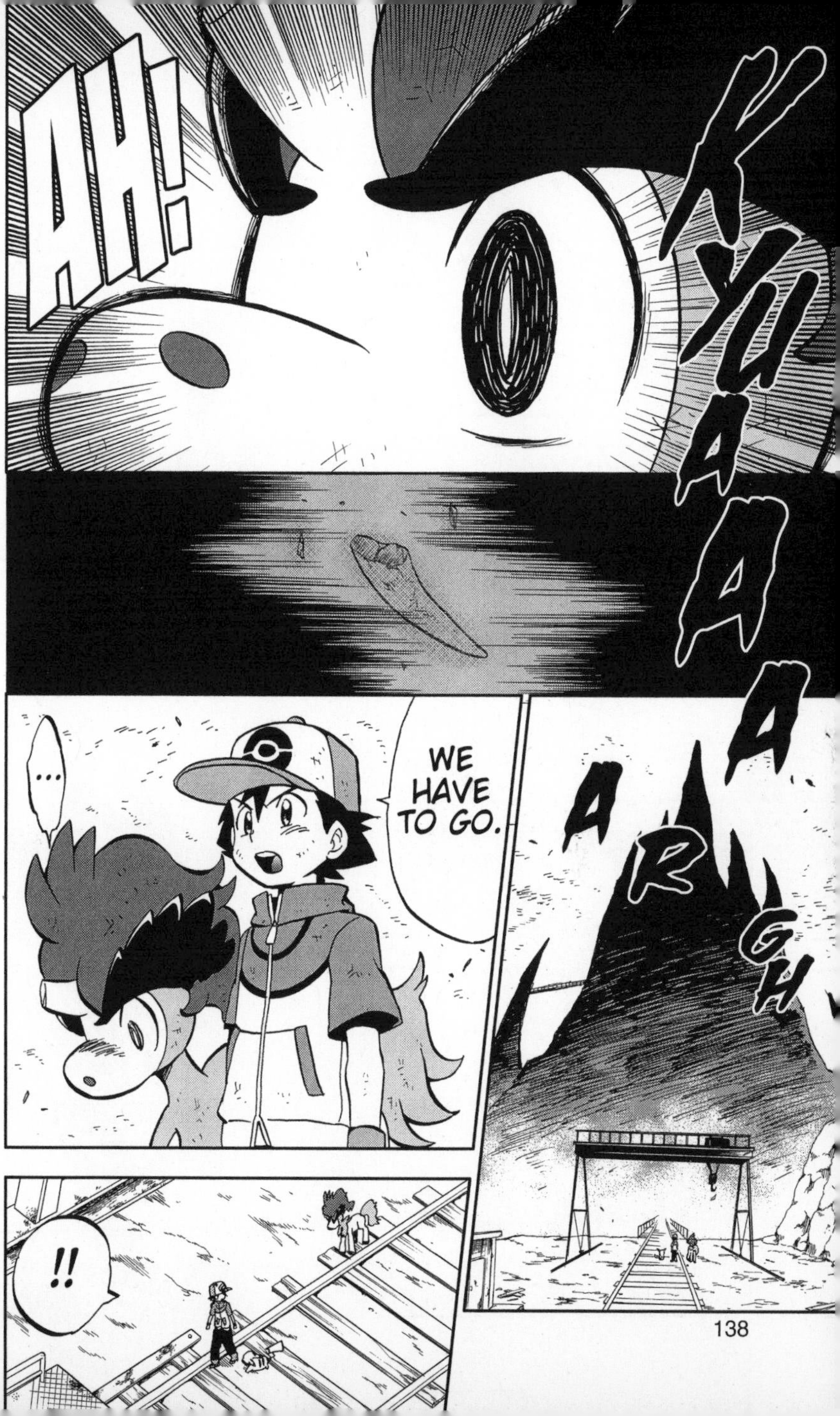
KYUAAAARGH
AH!
WE HAVE TO GO.
...
!!

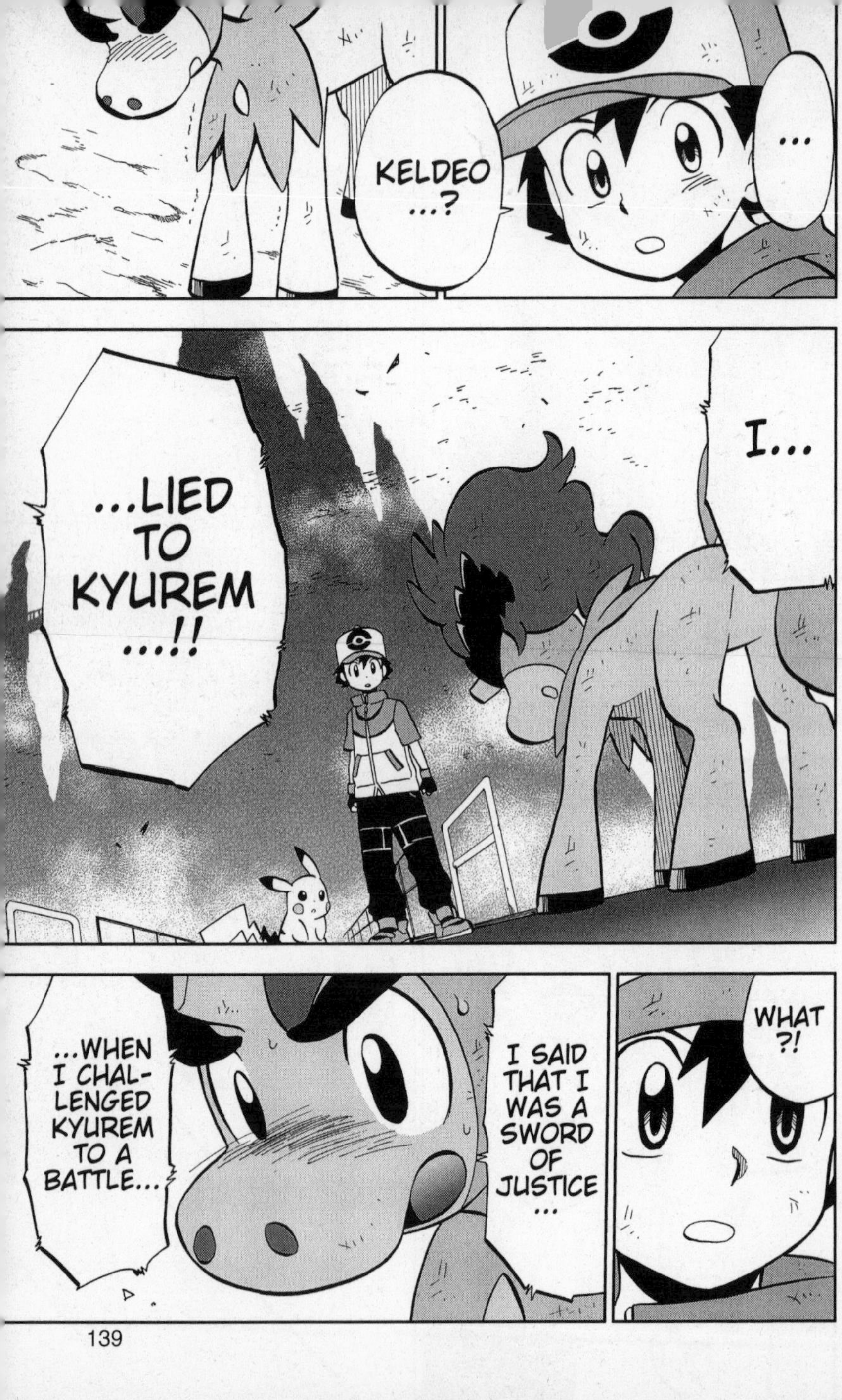
...
KELDEO ...?
I...
...LIED TO KYUREM ...!!
WHAT?!
I SAID THAT I WAS A SWORD OF JUSTICE ...
...WHEN I CHALLENGED KYUREM TO A BATTLE...

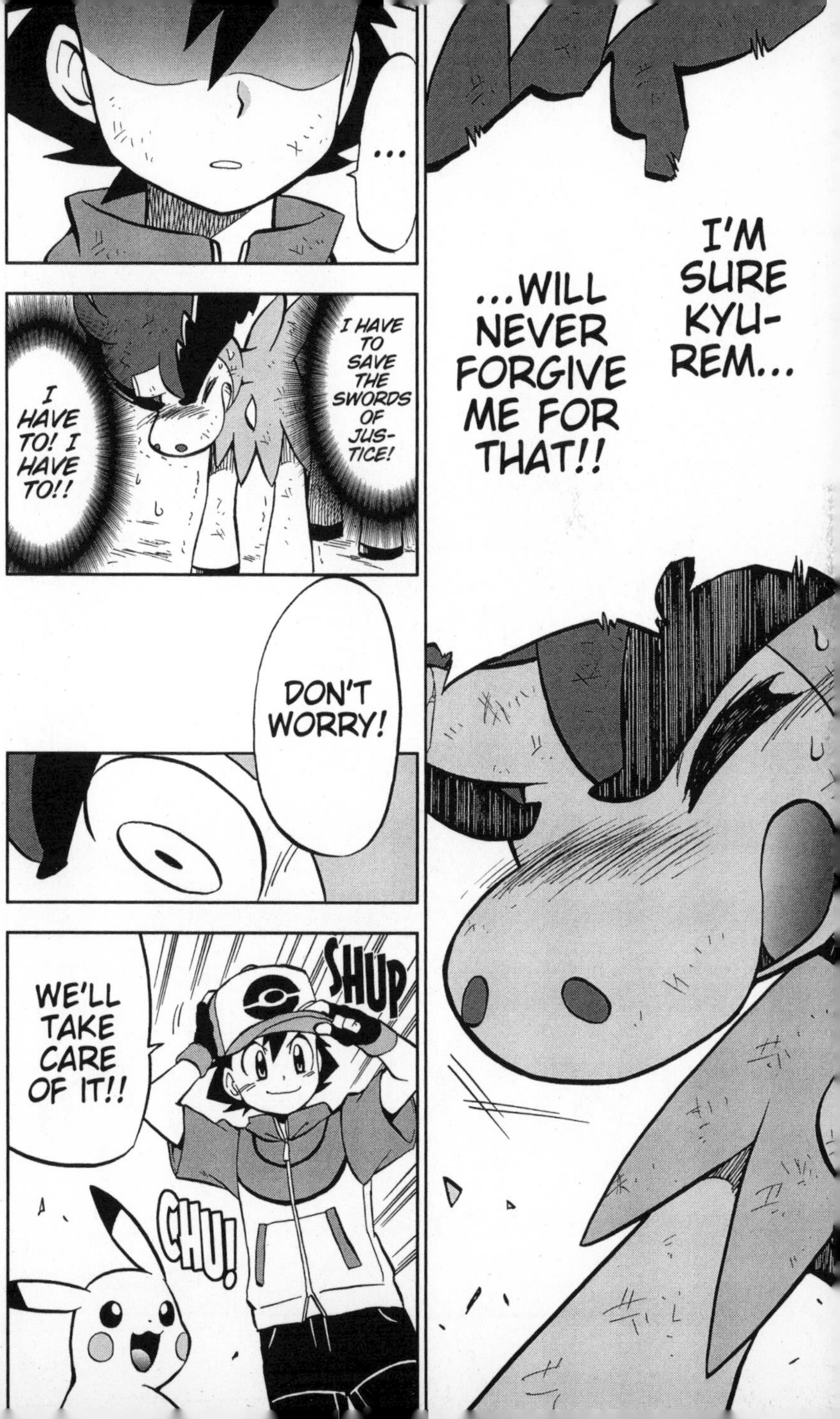
I'M SURE KYU-REM...
...WILL NEVER FORGIVE ME FOR THAT!!
...
I HAVE TO SAVE THE SWORDS OF JUS-TICE!
I HAVE TO! I HAVE TO!!
DON'T WORRY!
SHUP
WE'LL TAKE CARE OF IT!!
CHU!

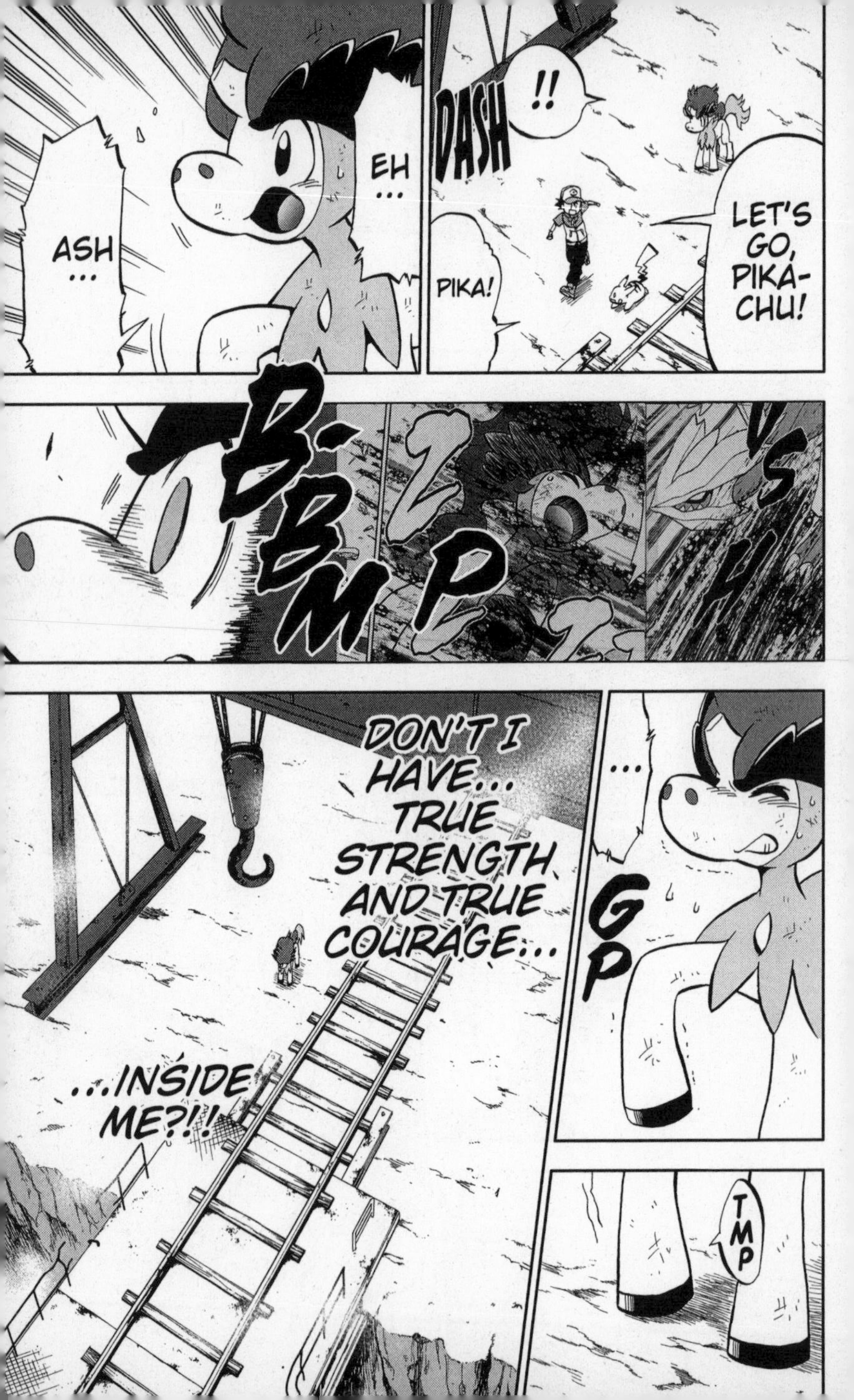
LET'S GO, PIKA-CHU!
PIKA!
!!
DASH
EH ...
ASH ...
B-BMP
...
GP
TMP
DON'T I HAVE... TRUE STRENGTH AND TRUE COURAGE...
...INSIDE ME?!!

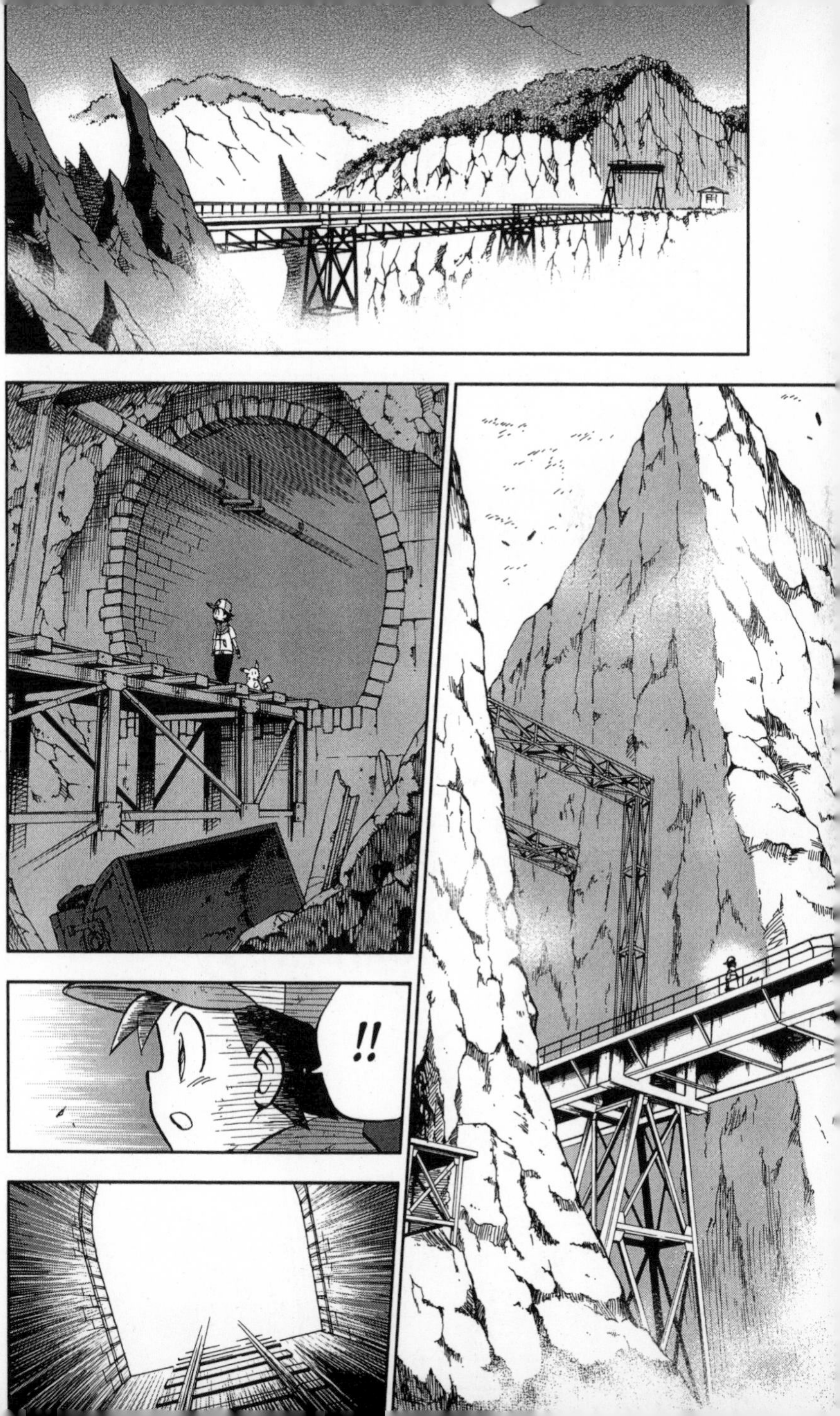
!!

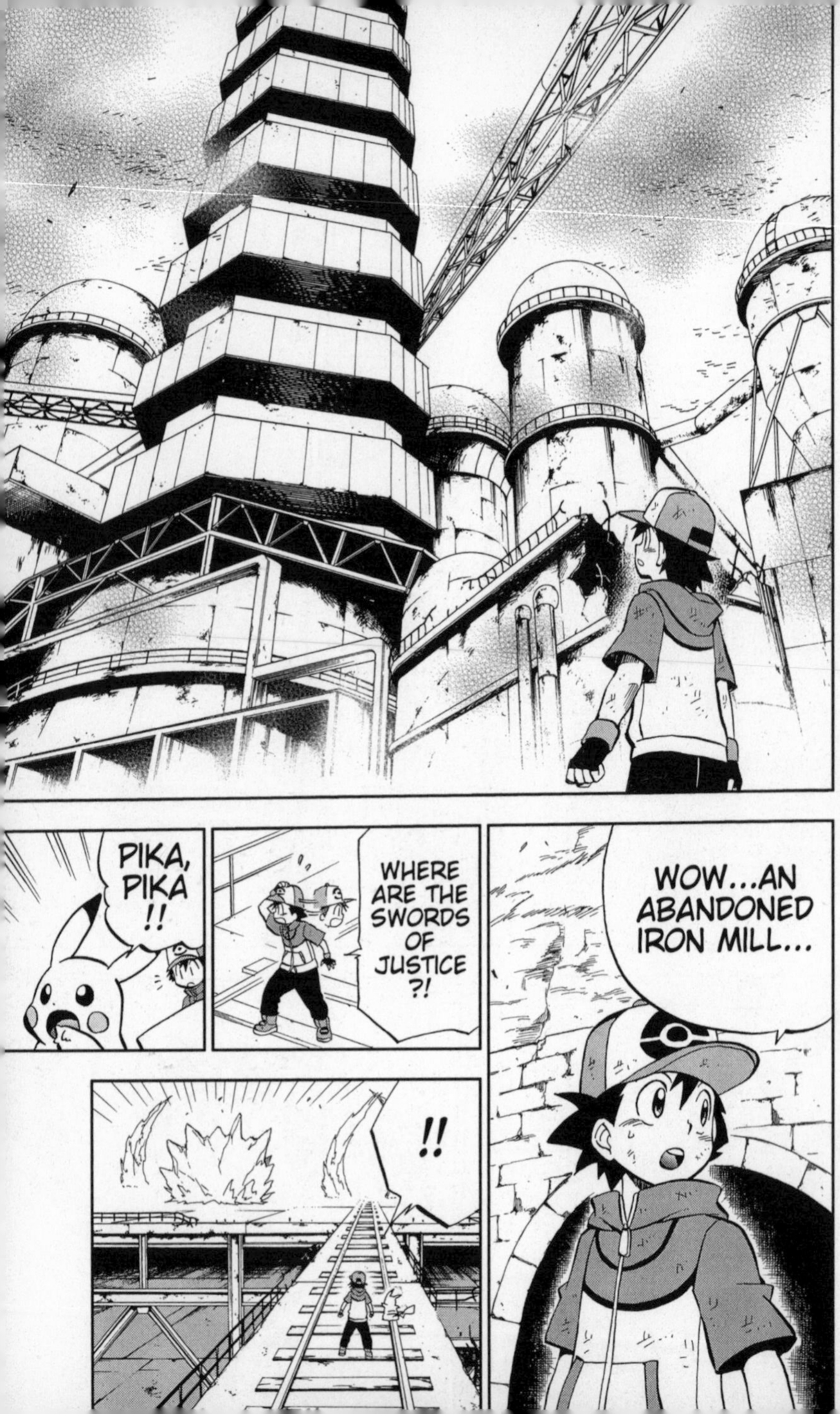
WOW...AN ABANDONED IRON MILL...
WHERE ARE THE SWORDS OF JUSTICE?!
PIKA, PIKA!!
!!

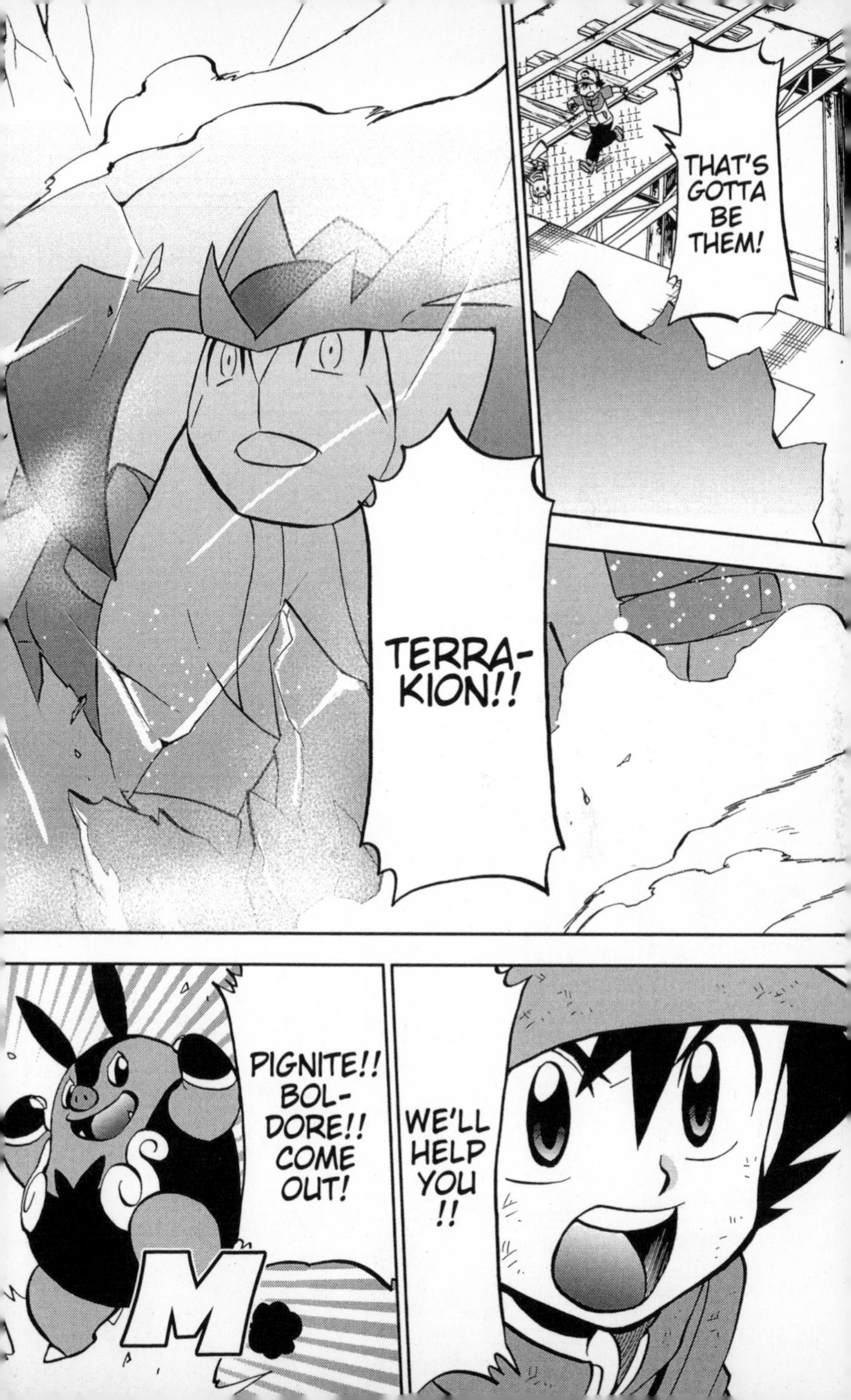
THAT'S GOTTA BE THEM!
TERRA-KION!!
WE'LL HELP YOU!!
PIGNITE!! BOL-DORE!! COME OUT!
M

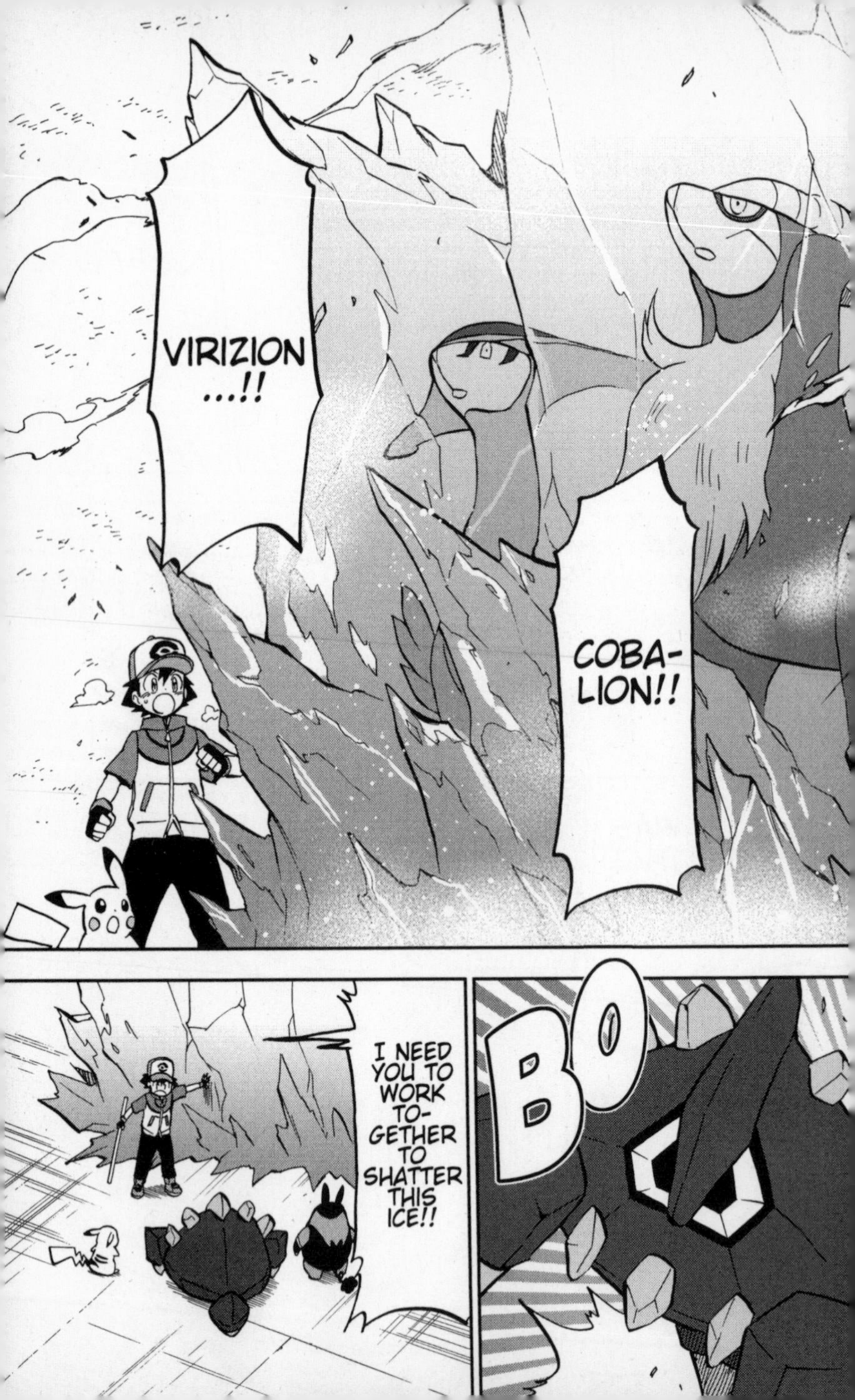
VIRIZION ...!!
COBA-LION!!
BO
I NEED YOU TO WORK TO-GETHER TO SHATTER THIS ICE!!

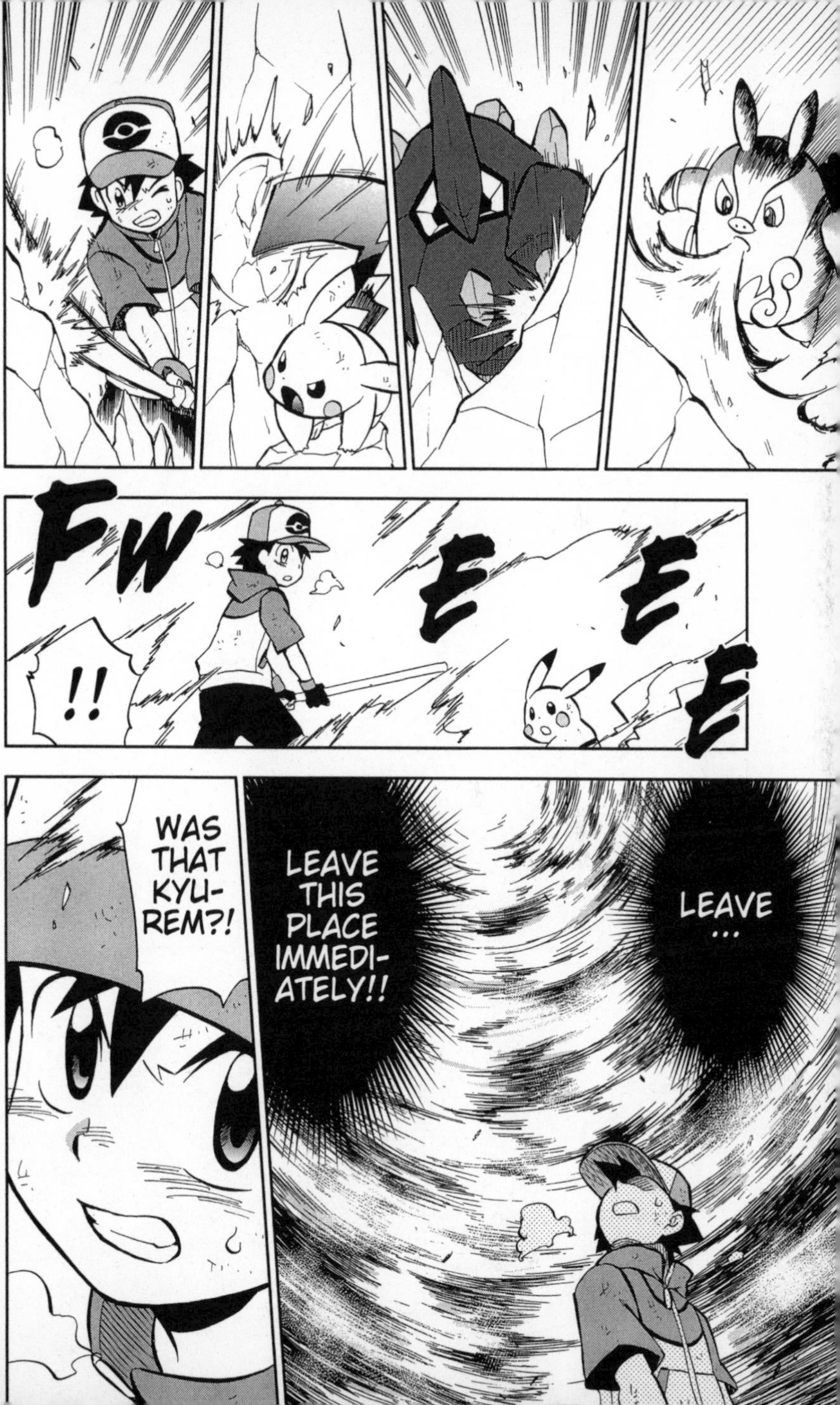
FWEEEE
!!
LEAVE ...
LEAVE THIS PLACE IMMEDIATELY!!
WAS THAT KYUREM?!

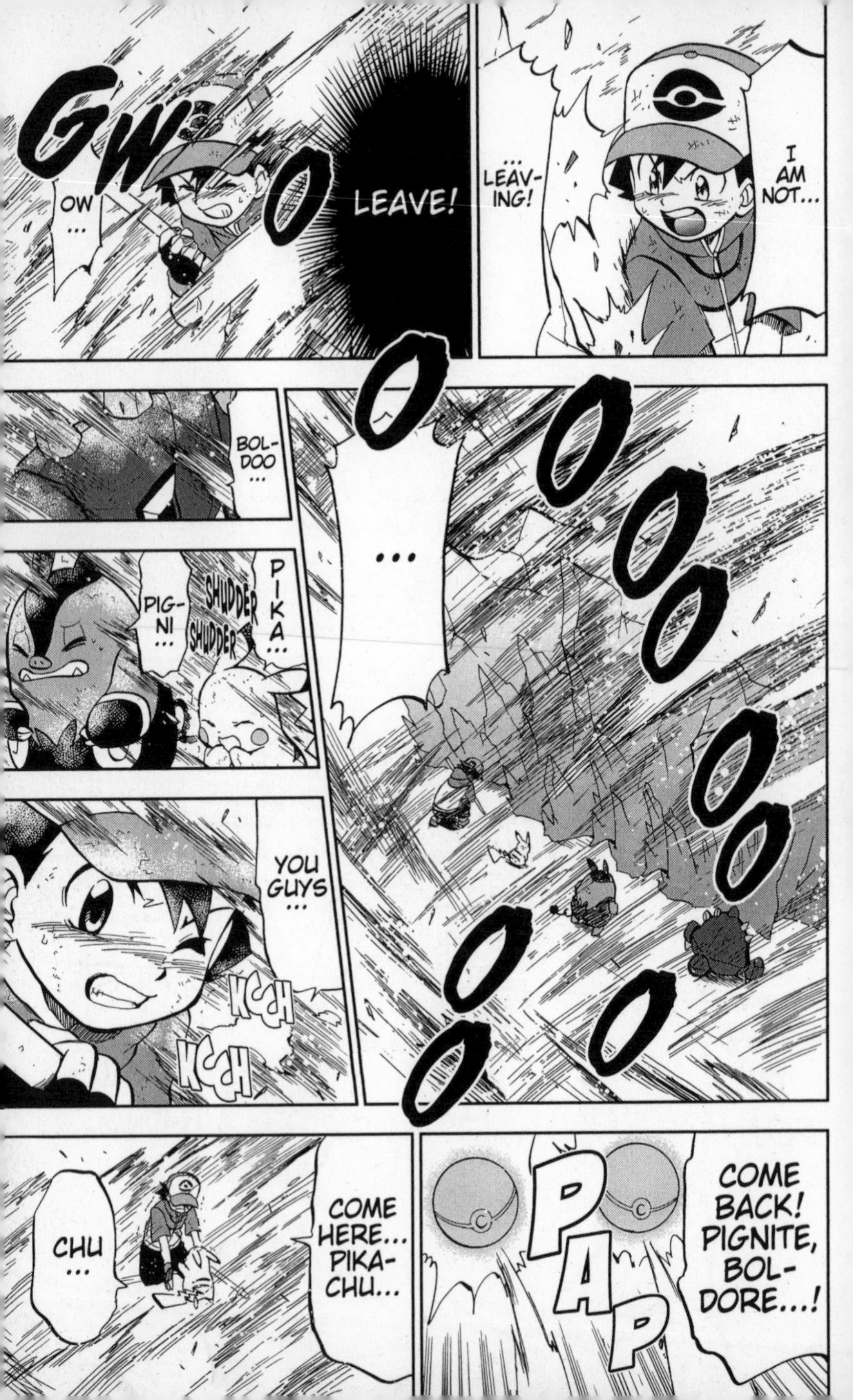
I AM NOT...
...LEAVING!
GWOOOOOOOOOO
LEAVE!
OW...
...
BOLDOO...
PIKA...
SHUDDER
SHUDDER
PIGNI...
YOU GUYS...
KCCH
KCCH
COME BACK! PIGNITE, BOLDORE...!
PAP
COME HERE... PIKACHU...
CHU...

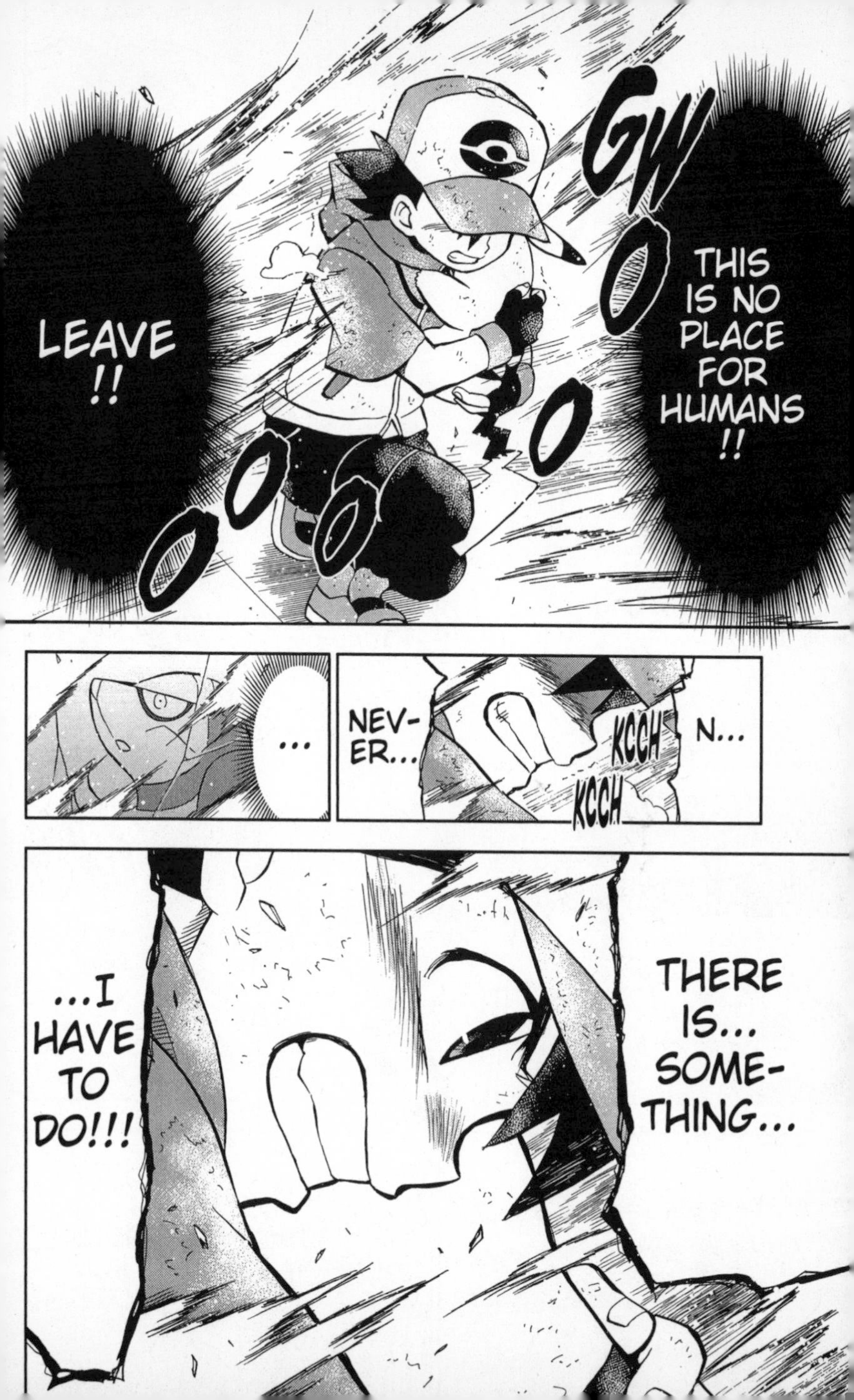
THIS IS NO PLACE FOR HUMANS!!
GW
LEAVE!!
N...
KCCH
KCCH
NEV- ER...
...
THERE IS... SOME- THING...
...I HAVE TO DO!!!

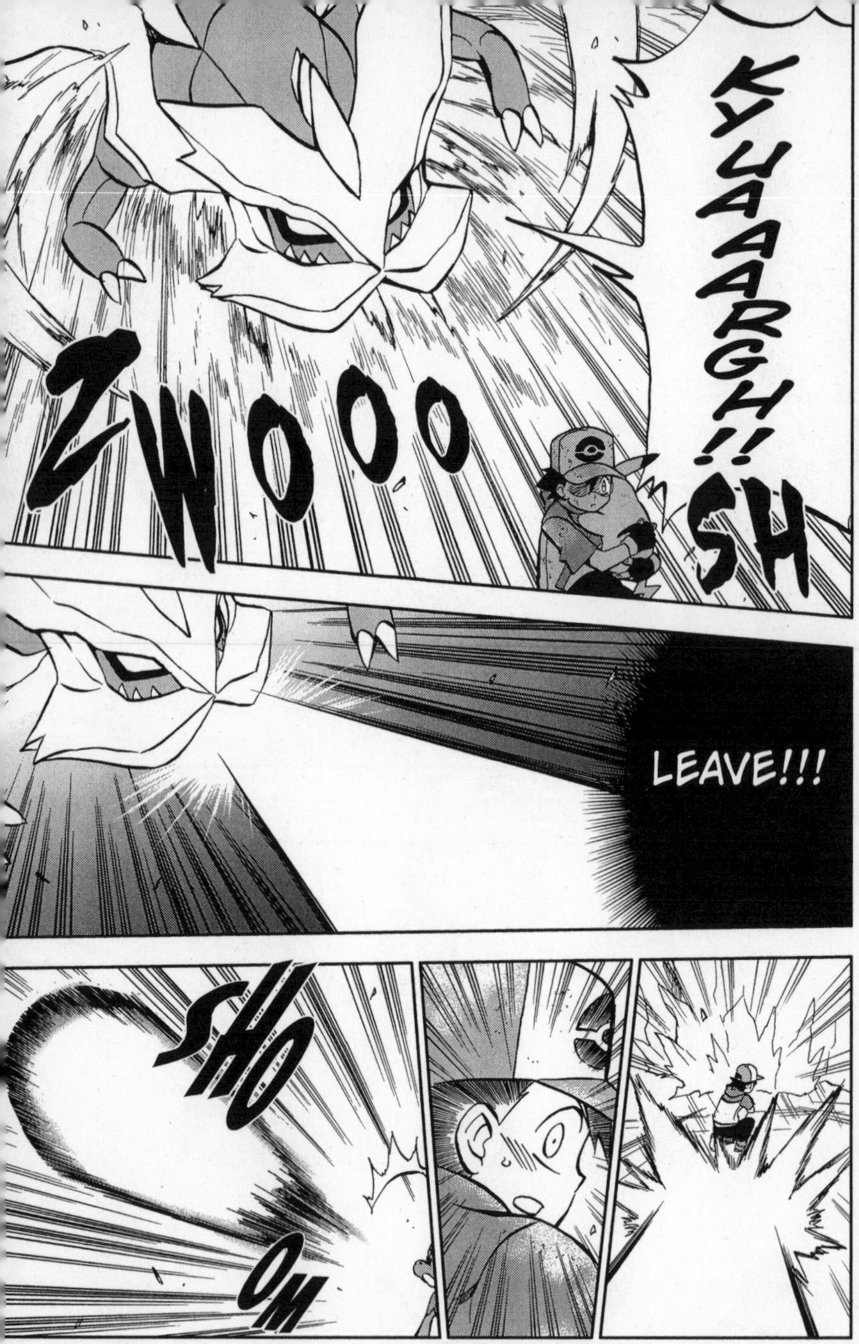
KYUAAAARGH!!
ZWOOOSH
LEAVE!!!
SHOOM

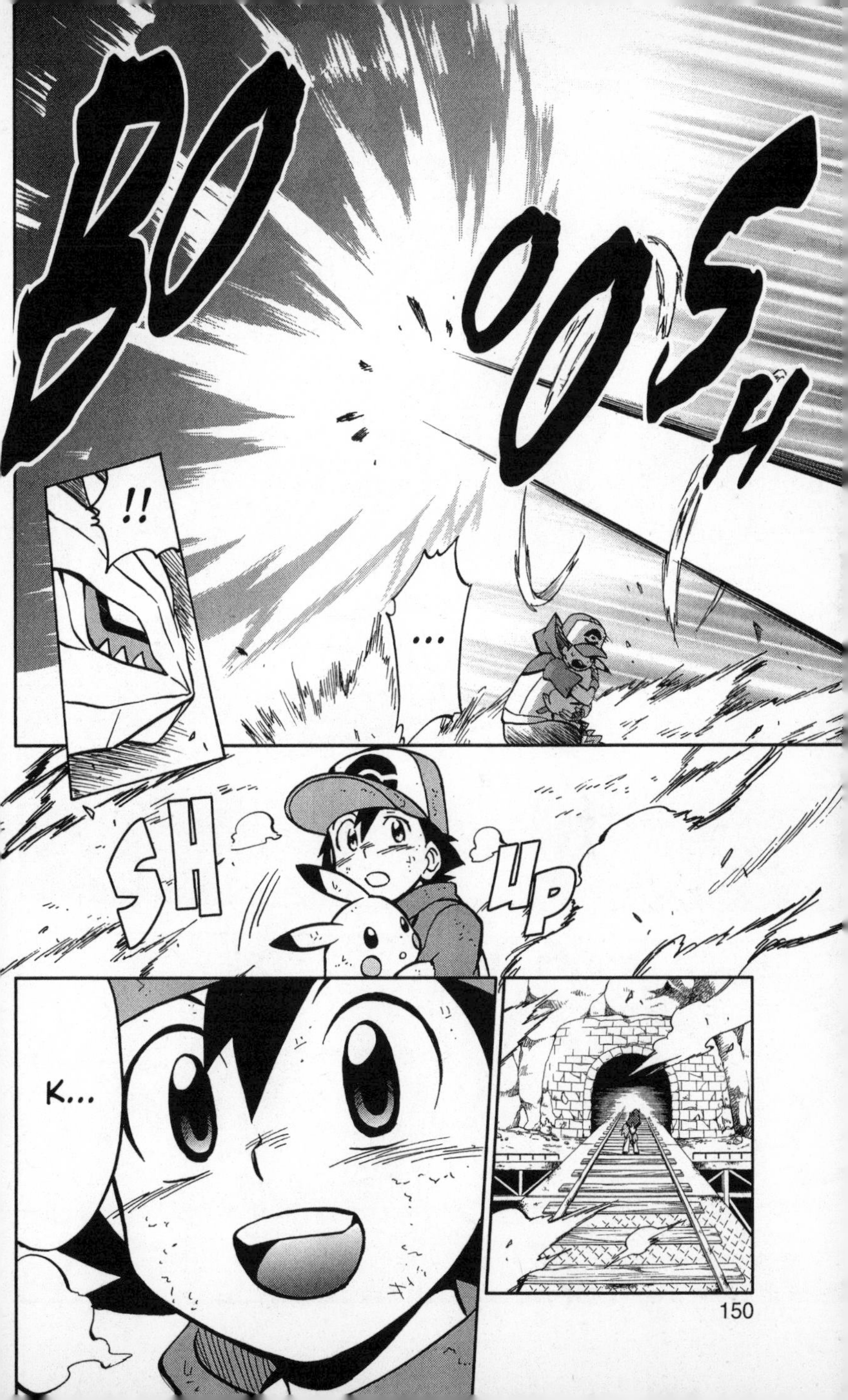
BOOOSH
...
!!
SHUP
K...

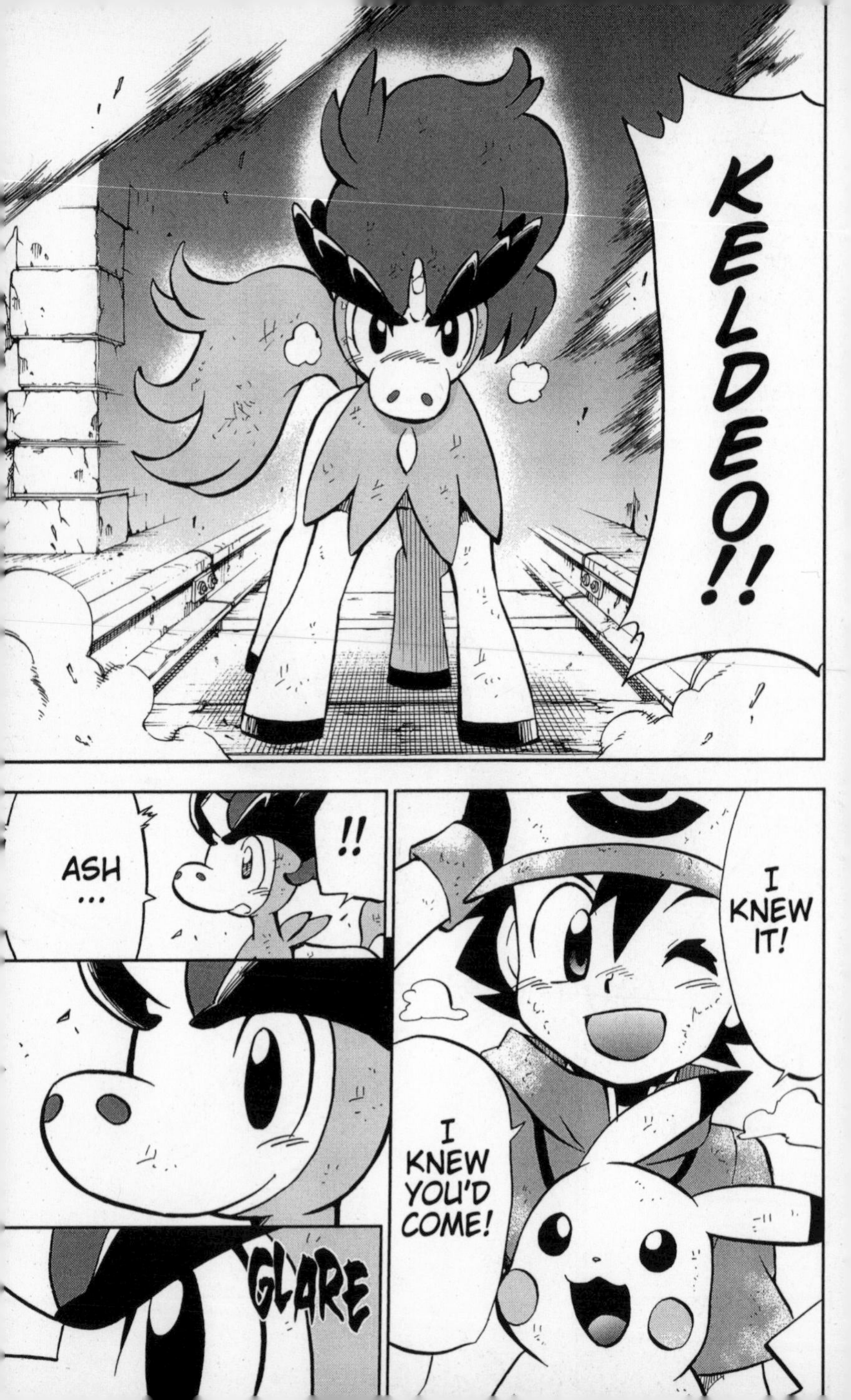
KELDEO!!
I KNEW IT!
I KNEW YOU'D COME!
ASH ...
!!
GLARE

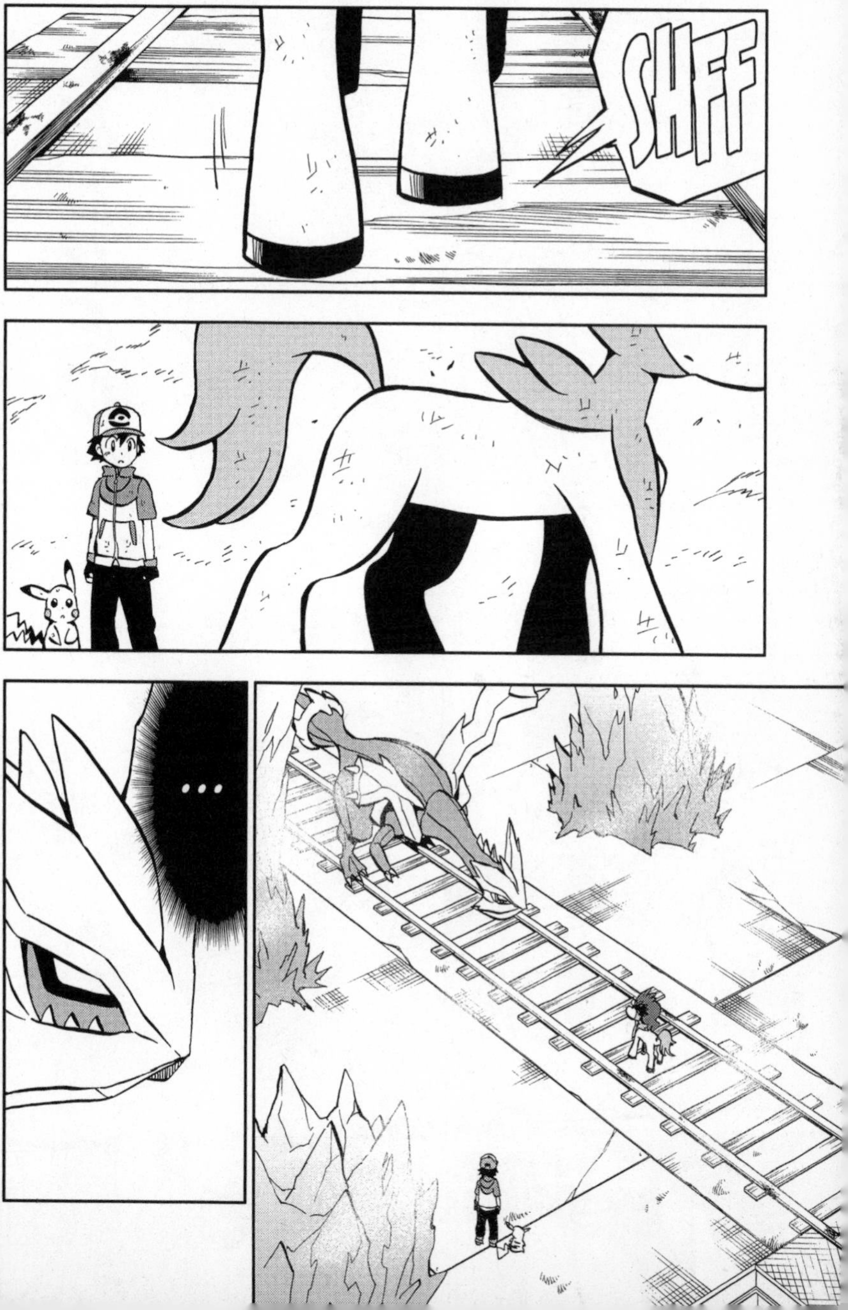
SHFF
...

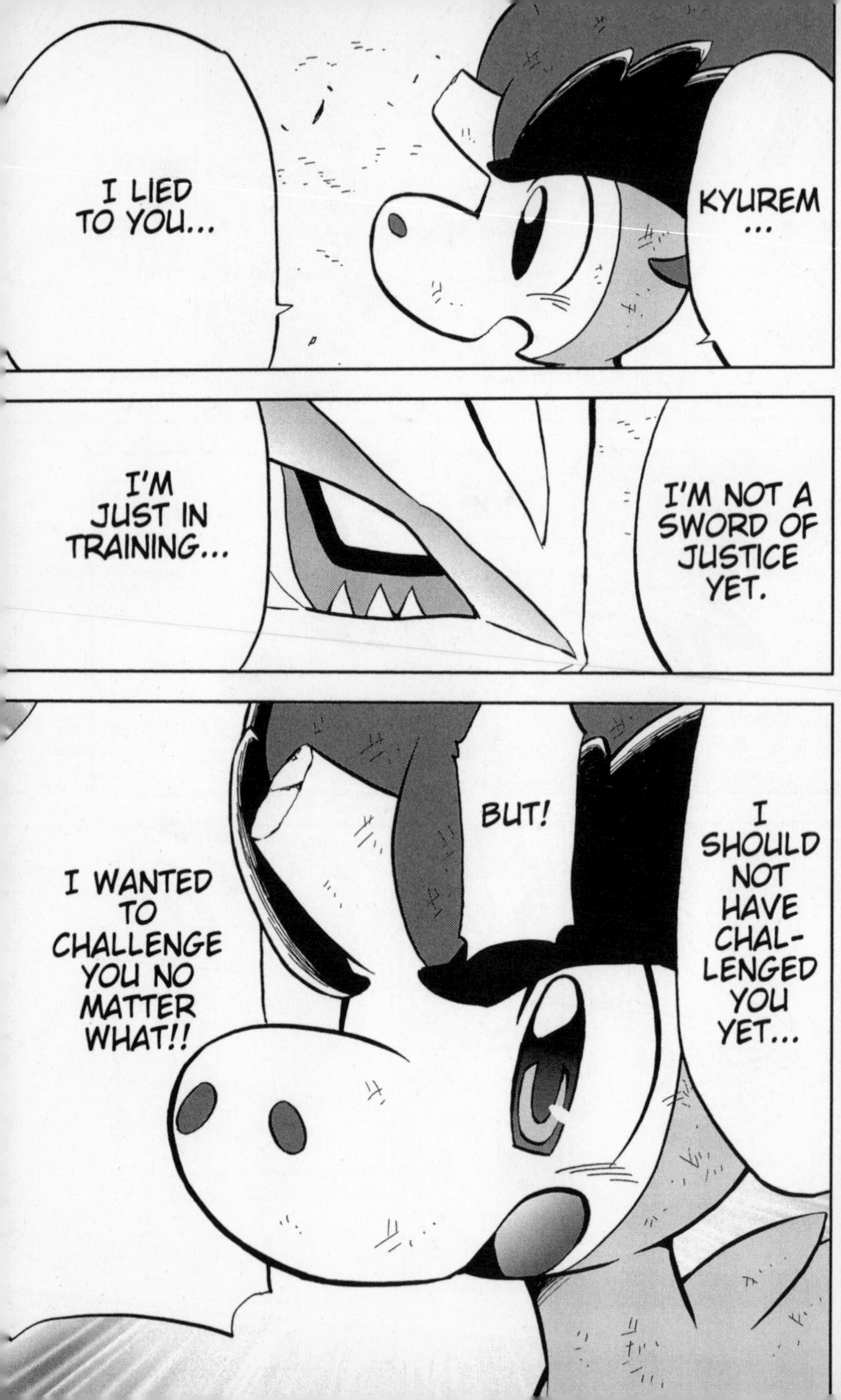
KYUREM ...
I LIED TO YOU...
I'M NOT A SWORD OF JUSTICE YET.
I'M JUST IN TRAINING...
I SHOULD NOT HAVE CHAL-LENGED YOU YET...
BUT!
I WANTED TO CHALLENGE YOU NO MATTER WHAT!!

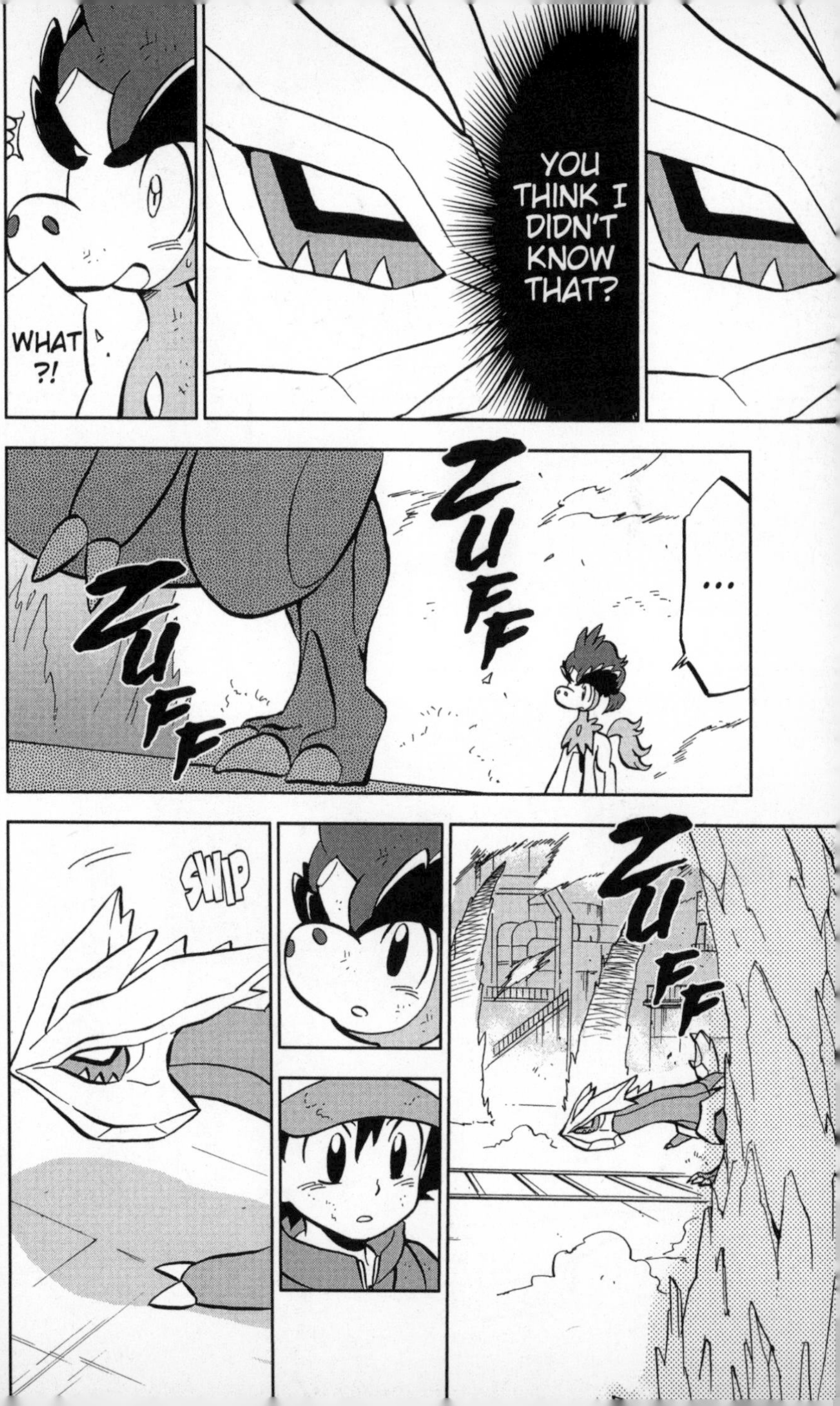
YOU THINK I DIDN'T KNOW THAT?
WHAT ?!
...
ZUFF
ZUFF
ZUFF
SWIP

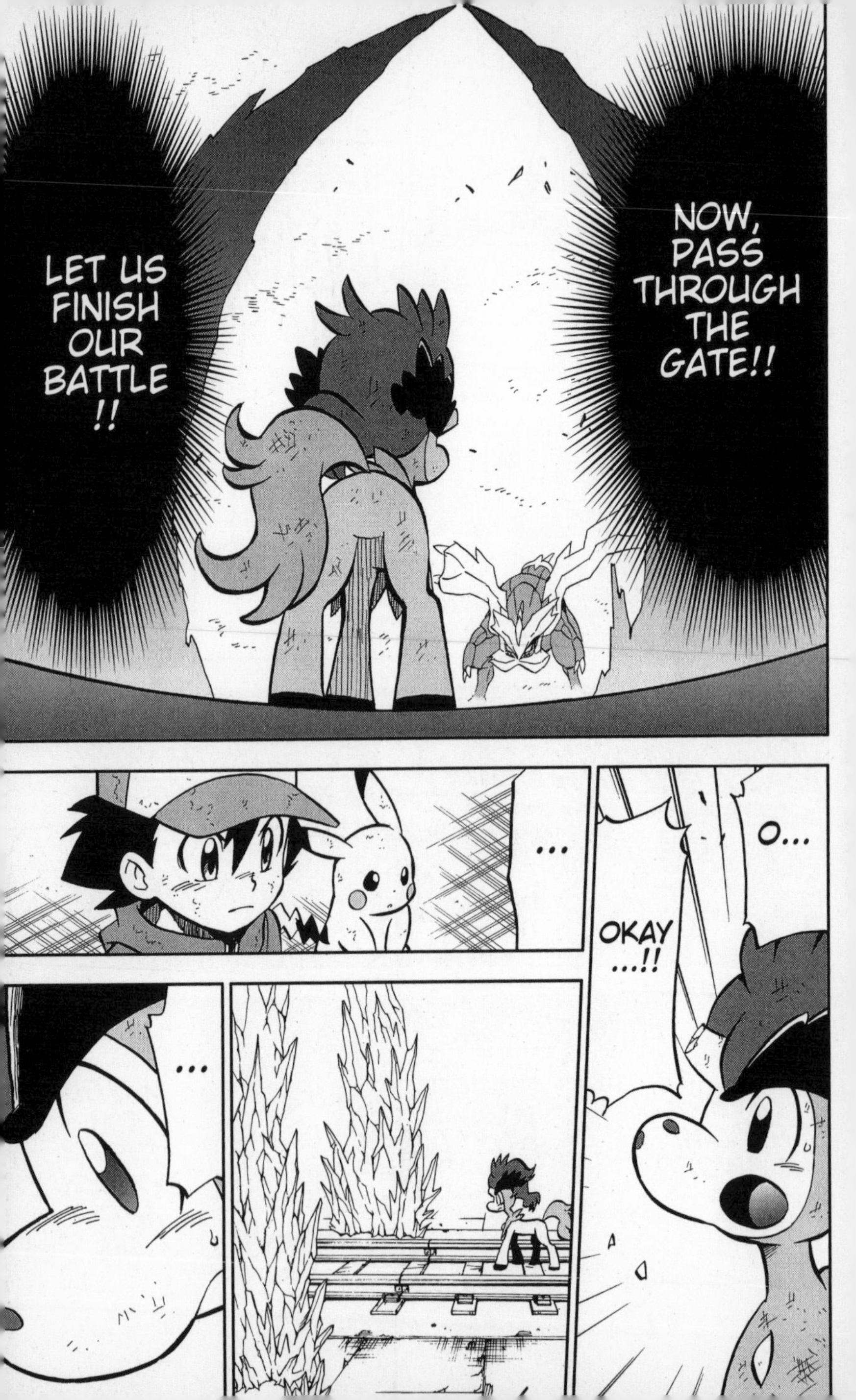
NOW, PASS THROUGH THE GATE!!
LET US FINISH OUR BATTLE!!
O...
OKAY ...!!
...
...

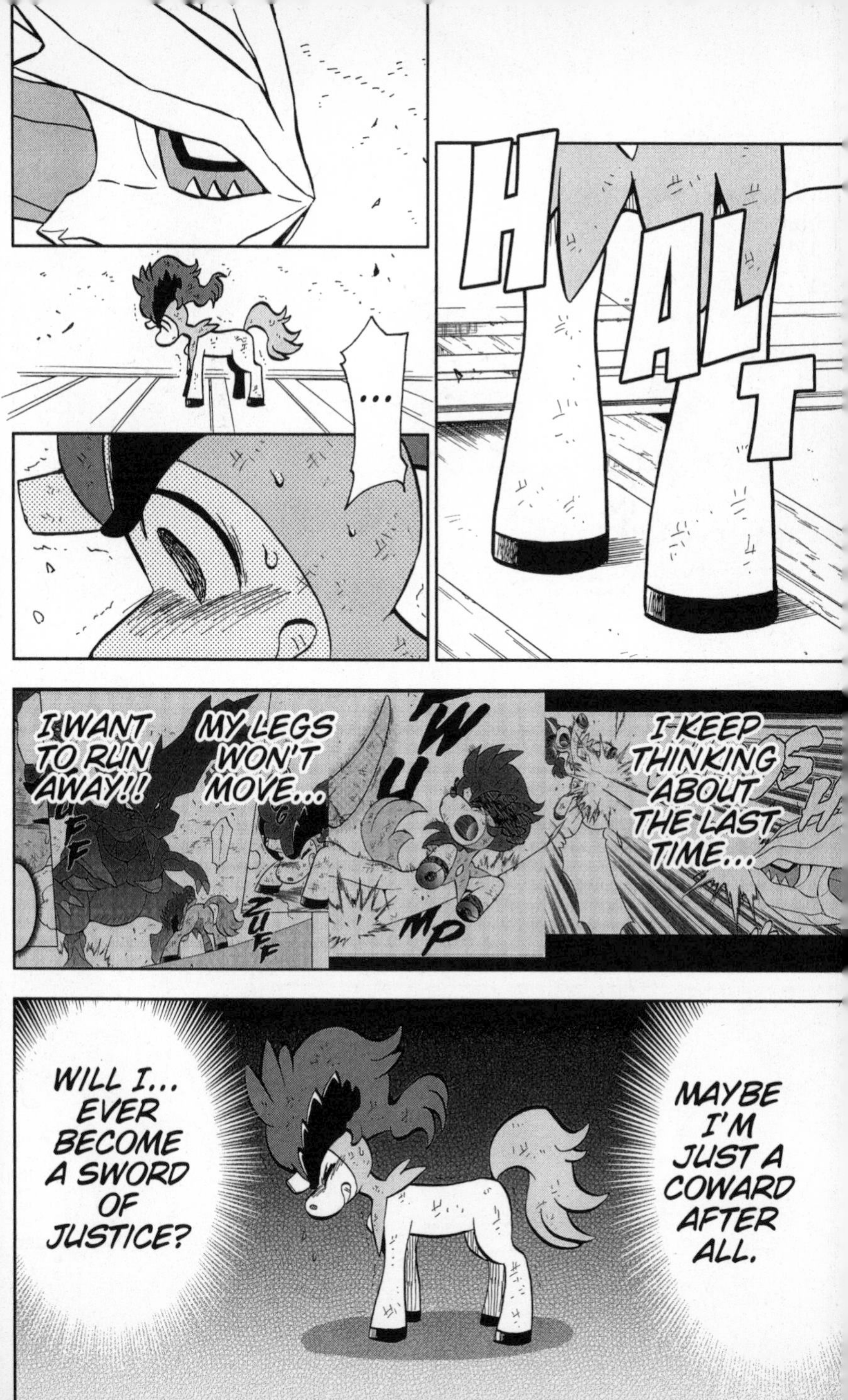
HALT
...
I KEEP THINKING ABOUT THE LAST TIME...
WUMP
MY LEGS WON'T MOVE...
ZUFF
I WANT TO RUN AWAY!!
MAYBE I'M JUST A COWARD AFTER ALL.
WILL I... EVER BECOME A SWORD OF JUSTICE?

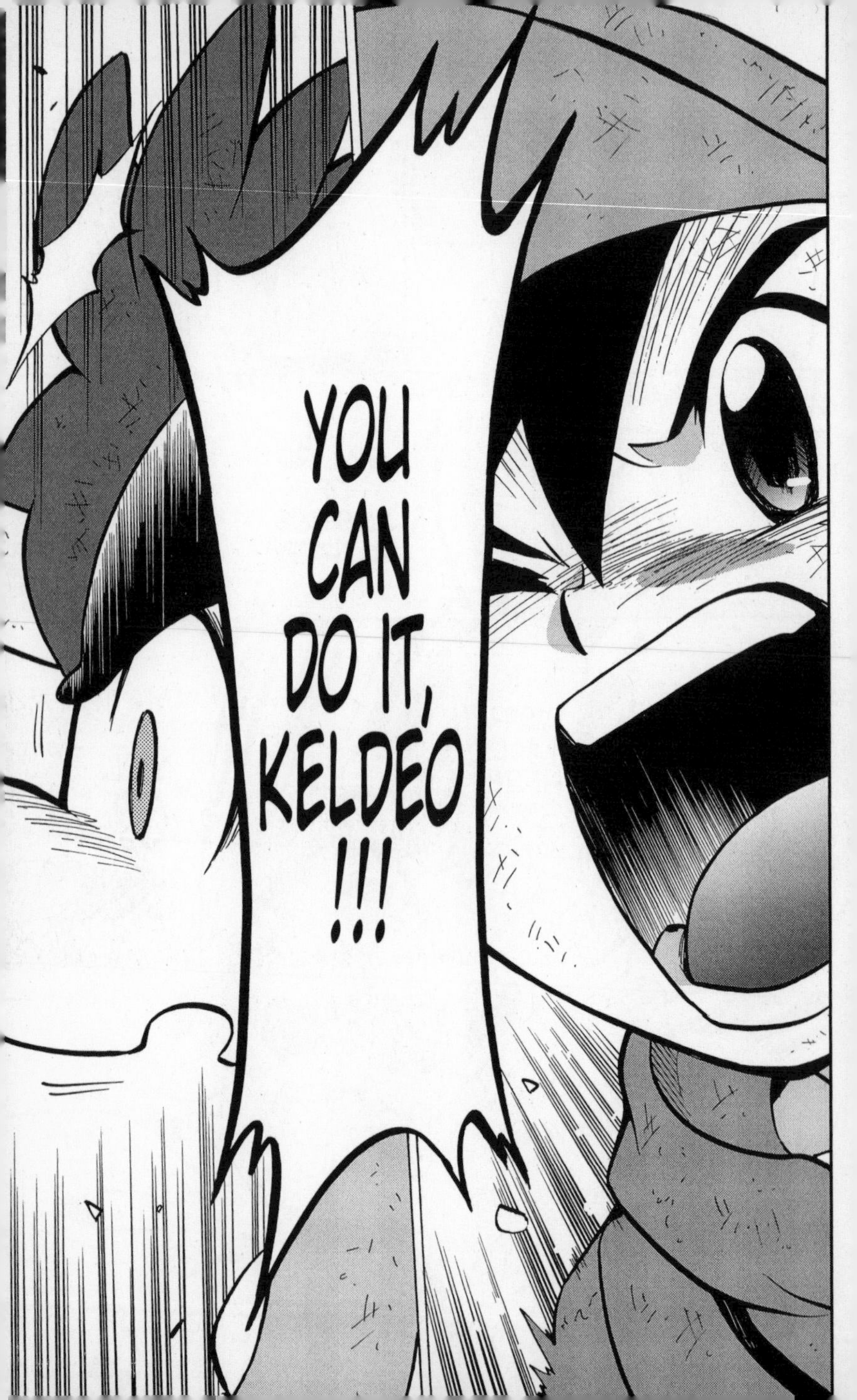
YOU CAN DO IT, KELDEO !!!

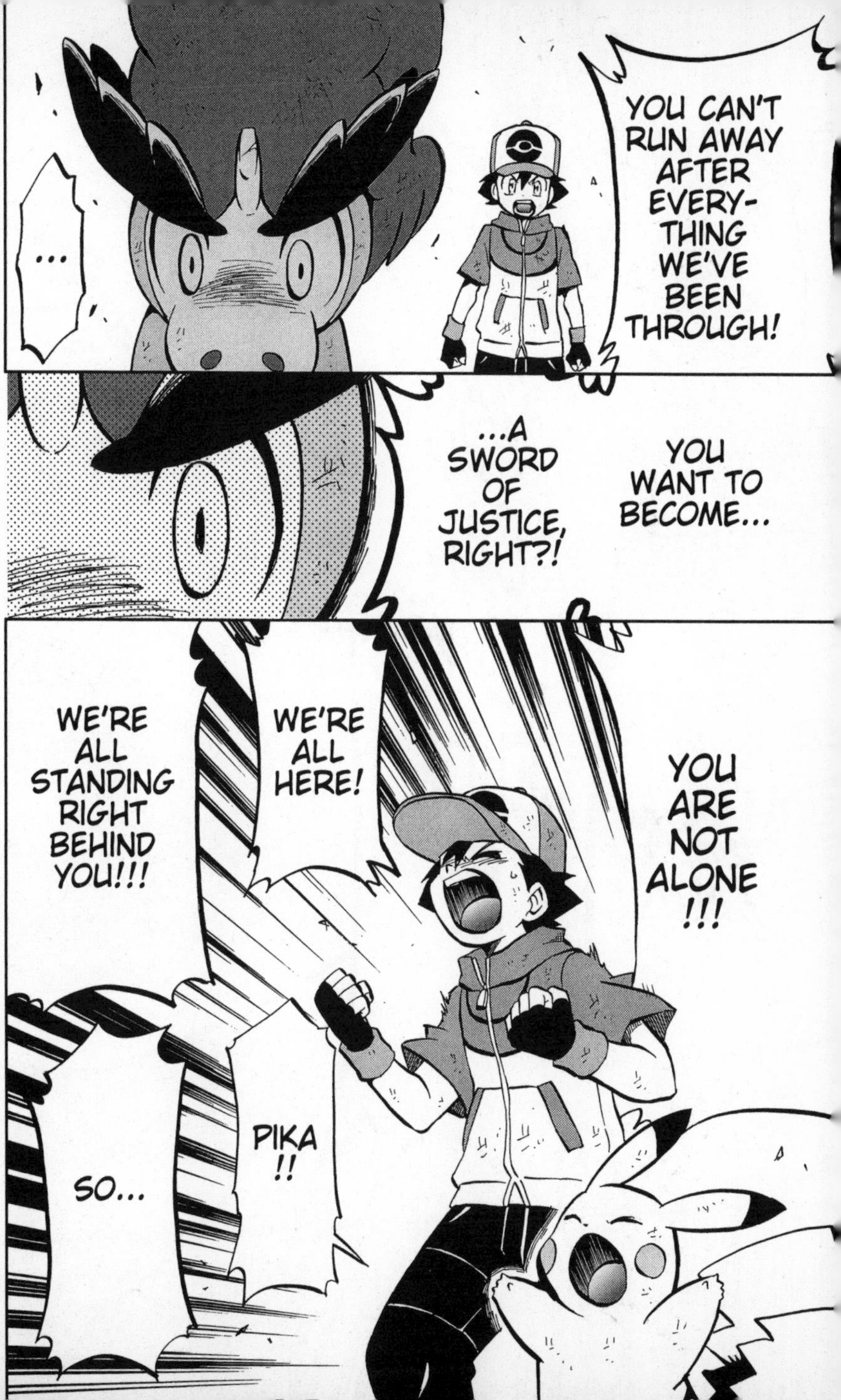
YOU CAN'T RUN AWAY AFTER EVERY-THING WE'VE BEEN THROUGH!
...
YOU WANT TO BECOME...
...A SWORD OF JUSTICE, RIGHT?!
YOU ARE NOT ALONE!!!
WE'RE ALL HERE!
WE'RE ALL STANDING RIGHT BEHIND YOU!!!
PIKA!!
SO...

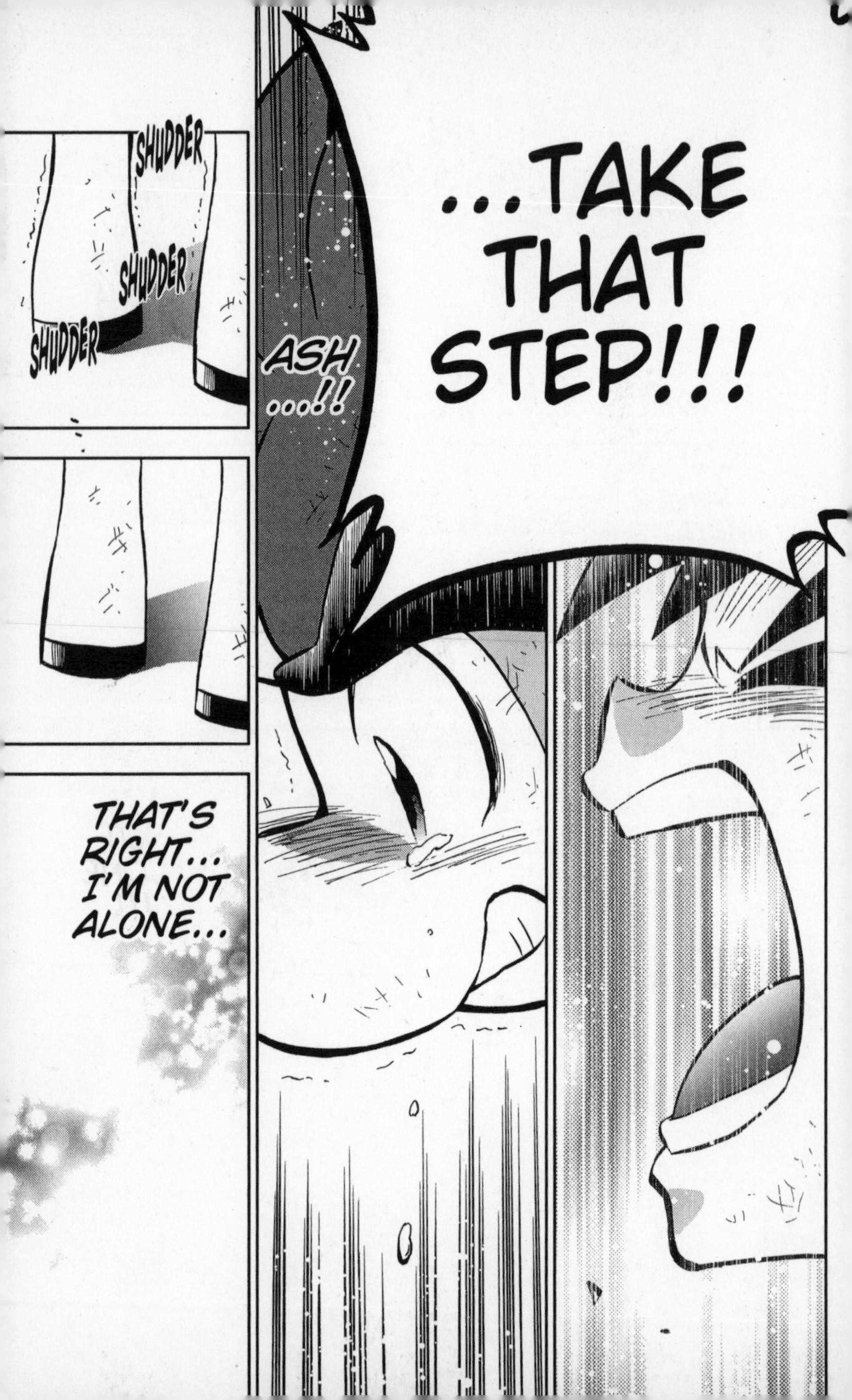
...TAKE THAT STEP!!!
ASH ...!!
SHUDDER
SHUDDER
SHUDDER
THAT'S RIGHT... I'M NOT ALONE...

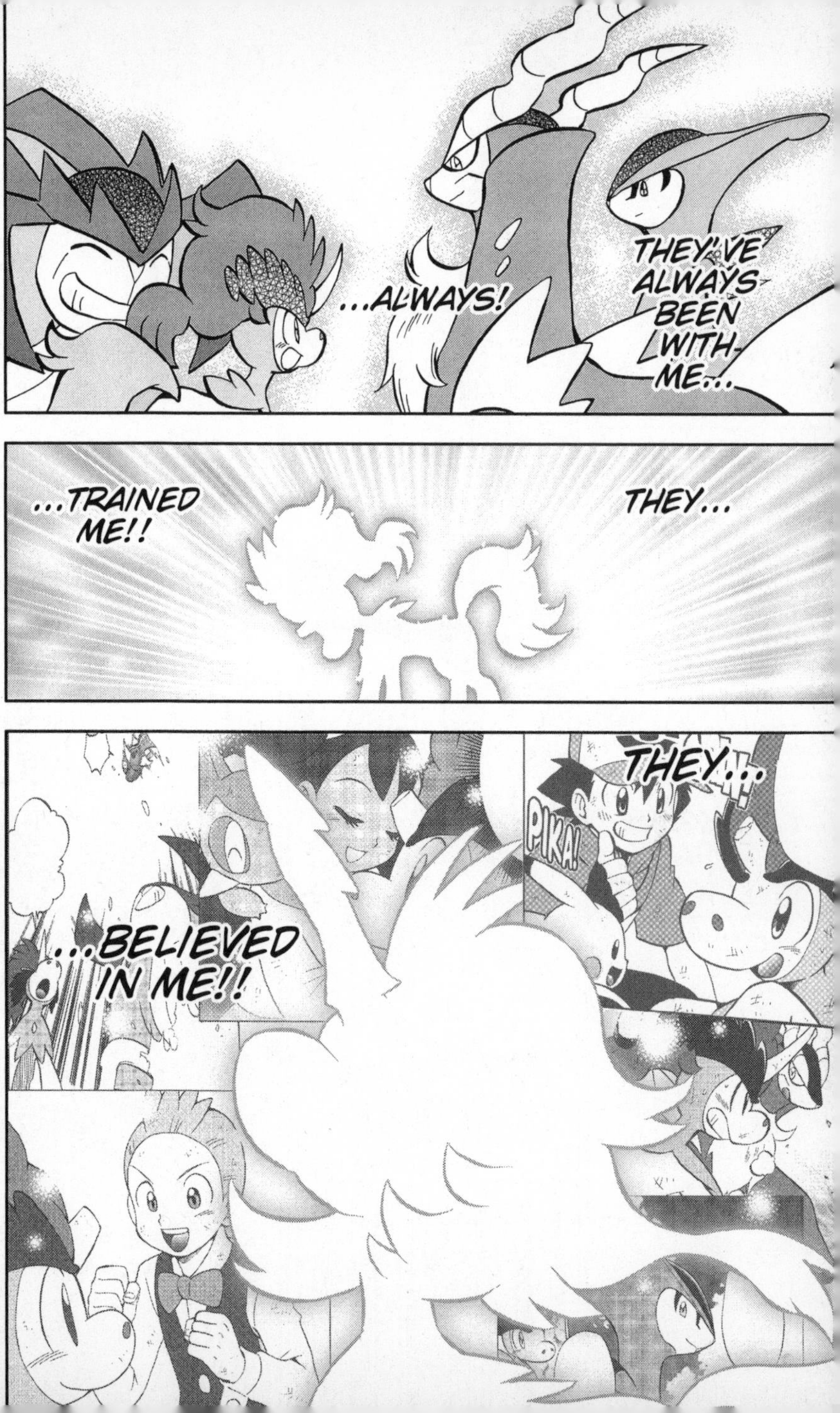
THEY'VE ALWAYS BEEN WITH ME...
...ALWAYS!
THEY...
...TRAINED ME!!
THEY...
PIKA!
...BELIEVED IN ME!!

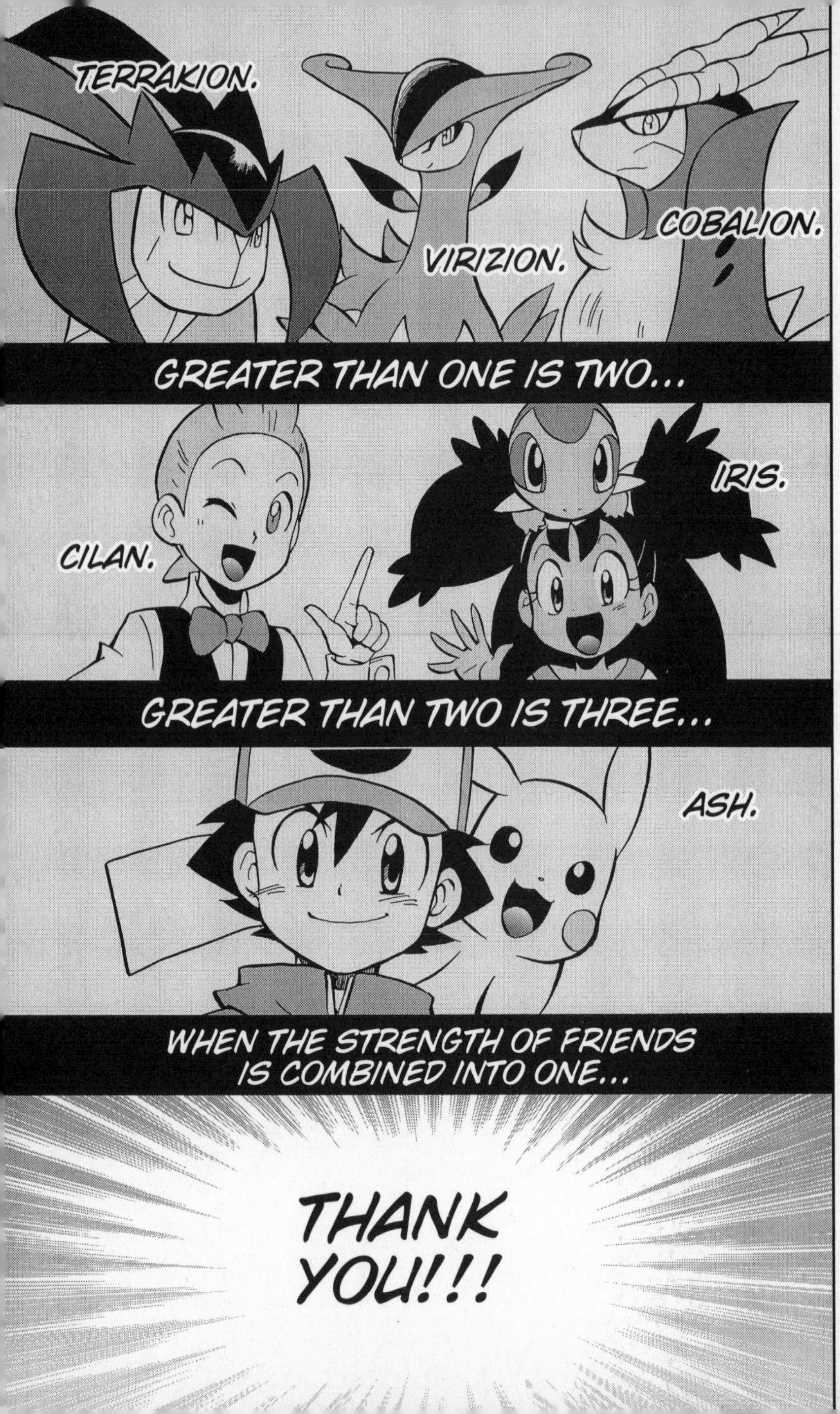
COBALION.
VIRIZION.
TERRAKION.
GREATER THAN ONE IS TWO...
IRIS.
CILAN.
GREATER THAN TWO IS THREE...
ASH.
WHEN THE STRENGTH OF FRIENDS IS COMBINED INTO ONE...
THANK YOU!!!

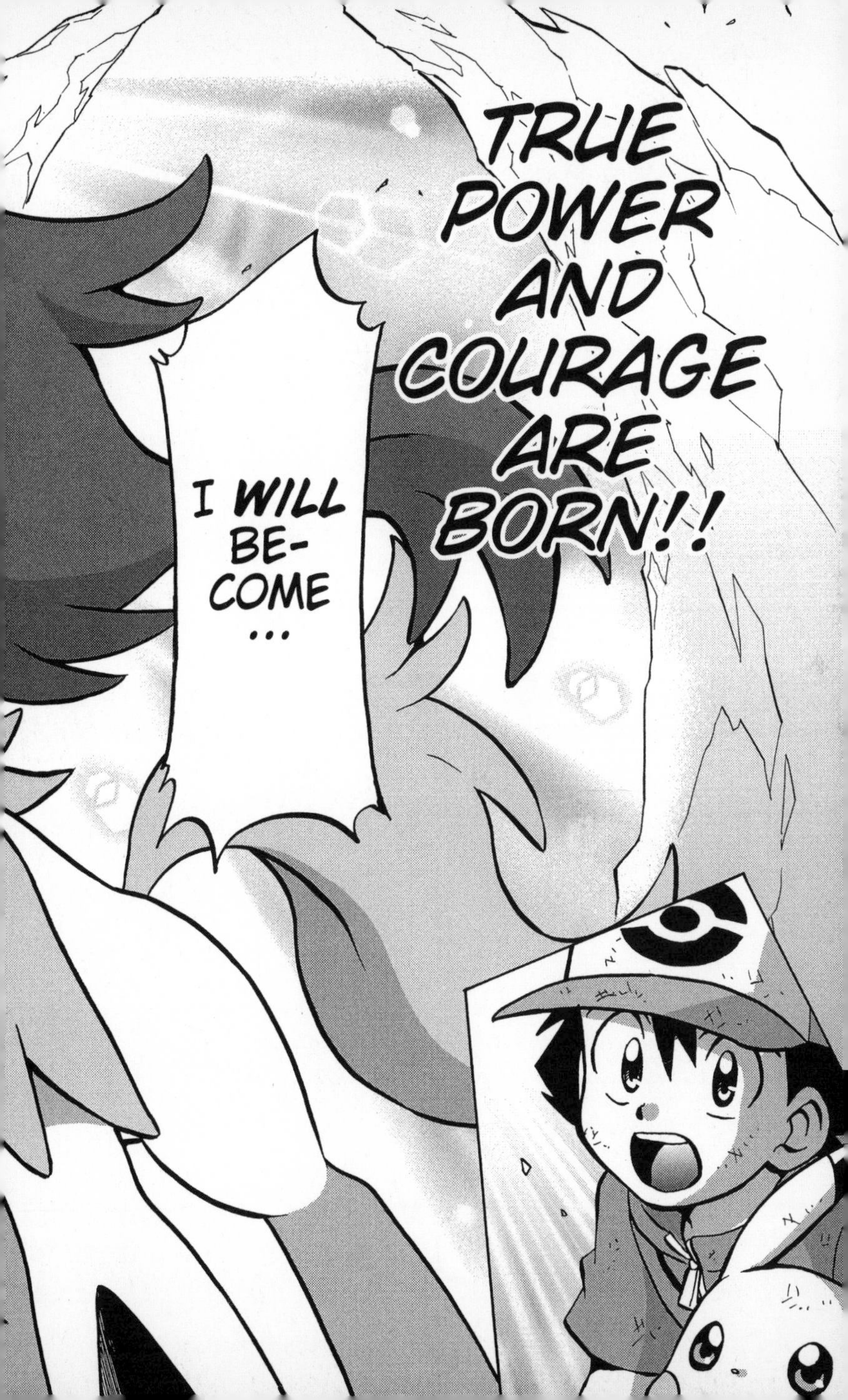
TRUE POWER AND COURAGE ARE BORN!!
I WILL BE-COME...

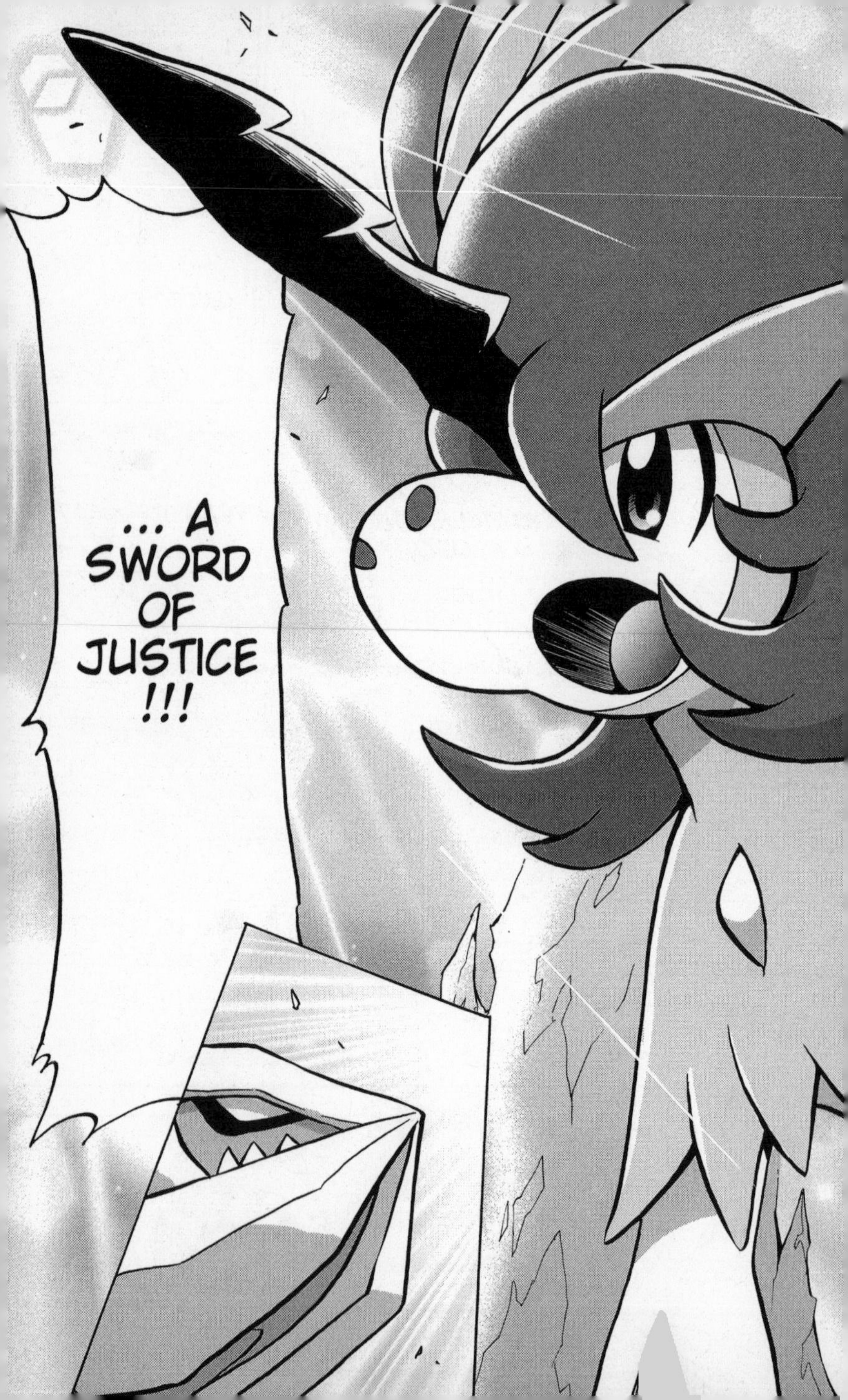
... A SWORD OF JUSTICE !!!

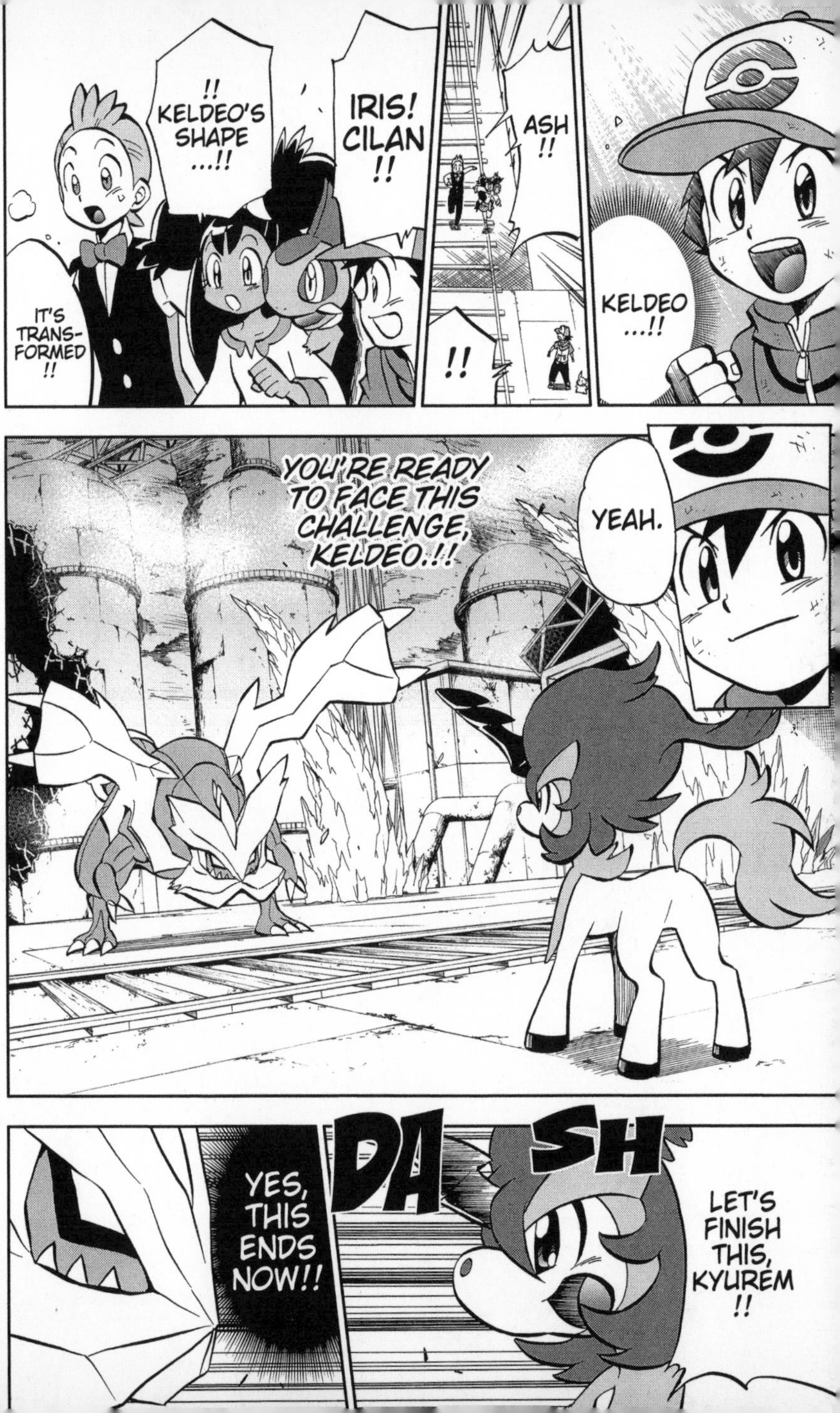
KELDEO ...!!
ASH !!
!!
IRIS! CILAN !!
!! KELDEO'S SHAPE ...!!
IT'S TRANS-FORMED !!
YEAH.
YOU'RE READY TO FACE THIS CHALLENGE, KELDEO.!!
LET'S FINISH THIS, KYUREM !!
DASH
YES, THIS ENDS NOW!!

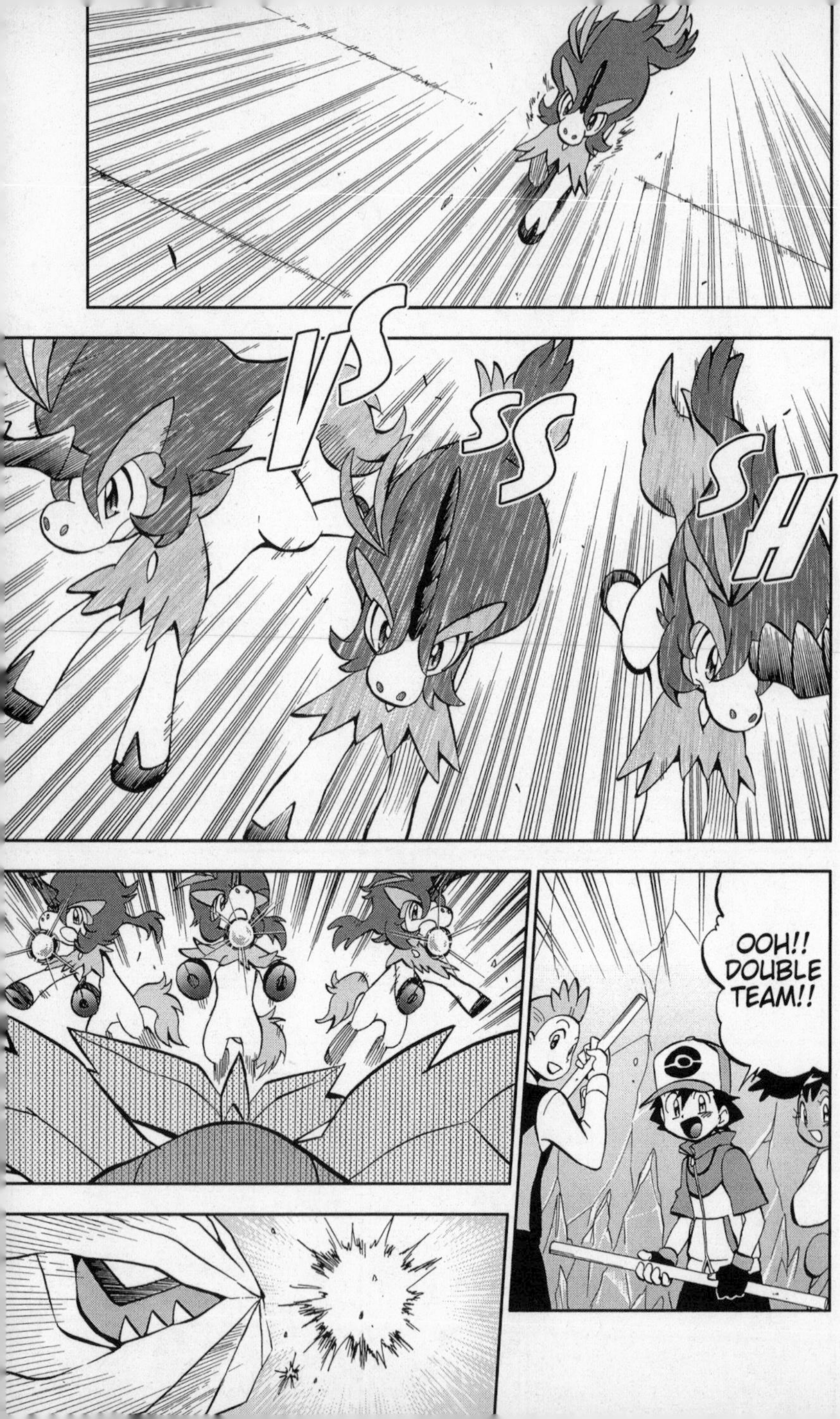
VSSSH
OOH!! DOUBLE TEAM!!

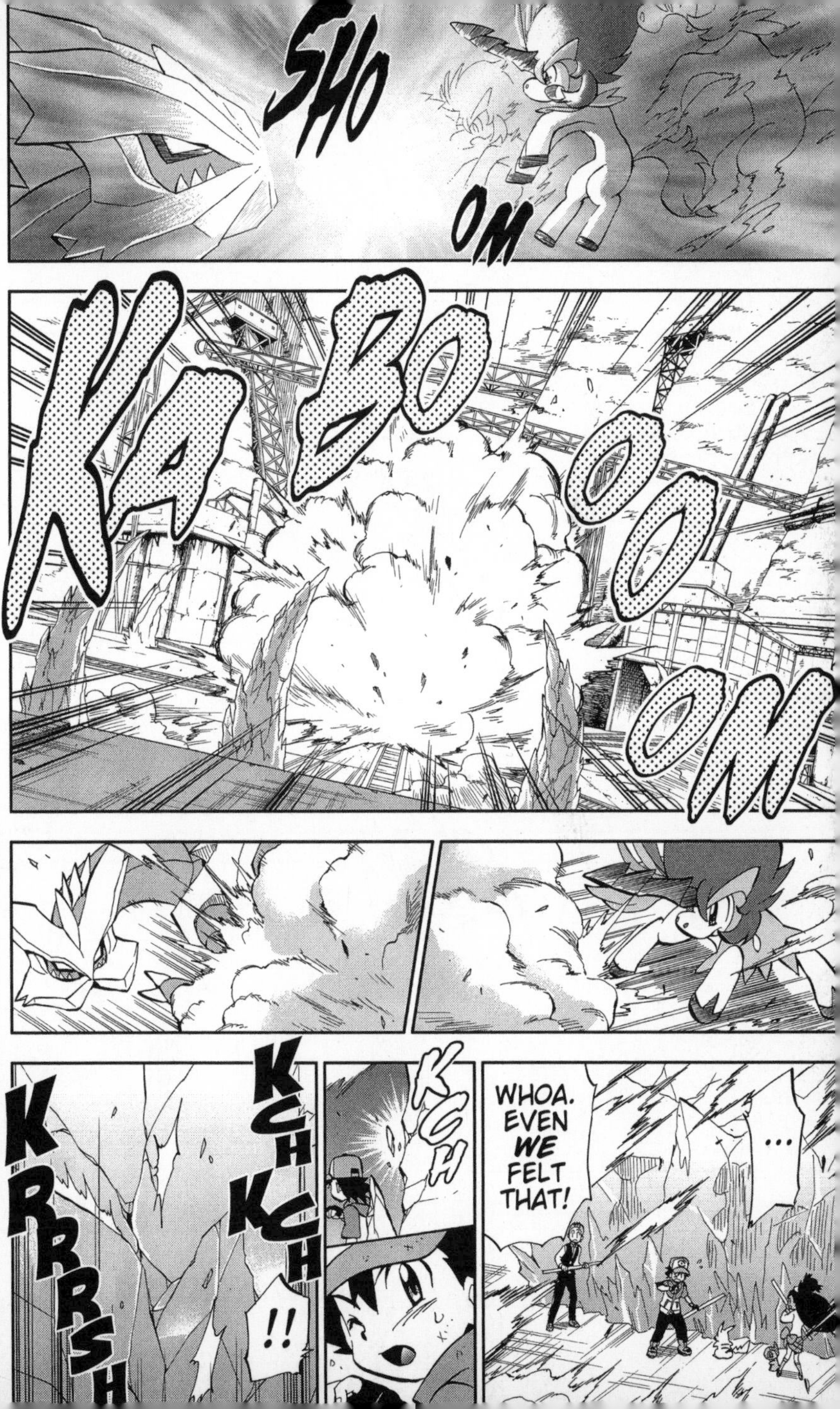
SHOOM
KABOOOOM
...
WHOA. EVEN WE FELT THAT!
KCH
!!
KCH KCH
KRRRSH

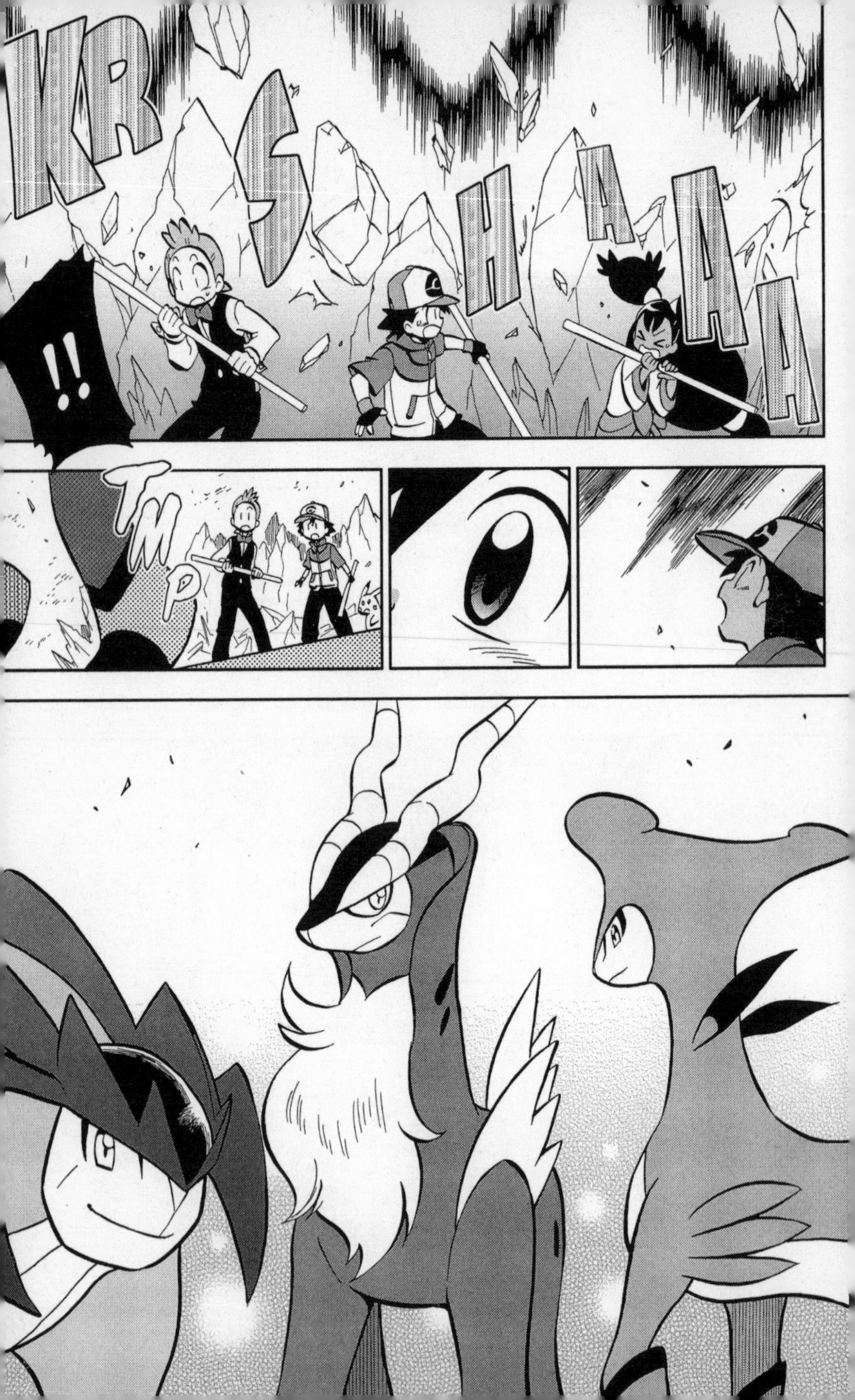
KRSHAAAA
!!
TMP

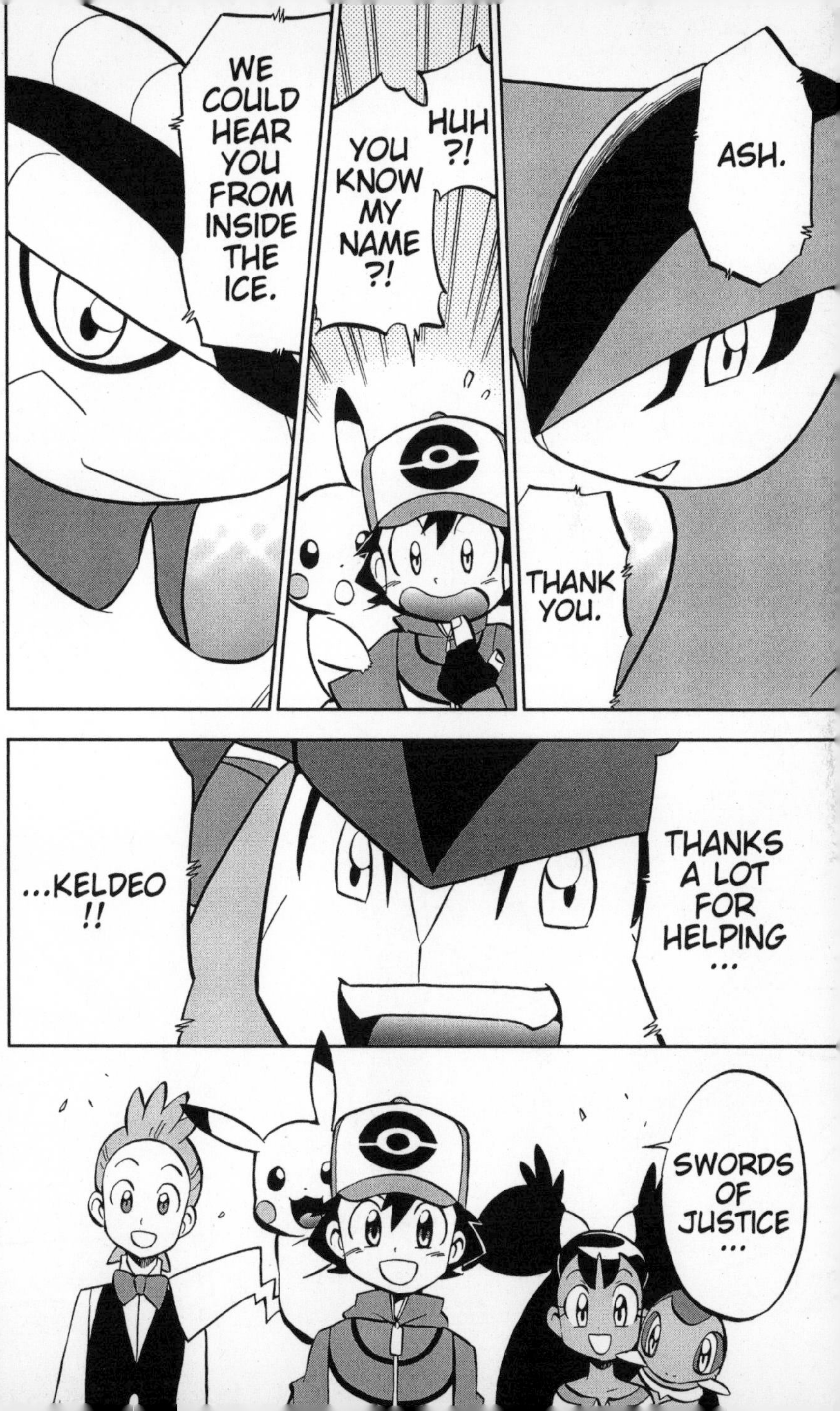
ASH.
THANK YOU.
HUH ?!
YOU KNOW MY NAME ?!
WE COULD HEAR YOU FROM INSIDE THE ICE.
THANKS A LOT FOR HELPING ...
...KELDEO !!
SWORDS OF JUSTICE ...

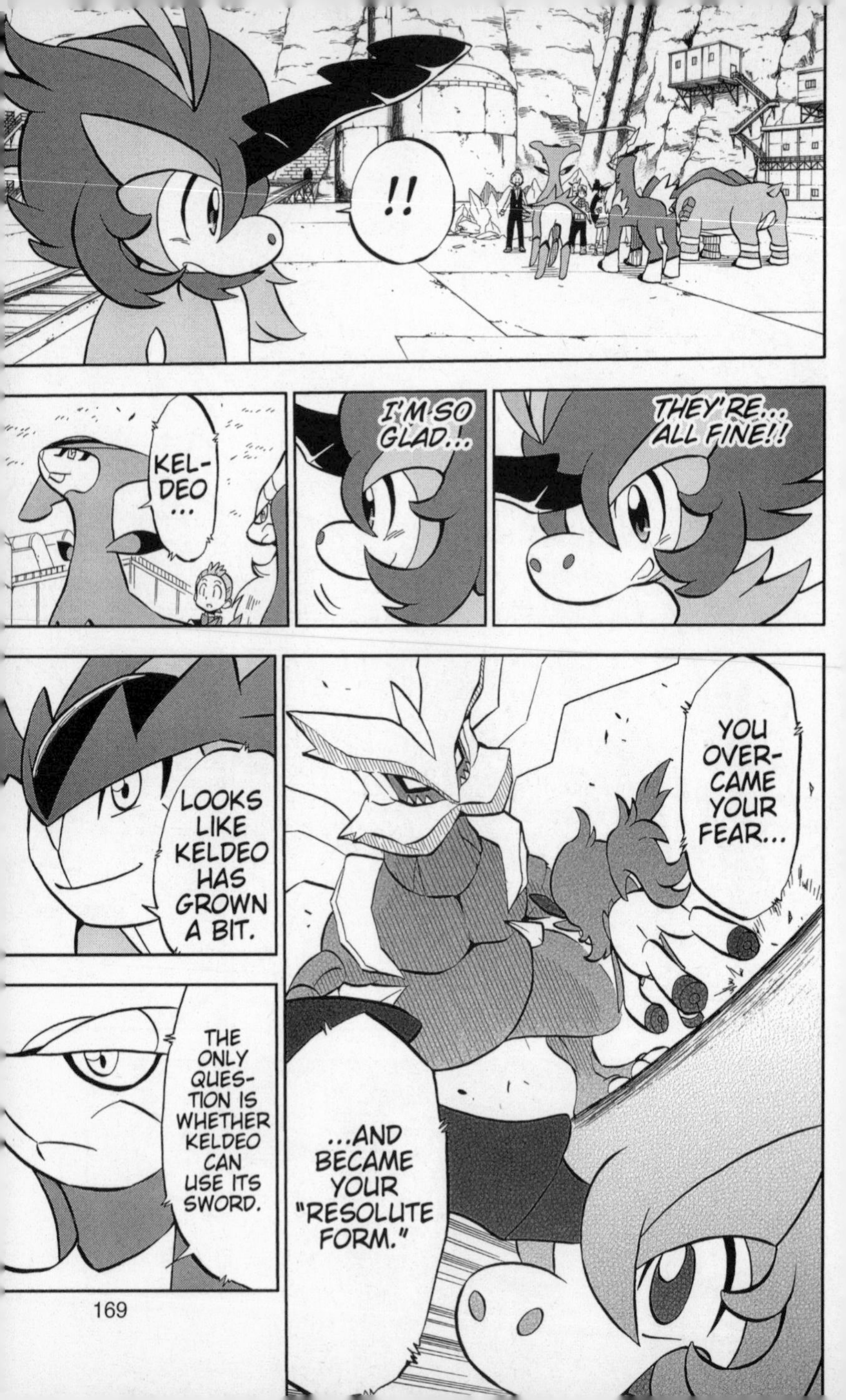
!!
THEY'RE... ALL FINE!!
I'M SO GLAD...
KEL-DEO...
YOU OVER-CAME YOUR FEAR...
...AND BECAME YOUR "RESOLUTE FORM."
LOOKS LIKE KELDEO HAS GROWN A BIT.
THE ONLY QUES-TION IS WHETHER KELDEO CAN USE ITS SWORD.

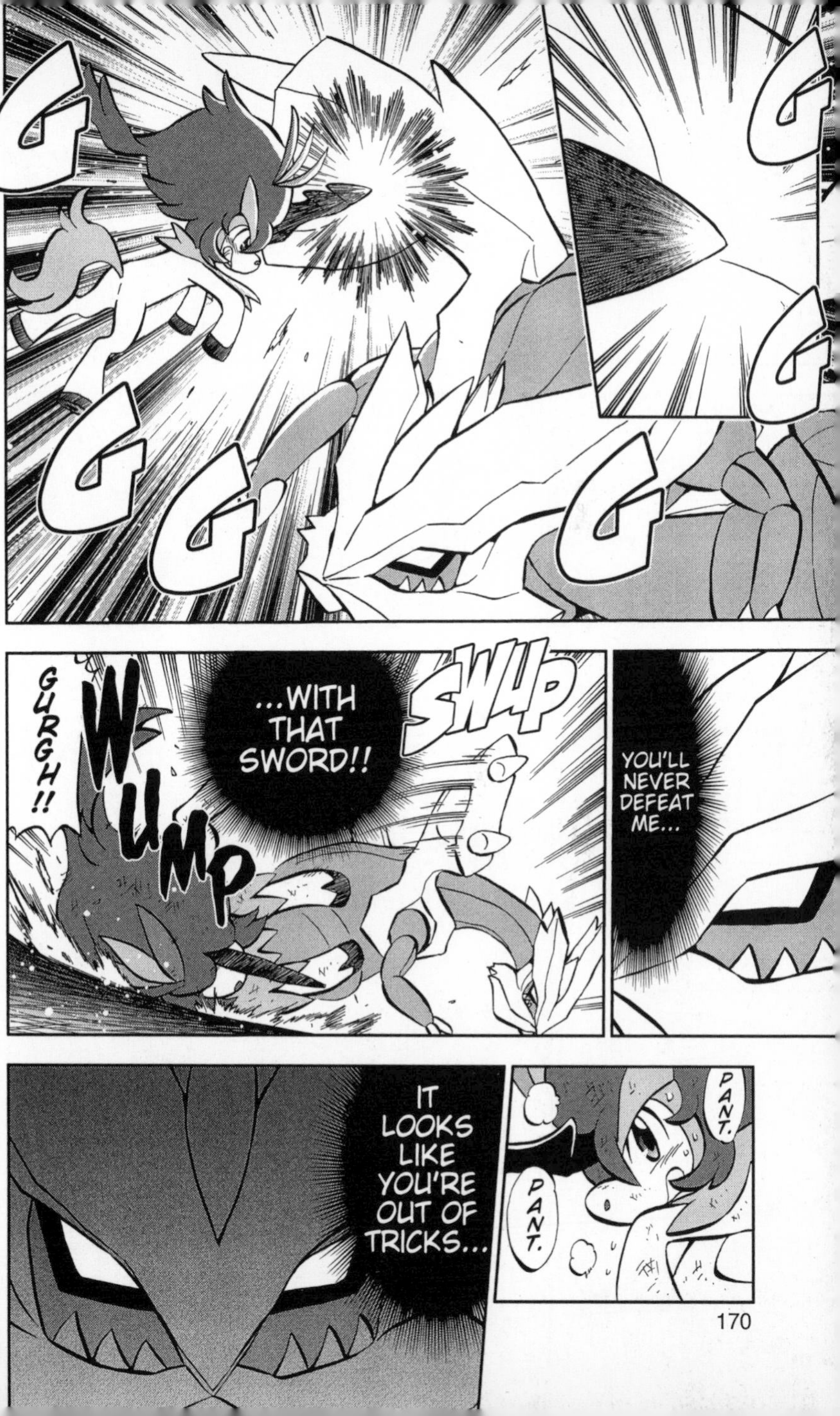
GGGGGG
YOU'LL NEVER DEFEAT ME...
...WITH THAT SWORD!!
SWUP
WUMP
GURGH!!
PANT. PANT.
IT LOOKS LIKE YOU'RE OUT OF TRICKS...

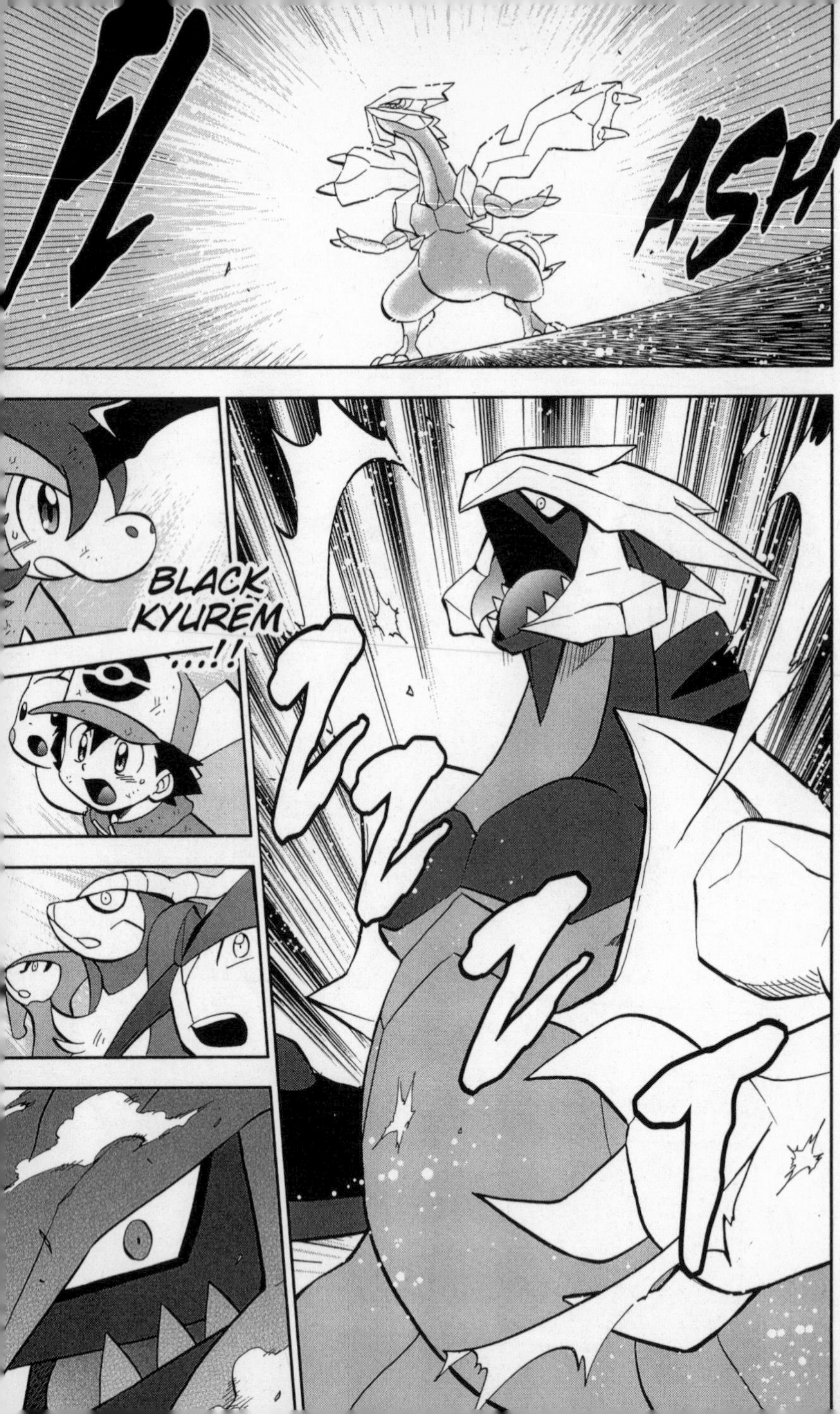
FLASH
BLACK KYUREM ...!!

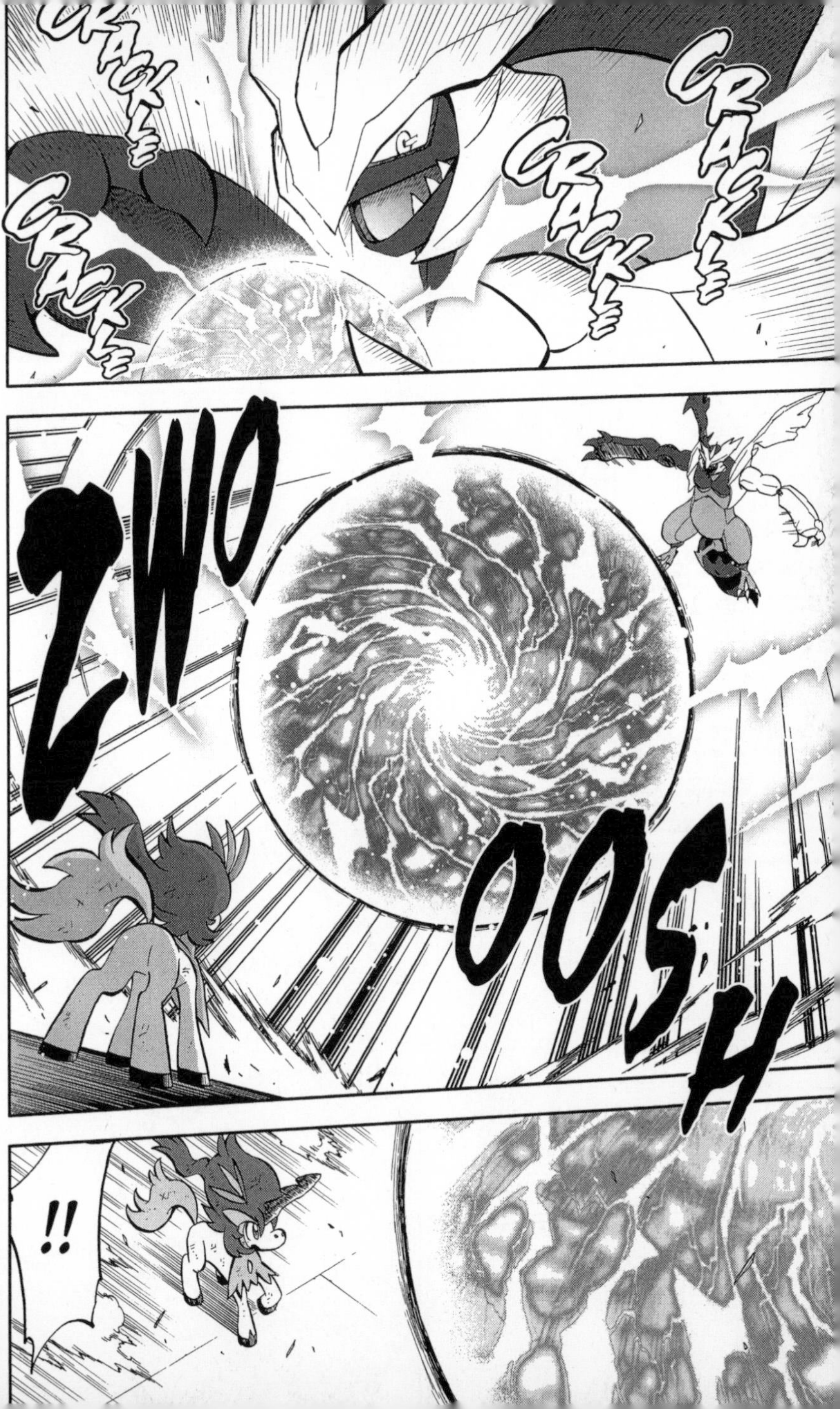
CRACKLE
CRACKLE
CRACKLE
CRACKLE
ZWOOOSH
!!

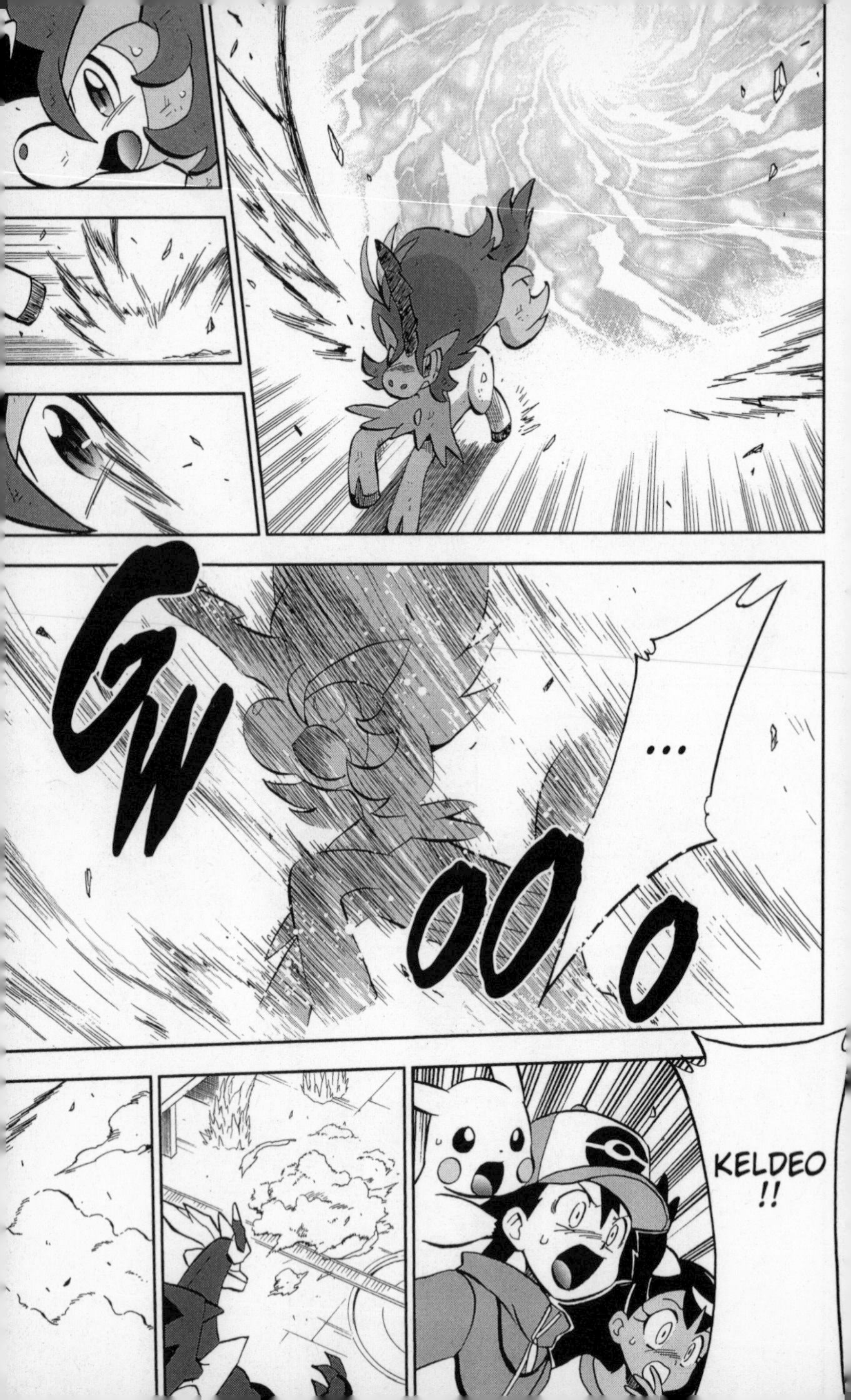

GWOOOO
...
KELDEO!!

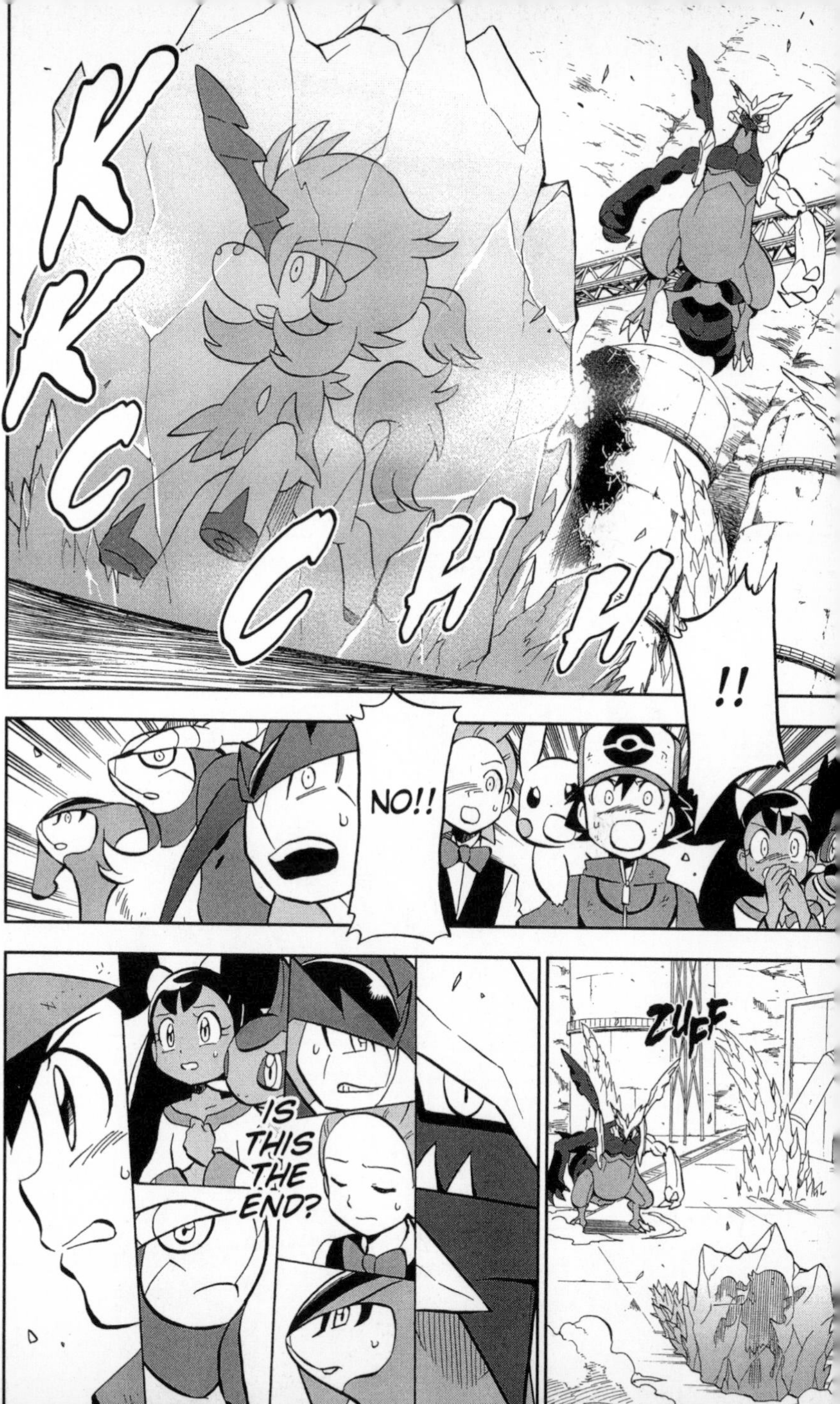
KKKCCHH
!!
NO!!
ZUFF
IS THIS THE END?

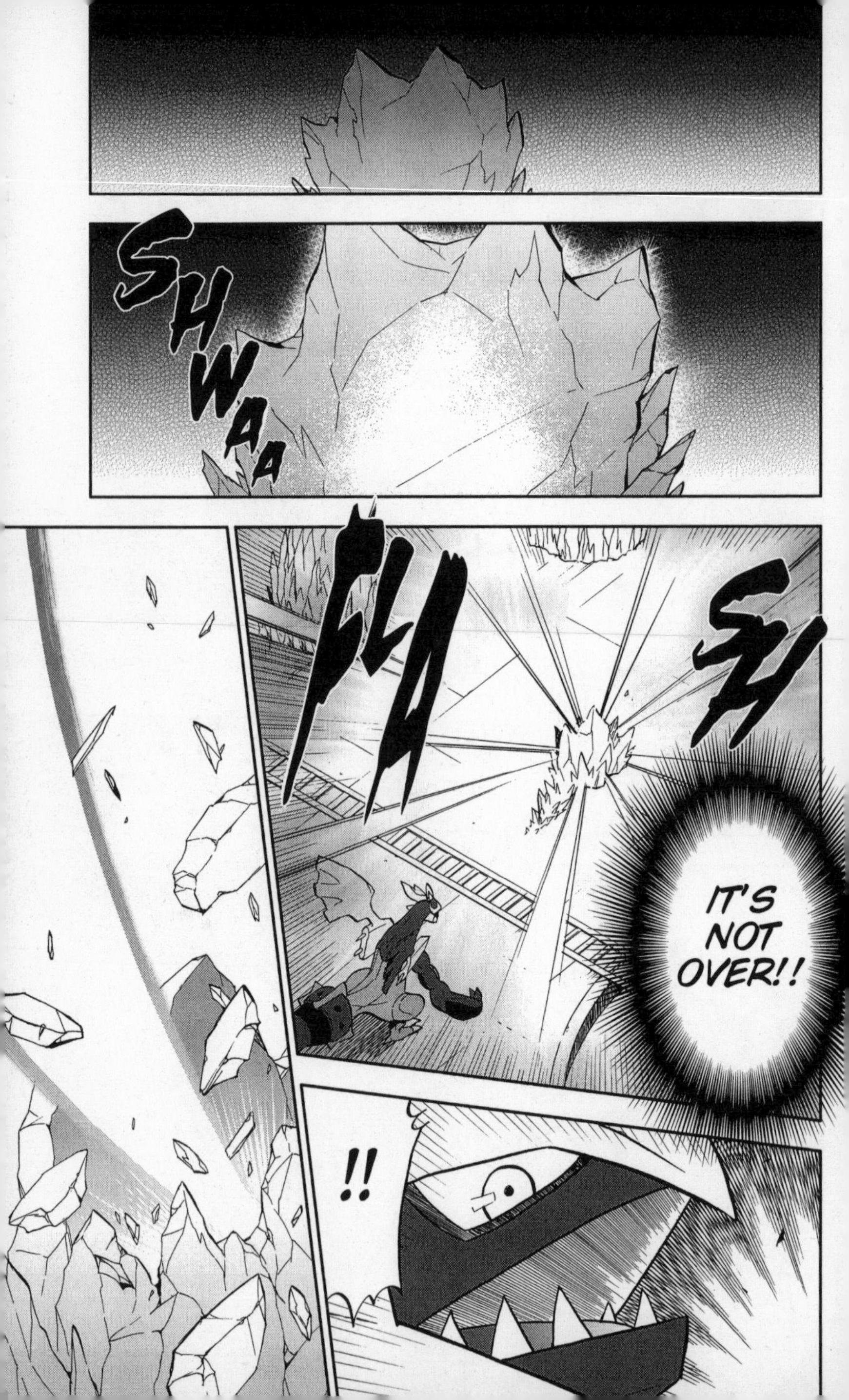

SHWAA
FLA
SH
IT'S NOT OVER!!
!!

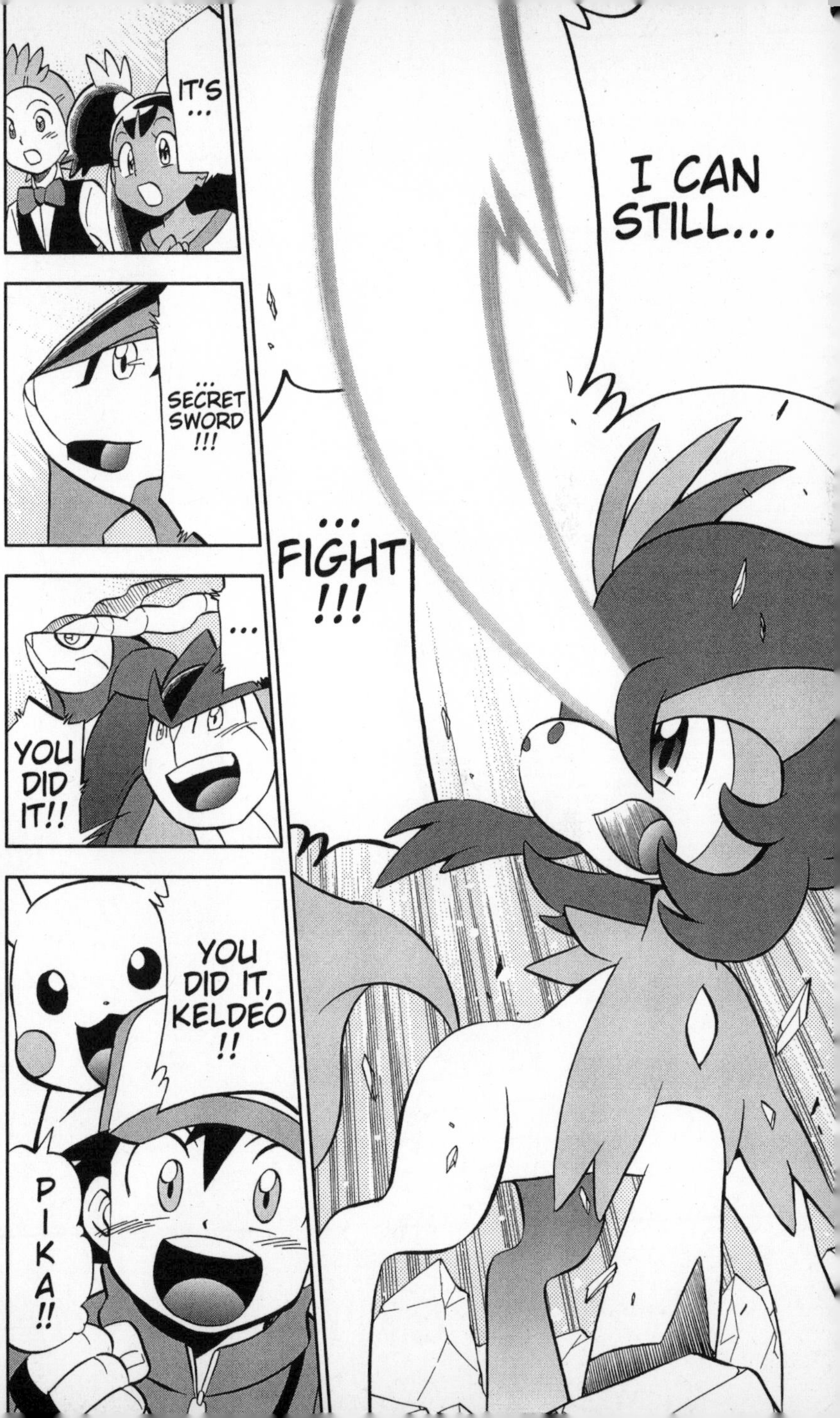
I CAN STILL...
...FIGHT!!!
IT'S...
...SECRET SWORD!!!
...
YOU DID IT!!
YOU DID IT, KELDEO!!
PIKA!!

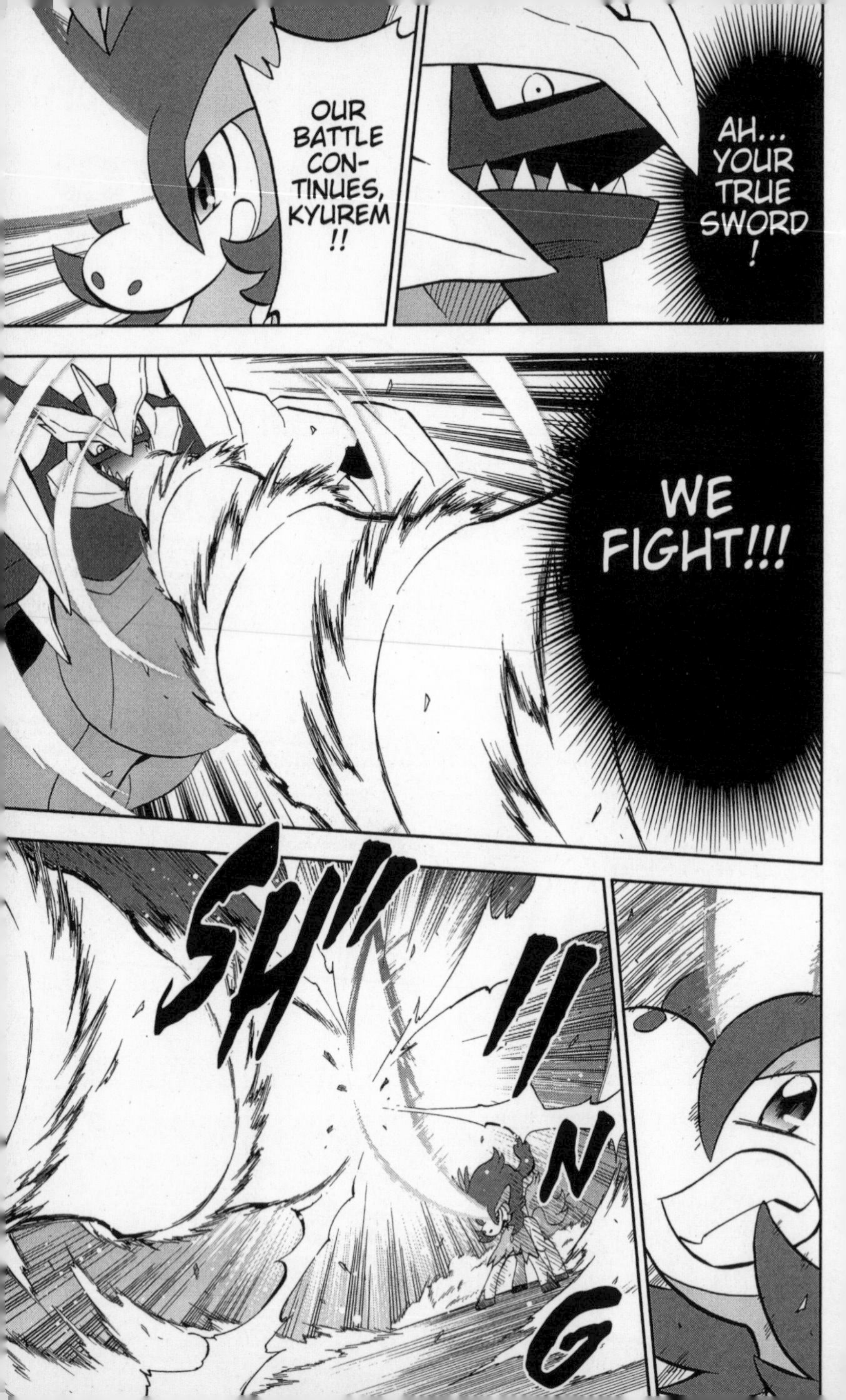
AH... YOUR TRUE SWORD!
OUR BATTLE CONTINUES, KYUREM!!
WE FIGHT!!!
SHIIIING

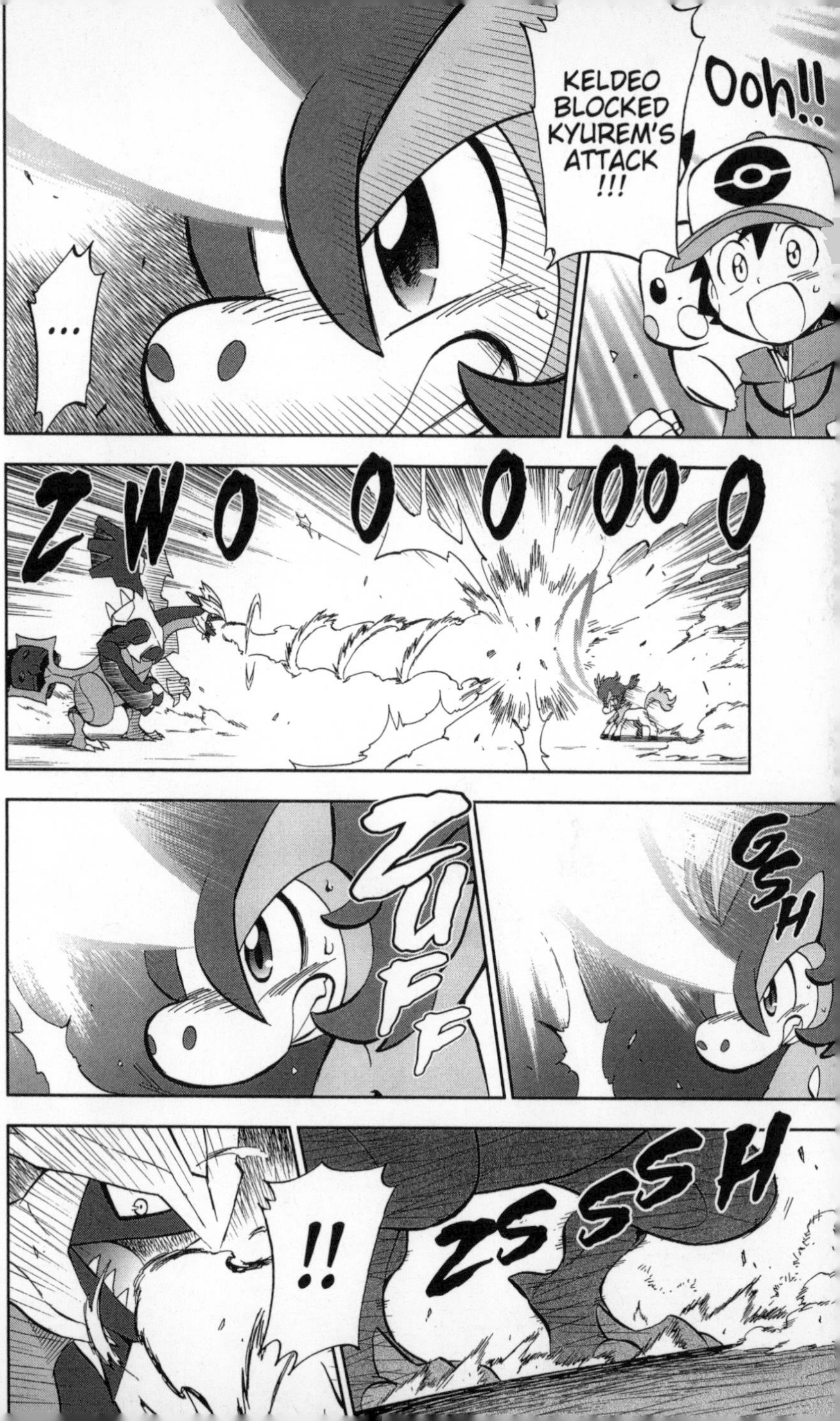
Ooh!!
KELDEO BLOCKED KYUREM'S ATTACK !!!
...
ZWOOOOOO
GSH
ZUFF
ZSSSSH
!!

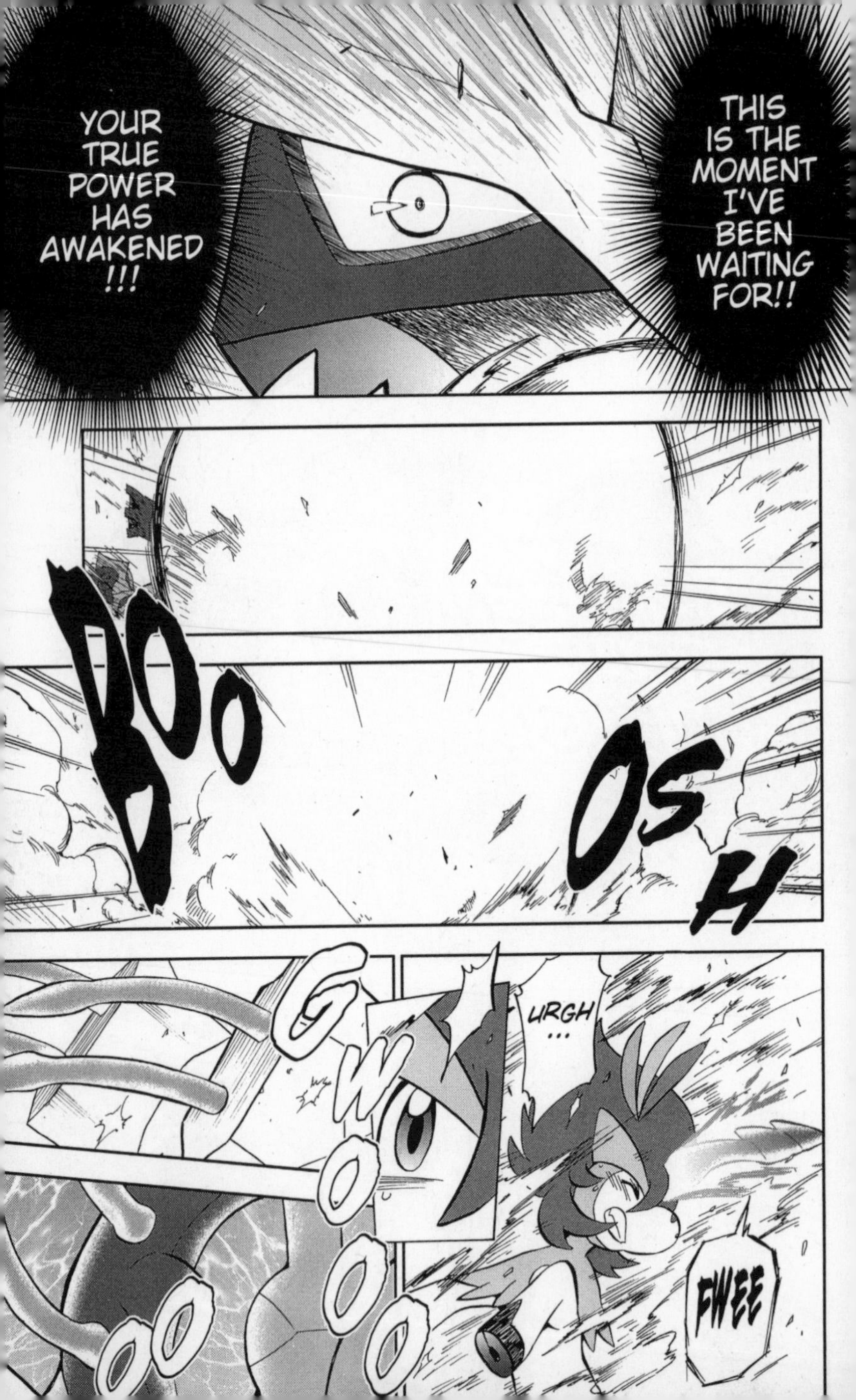
THIS IS THE MOMENT I'VE BEEN WAITING FOR!!
YOUR TRUE POWER HAS AWAKENED!!!
BOOOSH
URGH...
FWEE
GWOOOOOO

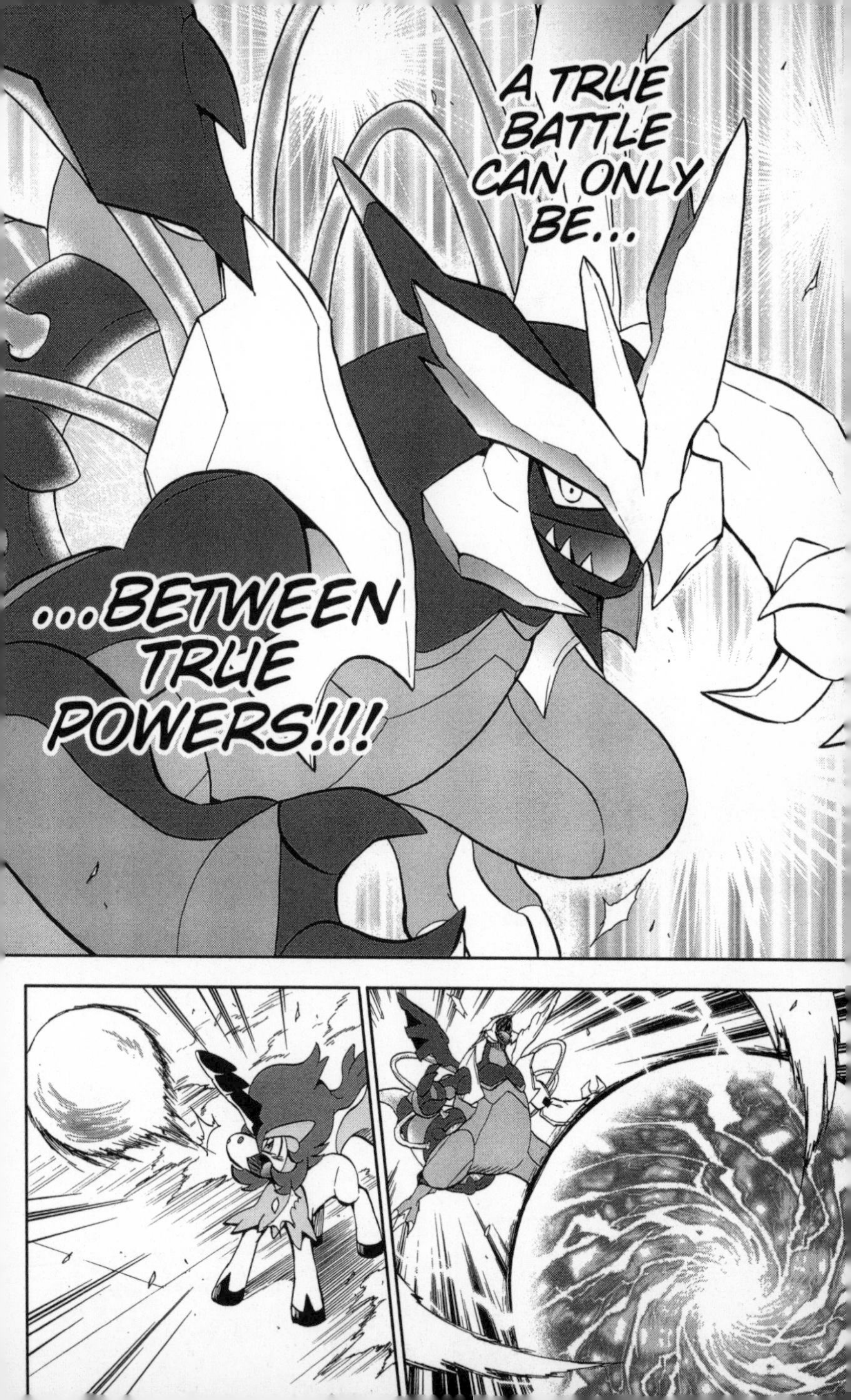
A TRUE BATTLE CAN ONLY BE...
...BETWEEN TRUE POWERS!!!

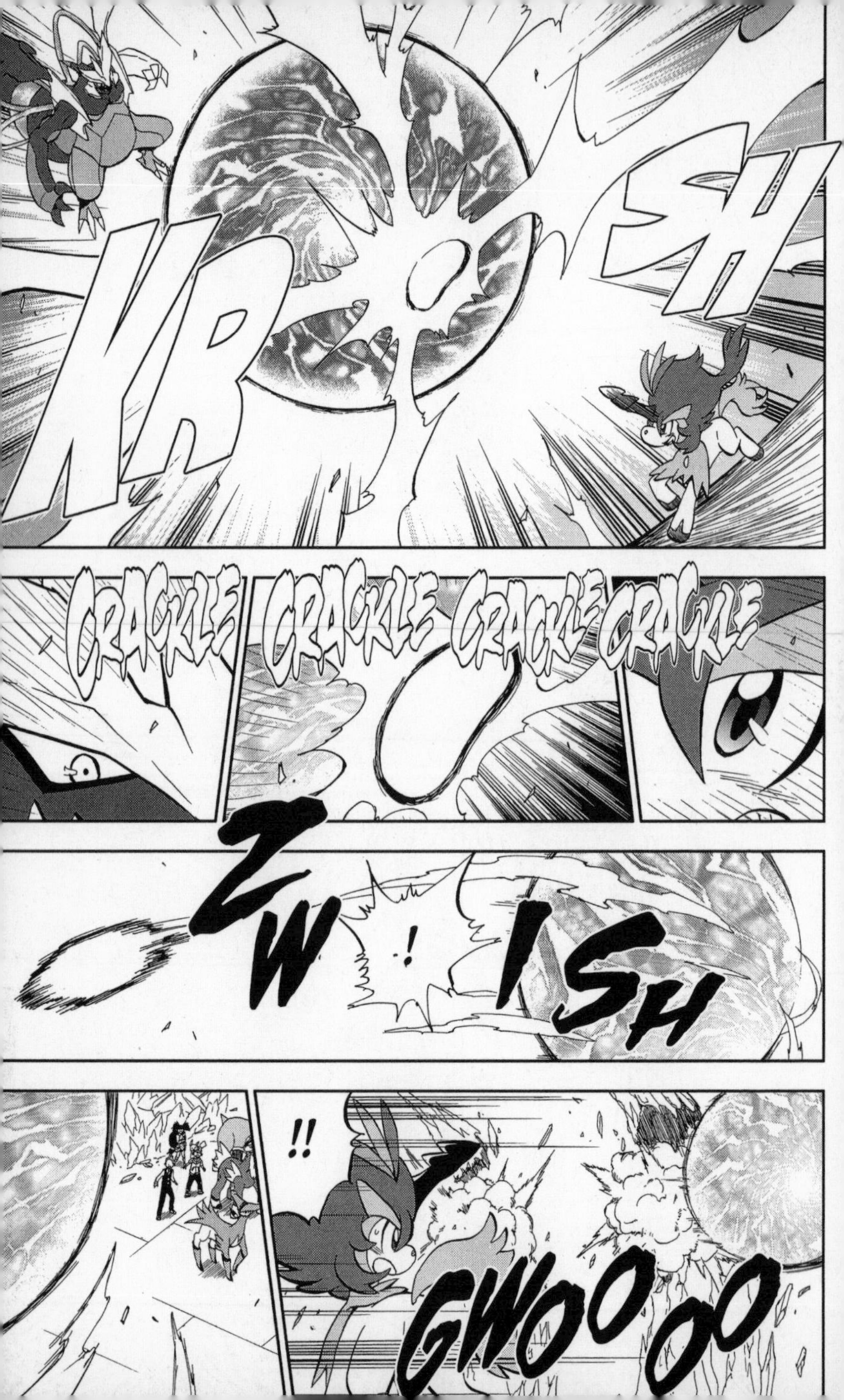
KRASH
CRACKLE CRACKLE CRACKLE CRACKLE
ZWISH
!
!!
GWOOOO

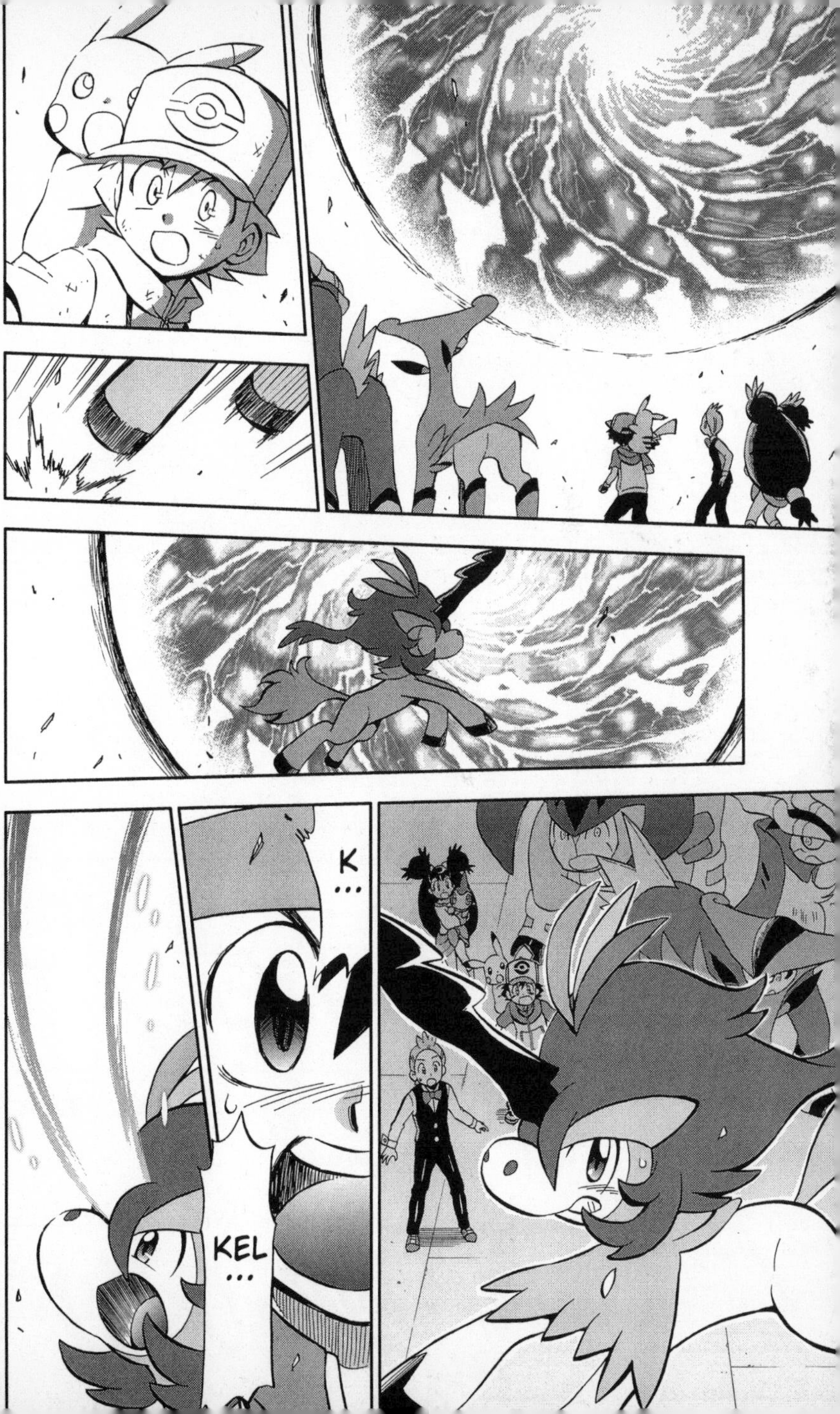
K...
KEL...

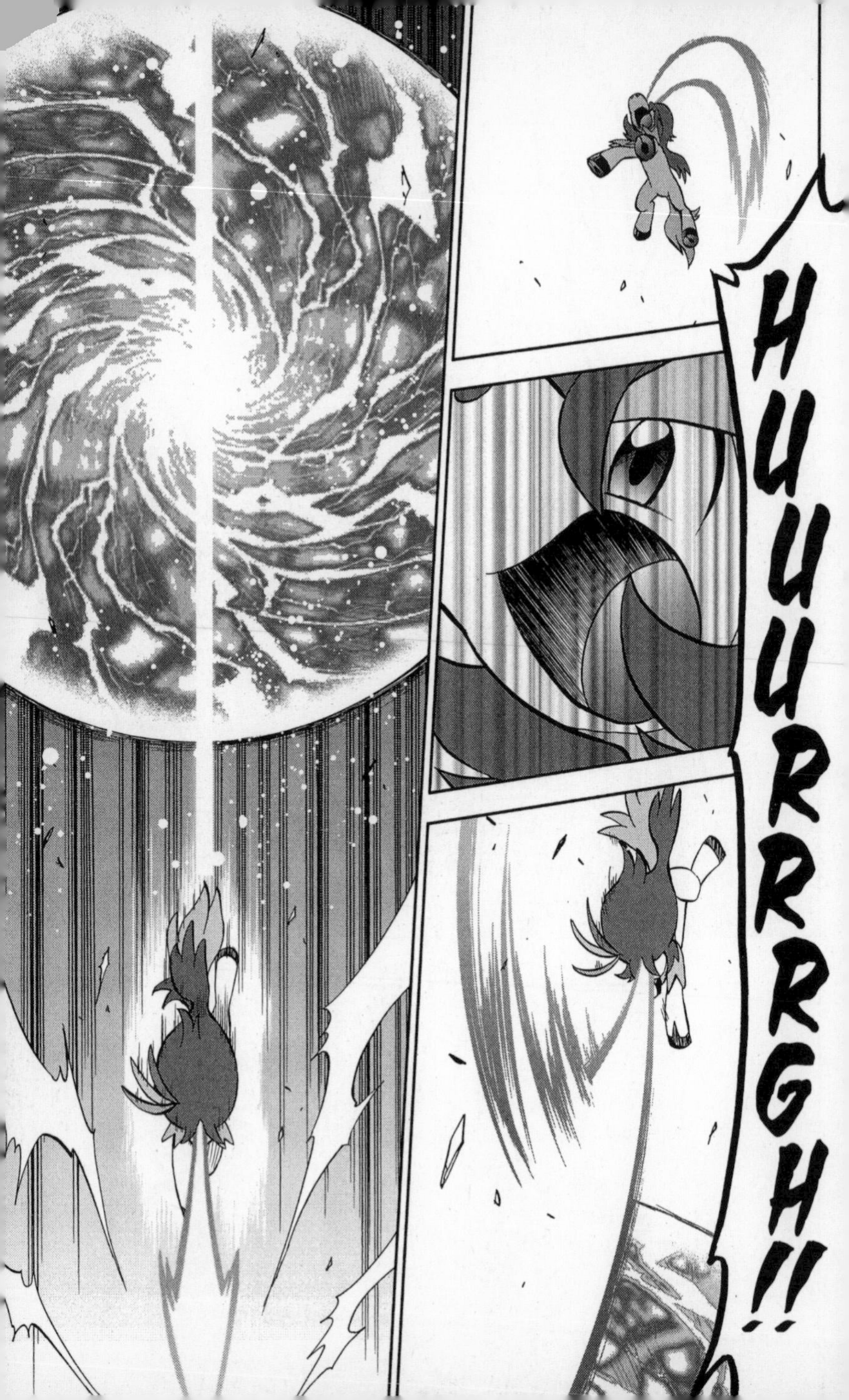
HURURRRGH!!

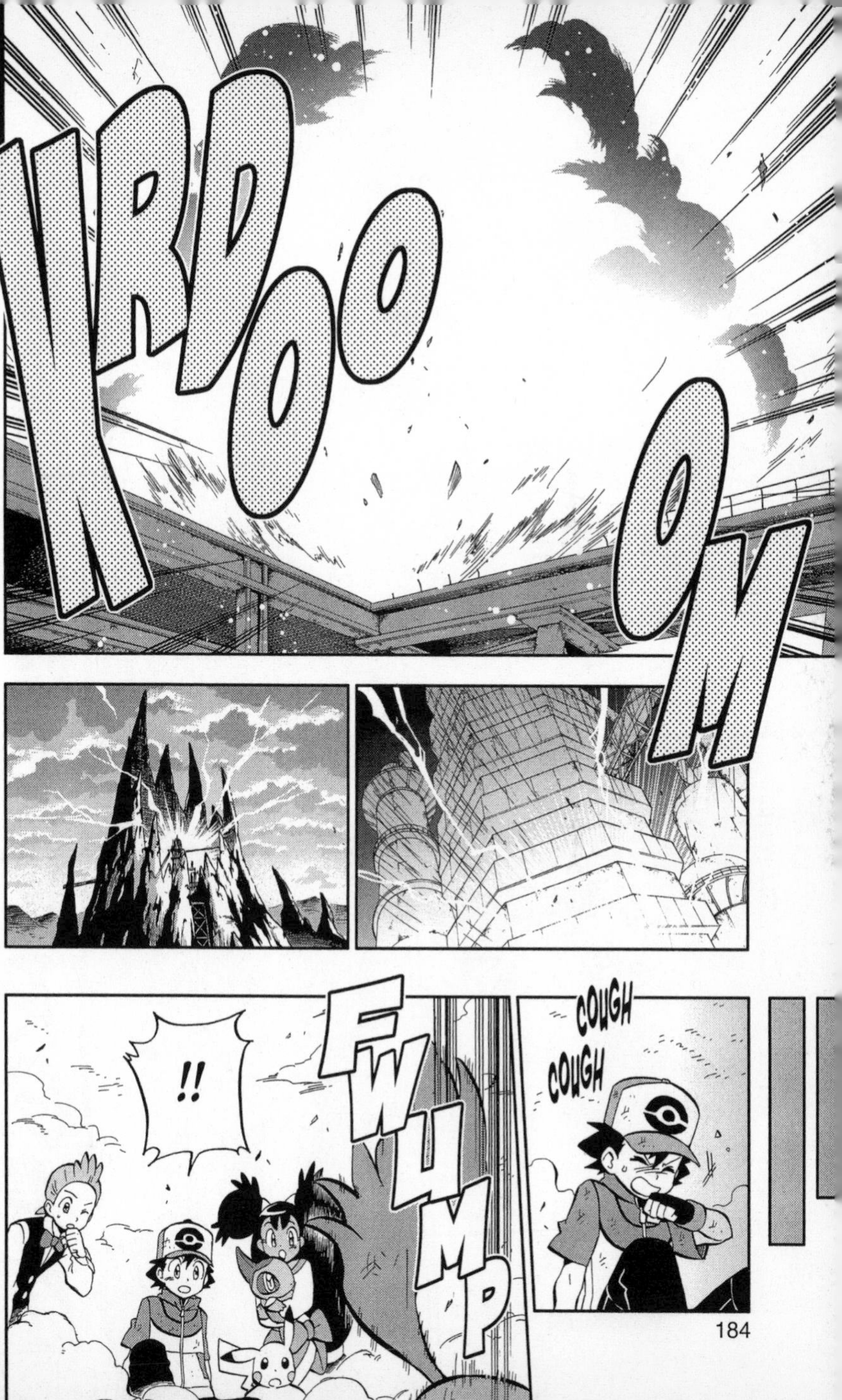
KRDOOOM
COUGH
COUGH
FWUMP
!!

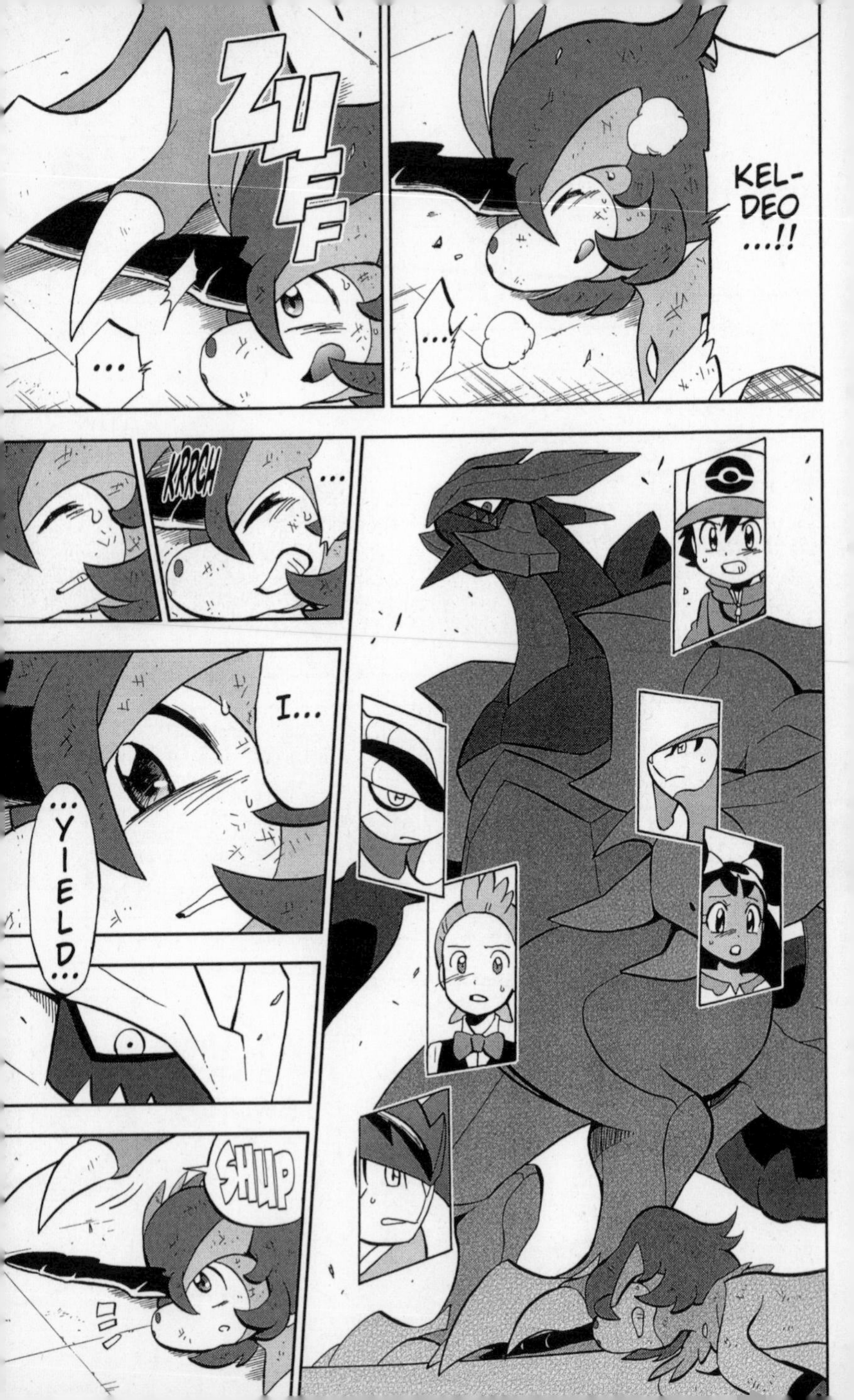
KEL-DEO ...!!
...
ZUFF
...
KRRCH
...
I...
...YIELD...
SHUP

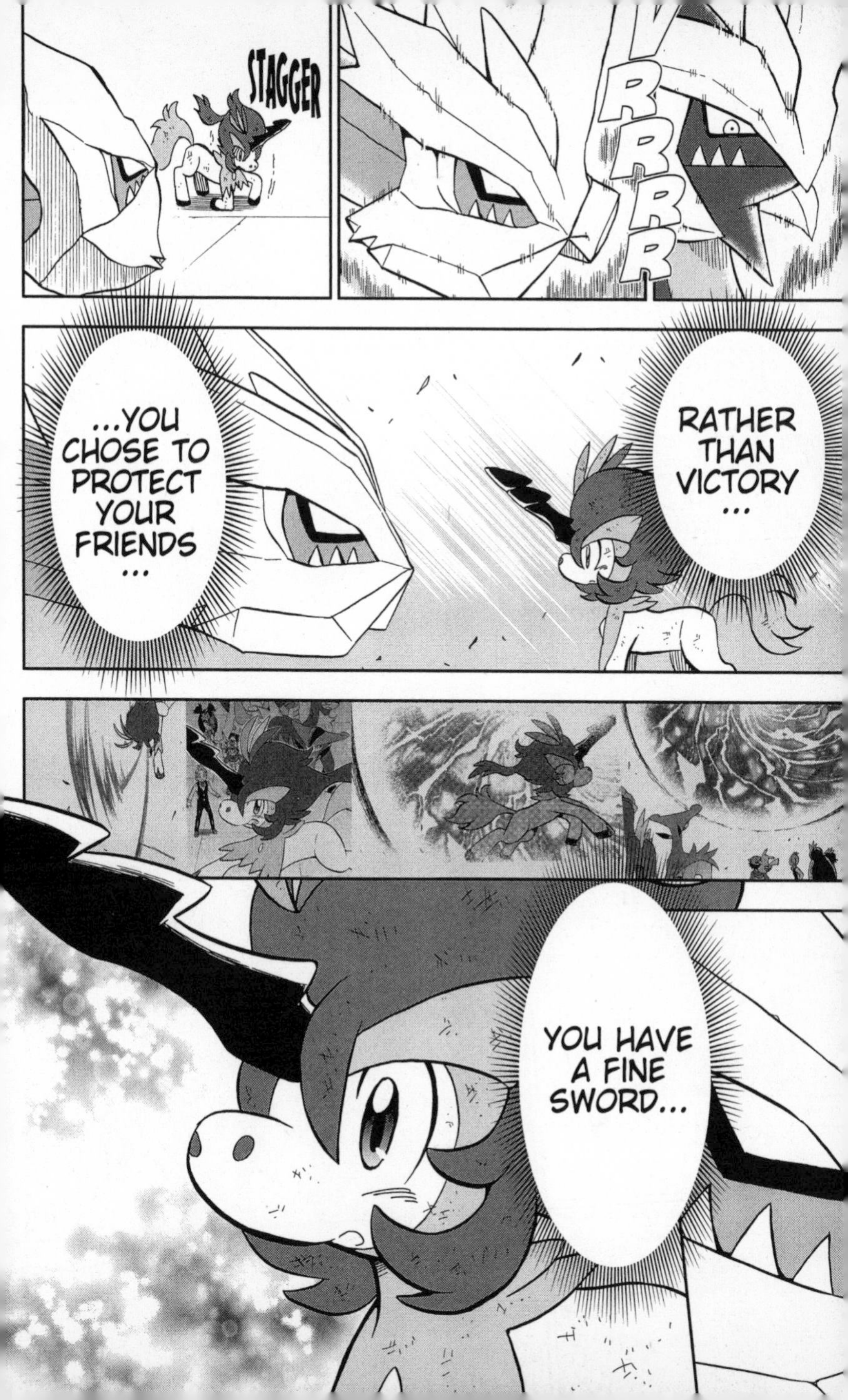
VRRRR
STAGGER
RATHER THAN VICTORY...
...YOU CHOSE TO PROTECT YOUR FRIENDS...
YOU HAVE A FINE SWORD...

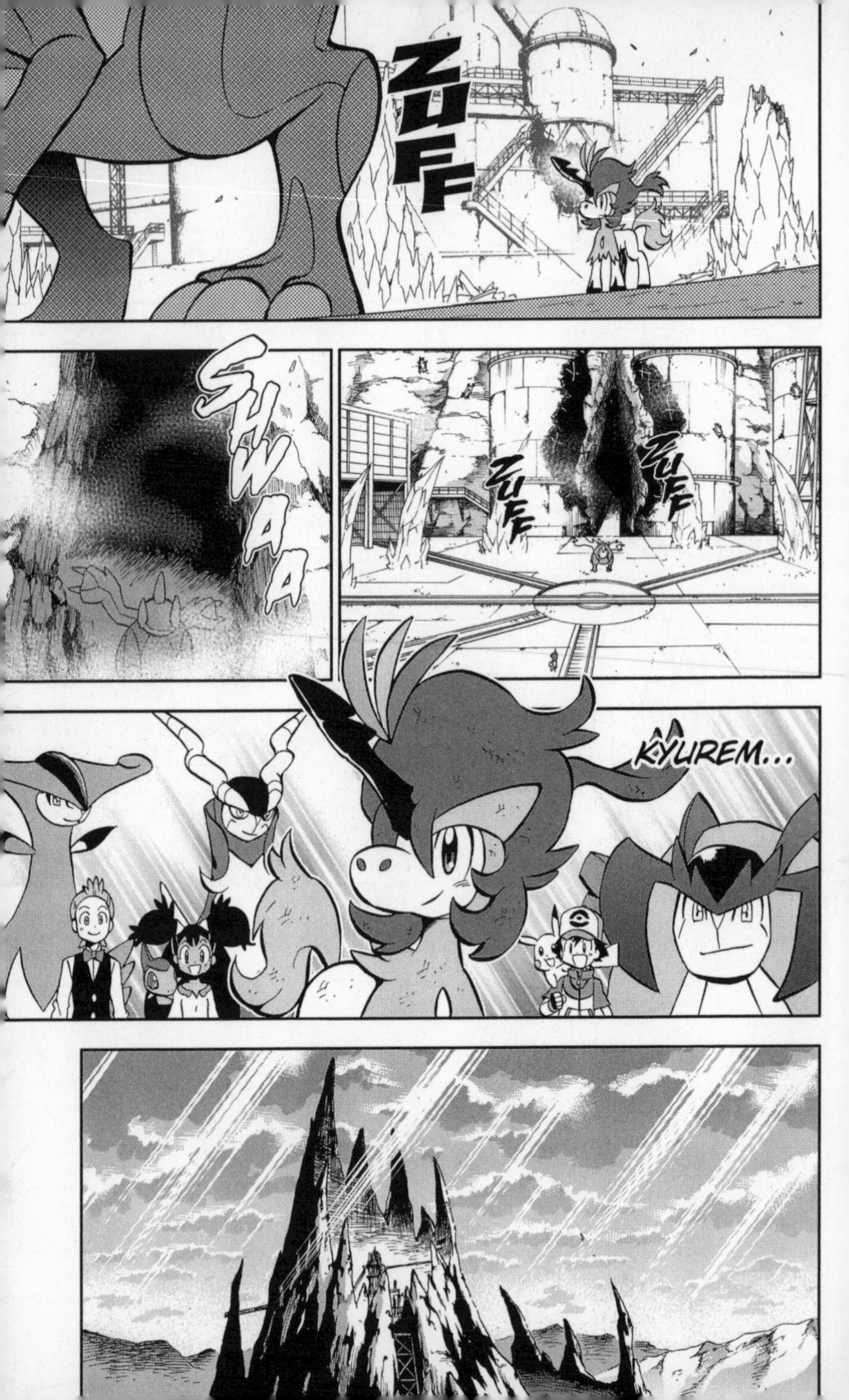
ZUFF
ZUFF
ZUFF
SHWAA
KYUREM...

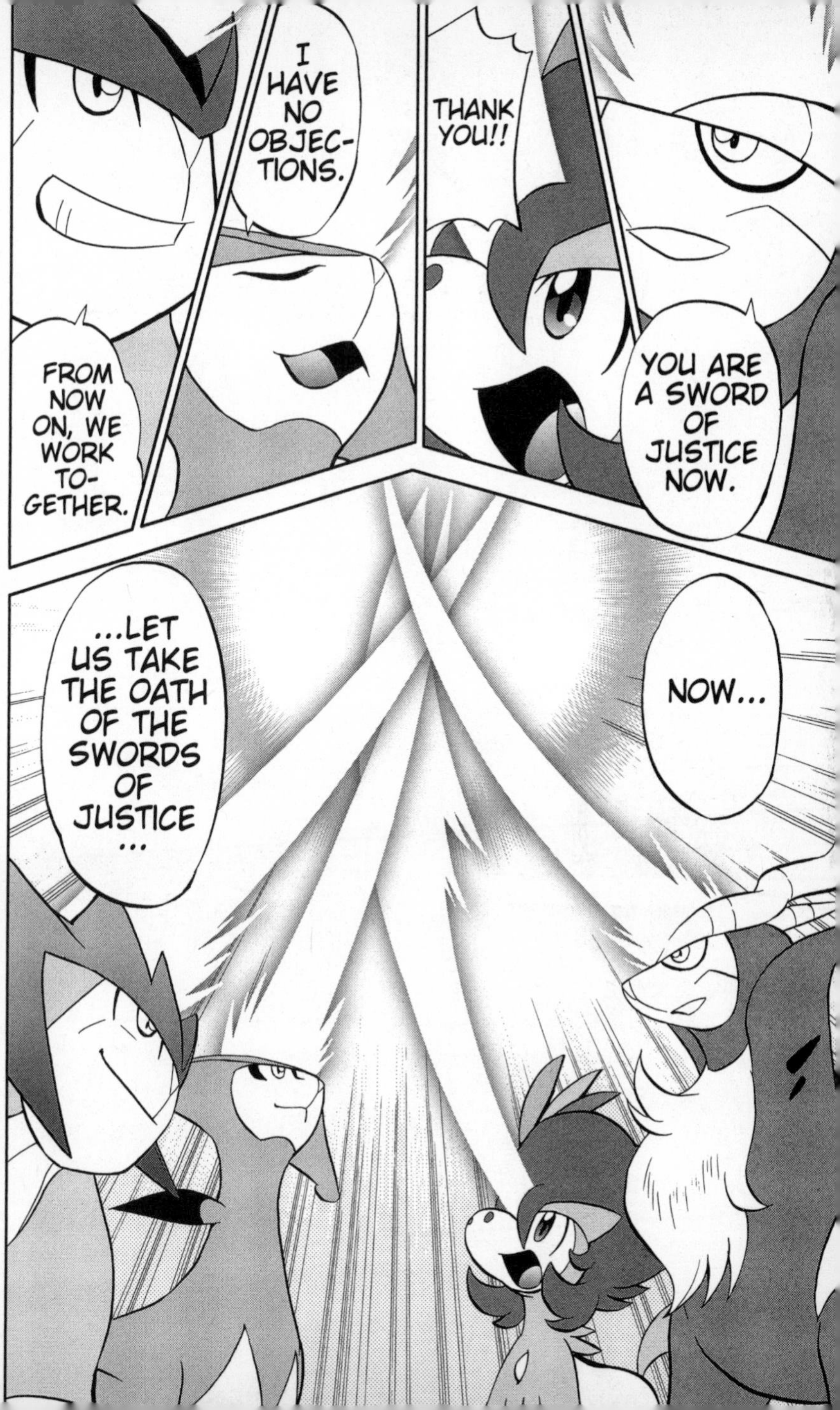

YOU ARE A SWORD OF JUSTICE NOW.
THANK YOU!!
I HAVE NO OBJECTIONS.
FROM NOW ON, WE WORK TOGETHER.
NOW...
...LET US TAKE THE OATH OF THE SWORDS OF JUSTICE...

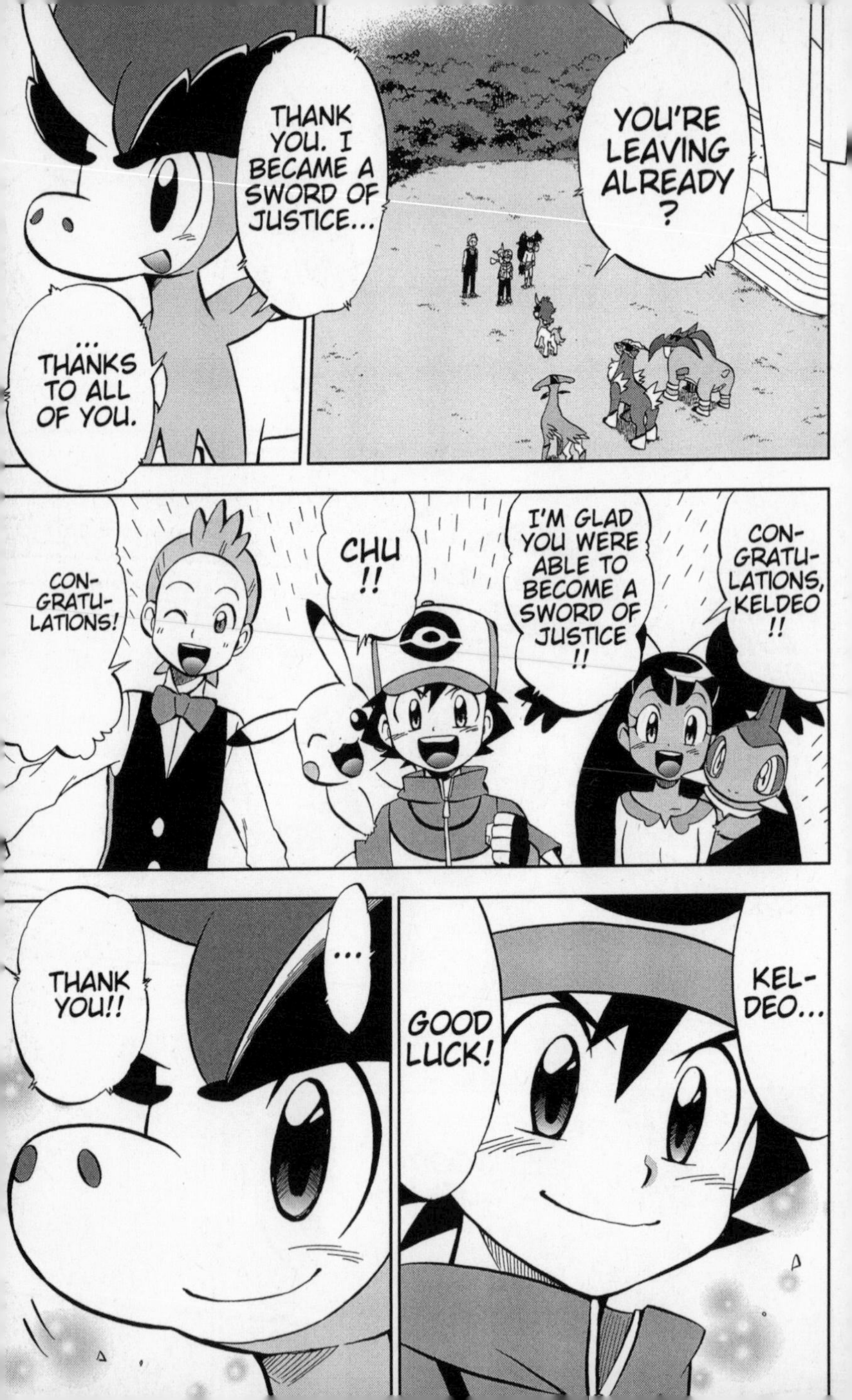
YOU'RE LEAVING ALREADY?
THANK YOU. I BECAME A SWORD OF JUSTICE...
...THANKS TO ALL OF YOU.
CONGRATULATIONS, KELDEO!!
I'M GLAD YOU WERE ABLE TO BECOME A SWORD OF JUSTICE!!
CHU!!
CONGRATULATIONS!
KELDEO...
GOOD LUCK!
...
THANK YOU!!

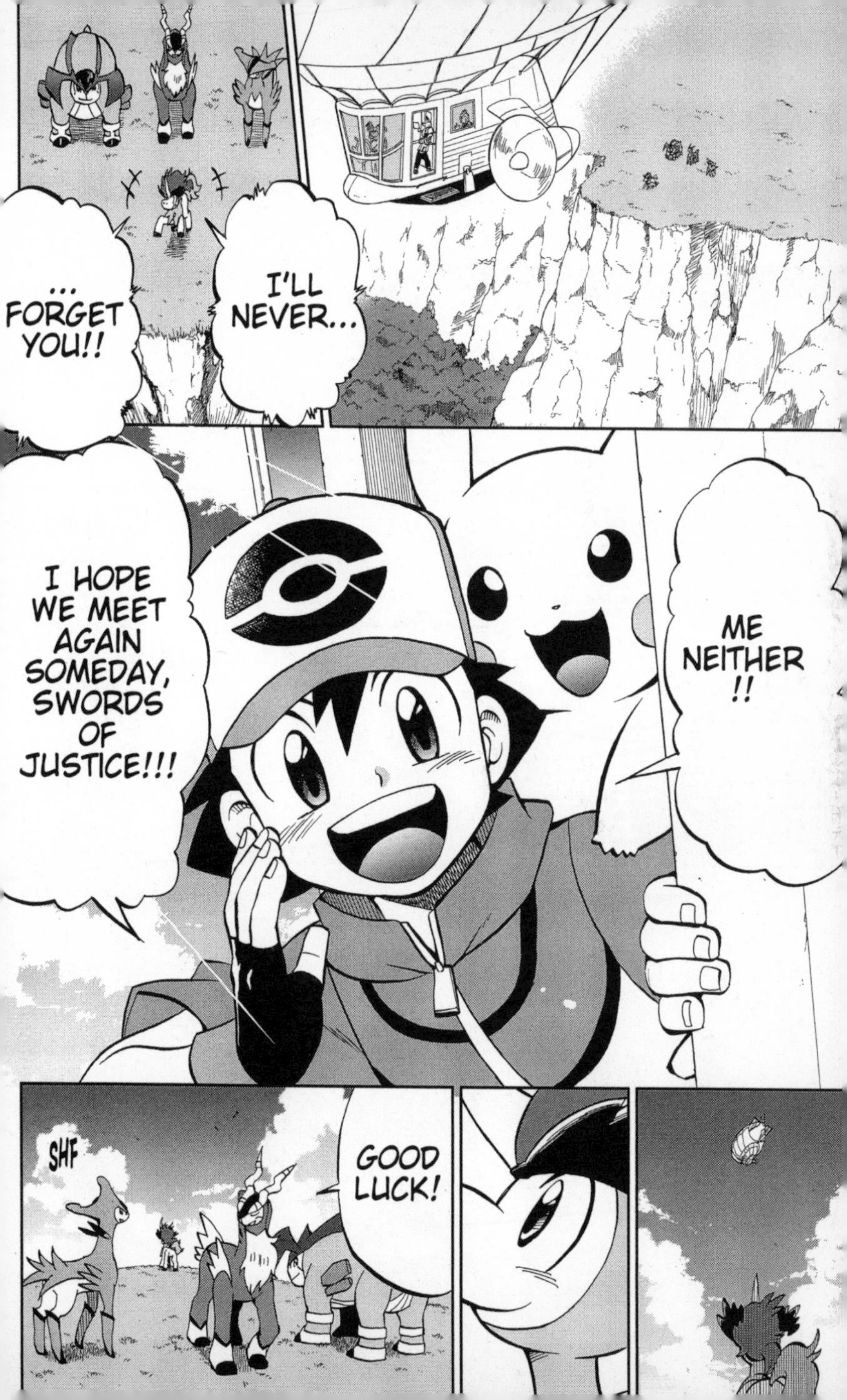
I'LL NEVER...
... FORGET YOU!!
ME NEITHER !!
I HOPE WE MEET AGAIN SOMEDAY, SWORDS OF JUSTICE!!!
GOOD LUCK!
SHF

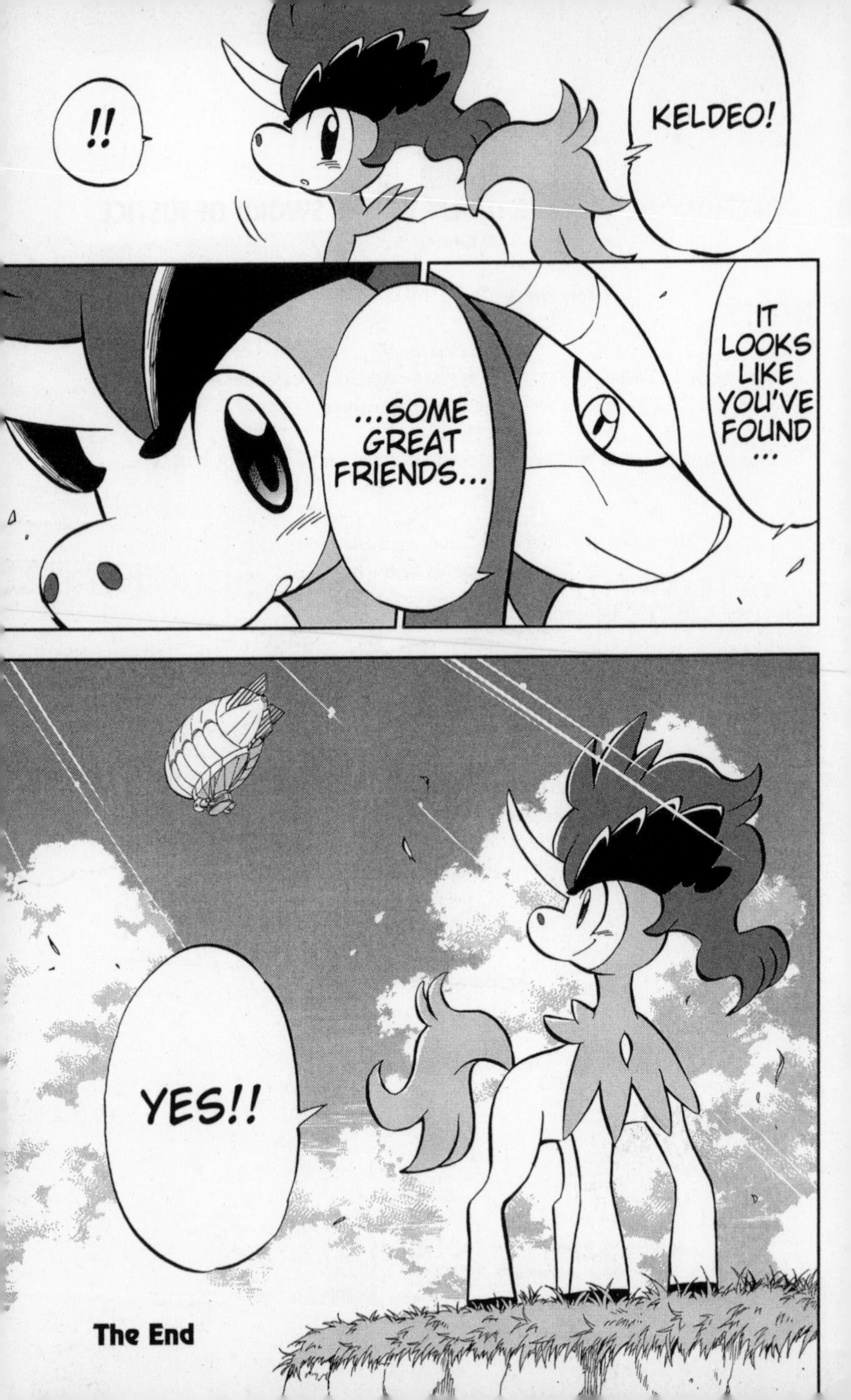
KELDEO!
!!
IT LOOKS LIKE YOU'VE FOUND ...
...SOME GREAT FRIENDS...
YES!!
The End

POKÉMON THE MOVIE: KYUREM

VIZ Kids Edition

Story and Art by **MOMOTA INOUE**

© 2013 Pokémon.
© 1998-2012 PIKACHU PROJECT. TM, ®, and character names are trademarks of Nintendo.
© 2012 Momota INOUE/Shogakukan
All rights reserved.
Original Japanese edition "KYUREM VS. SEIKENSHI KERUDIO" published by SHOGAKUKAN Inc.

Translation/Tetsuichiro Miyaki
Touch-up & Lettering/Stephen Dutro
Design/Shawn Carrico
Editor/Traci N. Todd

Printed in the U.S.A.

Published by VIZ Media, LLC
P.O. Box 77010
San Francisco, CA 94107

10 9 8 7 6 5 4 3 2 1
First printing, March 2013

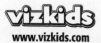